P9-CLR-337

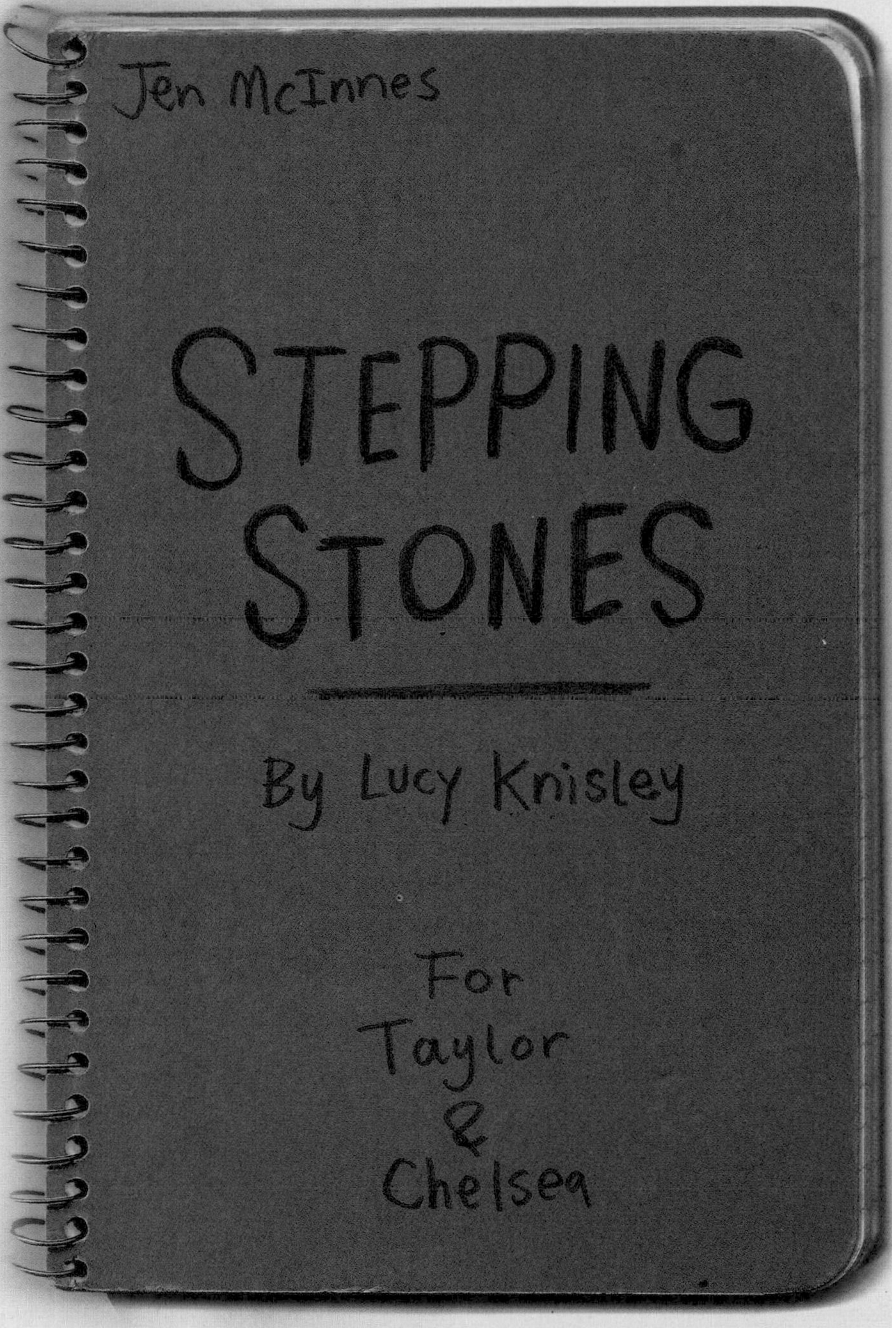
Jen McInnes
STEPPING STONES
By Lucy Knisley
For Taylor & Chelsea

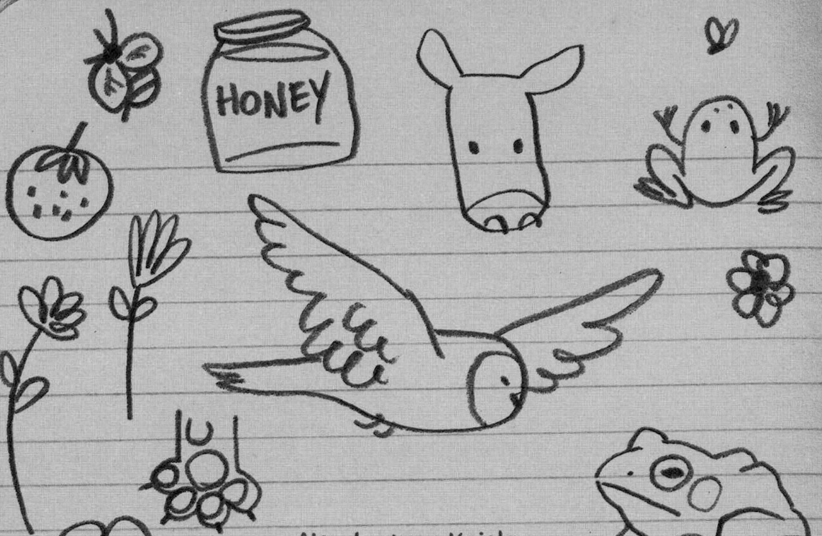
HONEY

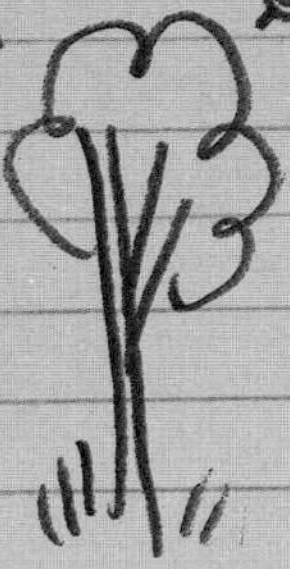

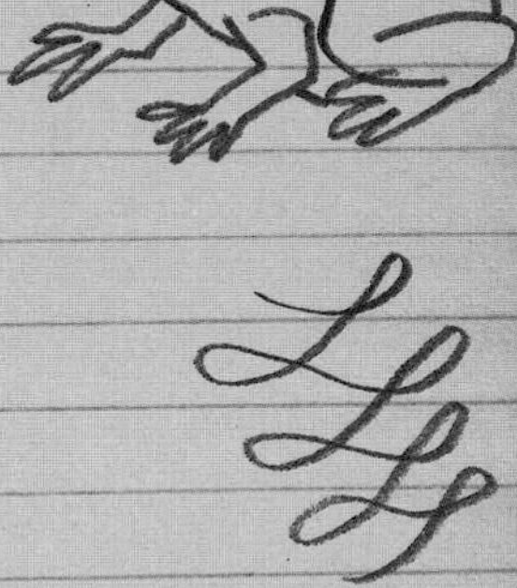

Also by Lucy Knisley

French Milk

Relish

An Age of License

Displacement

Something New

Kid Gloves

Picture Books

You Are New

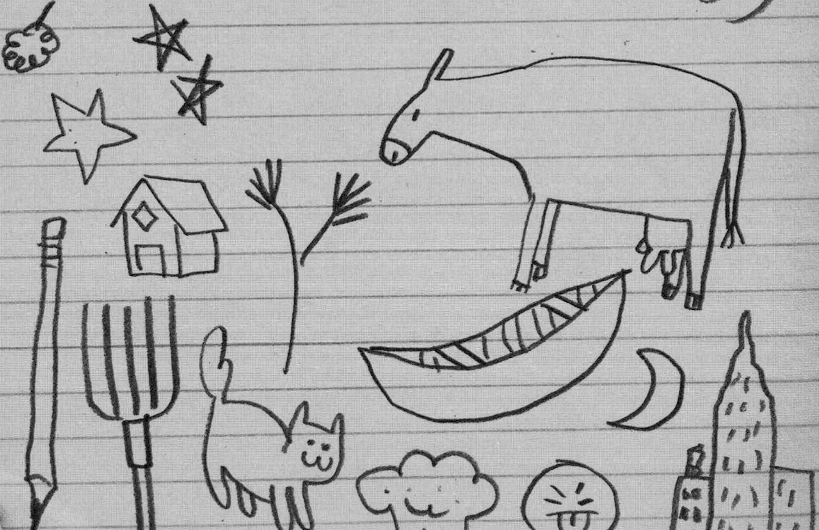

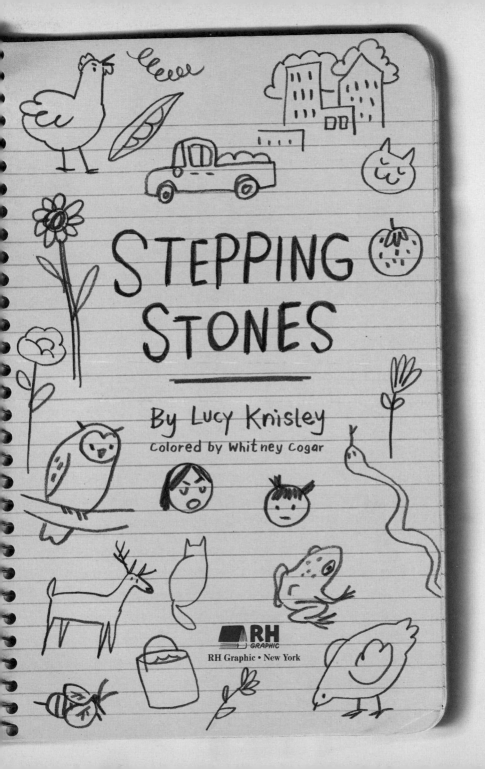

STEPPING STONES

By Lucy Knisley

Colored by Whitney Cogar

RH GRAPHIC

RH Graphic • New York

Text, cover art, and interior art copyright © 2020 by Lucy Knisley
All rights reserved. Published in the United States by RH Graphic, an imprint of Random House Children's Books, a division of Penguin Random House LLC, New York.

RH Graphic with the book design is a trademark of Penguin Random House LLC.

Visit us on the Web! RHKidsGraphic.com • @RHKidsGraphic

Educators and librarians, for a variety of teaching tools, visit us at RHTeachersLibrarians.com

Library of Congress Cataloging-in-Publication Data
Names: Knisley, Lucy, author, artist. Title: Stepping stones / Lucy Knisley.
Description: First edition. | New York : RH Graphic, [2020] | Audience: Ages 8–12 | Audience: Grades 4–6 | Summary: "Jen moves out to the country and has to put up with her mom and her mom's new boyfriend, as well as his kids. Suddenly part of a larger family in a new place, Jen isn't sure there is a place for her in this different world"—Provided by publisher.
Identifiers: LCCN 2019026160 | ISBN 978-1-9848-9684-1 (paperback) | ISBN 978-0-593-12524-3 (hardcover) | ISBN 978-1-9848-9685-8 (library binding) | ISBN 978-1-9848-9686-5 (ebook)
Subjects: LCSH: Graphic novels. | CYAC: Graphic novels. | Families—Fiction. | Country life—Fiction.
Classification: LCC PZ7.7.K663 St 2020 | DDC 741.5/973—dc23

Designed by Patrick Crotty
Colored by Whitney Cogar

MANUFACTURED IN CHINA
10 9 8 7 6 5 4 3 2 1
First Edition

A comic on every bookshelf.

Stepping Stones was drawn with
Blackwing *602* pencils on bristol and
colored digitally.

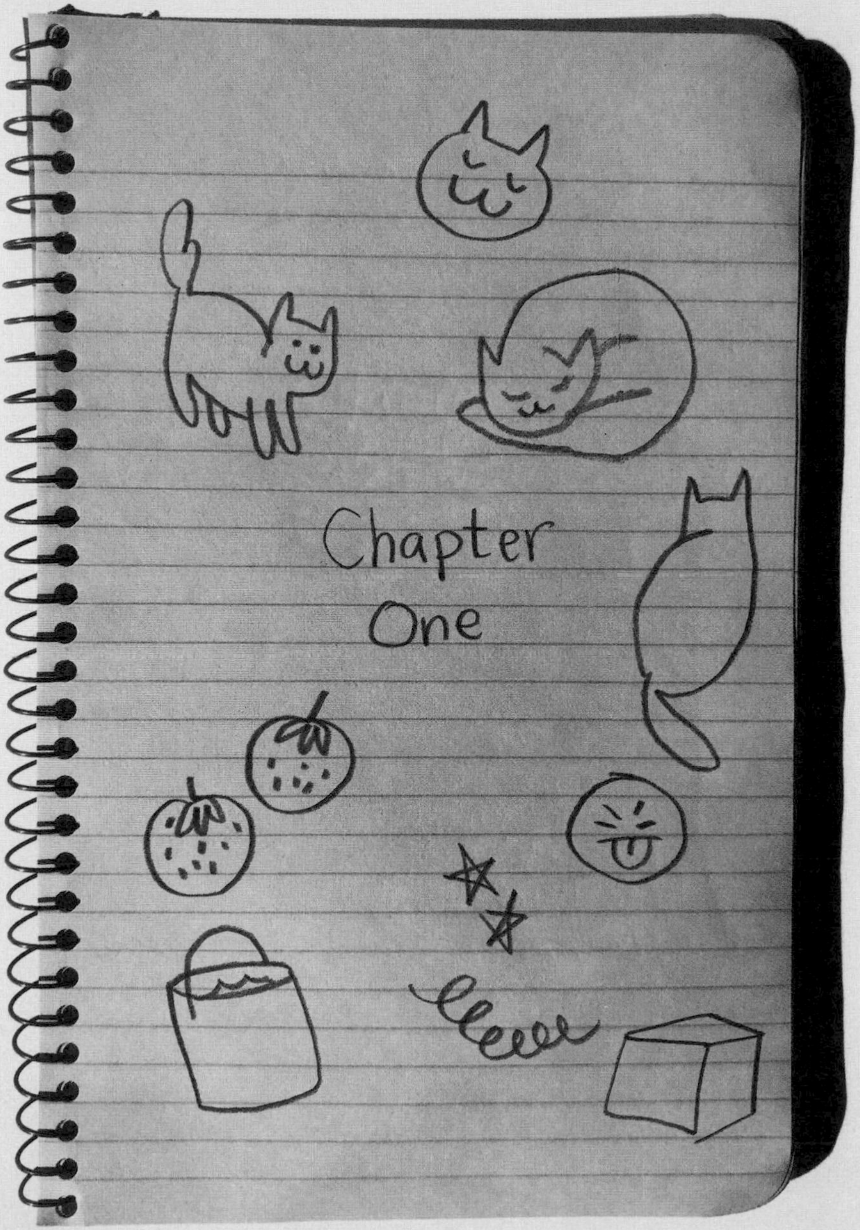
Chapter
One

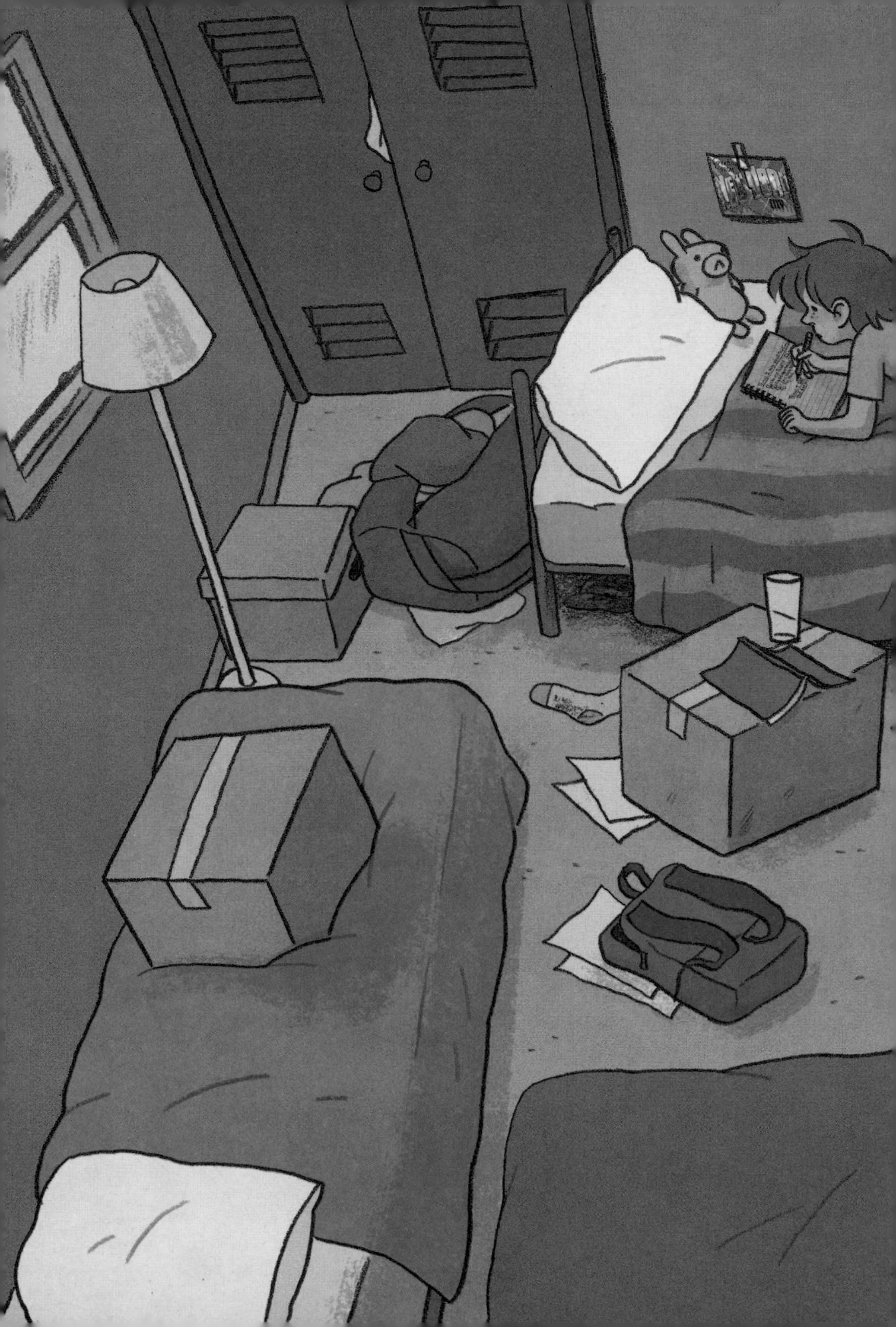

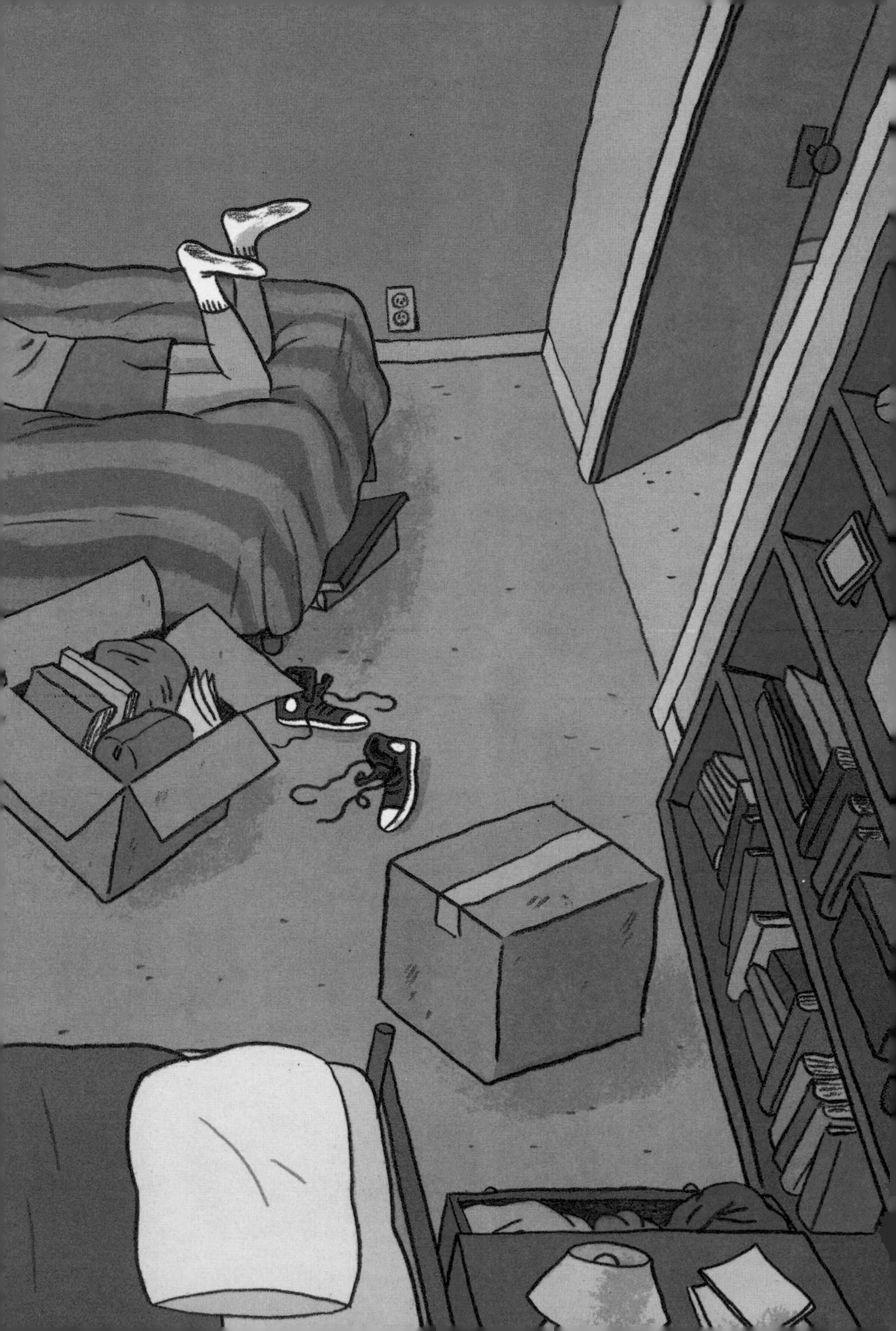

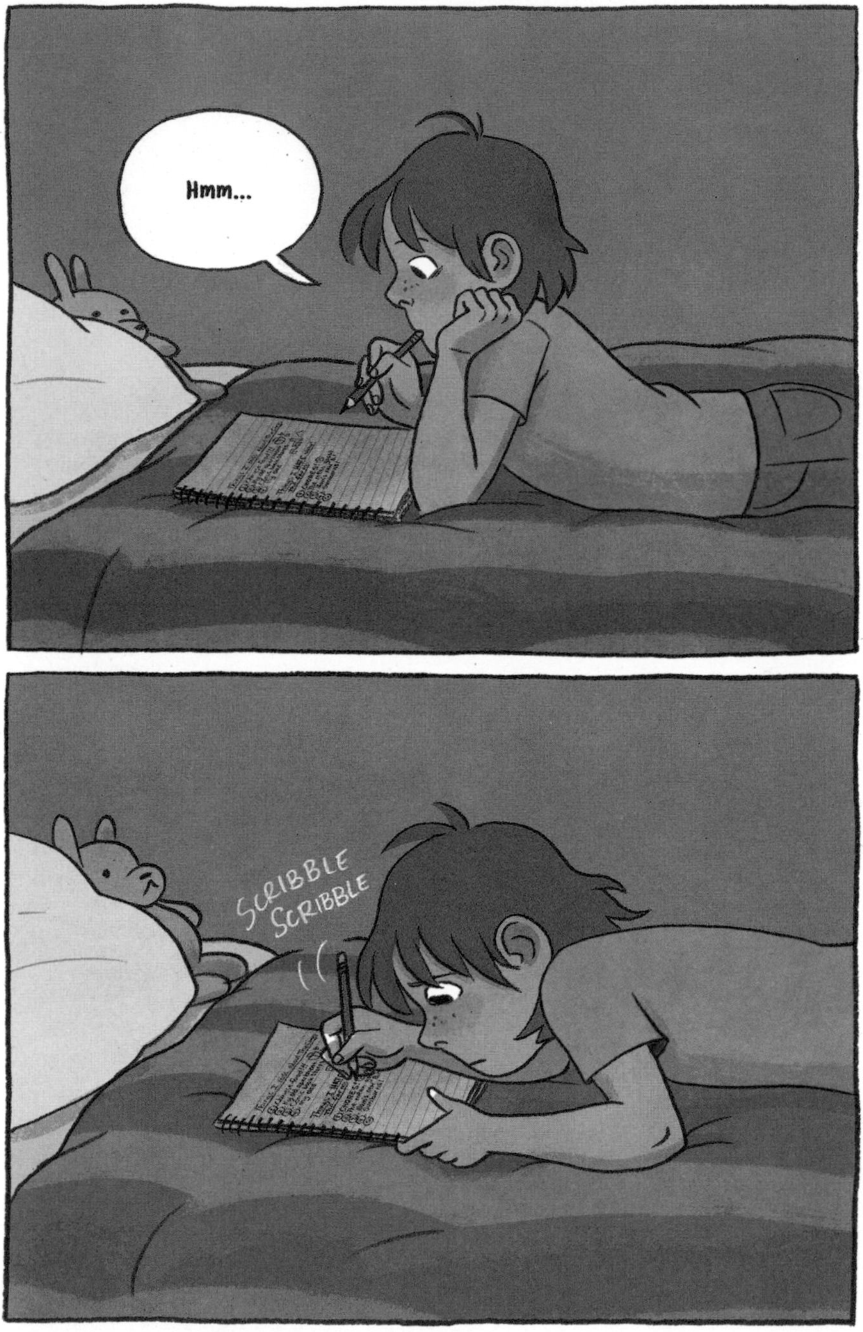
Hmm...
SCRIBBLE SCRIBBLE

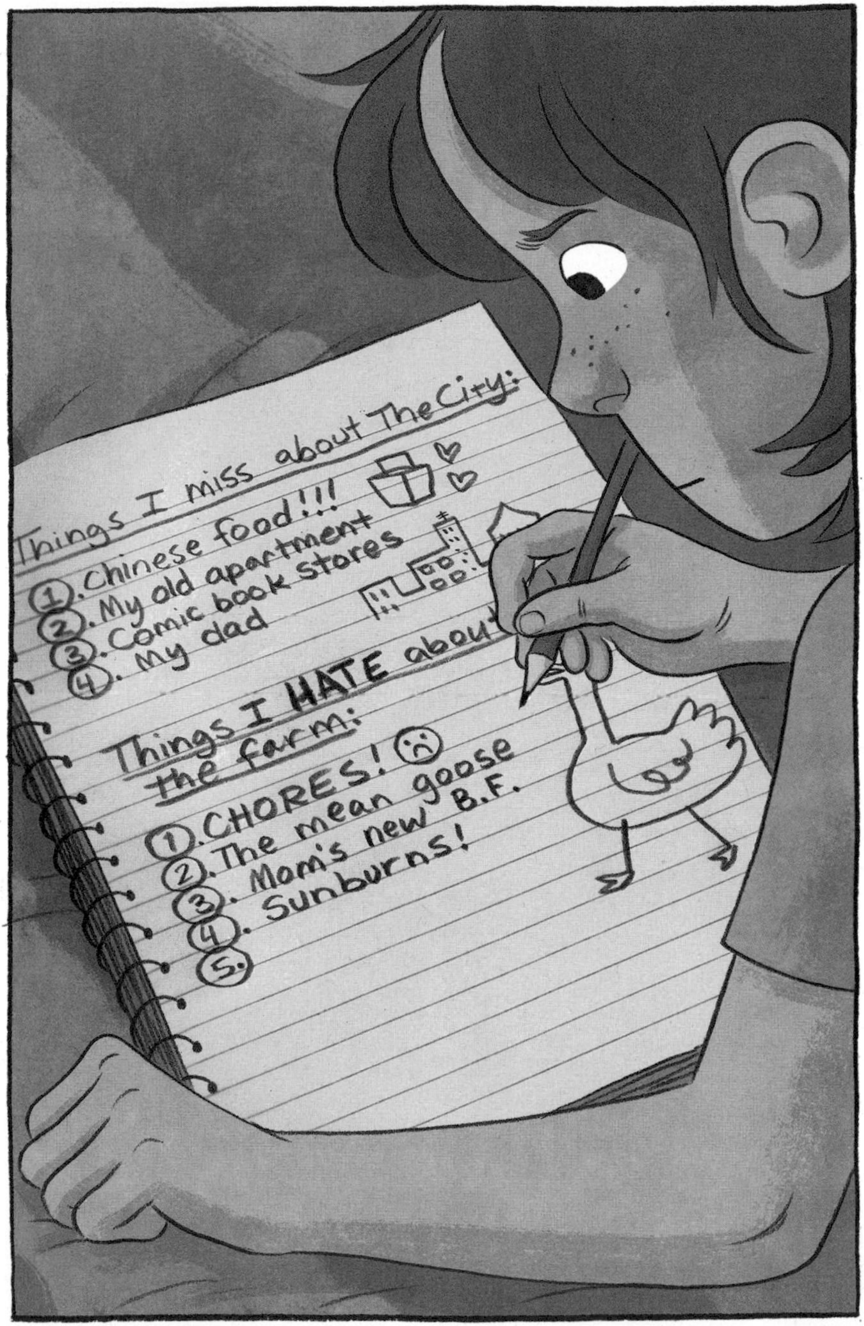
Things I miss about The City:
①. Chinese food!!!
②. My old apartment
③. Comic book stores
④. My dad
Things I HATE about the farm:
①. CHORES!
②. The mean goose
③. Mom's new B.F.
④. Sunburns!
⑤.

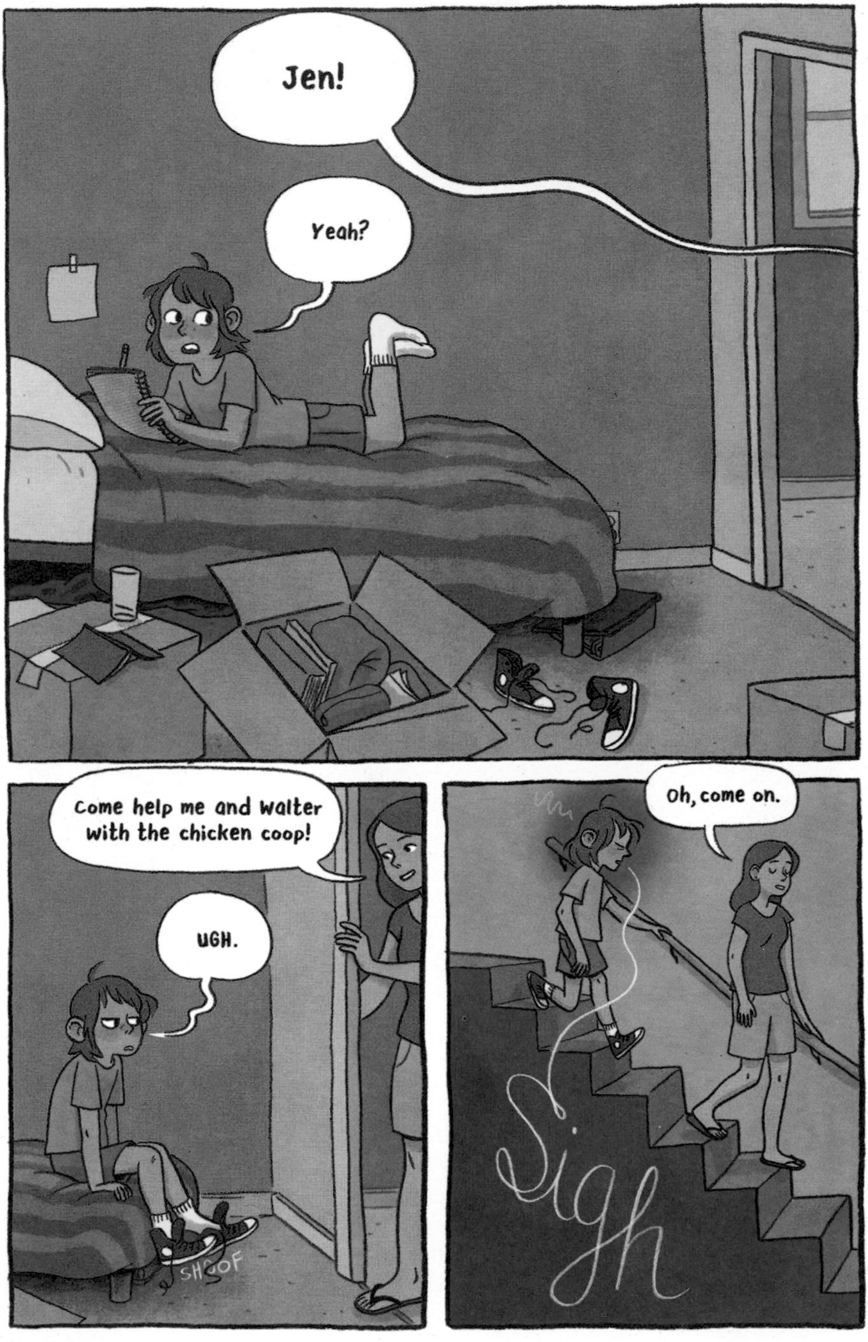
Jen!
Yeah?
Come help me and Walter with the chicken coop!
UGH.
Oh, come on.
Sigh

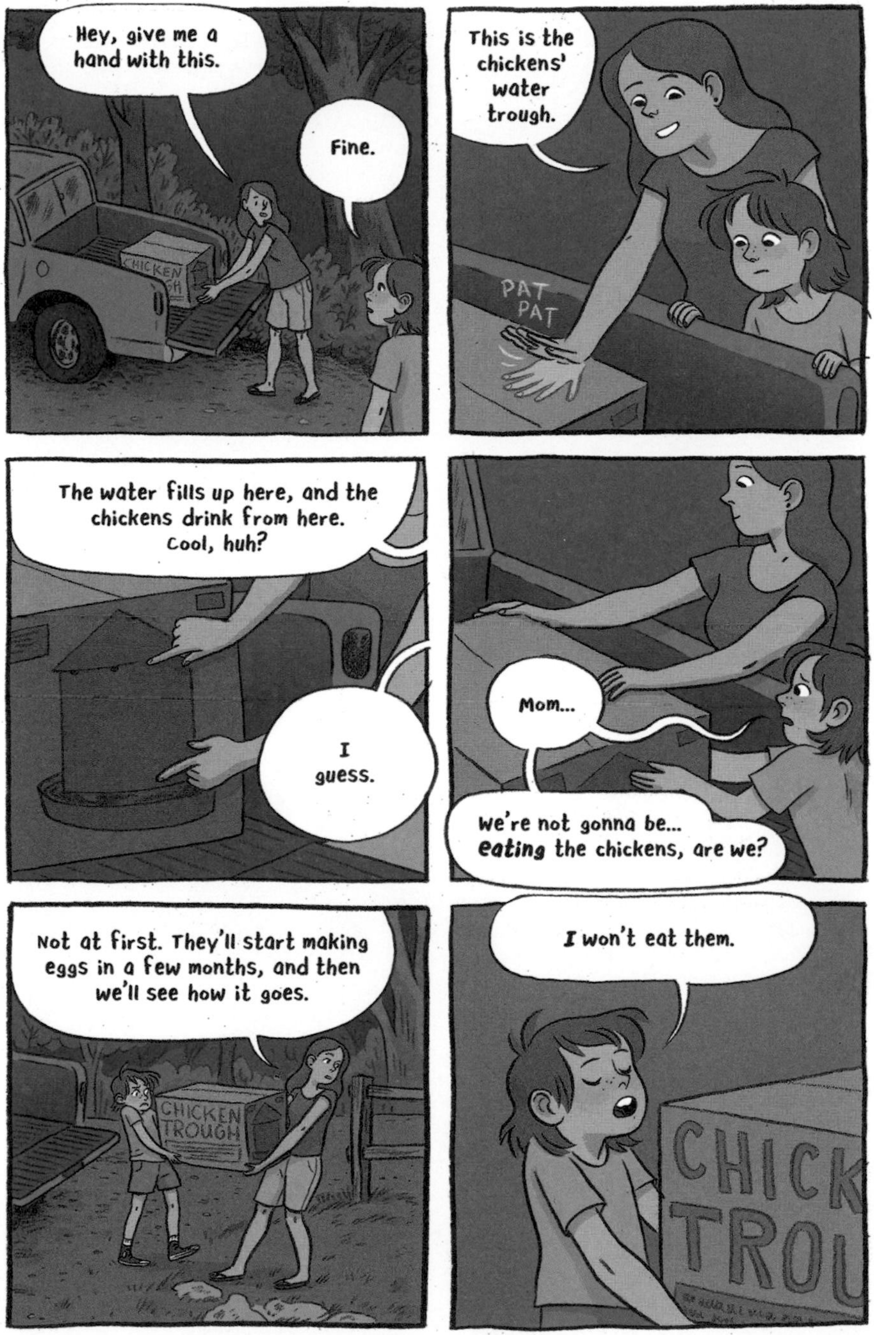
Hey, give me a hand with this.
Fine.
CHICKEN TROUGH
This is the chickens' water trough.
PAT PAT
The water fills up here, and the chickens drink from here. Cool, huh?
I guess.
Mom...
We're not gonna be... *eating* the chickens, are we?
Not at first. They'll start making eggs in a few months, and then we'll see how it goes.
CHICKEN TROUGH
I won't eat them.
CHICK TROU

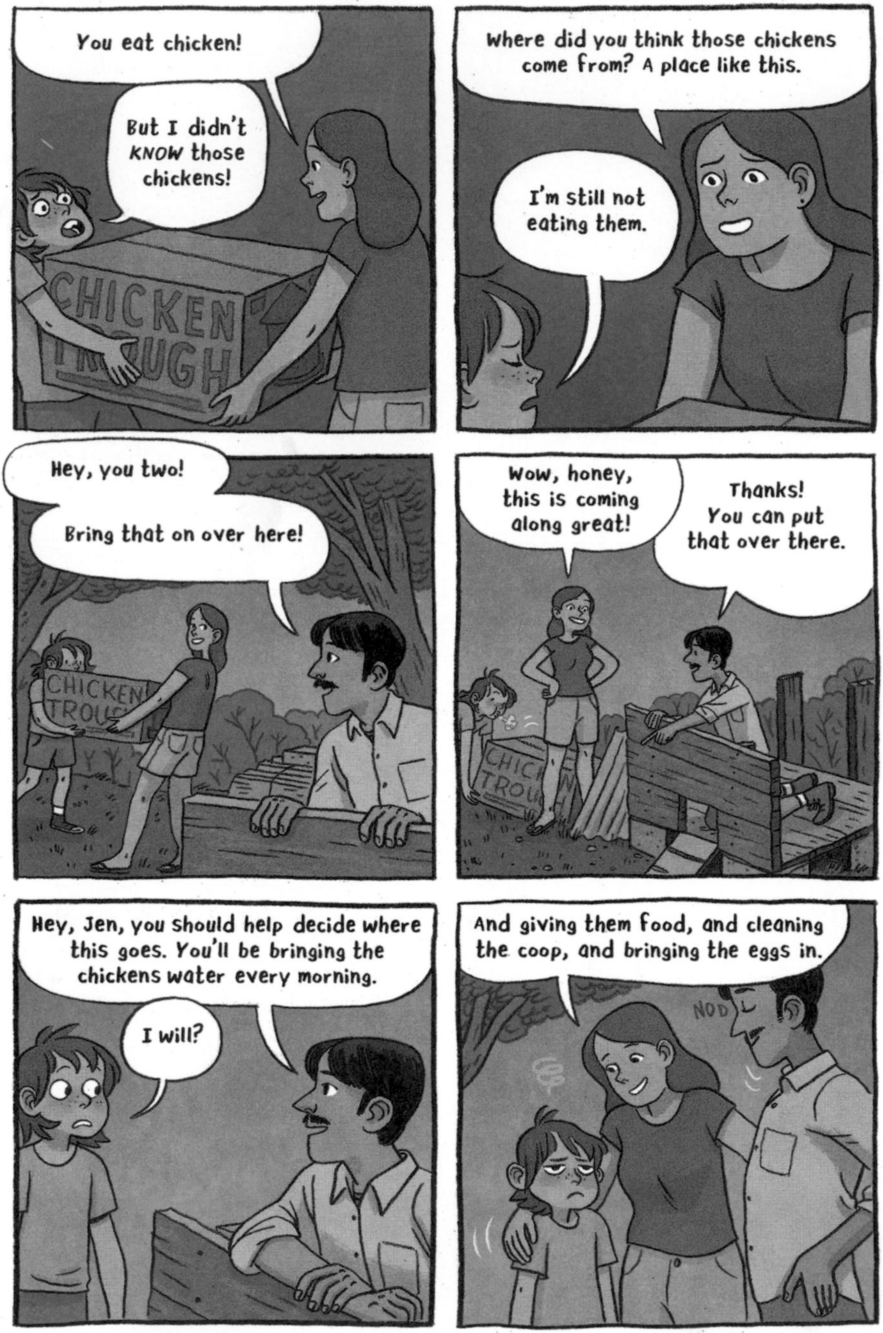
You eat chicken!
But I didn't KNOW those chickens!
CHICKEN TROUGH
Where did you think those chickens come from? A place like this.
I'm still not eating them.
Hey, you two!
Bring that on over here!
CHICKEN TROUG
Wow, honey, this is coming along great!
Thanks! You can put that over there.
Hey, Jen, you should help decide where this goes. You'll be bringing the chickens water every morning.
I will?
And giving them food, and cleaning the coop, and bringing the eggs in.
NOD

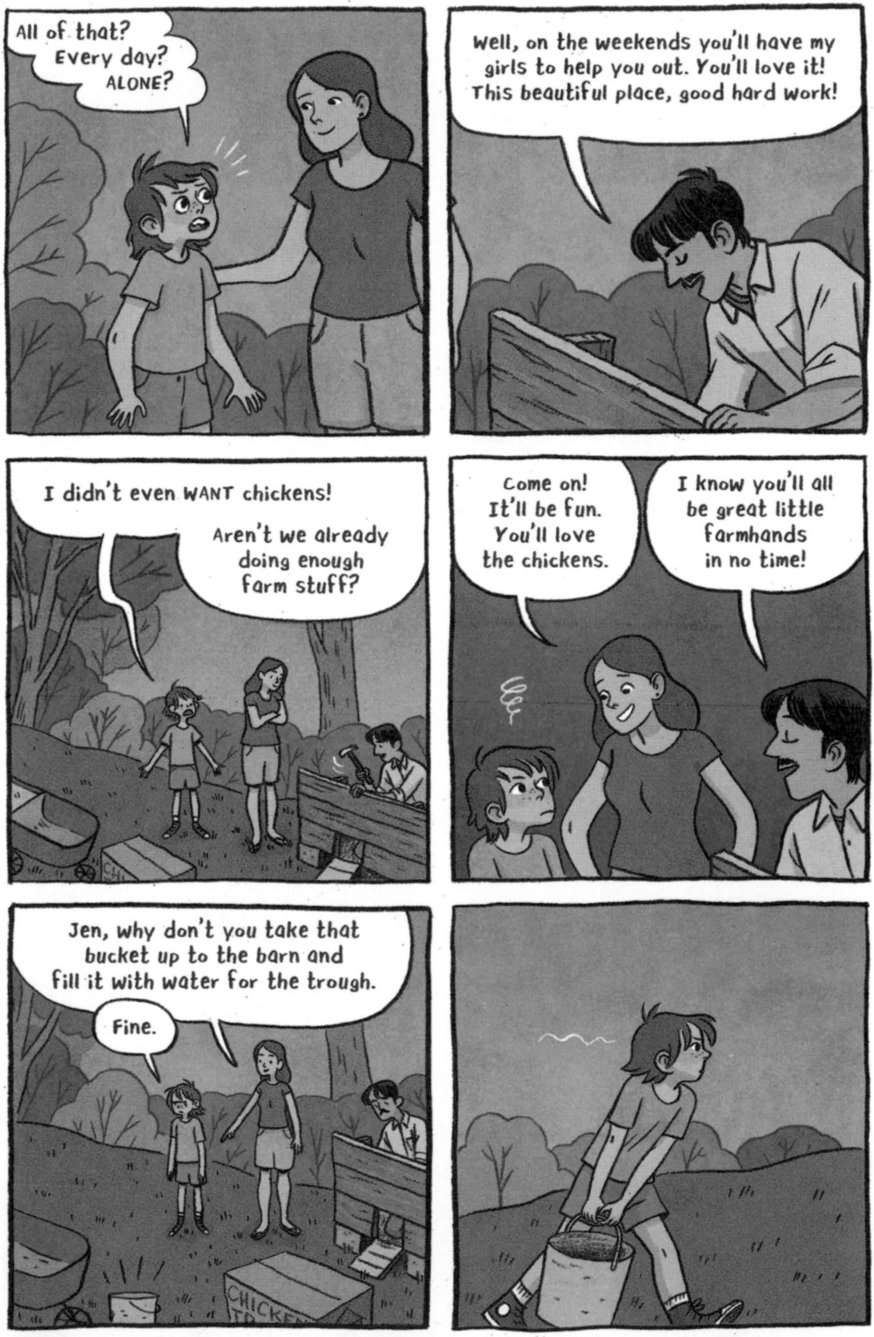
All of that? Every day? ALONE?
Well, on the weekends you'll have my girls to help you out. You'll love it! This beautiful place, good hard work!
I didn't even WANT chickens!
Aren't we already doing enough farm stuff?
Come on! It'll be fun. You'll love the chickens.
I know you'll all be great little farmhands in no time!
Jen, why don't you take that bucket up to the barn and fill it with water for the trough.
Fine.

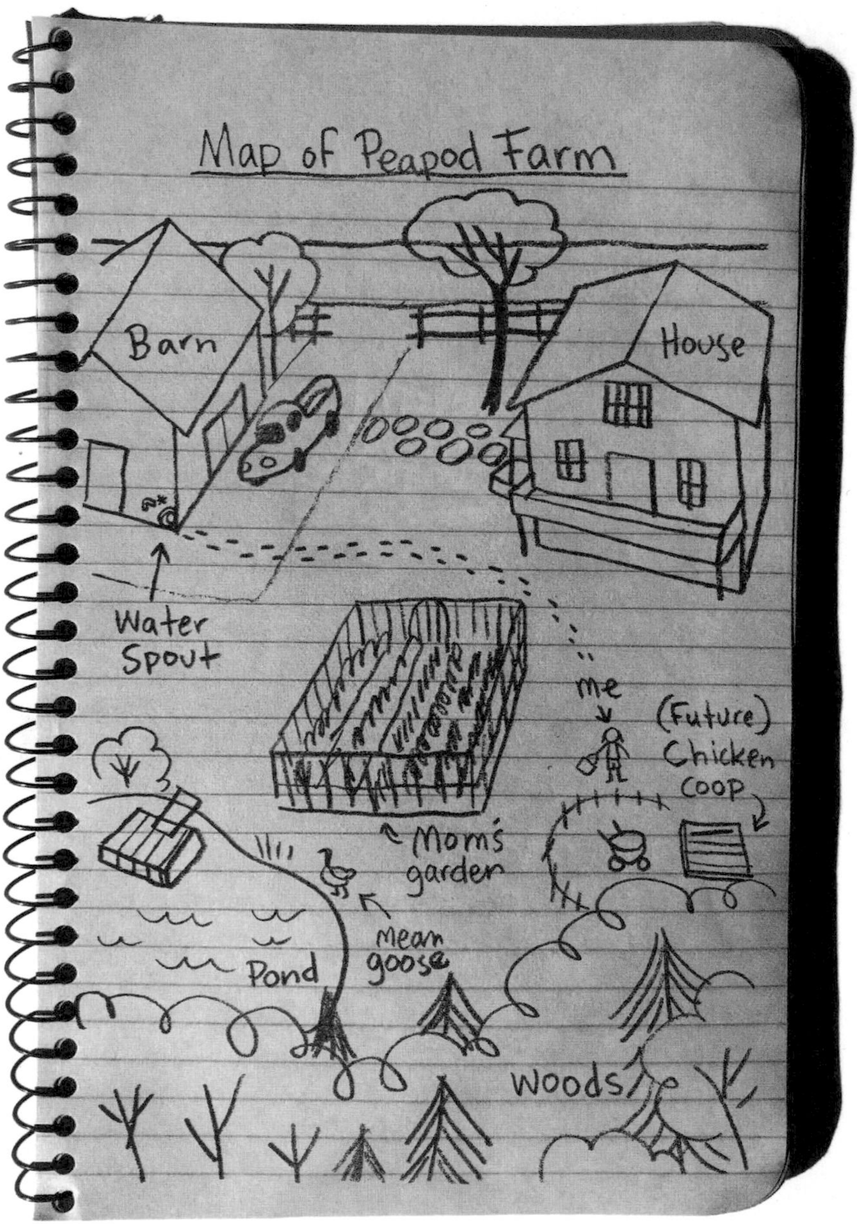

Map of Peapod Farm
Barn
House
Water Spout
me
(Future) Chicken coop
Mom's garden
mean goose
Pond
Woods

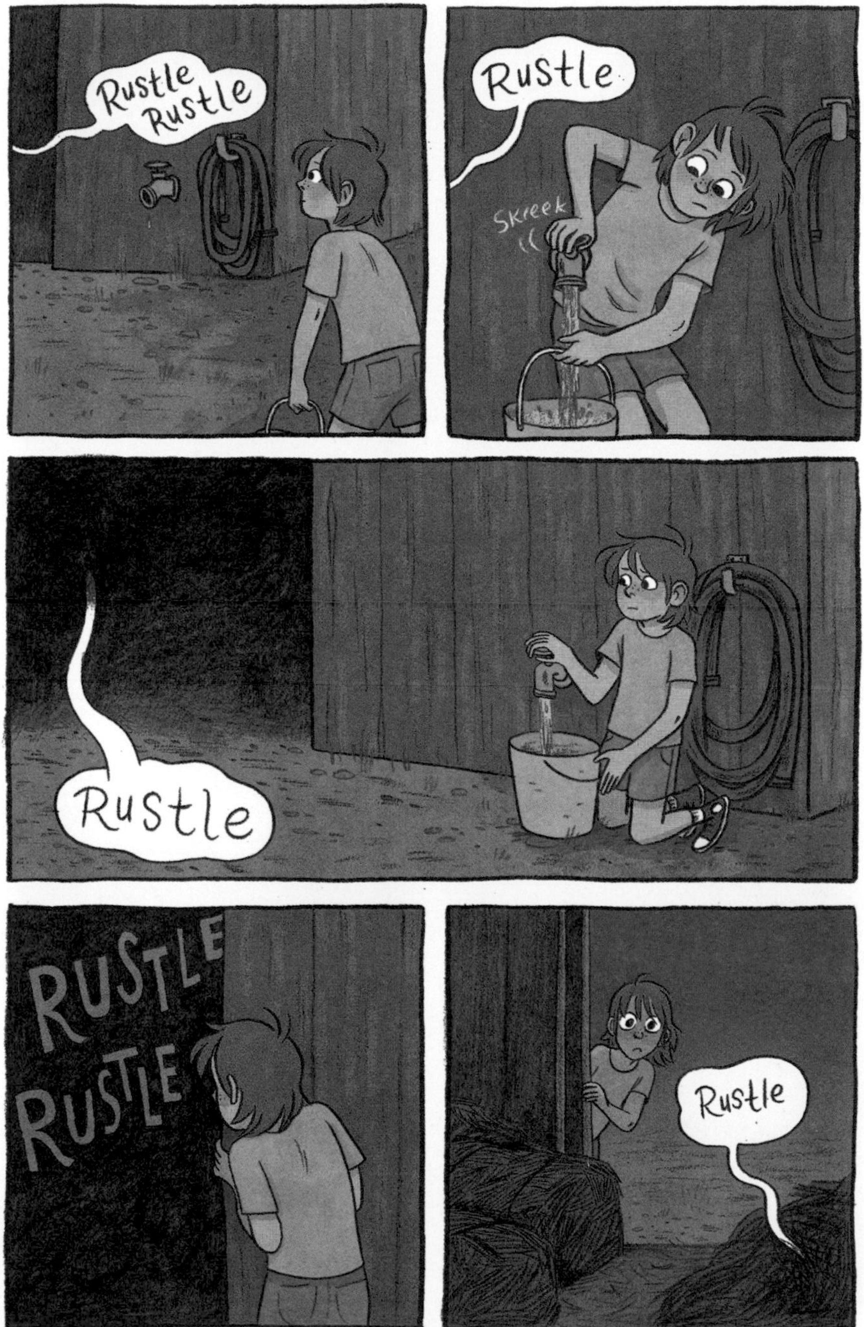
Rustle Rustle
Rustle
Skreek
Rustle
RUSTLE
RUSTLE
Rustle

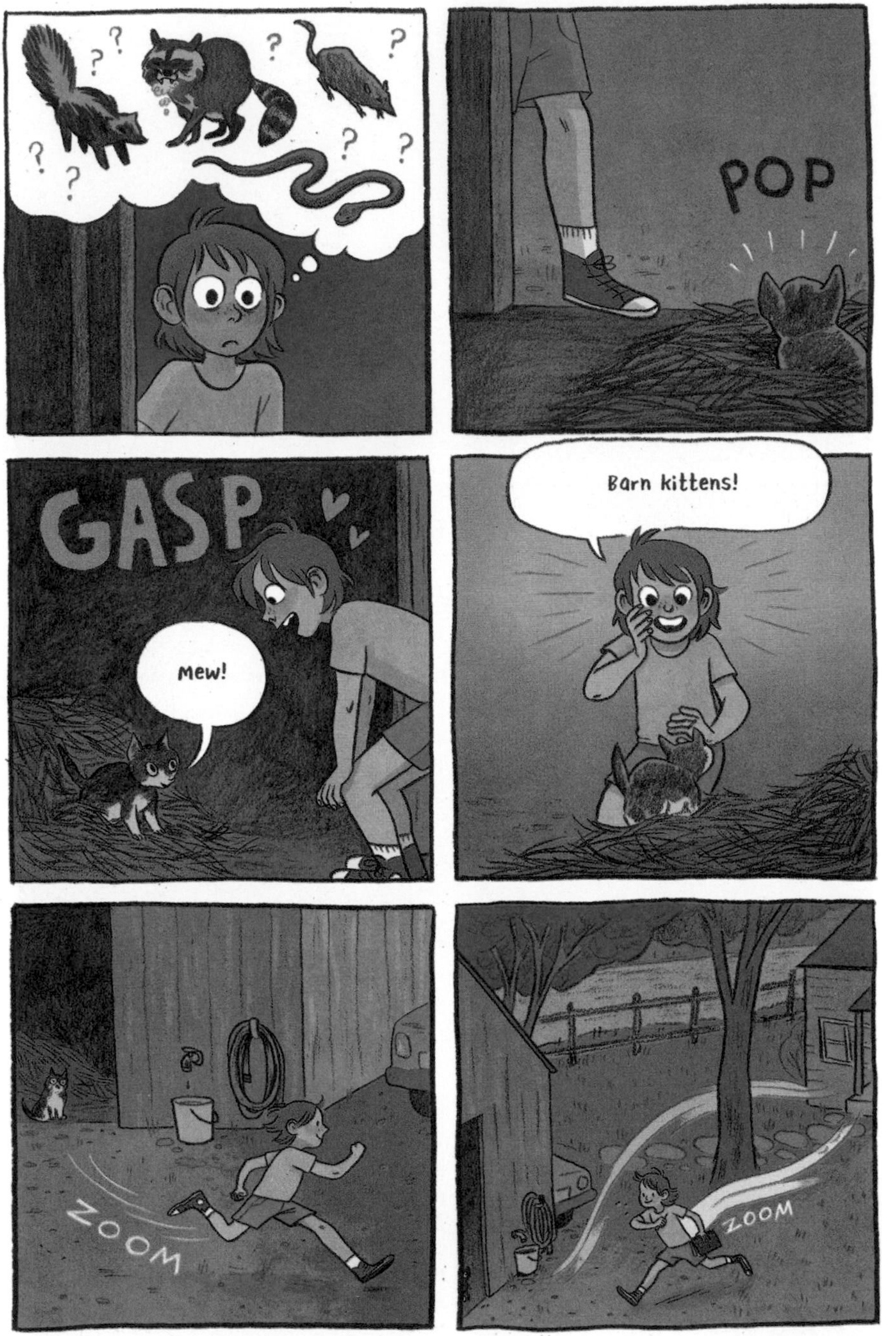
POP
GASP
Mew!
Barn kittens!
ZOOM
ZOOM

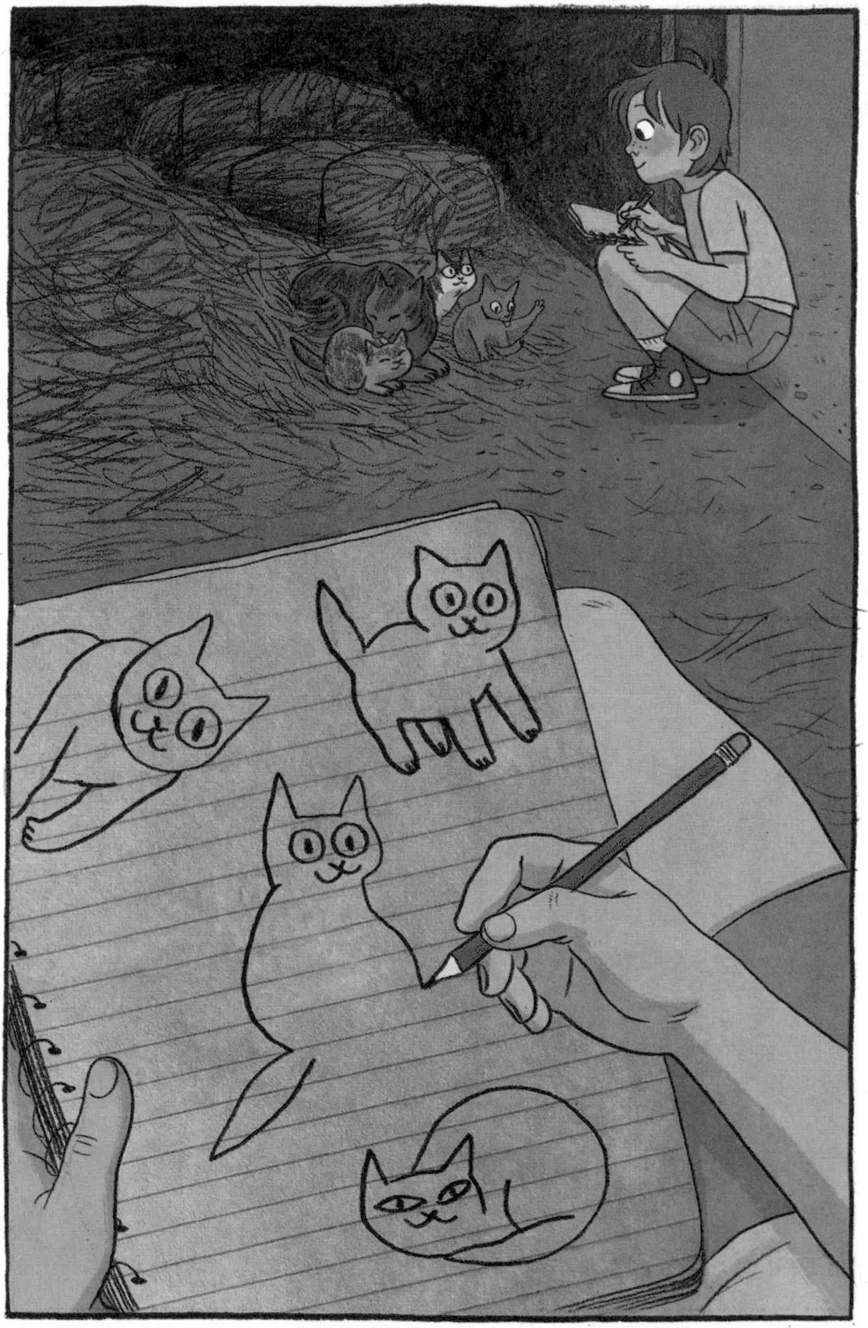

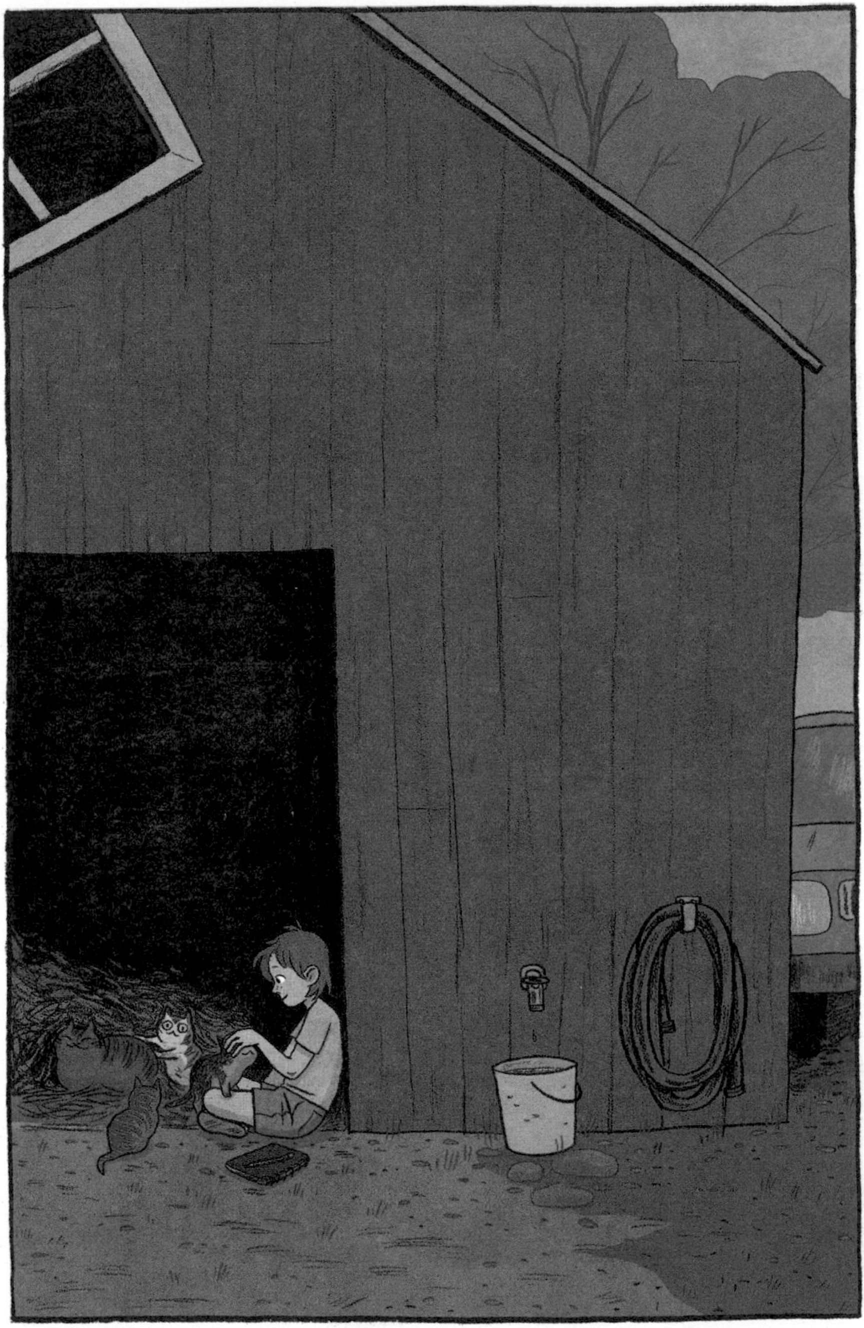

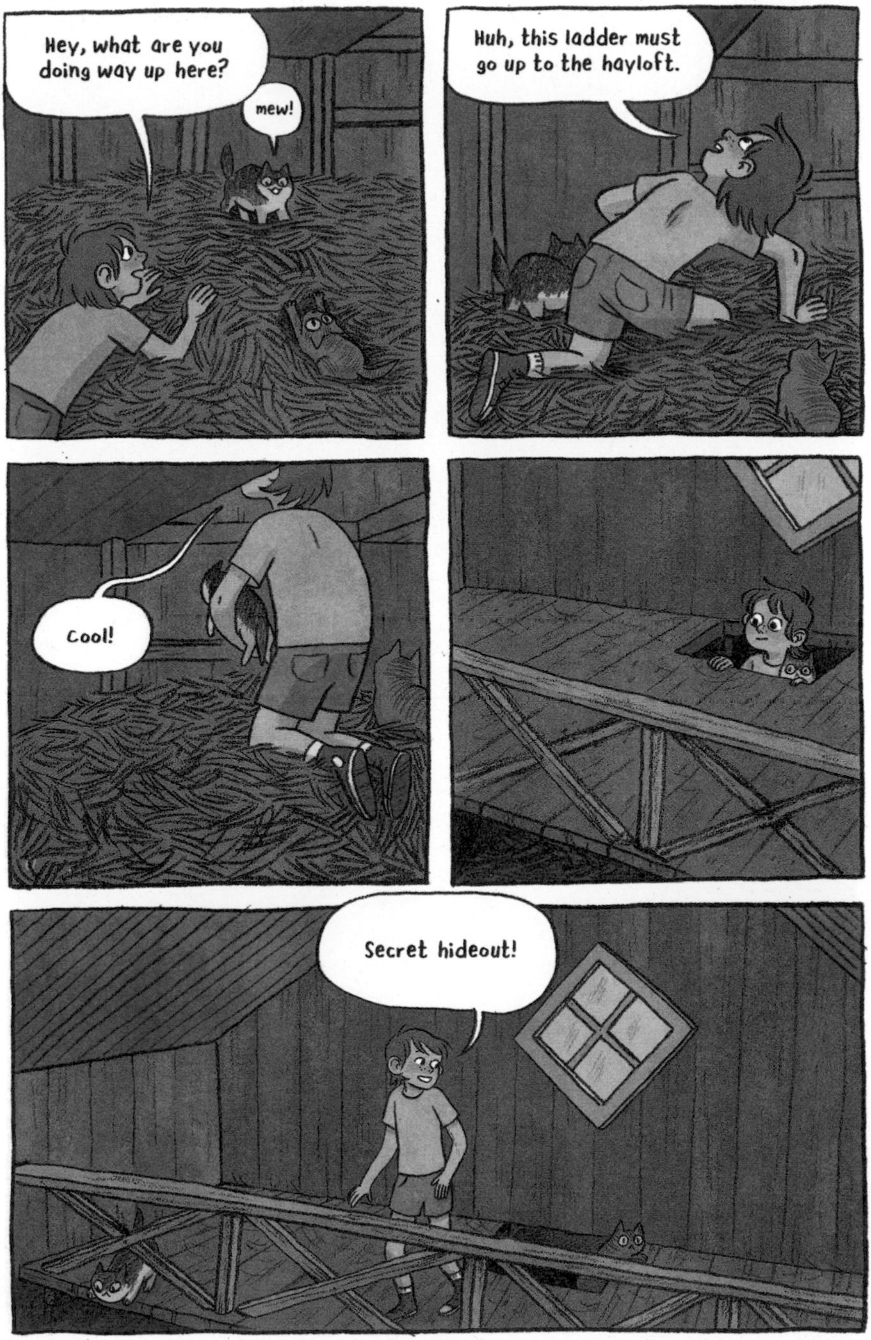
Hey, what are you doing way up here?
mew!
Huh, this ladder must go up to the hayloft.
Cool!
Secret hideout!

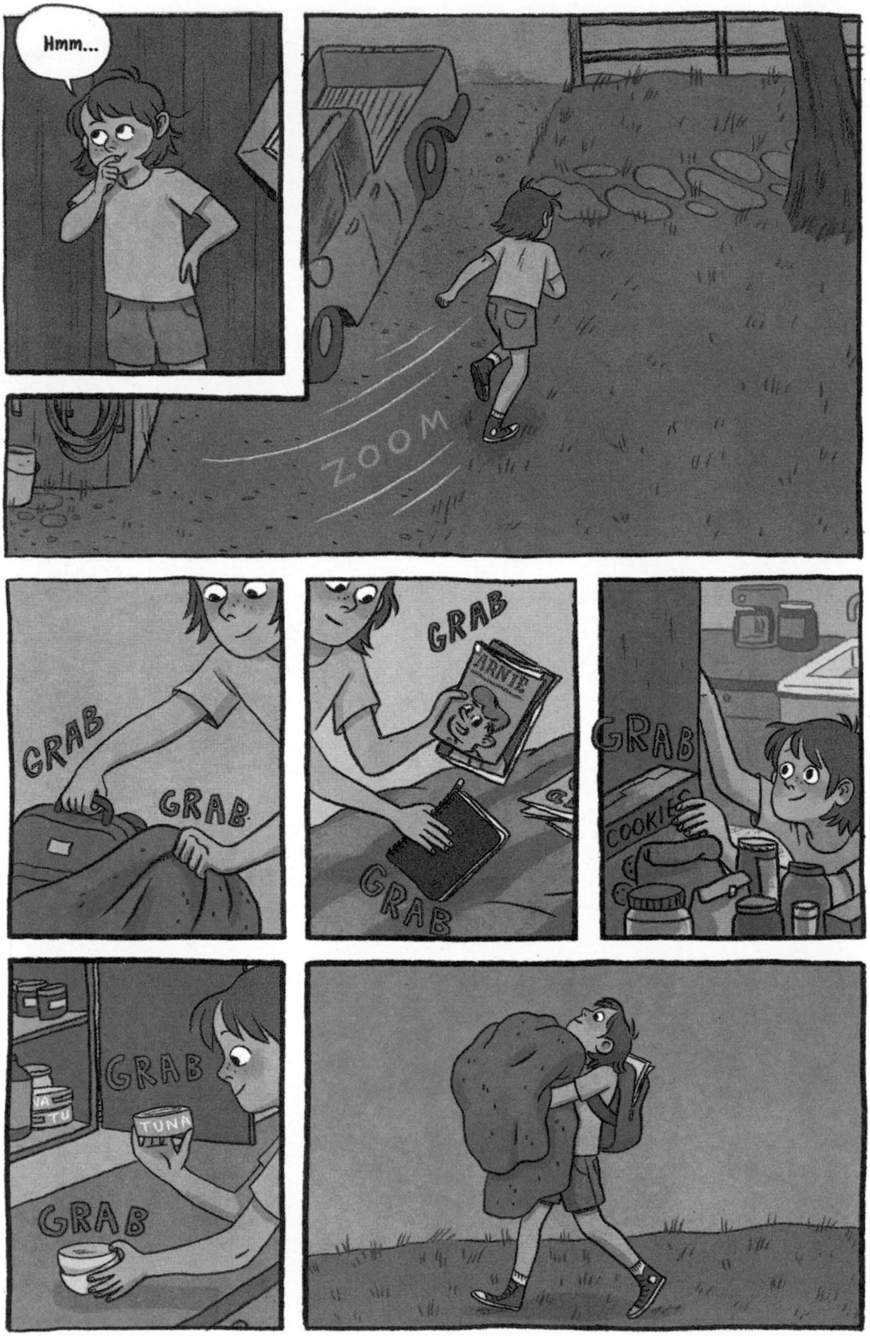
Hmm...
ZOOM
GRAB
GRAB
GRAB
ARNIE
GRAB
GRAB
COOKIES
GRAB
TUNA
GRAB

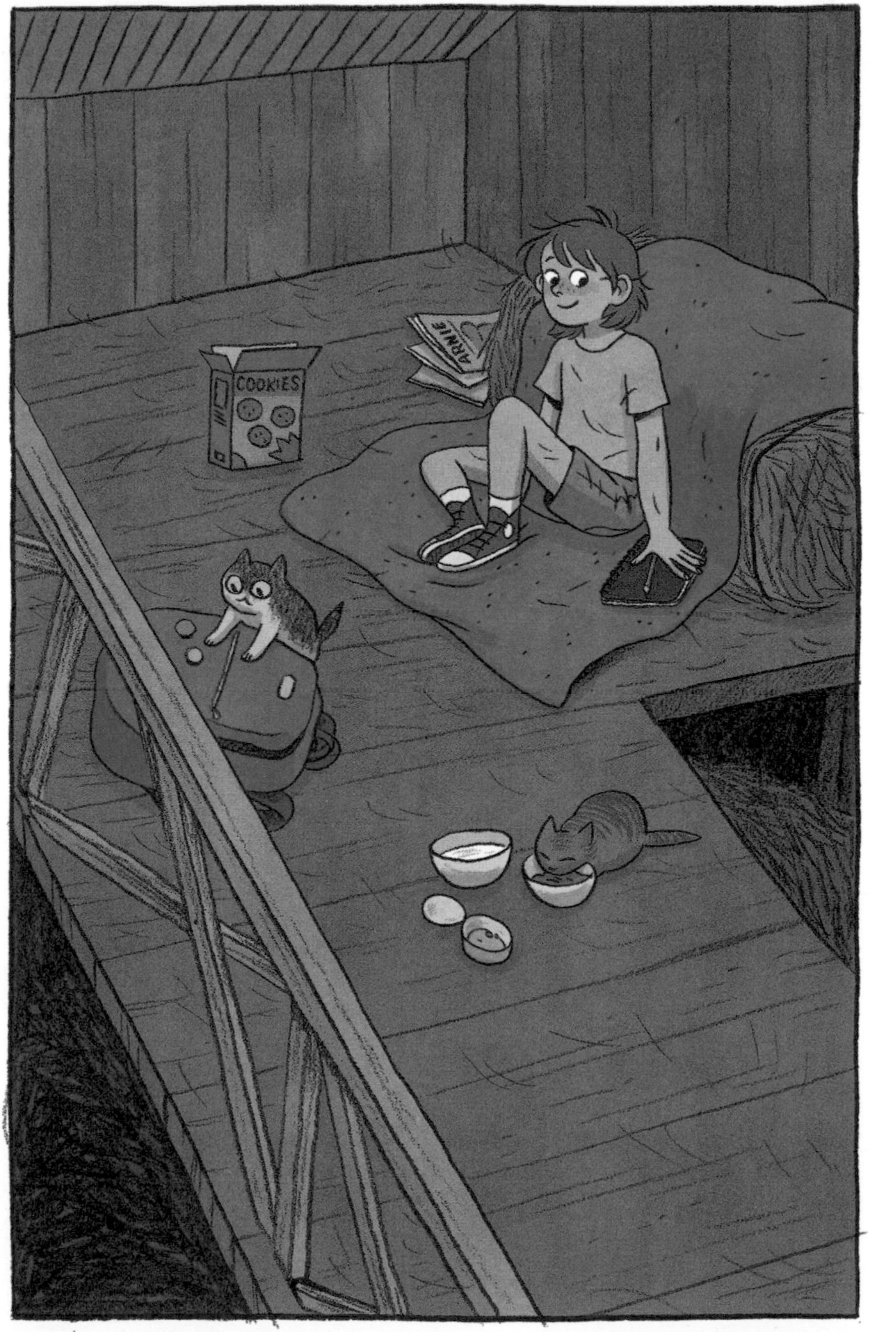
ARNIE
COOKIES

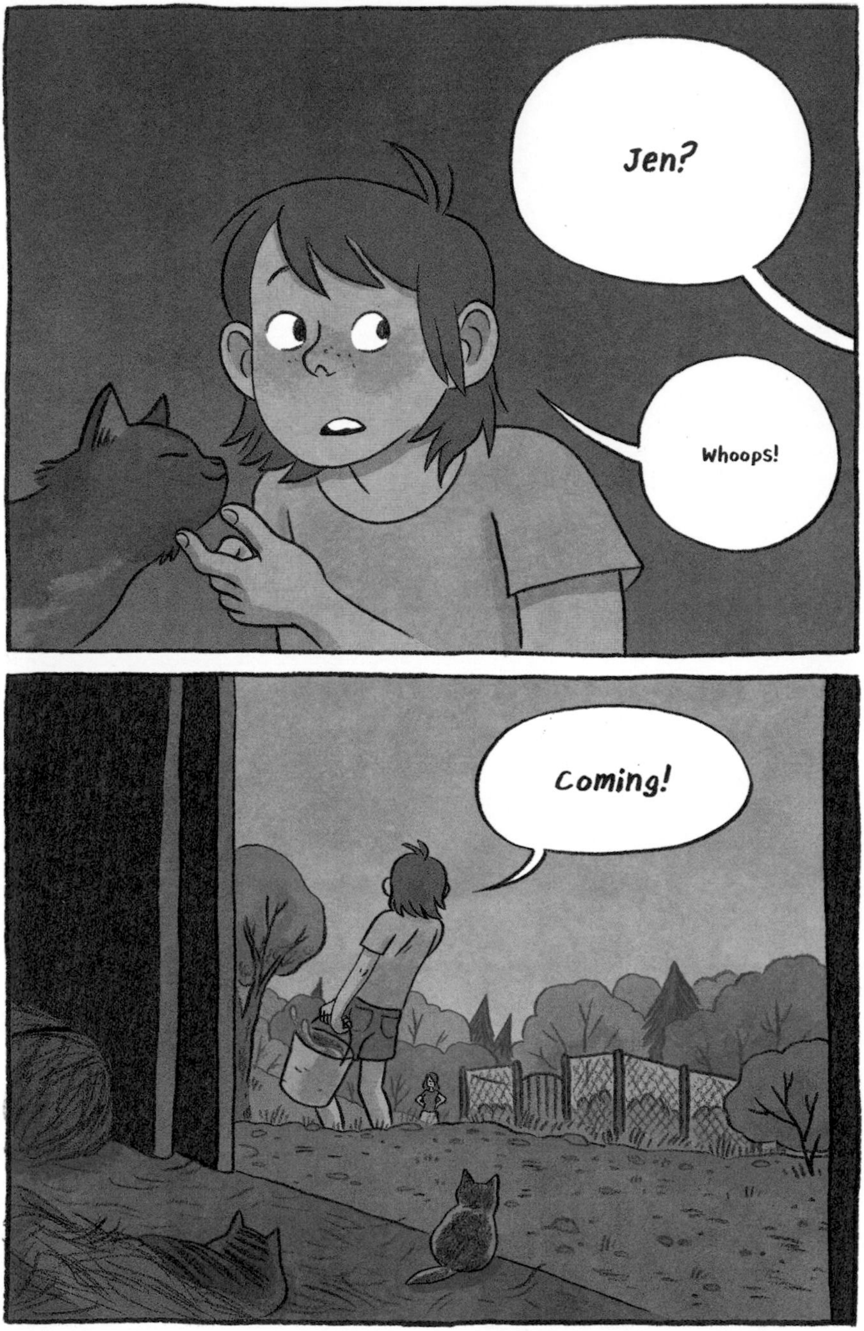
Jen?
Whoops!
Coming!

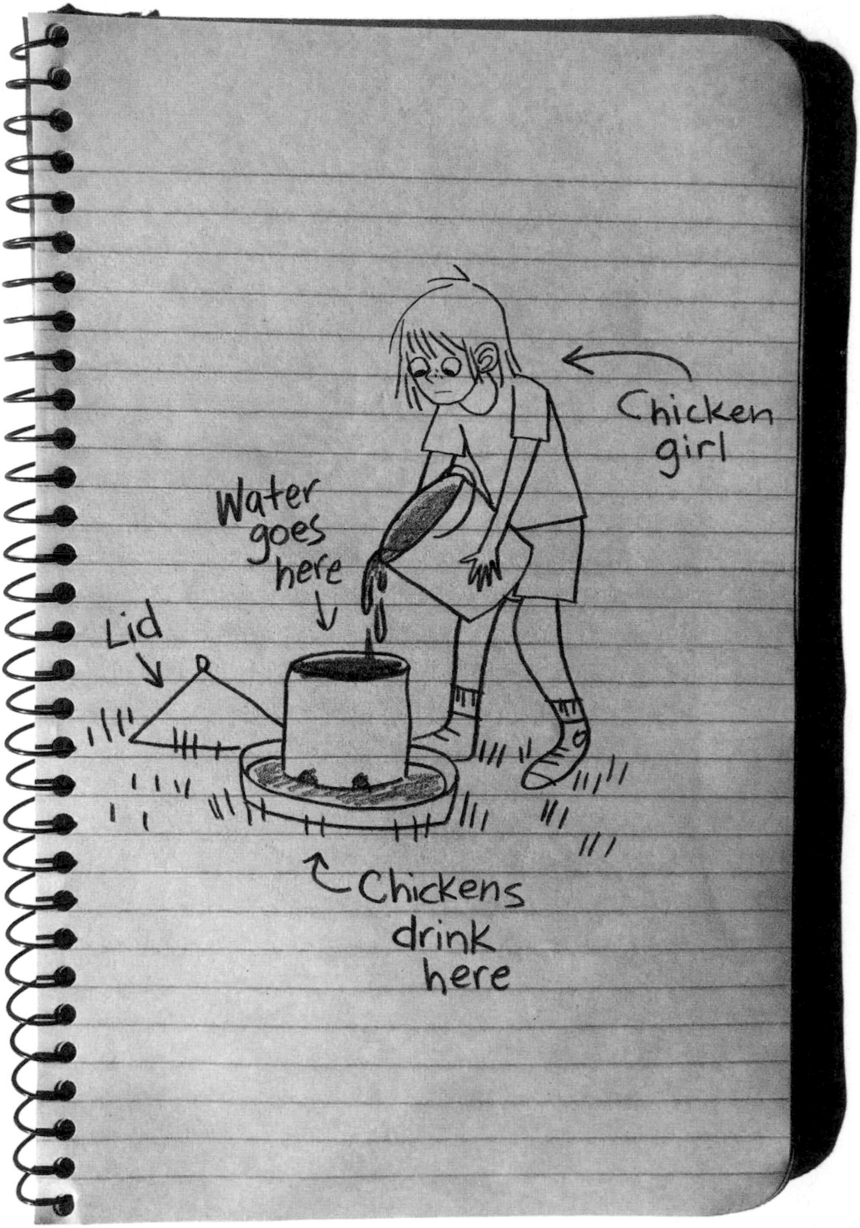
Chicken girl
Water goes here
Lid
Chickens drink here

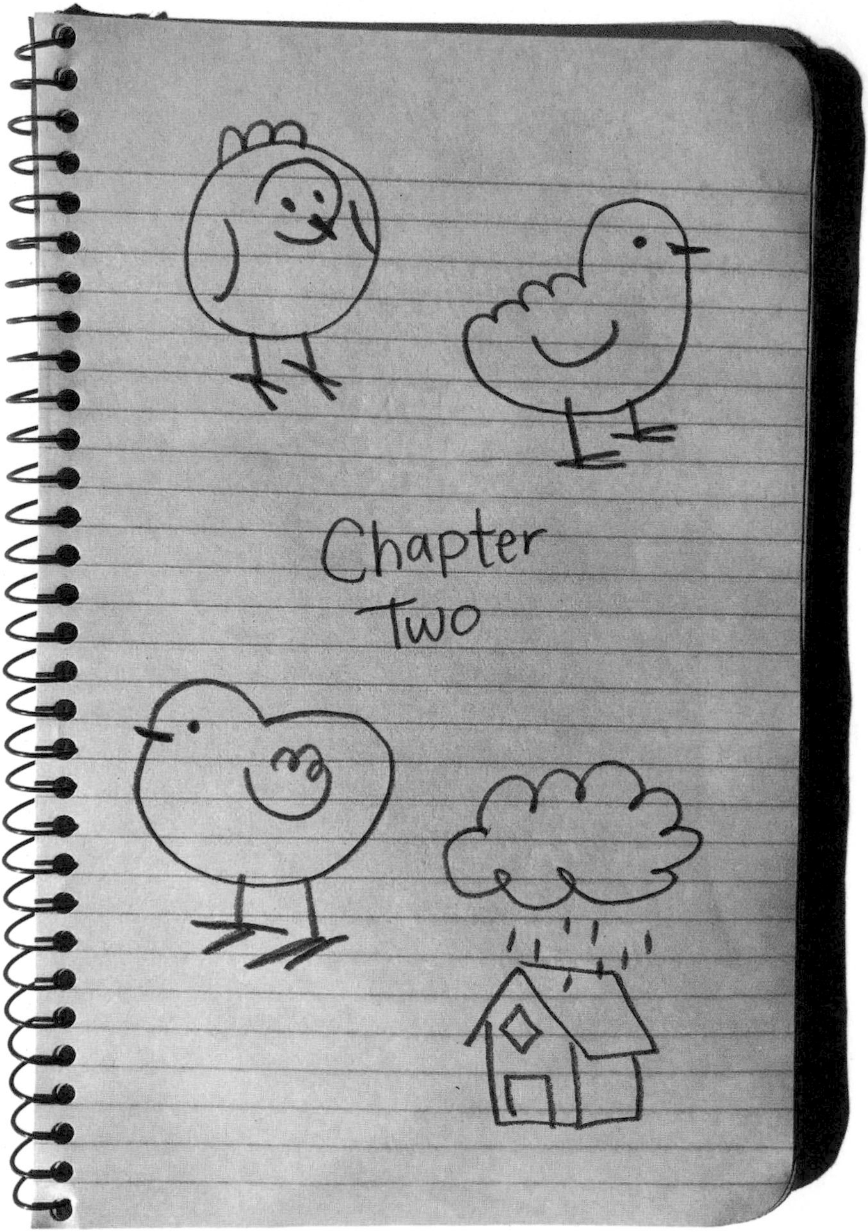
Chapter
Two

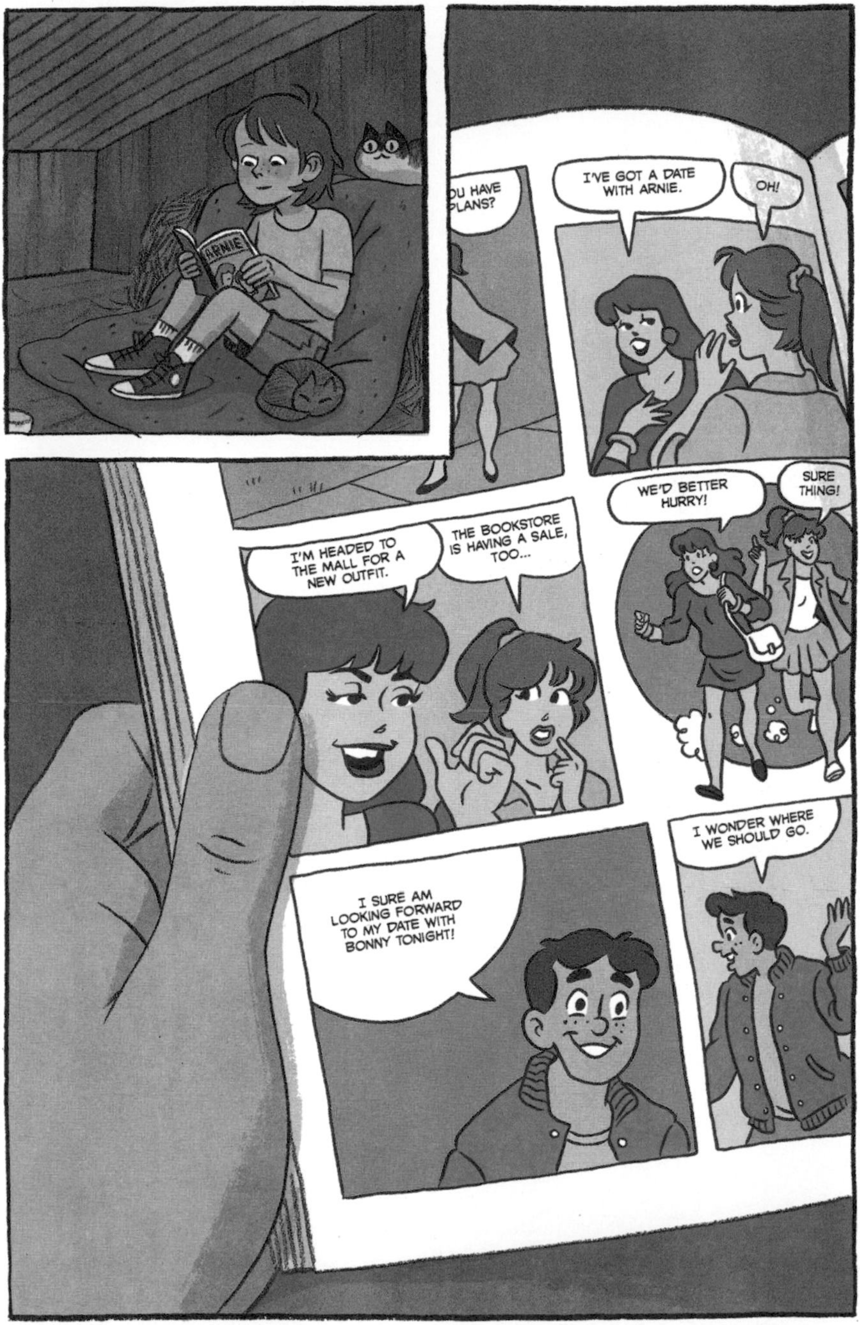
ARNIE
U HAVE PLANS?
I'VE GOT A DATE WITH ARNIE.
OH!
I'M HEADED TO THE MALL FOR A NEW OUTFIT.
THE BOOKSTORE IS HAVING A SALE, TOO...
WE'D BETTER HURRY!
SURE THING!
I SURE AM LOOKING FORWARD TO MY DATE WITH BONNY TONIGHT!
I WONDER WHERE WE SHOULD GO.

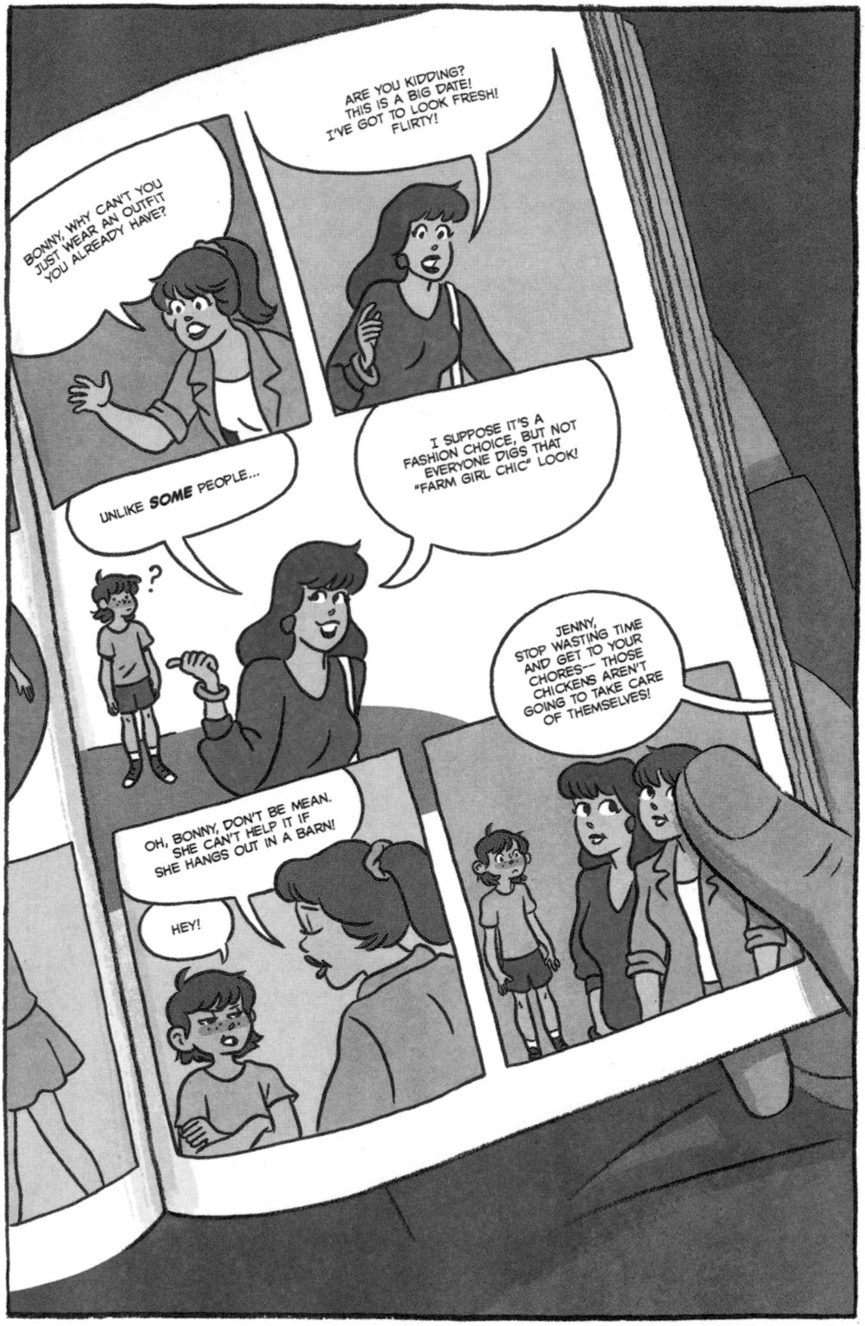
BONNY, WHY CAN'T YOU JUST WEAR AN OUTFIT YOU ALREADY HAVE?
ARE YOU KIDDING? THIS IS A BIG DATE! I'VE GOT TO LOOK FRESH! FLIRTY!
UNLIKE SOME PEOPLE...
I SUPPOSE IT'S A FASHION CHOICE, BUT NOT EVERYONE DIGS THAT "FARM GIRL CHIC" LOOK!
?
OH, BONNY, DON'T BE MEAN. SHE CAN'T HELP IT IF SHE HANGS OUT IN A BARN!
HEY!
JENNY, STOP WASTING TIME AND GET TO YOUR CHORES-- THOSE CHICKENS AREN'T GOING TO TAKE CARE OF THEMSELVES!

23

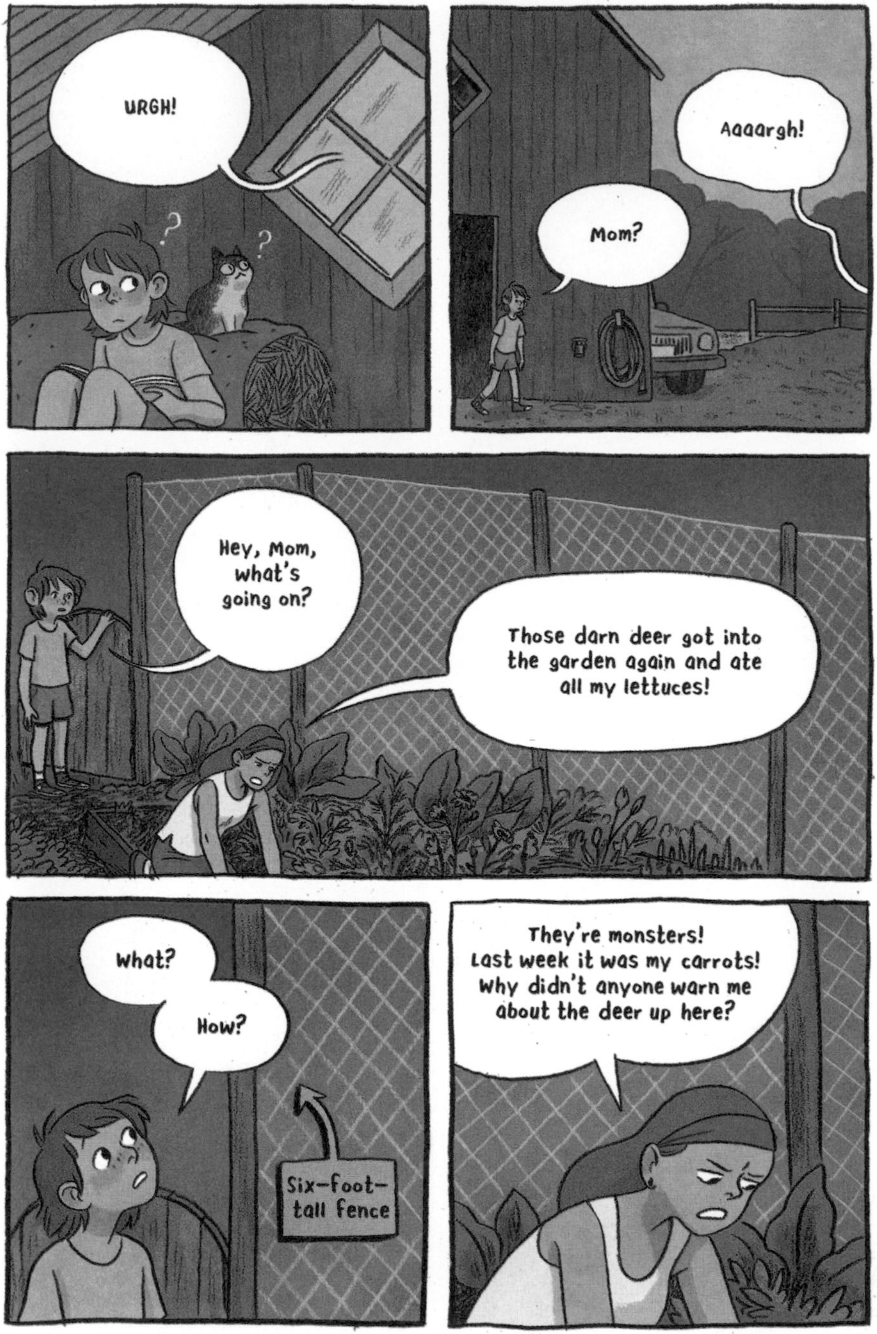
URGH!
Aaaargh!
Mom?
Hey, Mom, what's going on?
Those darn deer got into the garden again and ate all my lettuces!
What?
How?
Six-foot-tall fence
They're monsters! Last week it was my carrots! Why didn't anyone warn me about the deer up here?

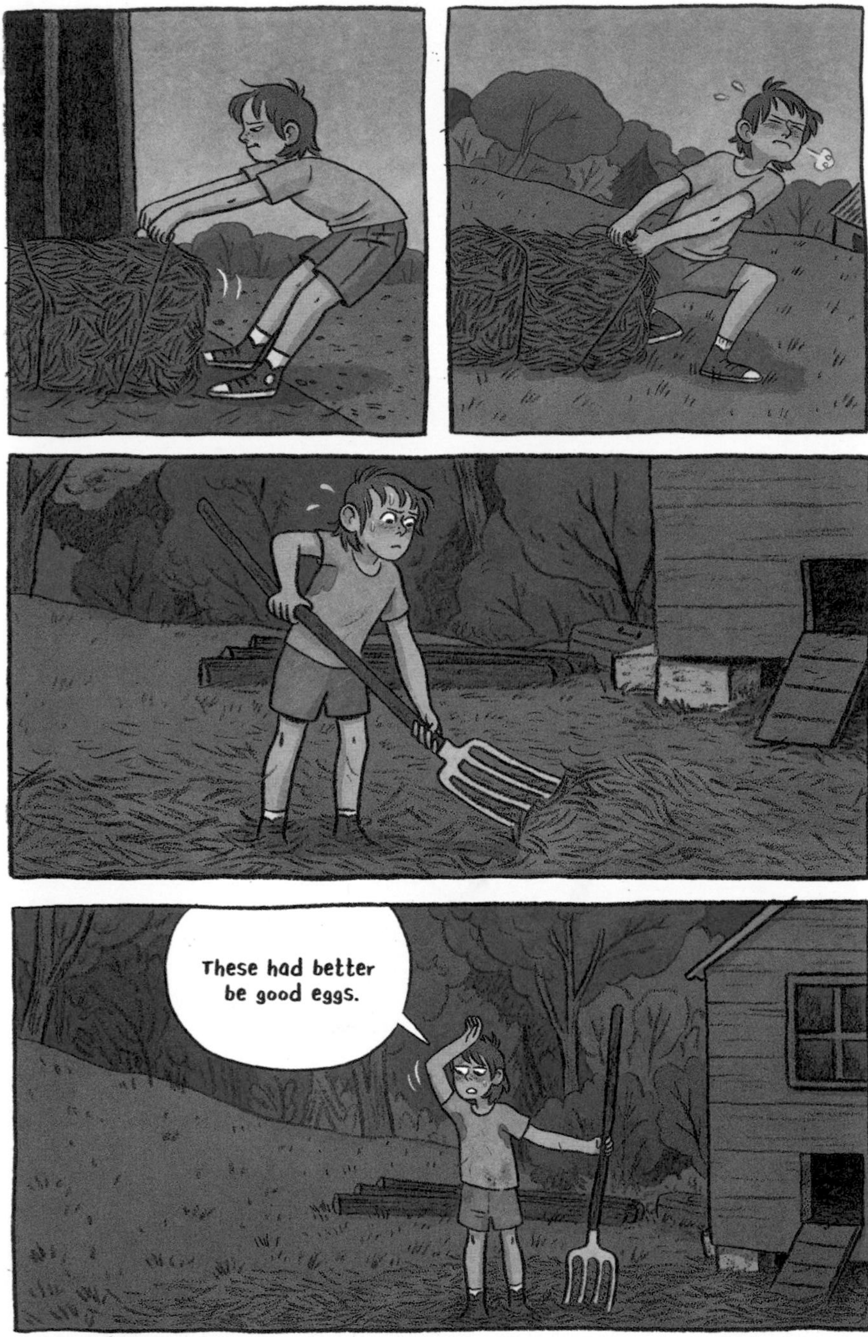
These had better be good eggs.

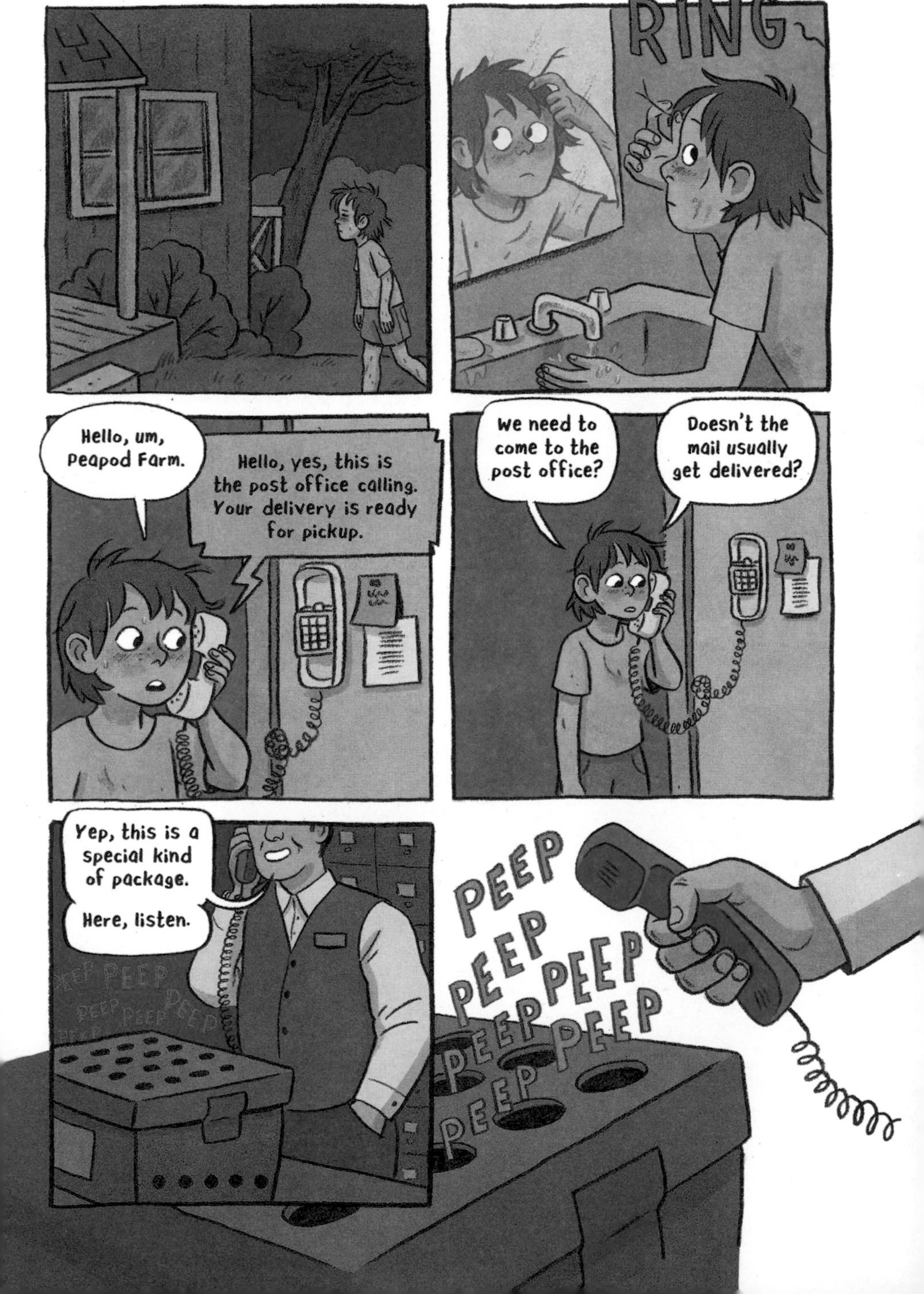
RING
Hello, um, Peapod Farm.
Hello, yes, this is the post office calling. Your delivery is ready for pickup.
We need to come to the post office?
Doesn't the mail usually get delivered?
Yep, this is a special kind of package.
Here, listen.
PEEP PEEP PEEP PEEP PEEP PEEP PEEP PEEP

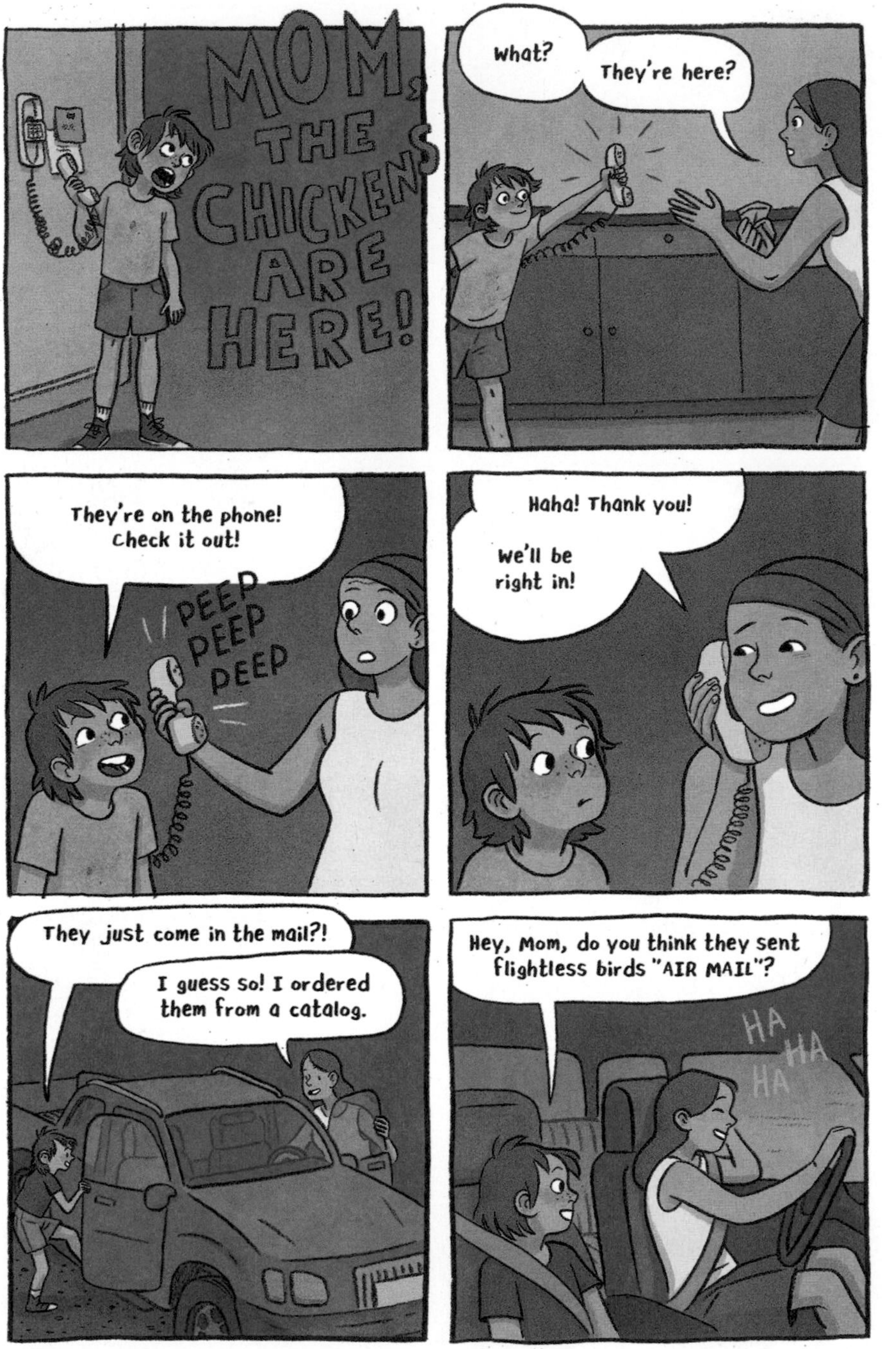
MOM, THE CHICKENS ARE HERE!
What?
They're here?
They're on the phone! Check it out!
PEEP PEEP PEEP
Haha! Thank you!
We'll be right in!
They just come in the mail?!
I guess so! I ordered them from a catalog.
Hey, Mom, do you think they sent flightless birds "AIR MAIL"?
HA HA HA

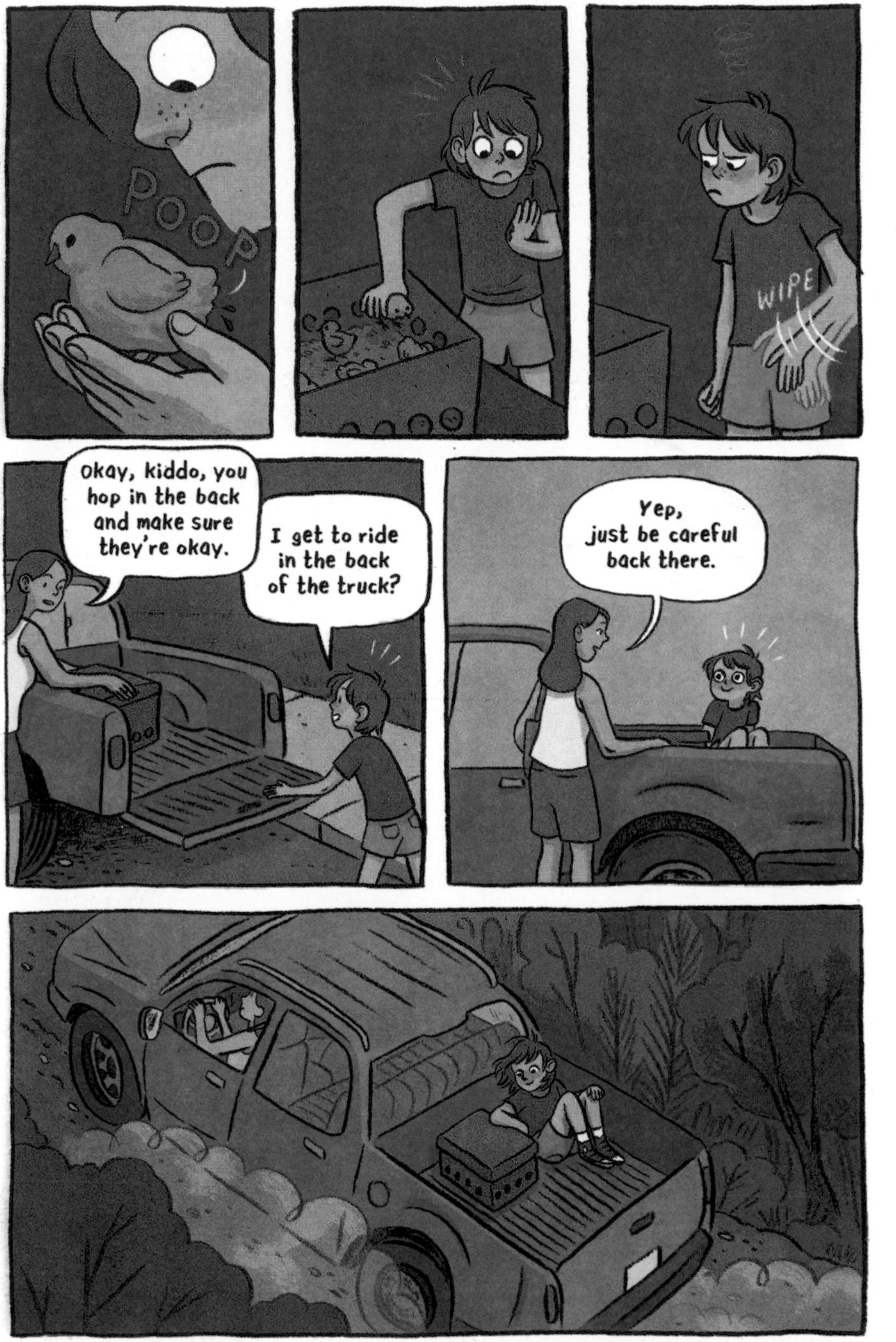
POOP
WIPE
Okay, kiddo, you hop in the back and make sure they're okay.
I get to ride in the back of the truck?
Yep, just be careful back there.

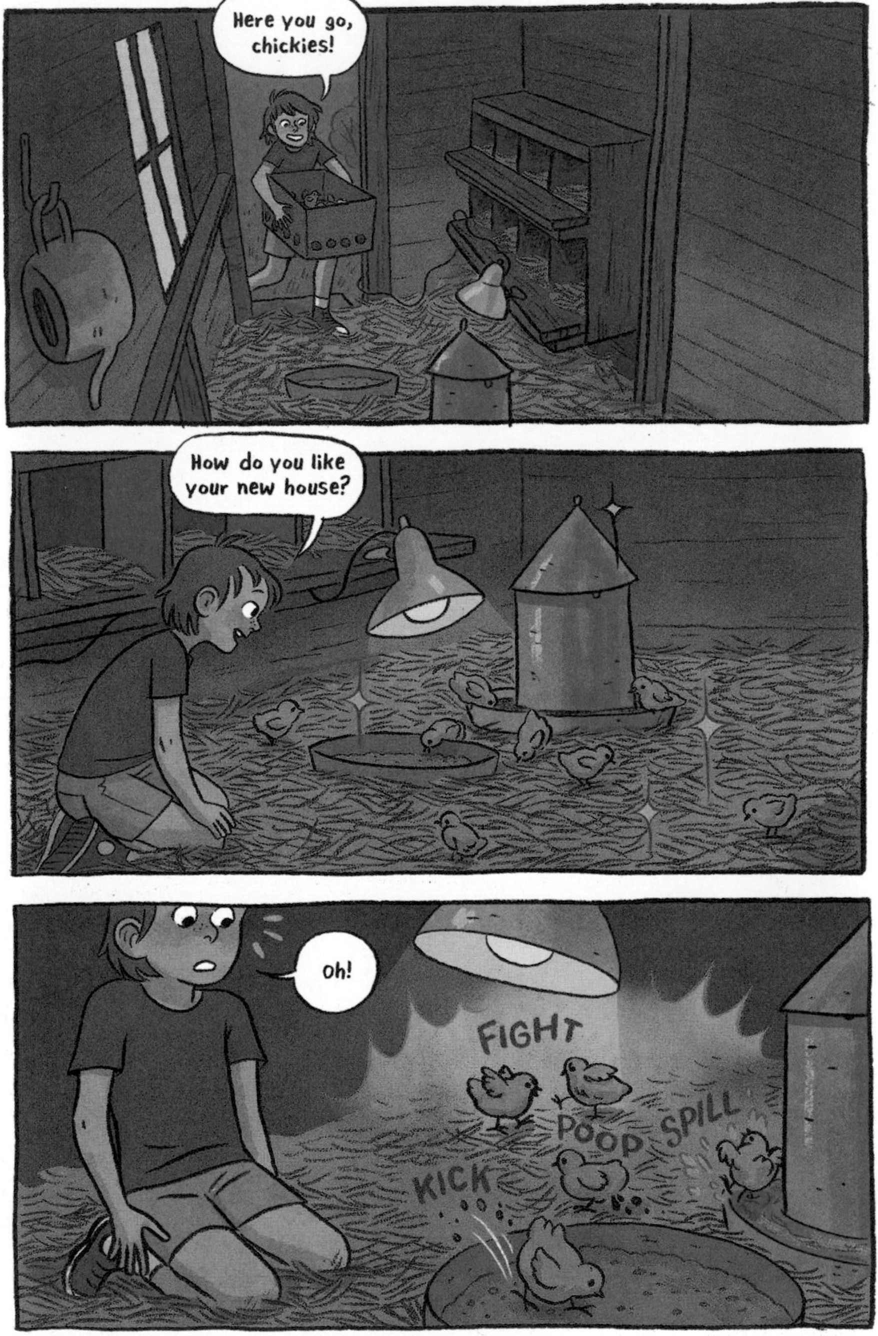
Here you go, chickies!
How do you like your new house?
Oh!
FIGHT
POOP
SPILL
KICK

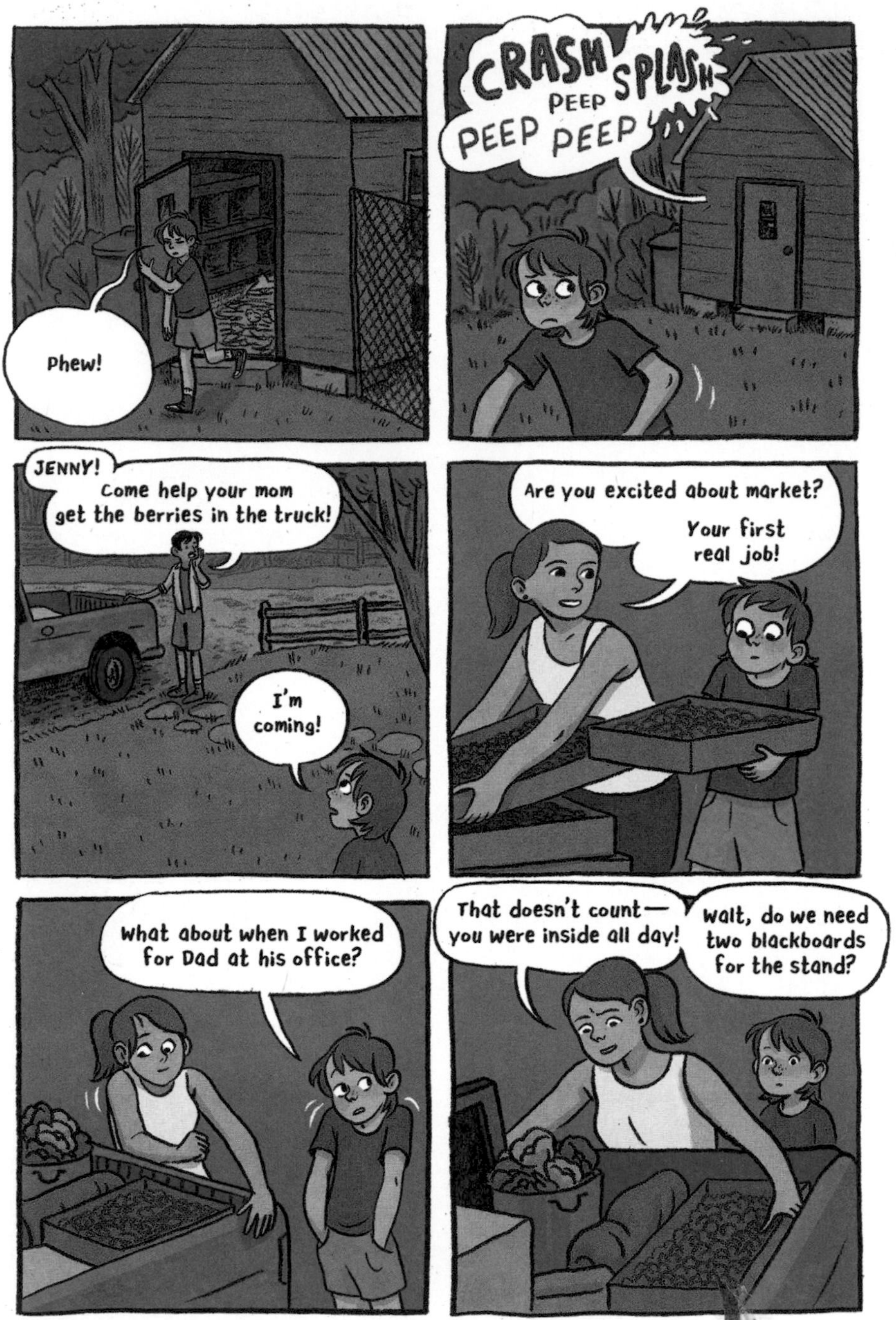
Phew!
CRASH SPLASH
PEEP PEEP PEEP
JENNY! Come help your mom get the berries in the truck!
I'm coming!
Are you excited about market?
Your first real job!
What about when I worked for Dad at his office?
That doesn't count— you were inside all day!
Walt, do we need two blackboards for the stand?

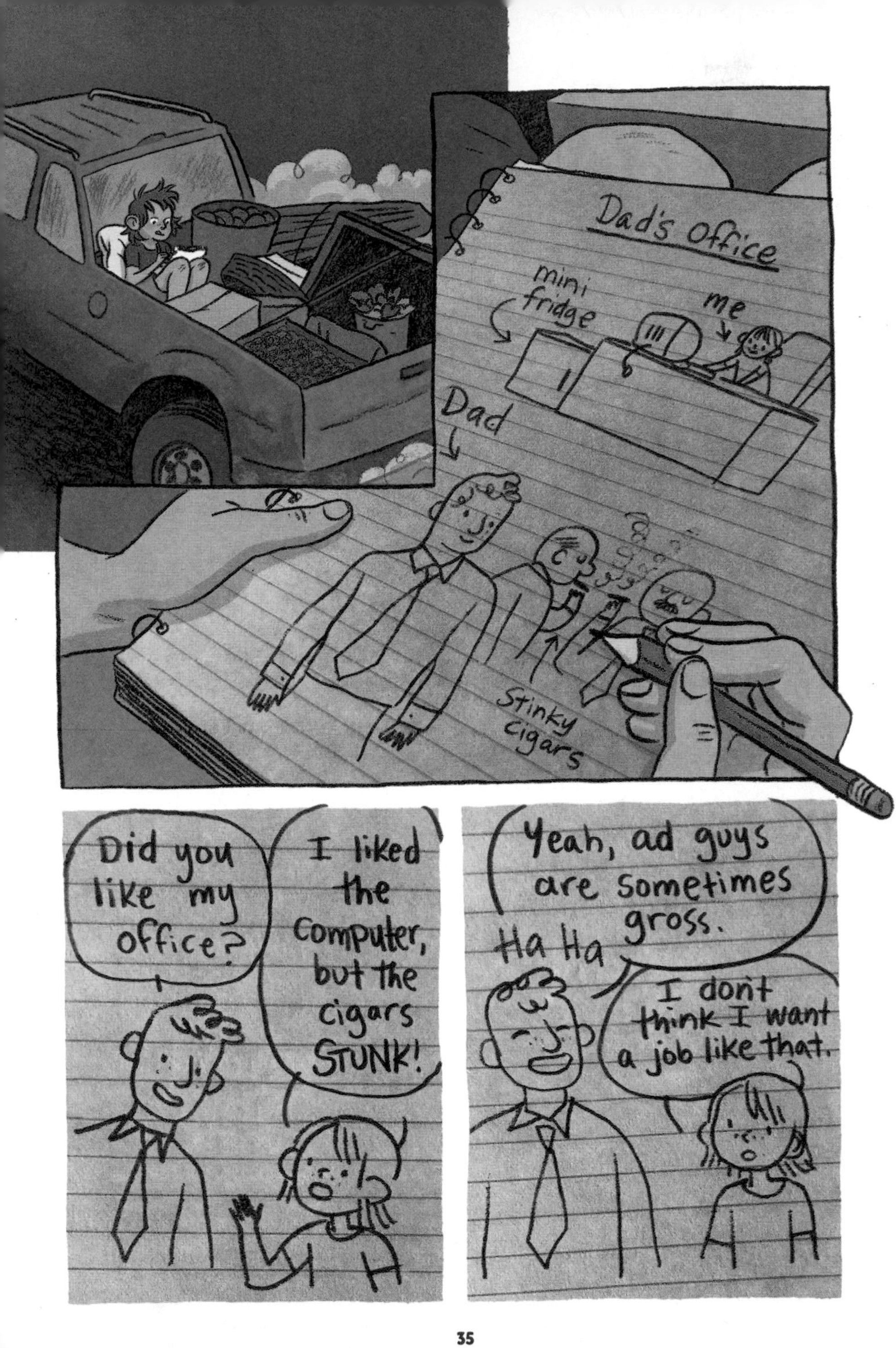
Dad's Office
mini fridge
me
Dad
Stinky cigars
Did you like my office?
I liked the computer, but the cigars STUNK!
Yeah, ad guys are sometimes gross.
Ha Ha
I don't think I want a job like that.

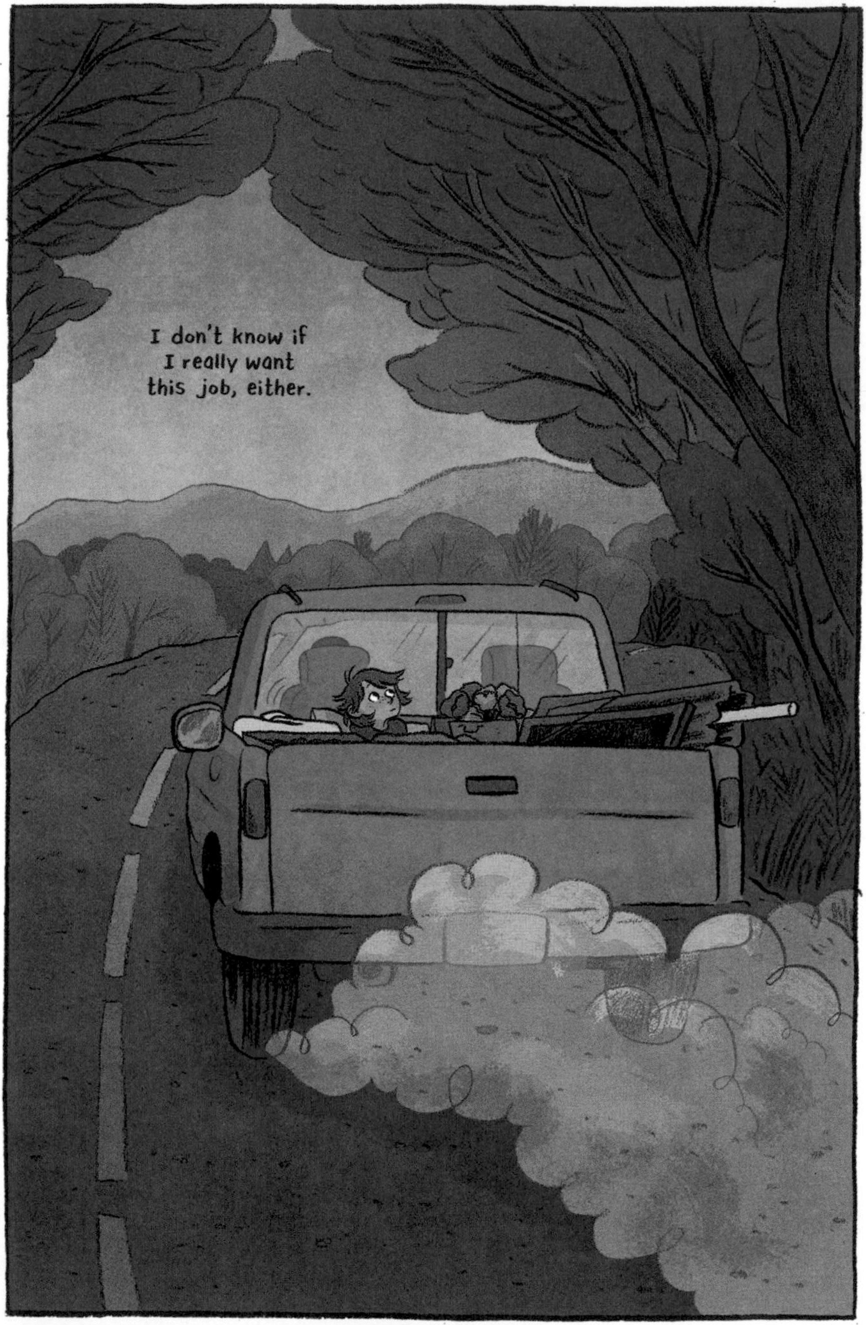
I don't know if
I really want
this job, either.

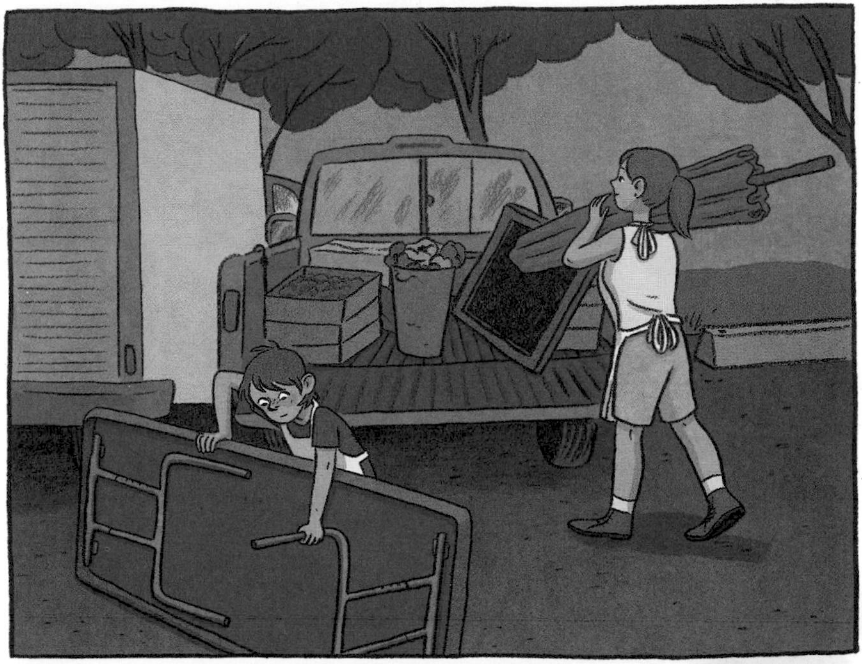

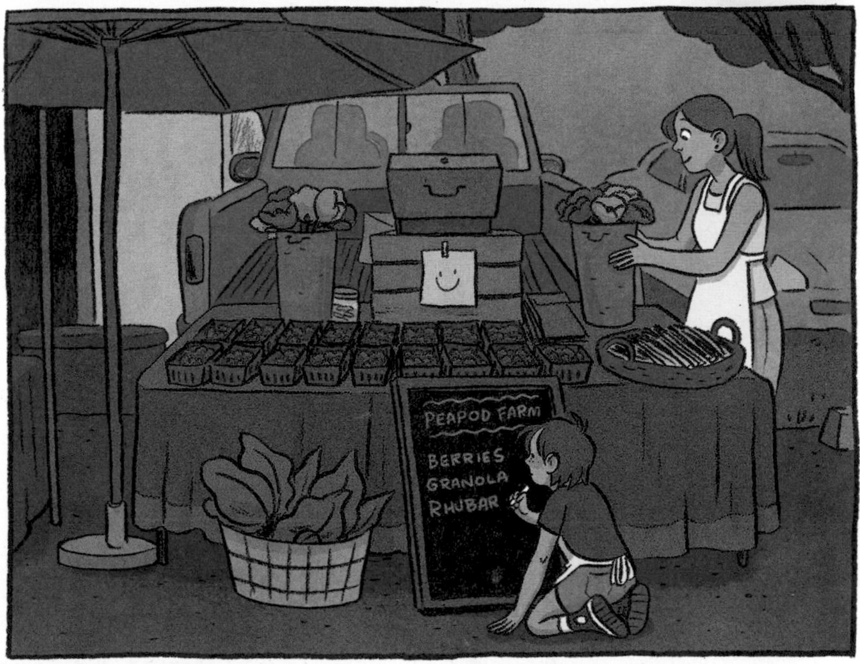
PEAPOD FARM
BERRIES
GRANOLA
RHUBAR

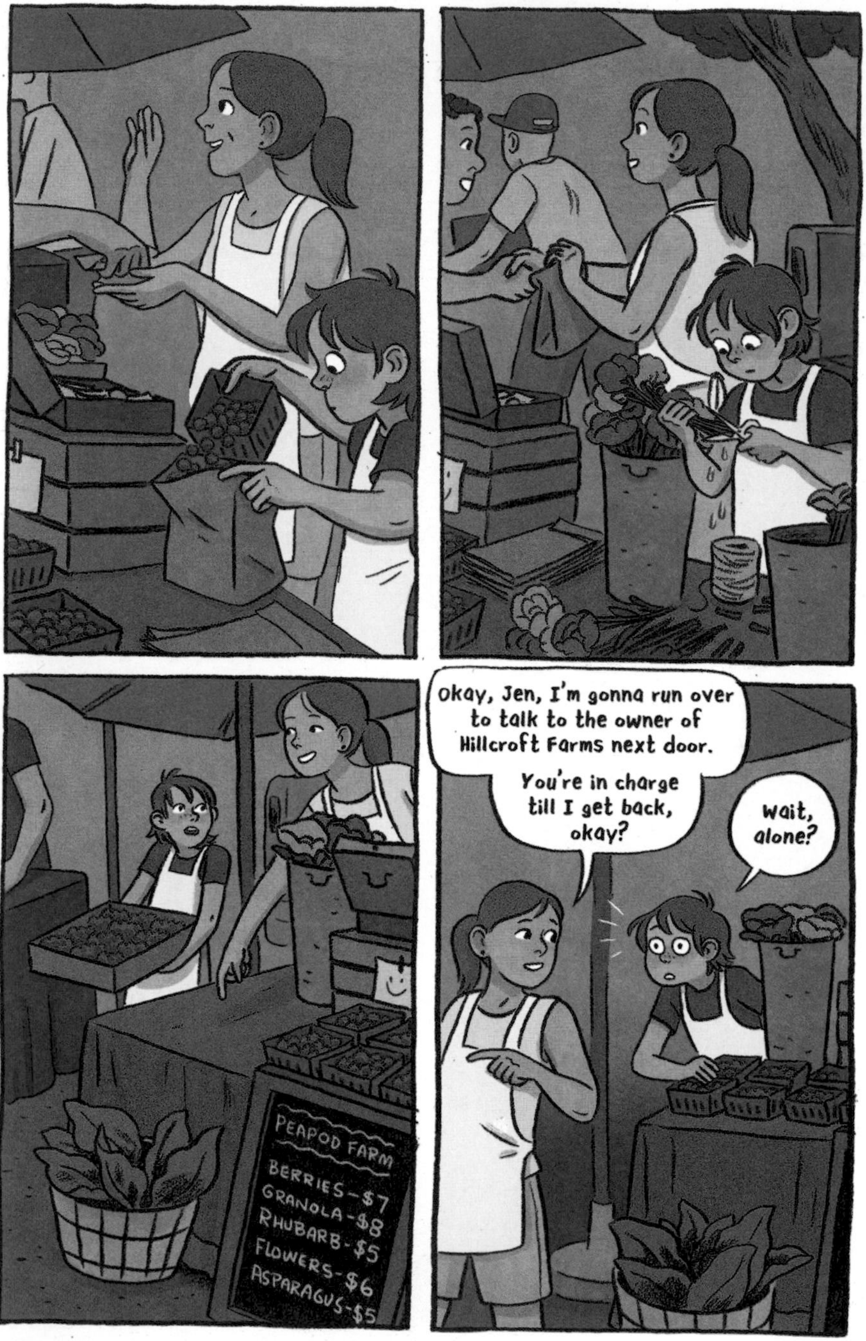
PEAPOD FARM
BERRIES-$7
GRANOLA-$8
RHUBARB-$5
FLOWERS-$6
ASPARAGUS-$5
Okay, Jen, I'm gonna run over to talk to the owner of Hillcroft Farms next door.
You're in charge till I get back, okay?
Wait, alone?

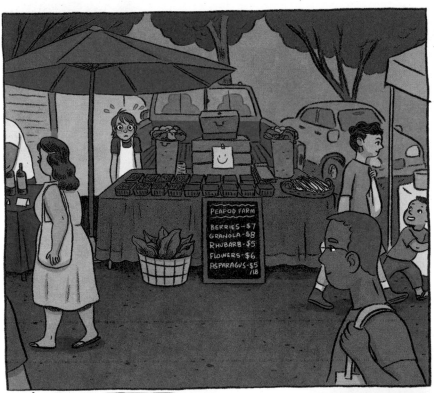

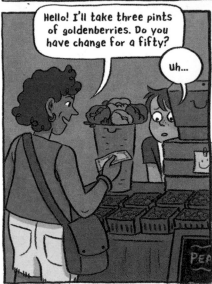

PEAPOD FARM
BERRIES-$7
GRANOLA-$8
RHUBARB-$5
FLOWERS-$6
ASPARAGUS-$5 /LB
Hello! I'll take three pints of goldenberries. Do you have change for a fifty?
uh...
uh, yes, um, here you go, uh...

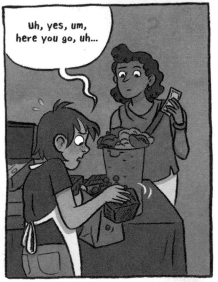

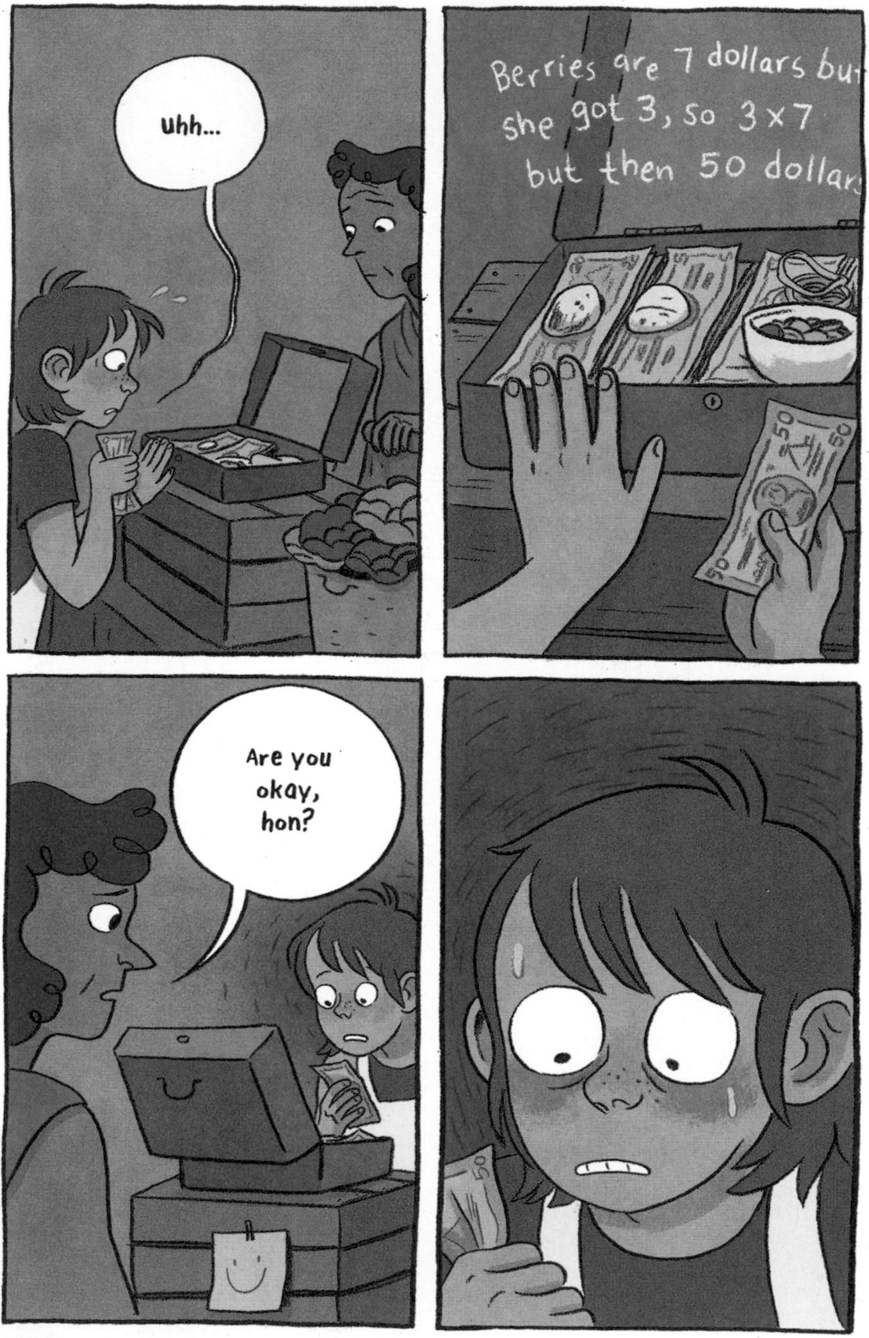
uhh...
Berries are 7 dollars bu
she got 3, so 3 x 7
but then 50 dollar
Are you okay, hon?

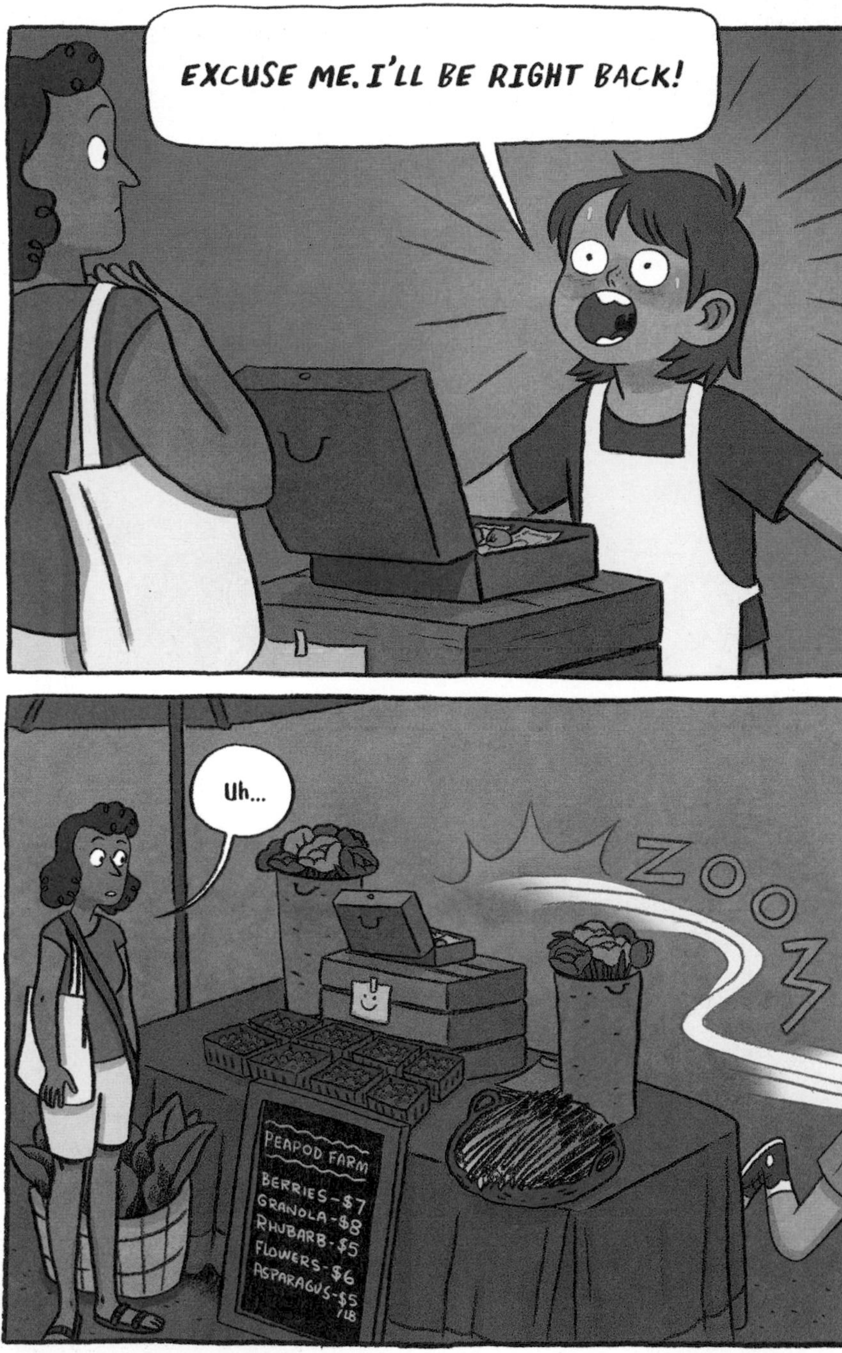
EXCUSE ME. I'LL BE RIGHT BACK!
Uh...
ZOOM
PEAPOD FARM
BERRIES-$7
GRANOLA-$8
RHUBARB-$5
FLOWERS-$6
ASPARAGUS-$5 /LB

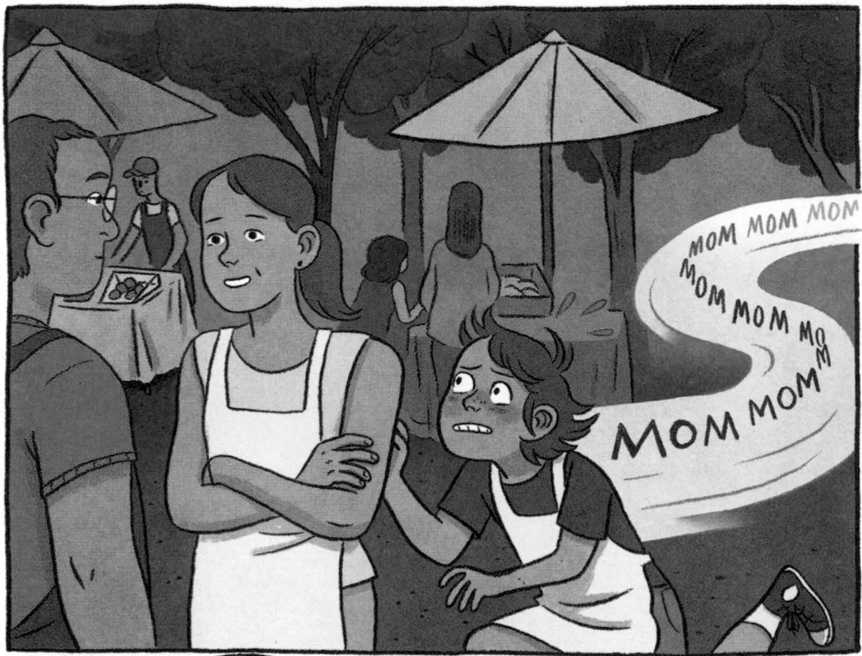
MOM MOM MOM
MOM MOM MO
MOM MOM M
MOM

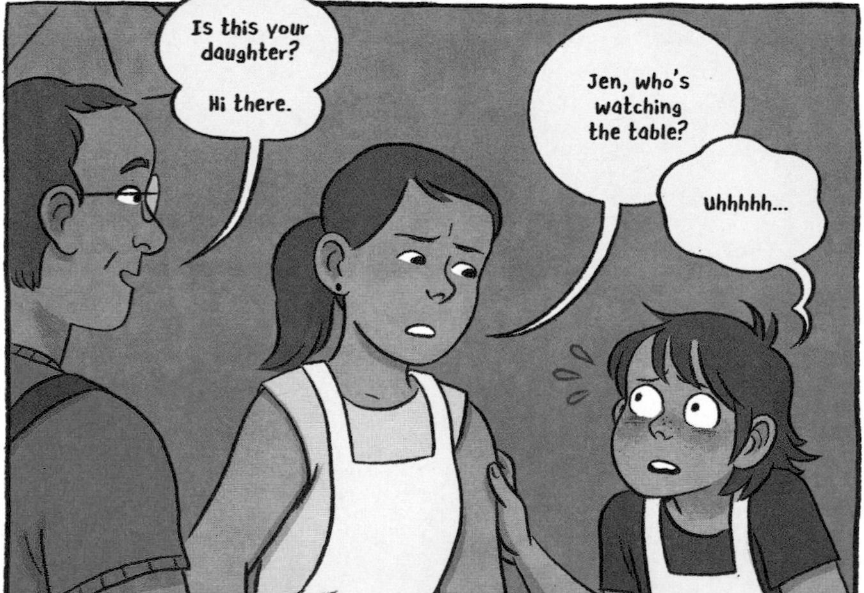
Is this your daughter?
Hi there.
Jen, who's watching the table?
Uhhhhh...

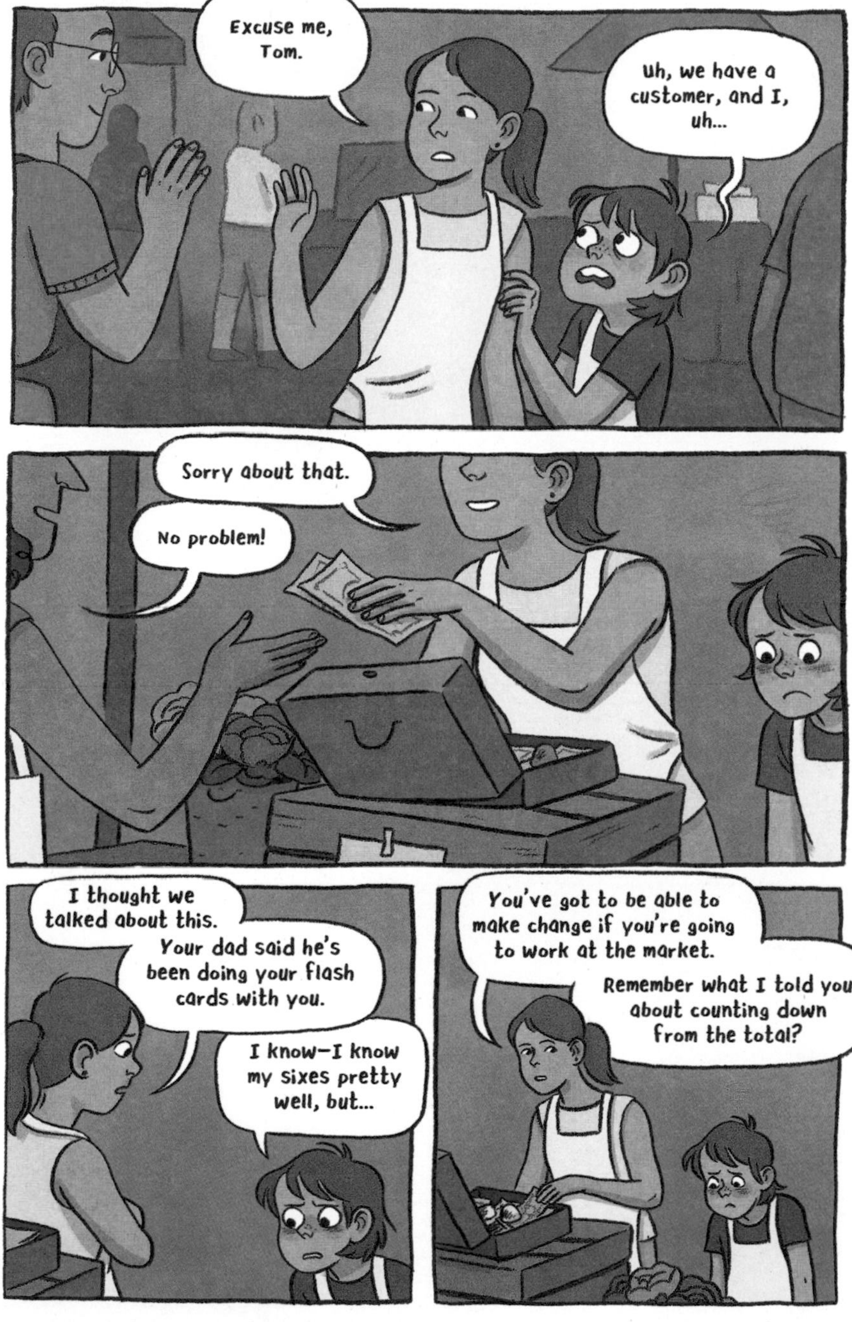
Excuse me, Tom.
Uh, we have a customer, and I, uh...
Sorry about that.
No problem!
I thought we talked about this.
Your dad said he's been doing your flash cards with you.
I know—I know my sixes pretty well, but...
You've got to be able to make change if you're going to work at the market.
Remember what I told you about counting down from the total?

I know, I know...

I can't be here all the time, Jen, and Walter has to work at the farm.

I know.

Keep at it, okay? I know you'll get it.

RHI

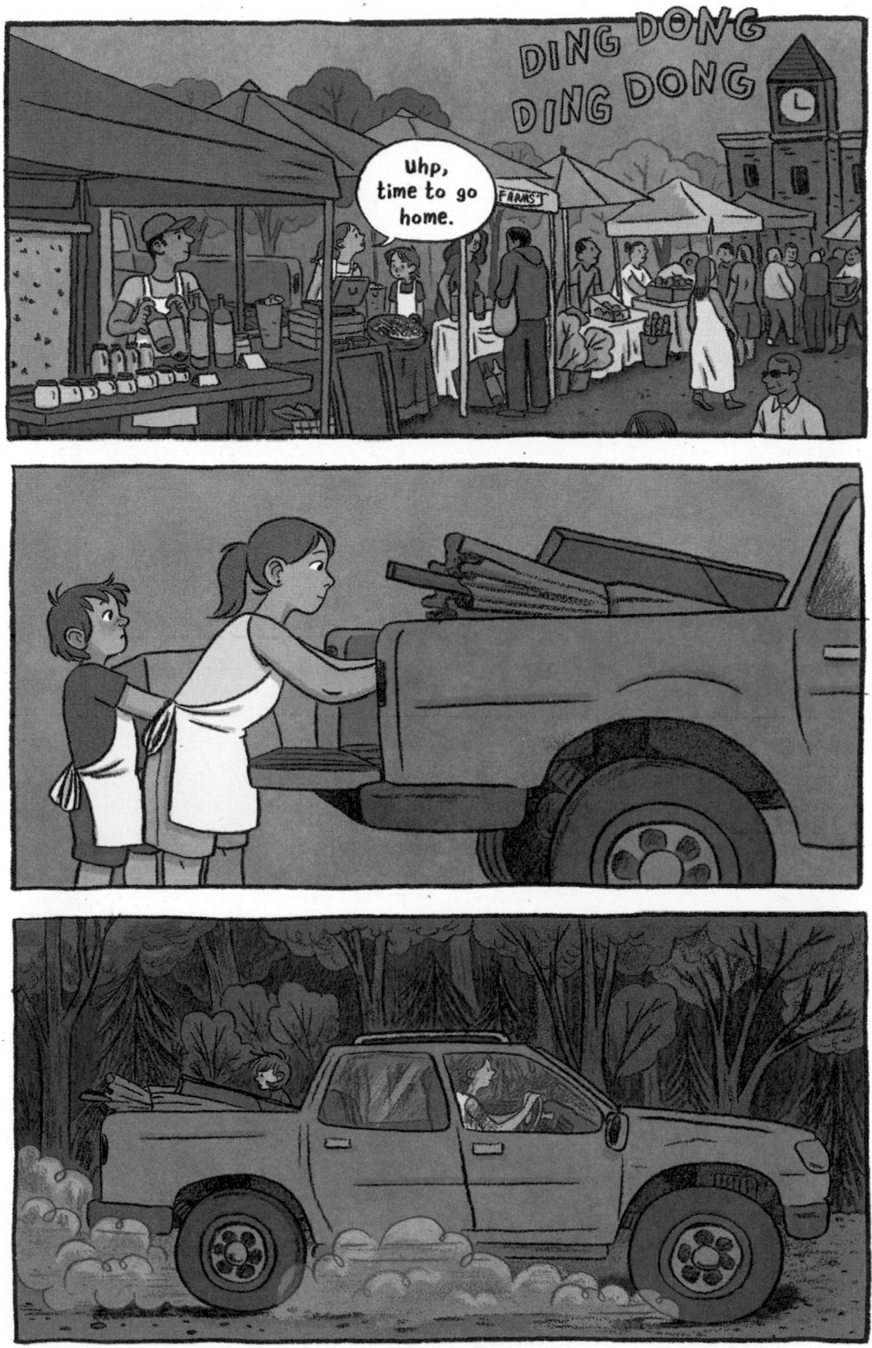
DING DONG
DING DONG
Uhp, time to go home.
FARMS

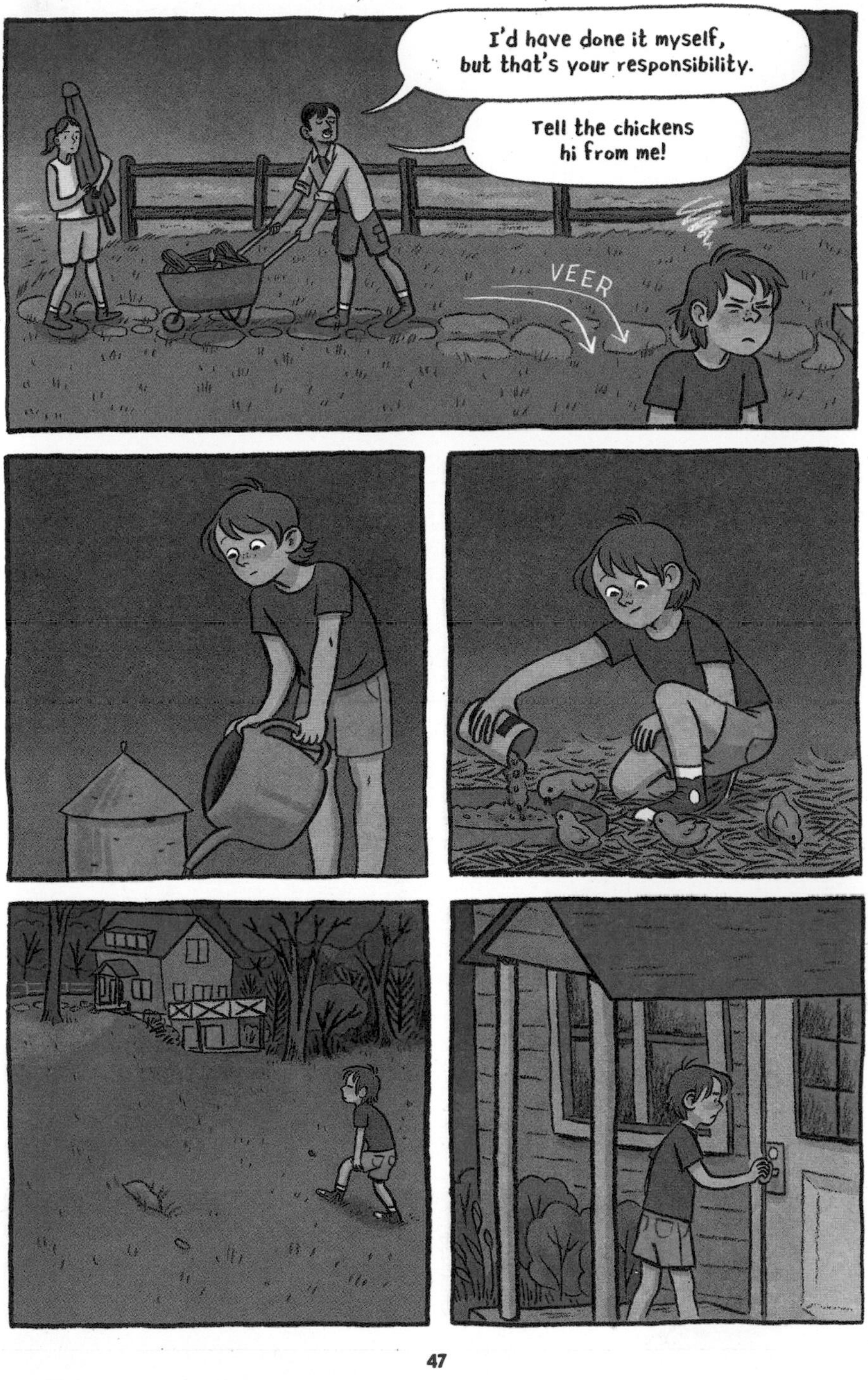

I'd have done it myself, but that's your responsibility.
Tell the chickens hi from me!
VEER

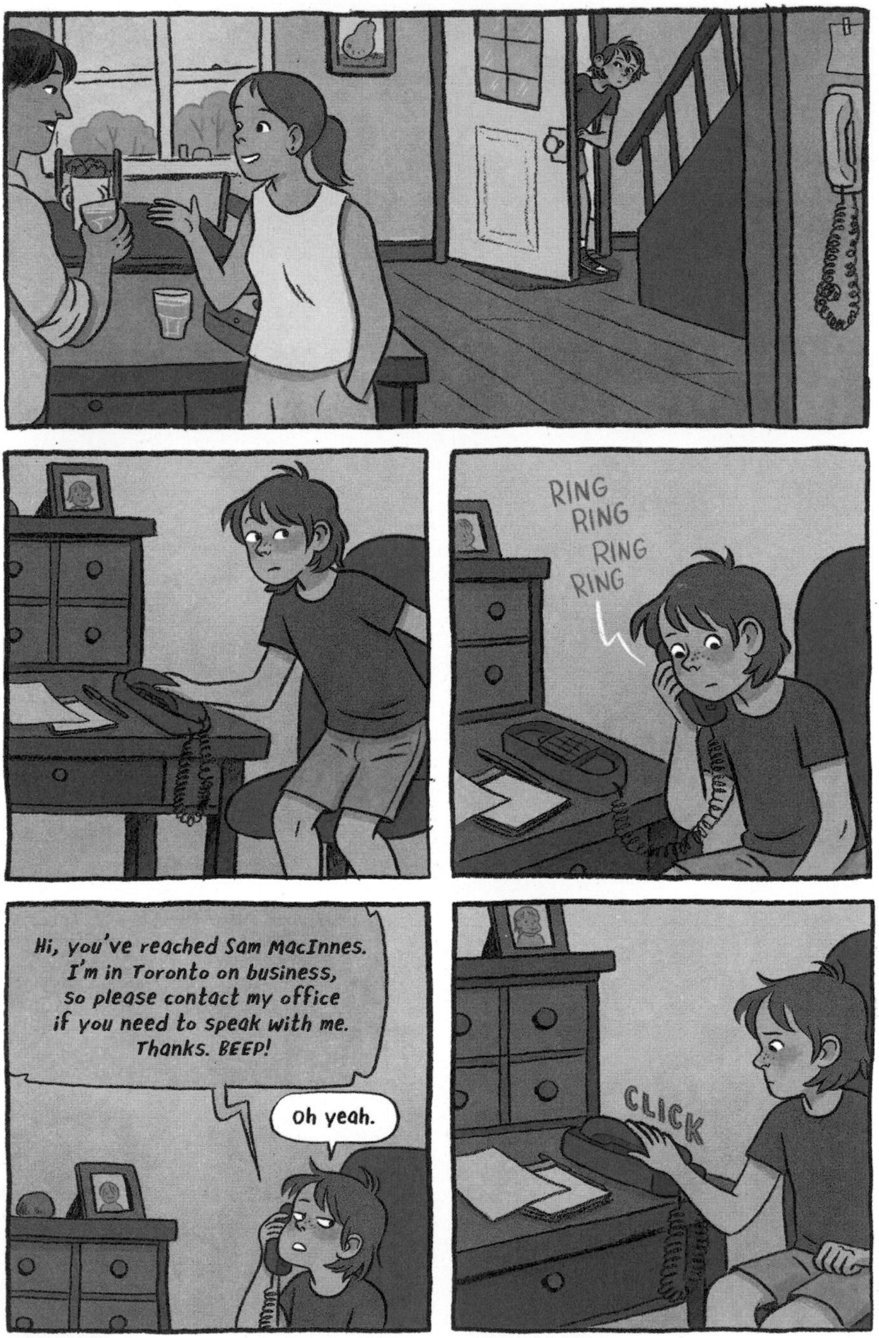
RING
RING
RING
RING
Hi, you've reached Sam MacInnes. I'm in Toronto on business, so please contact my office if you need to speak with me. Thanks. BEEP!
Oh yeah.
CLICK

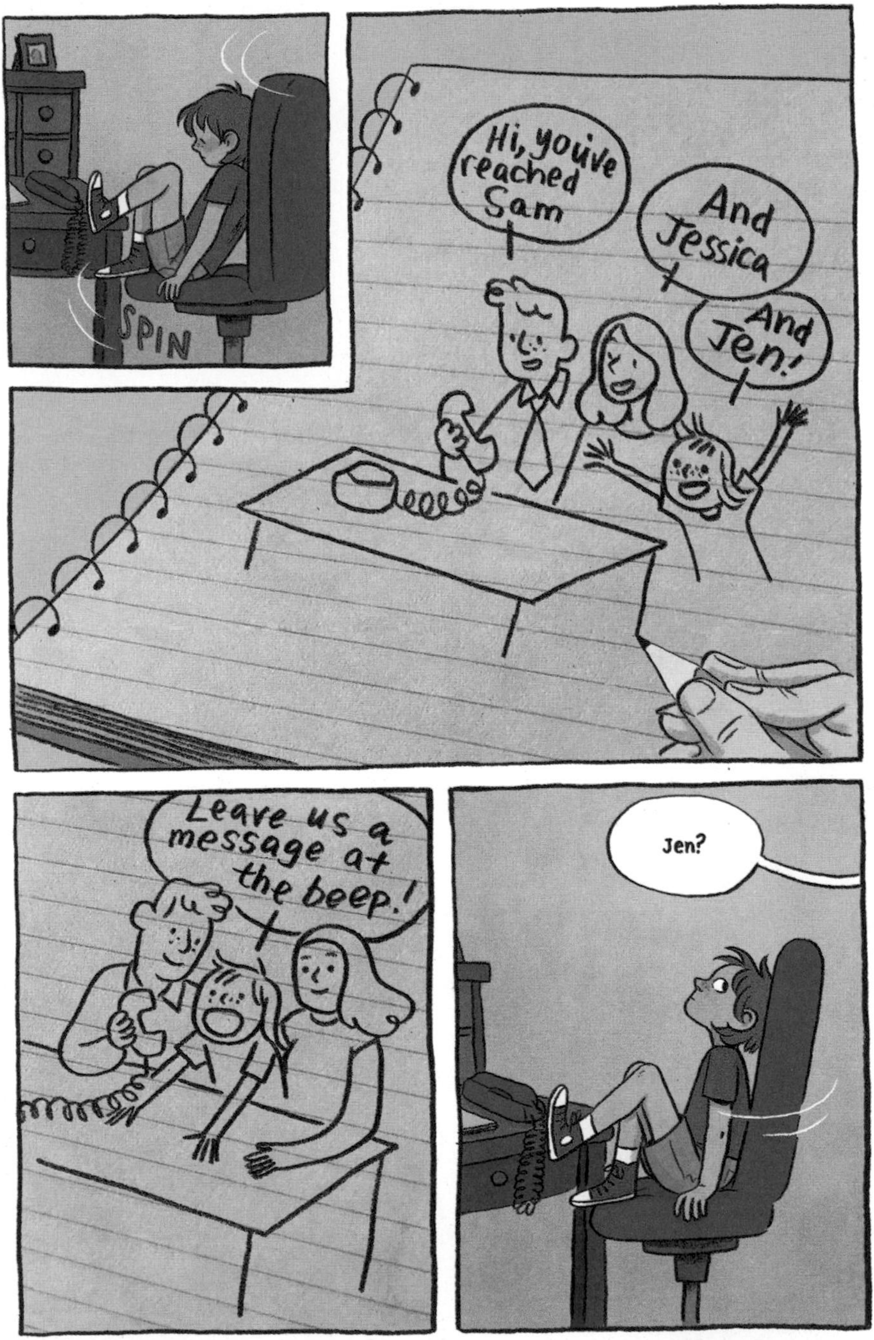
SPIN
Hi, you've reached Sam
And Jessica
And Jen!
Leave us a message at the beep.!
Jen?

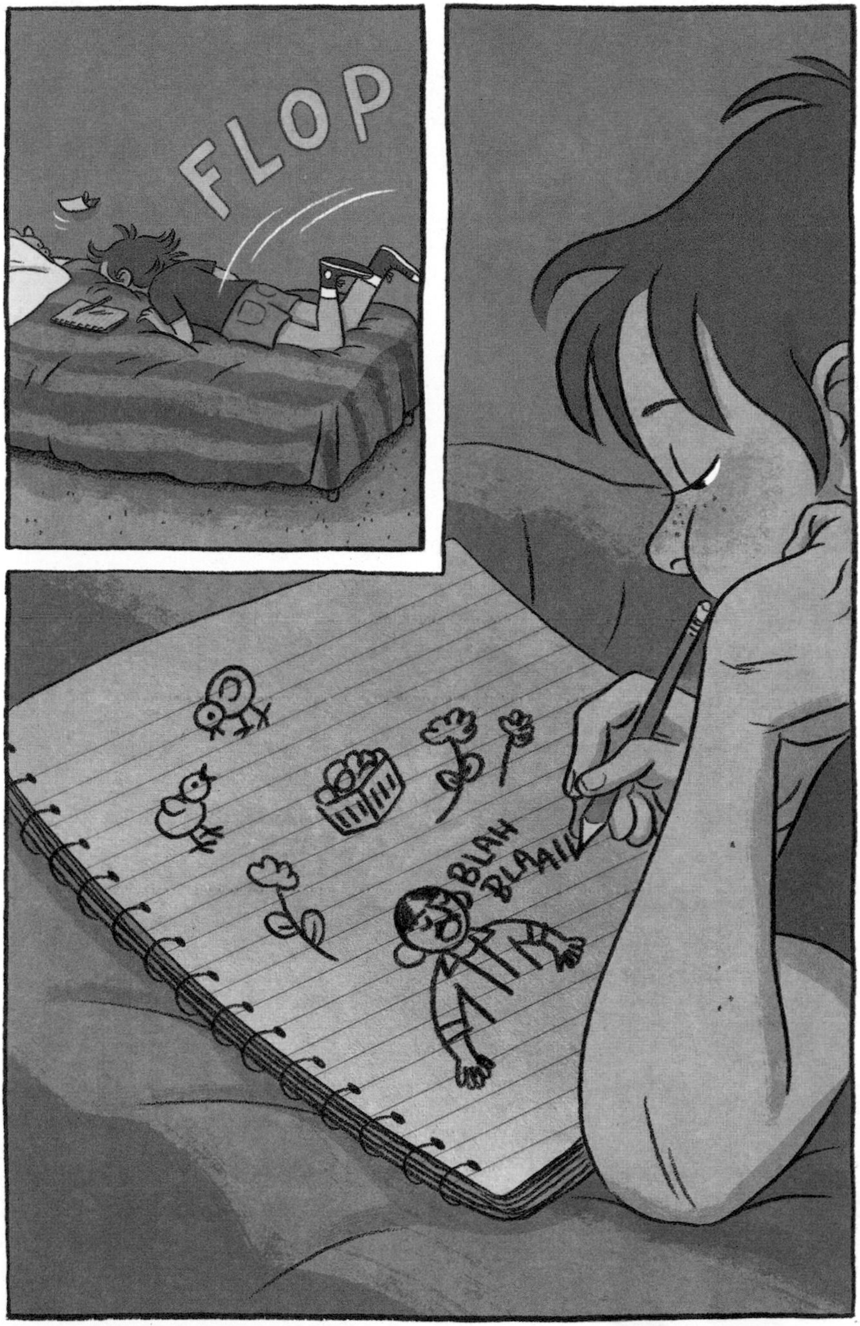
FLOP
BLAH BLAAH

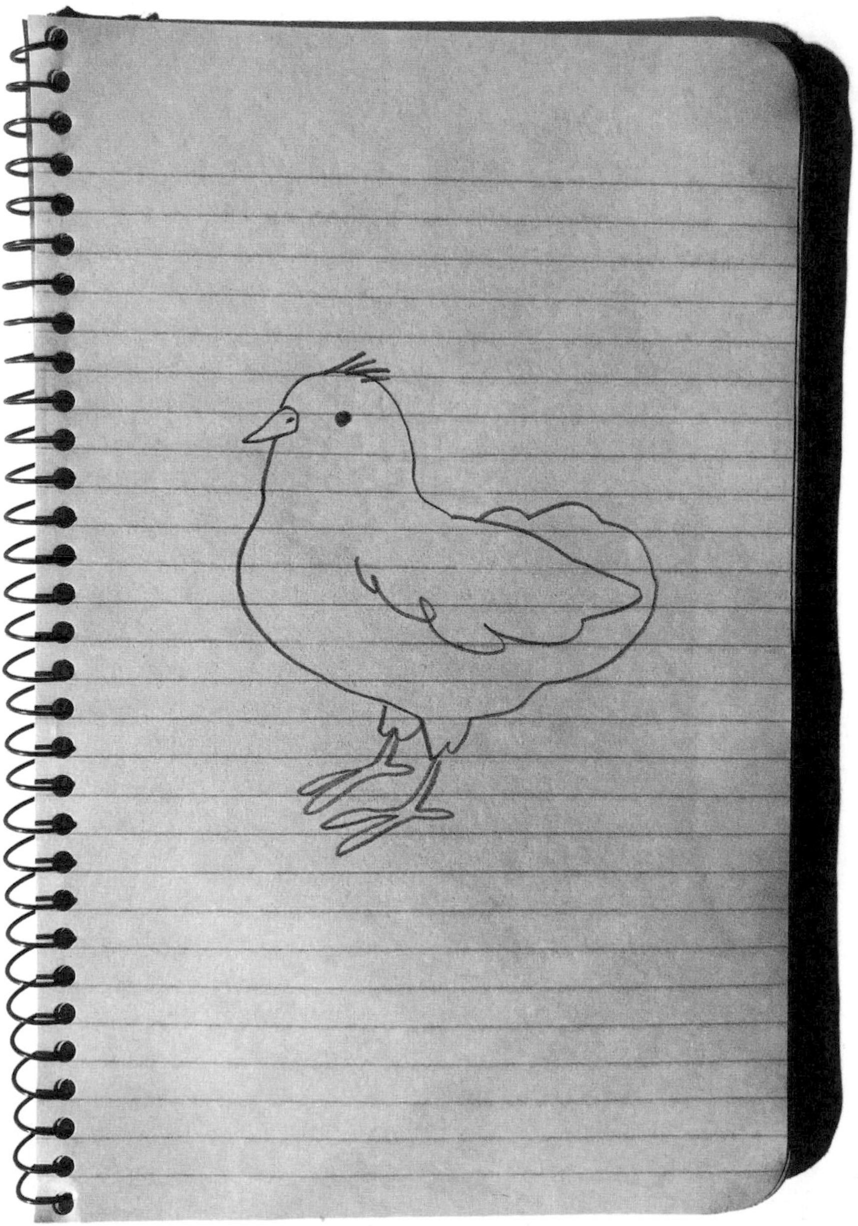

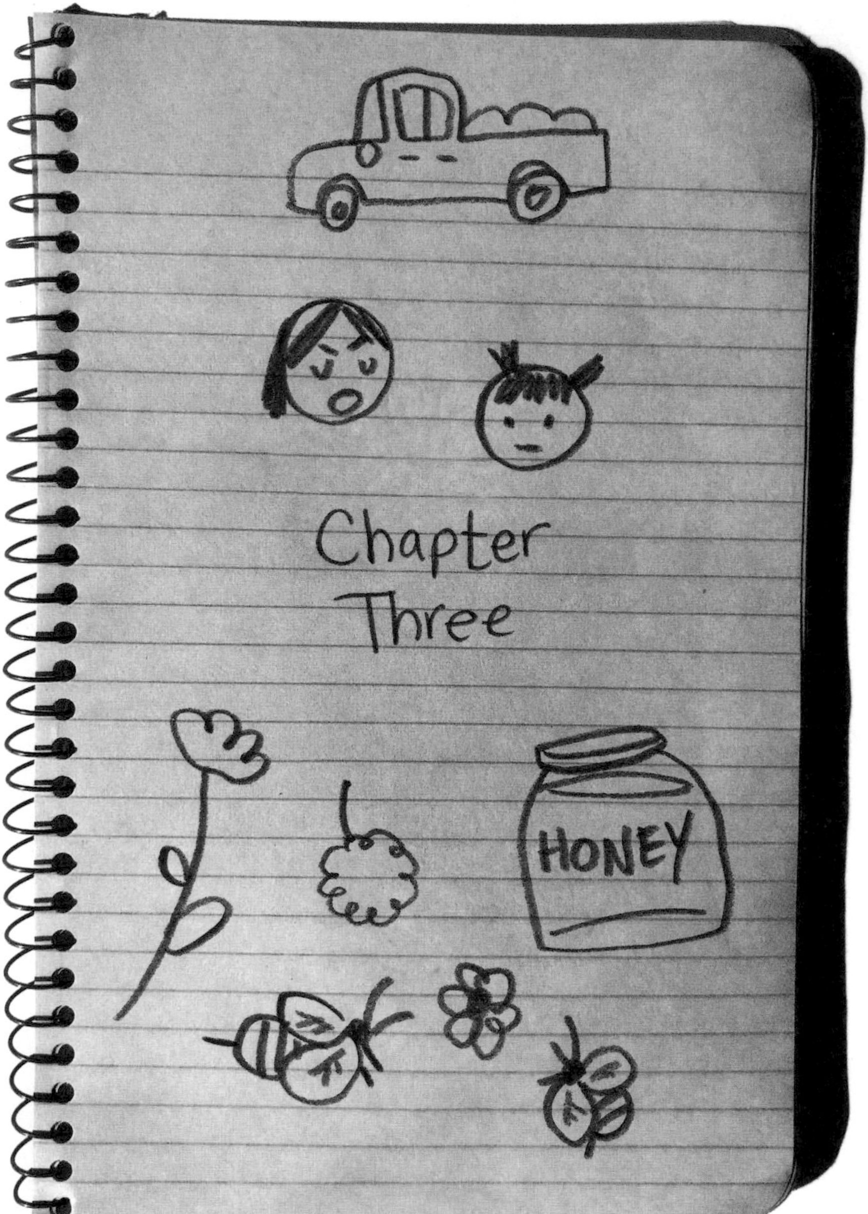
Chapter
Three
HONEY

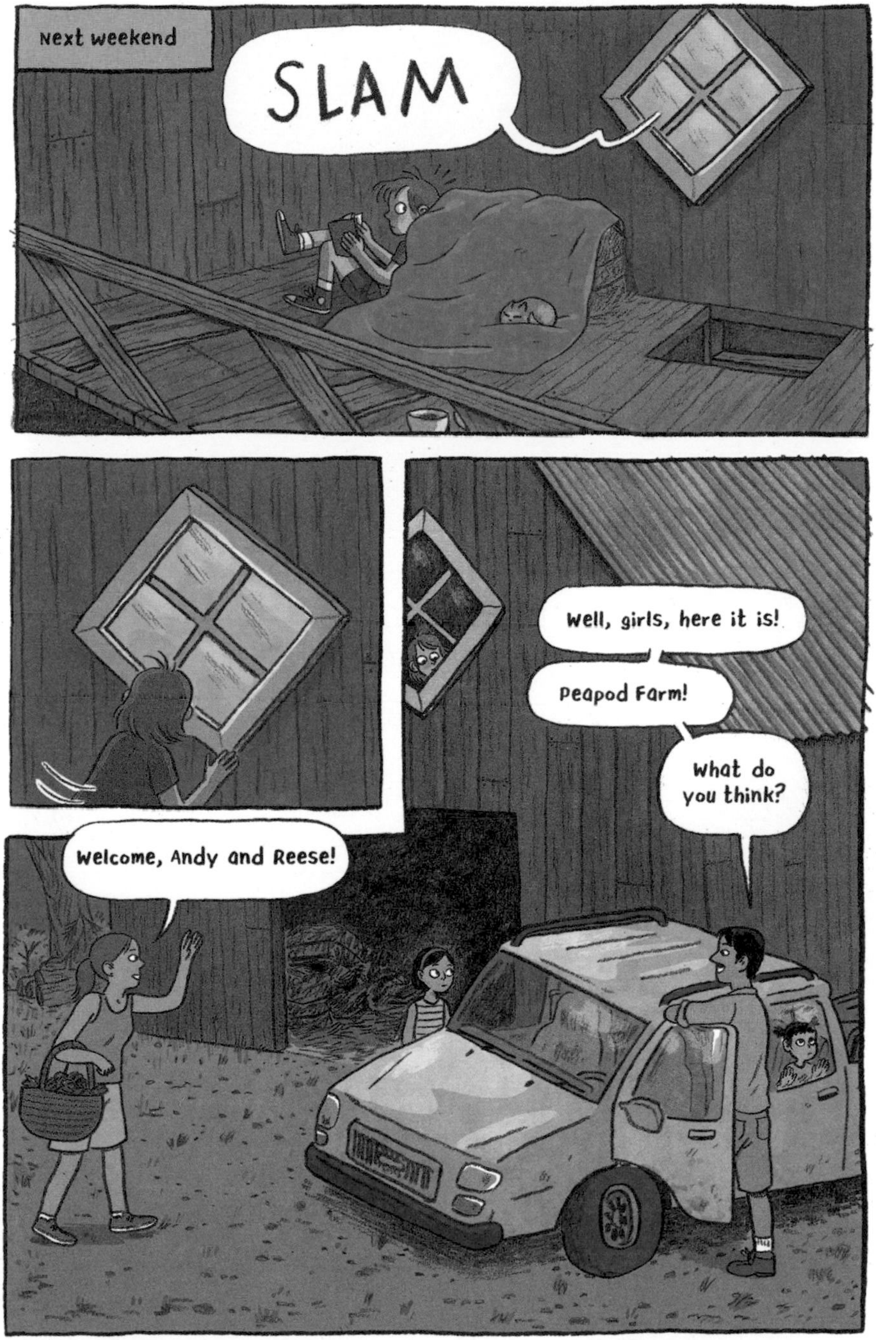
Next weekend
SLAM
Well, girls, here it is!
Peapod Farm!
What do you think?
Welcome, Andy and Reese!

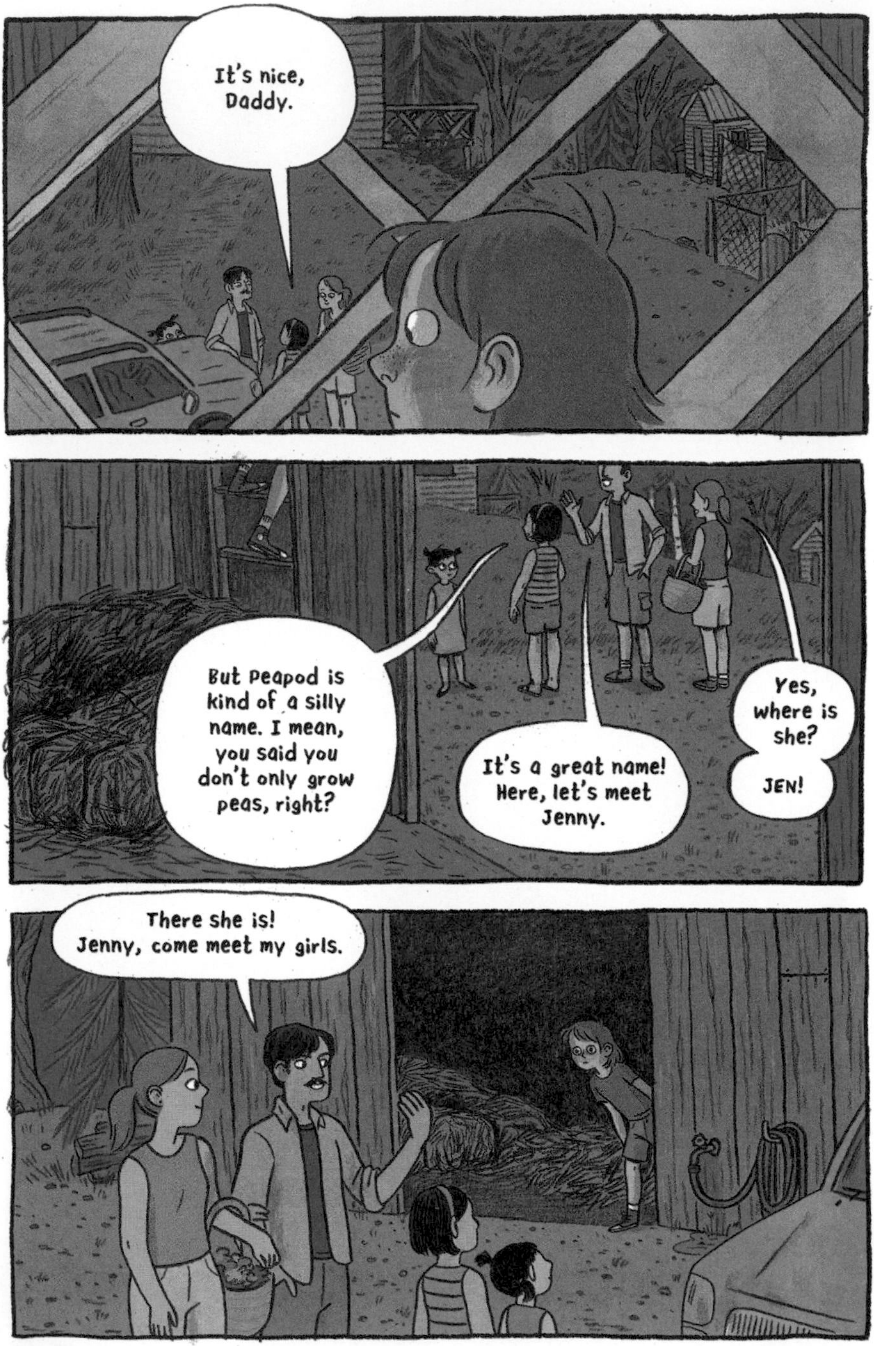
It's nice, Daddy.
But Peapod is kind of a silly name. I mean, you said you don't only grow peas, right?
It's a great name! Here, let's meet Jenny.
Yes, where is she?
JEN!
There she is! Jenny, come meet my girls.

57

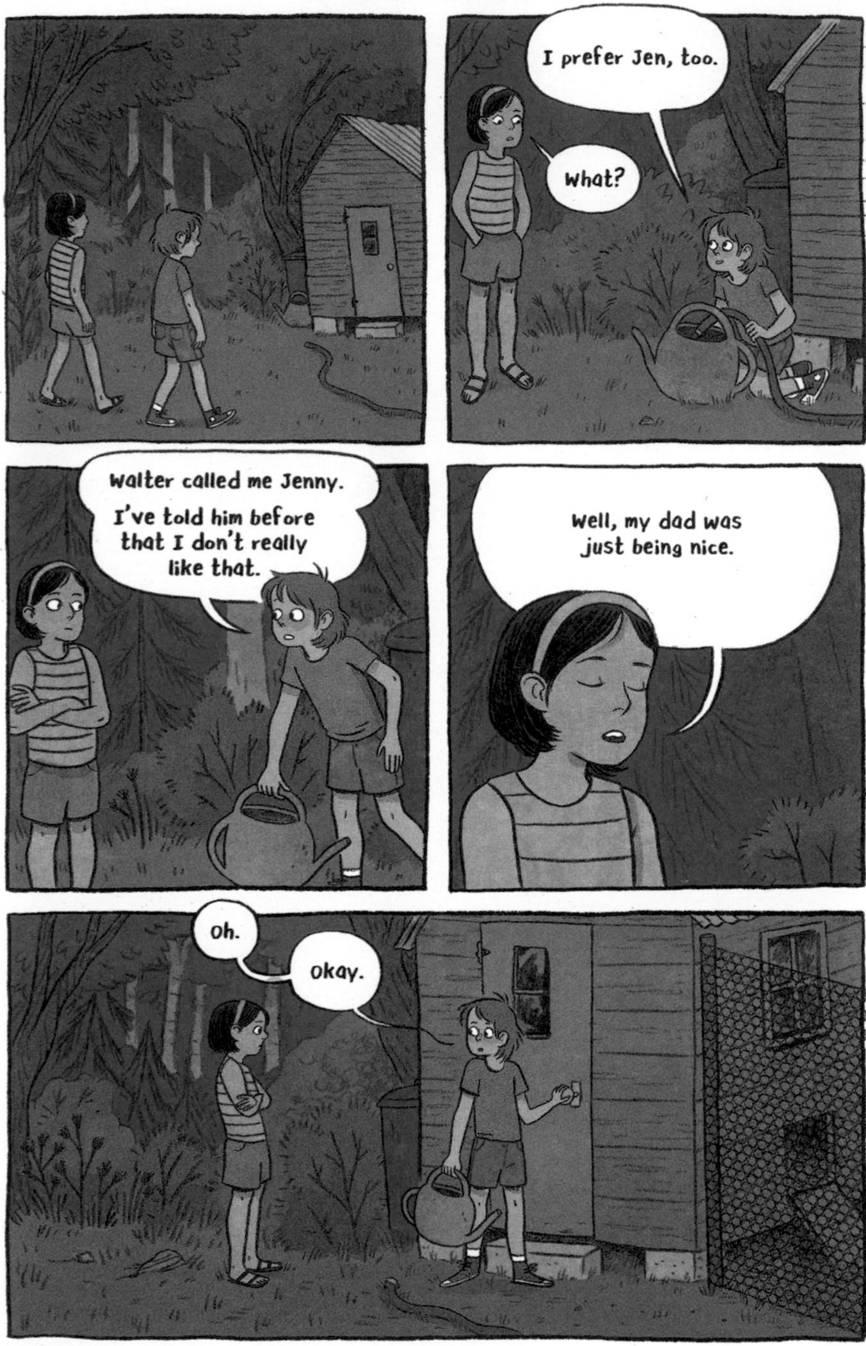
I prefer Jen, too.
What?
Walter called me Jenny.
I've told him before that I don't really like that.
Well, my dad was just being nice.
Oh.
Okay.

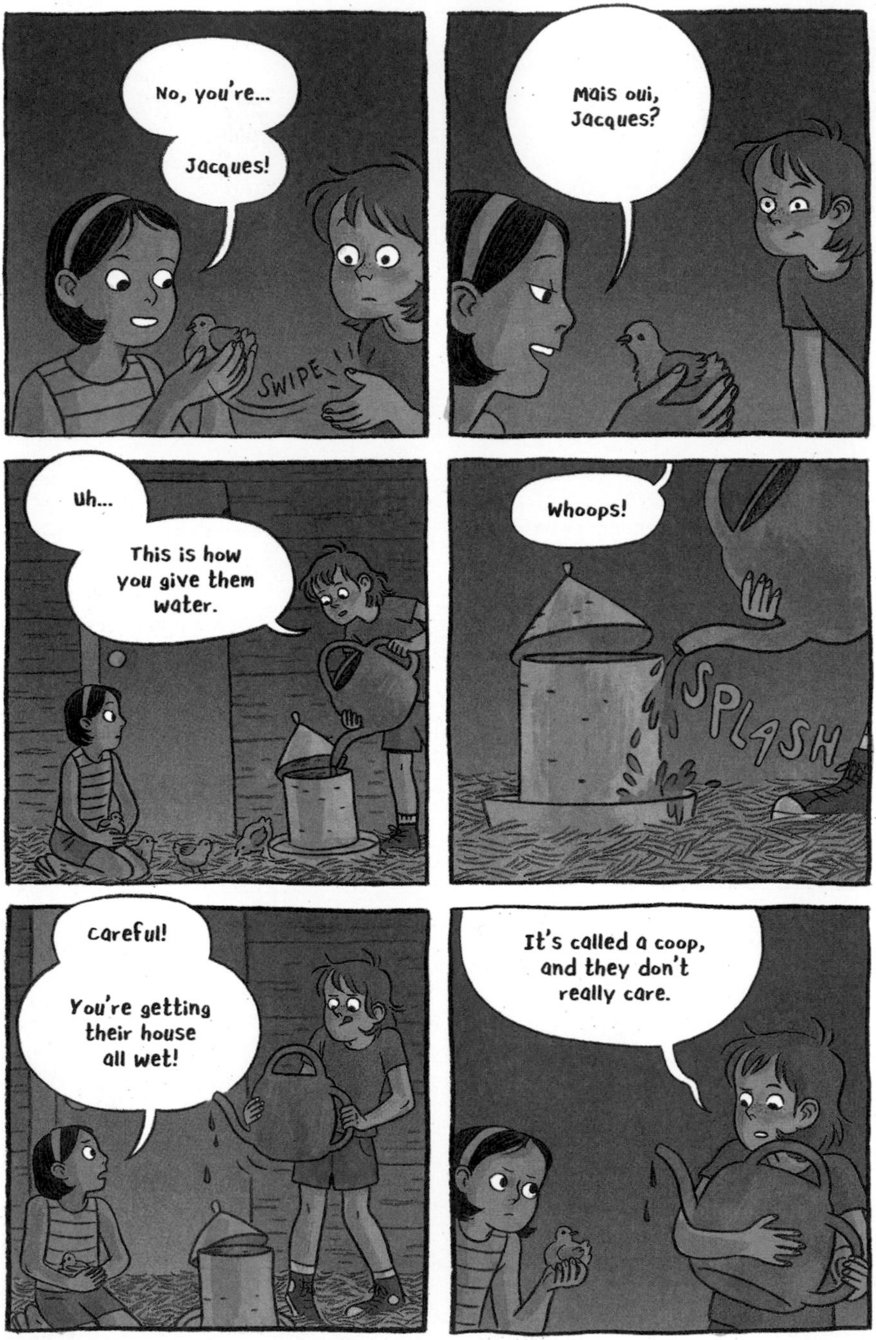
No, you're...
Jacques!
SWIPE
Mais oui, Jacques?
Uh...
This is how you give them water.
Whoops!
SPLASH
Careful!
You're getting their house all wet!
It's called a coop, and they don't really care.

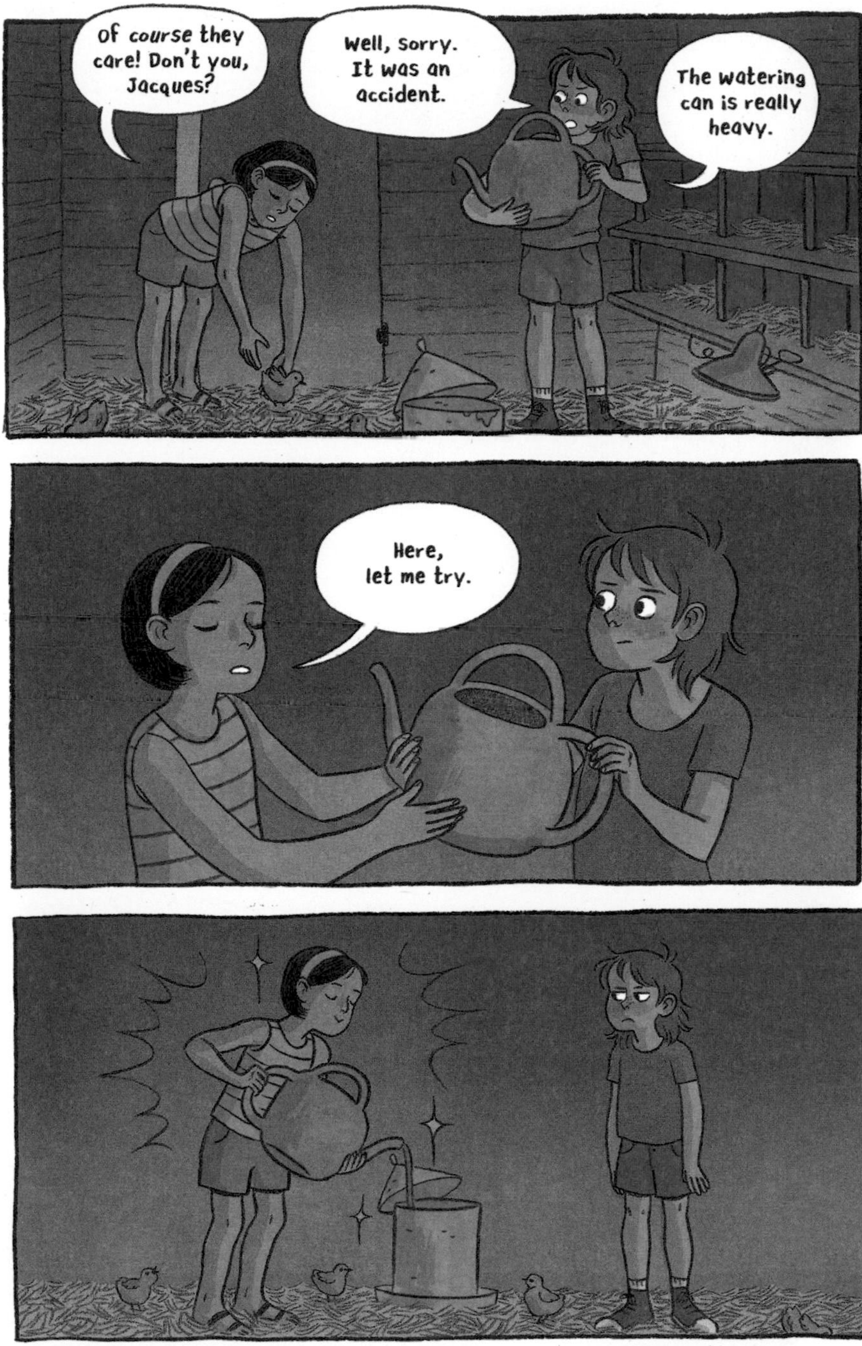
Of course they care! Don't you, Jacques?
Well, sorry. It was an accident.
The watering can is really heavy.
Here, let me try.

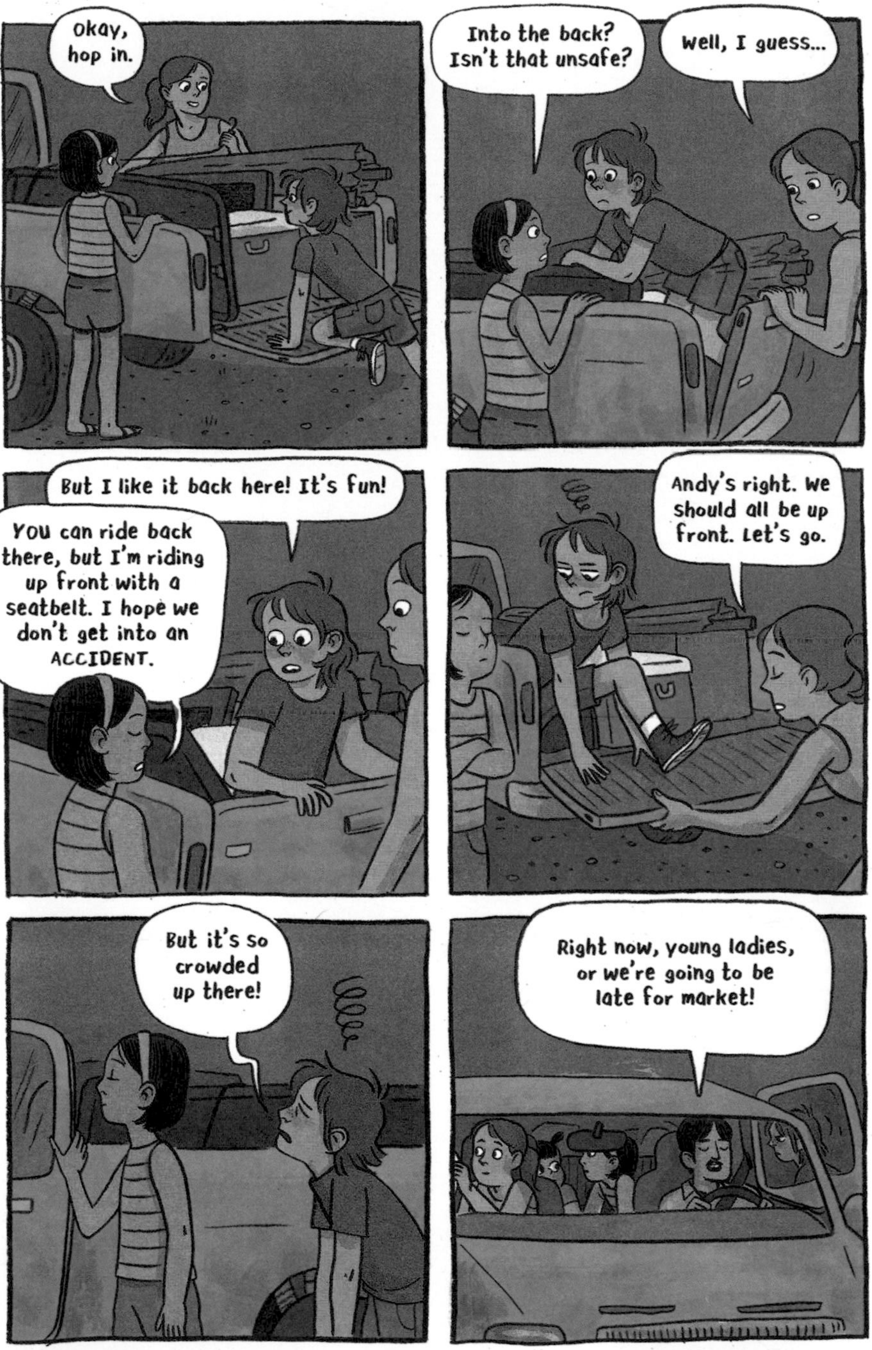
Okay, hop in.
Into the back? Isn't that unsafe?
Well, I guess...
But I like it back here! It's fun!
You can ride back there, but I'm riding up front with a seatbelt. I hope we don't get into an ACCIDENT.
Andy's right. We should all be up front. Let's go.
But it's so crowded up there!
Right now, young ladies, or we're going to be late for market!

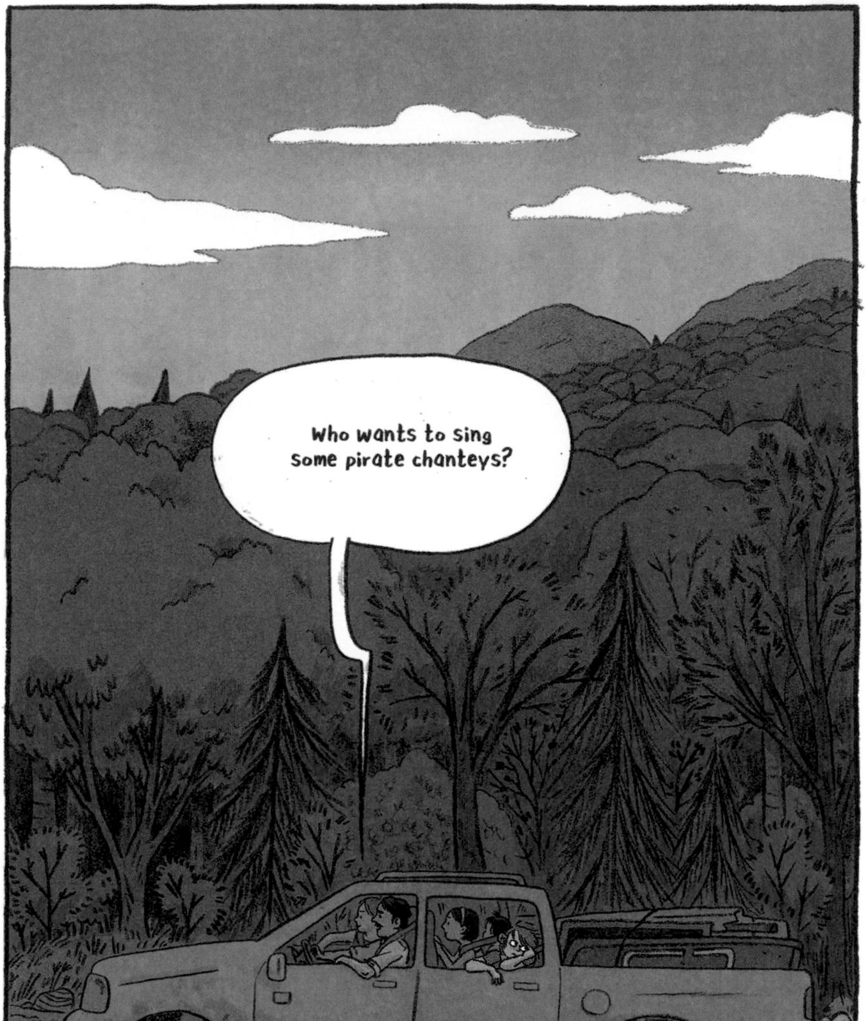
Who wants to sing
some pirate chanteys?

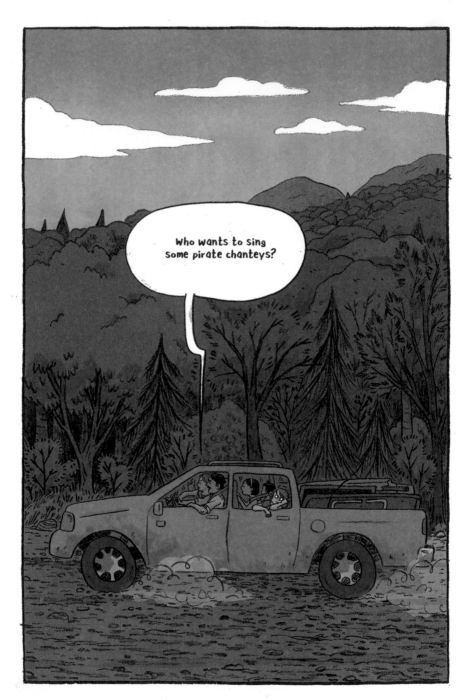

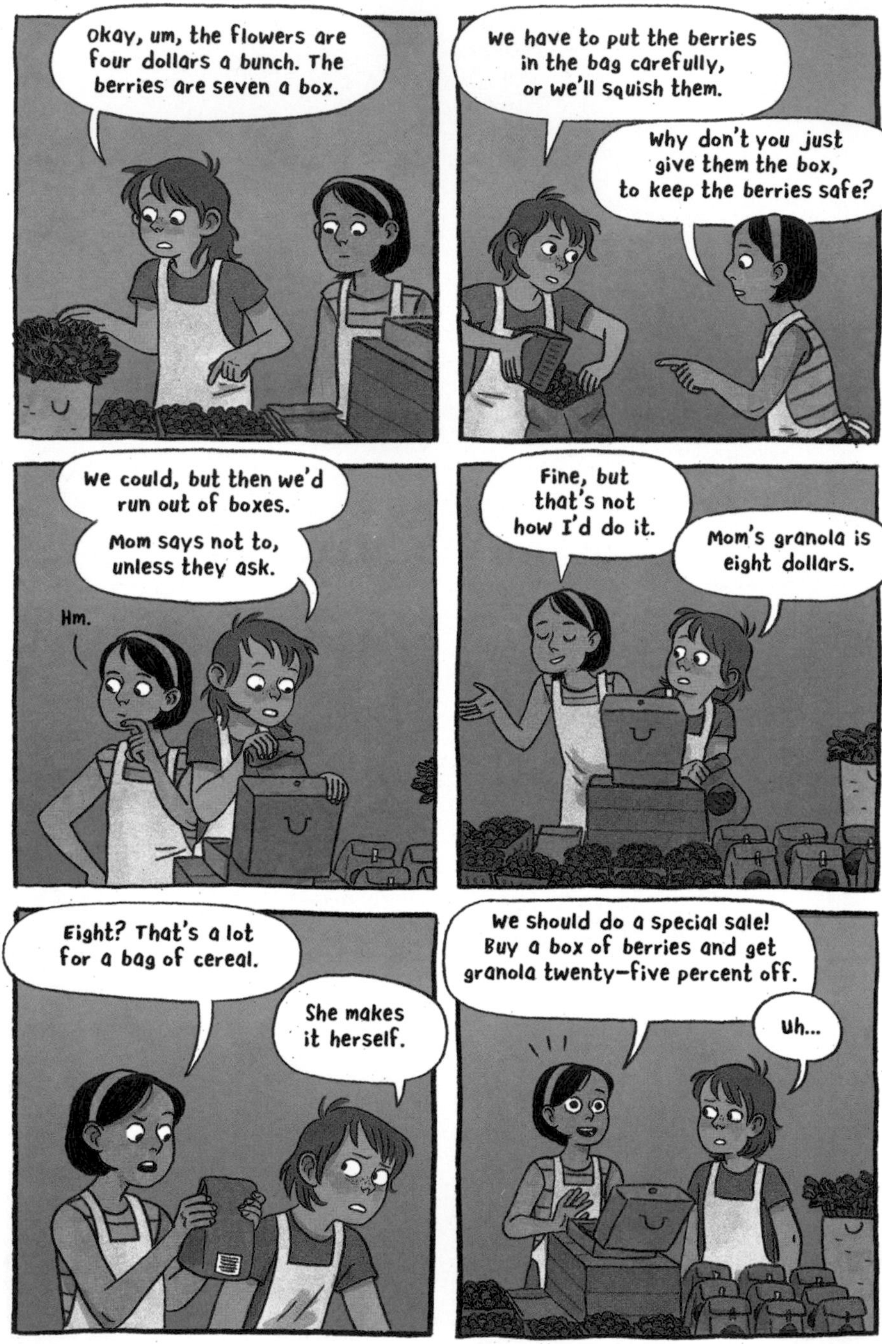
Okay, um, the flowers are four dollars a bunch. The berries are seven a box.
We have to put the berries in the bag carefully, or we'll squish them.
Why don't you just give them the box, to keep the berries safe?
We could, but then we'd run out of boxes.
Mom says not to, unless they ask.
Hm.
Fine, but that's not how I'd do it.
Mom's granola is eight dollars.
Eight? That's a lot for a bag of cereal.
She makes it herself.
We should do a special sale! Buy a box of berries and get granola twenty-five percent off.
Uh...

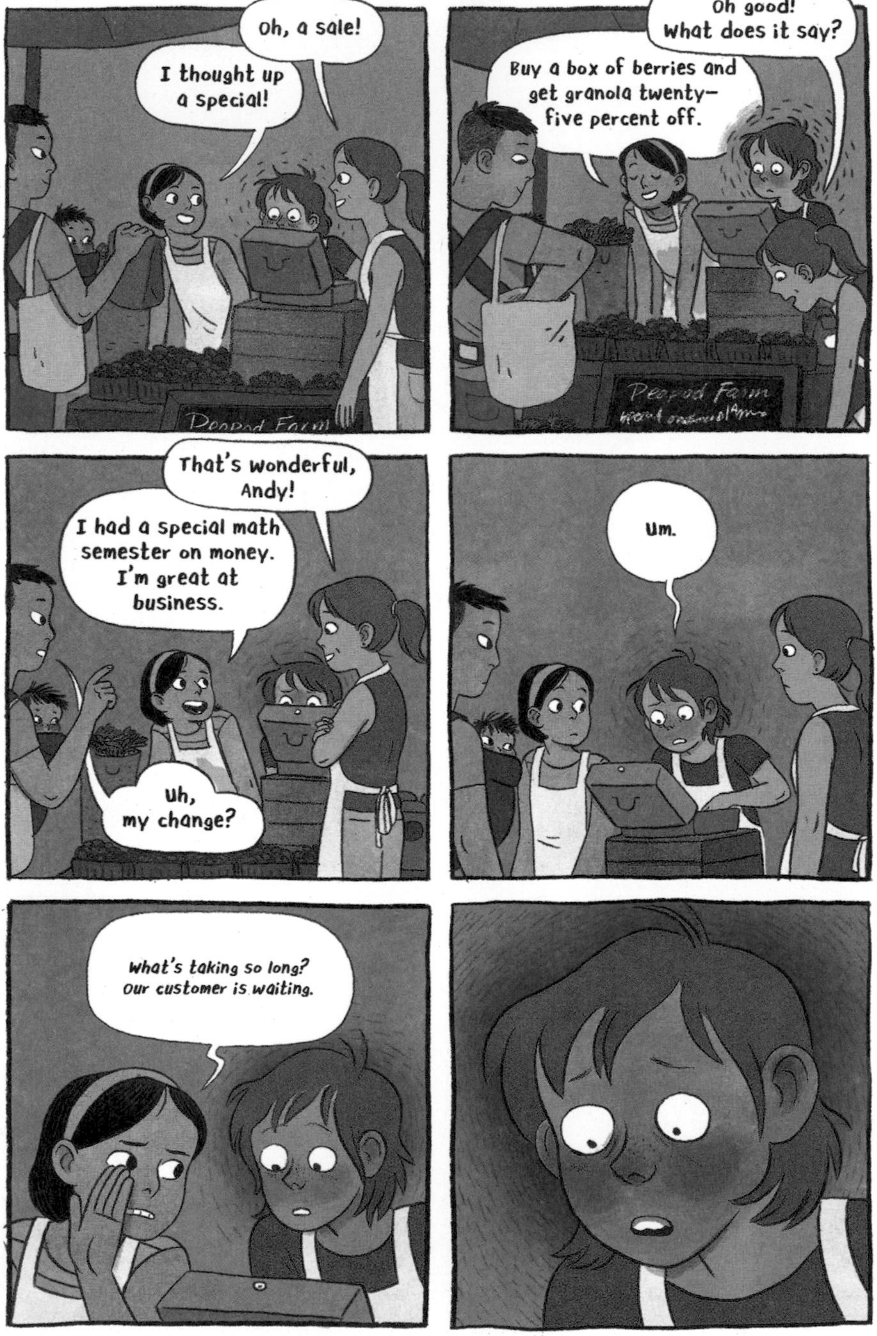

I thought up a special!
Oh, a sale!
Oh good! What does it say?
Buy a box of berries and get granola twenty-five percent off.
Peapod Farm
That's wonderful, Andy!
I had a special math semester on money. I'm great at business.
Uh, my change?
Um.
What's taking so long? Our customer is waiting.

What's twenty-five percent of eight?

What? That's like a basic fraction.

Here, let me.

Here you are, enjoy your purchases.

Andy, maybe you'd like to handle the cash box, since you're so good with numbers.

Jen, why don't you tidy up the sign a bit?

Of course!

I'll get this organized. I'm gonna be an engineer when I grow up!

Come to Peapod Farm for a special on granola!

Peapod Farm

Peapod Farm

BERRIES — $7
GRANOLA — $8
RHUBARB — $4
FLOWERS — $4

SPECIAL: BUY A BOX OF BERRIES & GET 25% OFF OF HOMEMADE GRANOLA

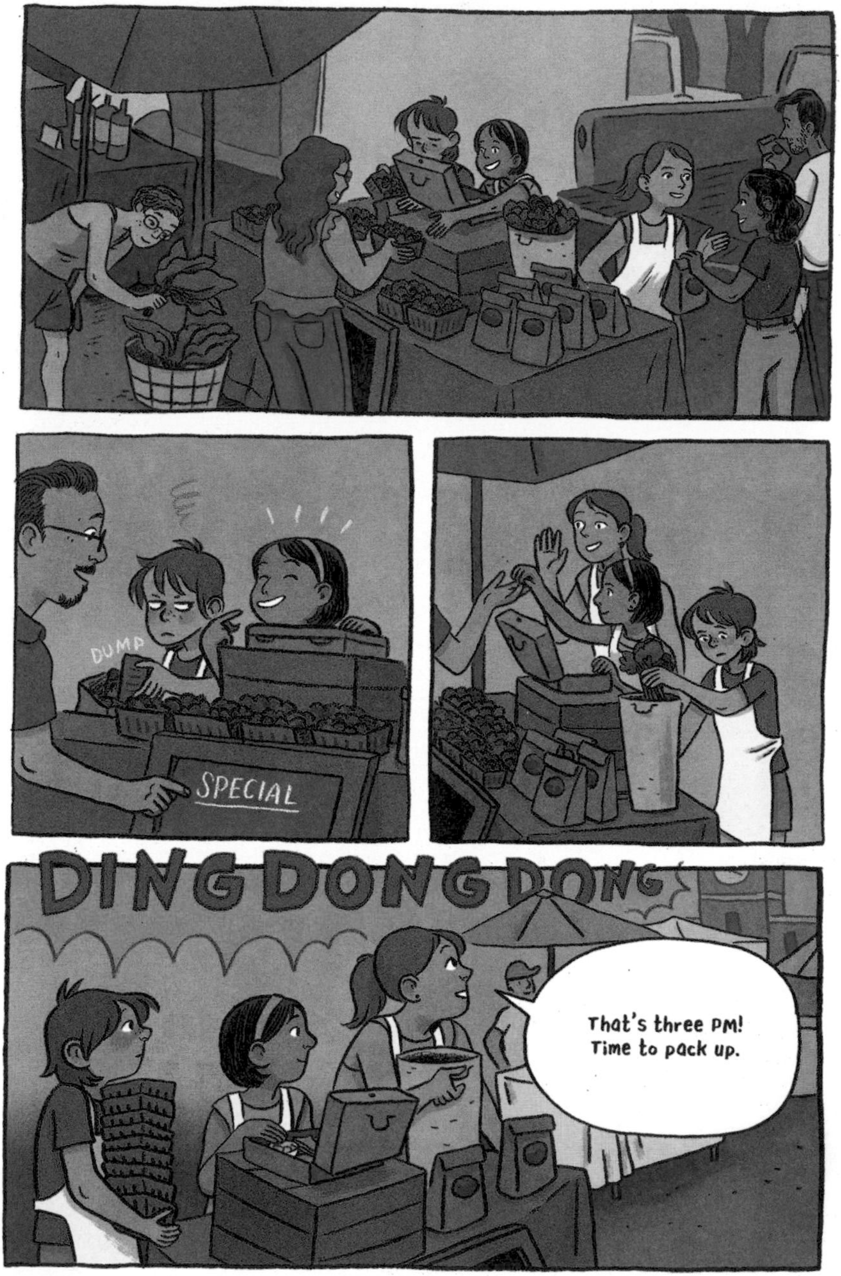
DUMP
SPECIAL
DINGDONGDONG
That's three PM! Time to pack up.

Hello there. What do you think of my bees?

They're so cool!

You work at a stand, too, right?

Yep. Over there.

You guys had a special today, didn't you?

Yeah.

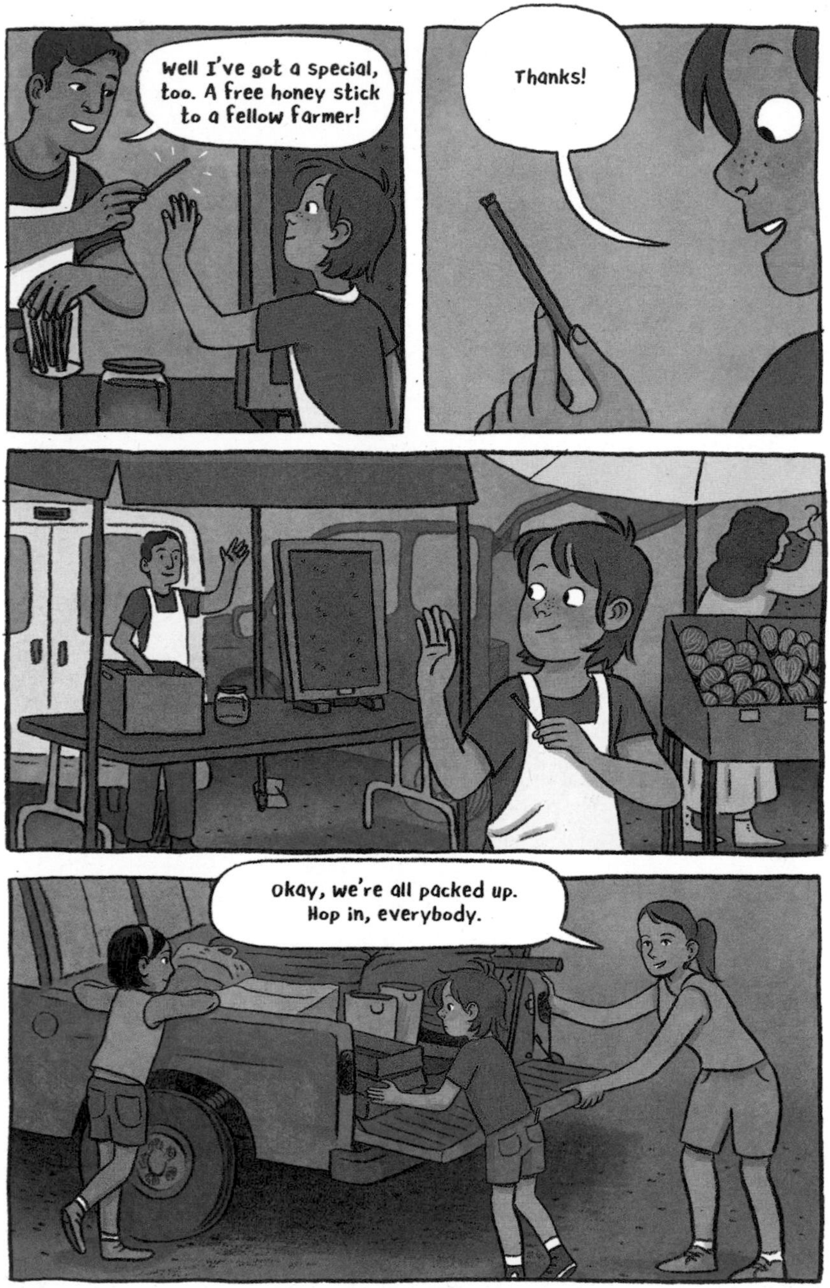
Well I've got a special, too. A free honey stick to a fellow farmer!
Thanks!
Okay, we're all packed up. Hop in, everybody.

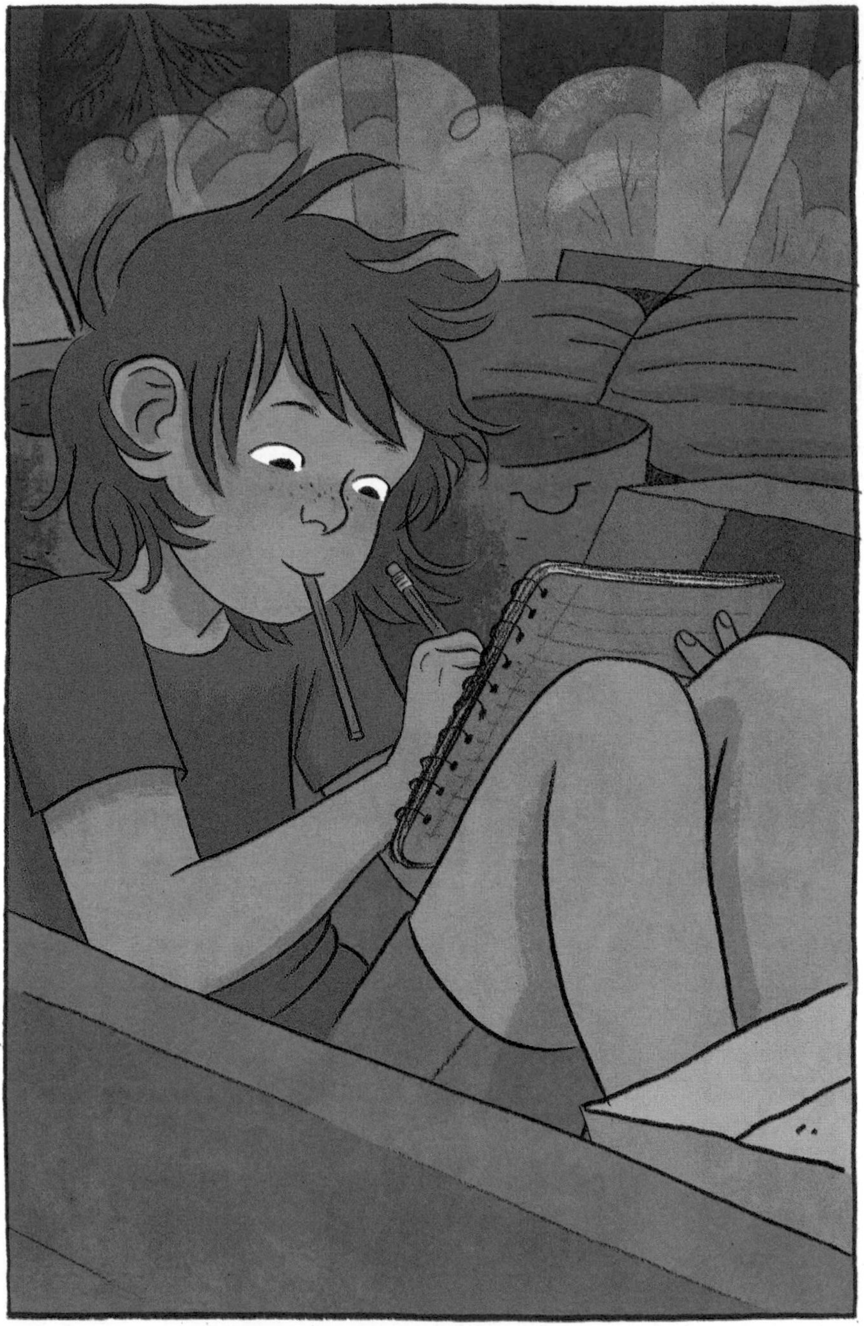

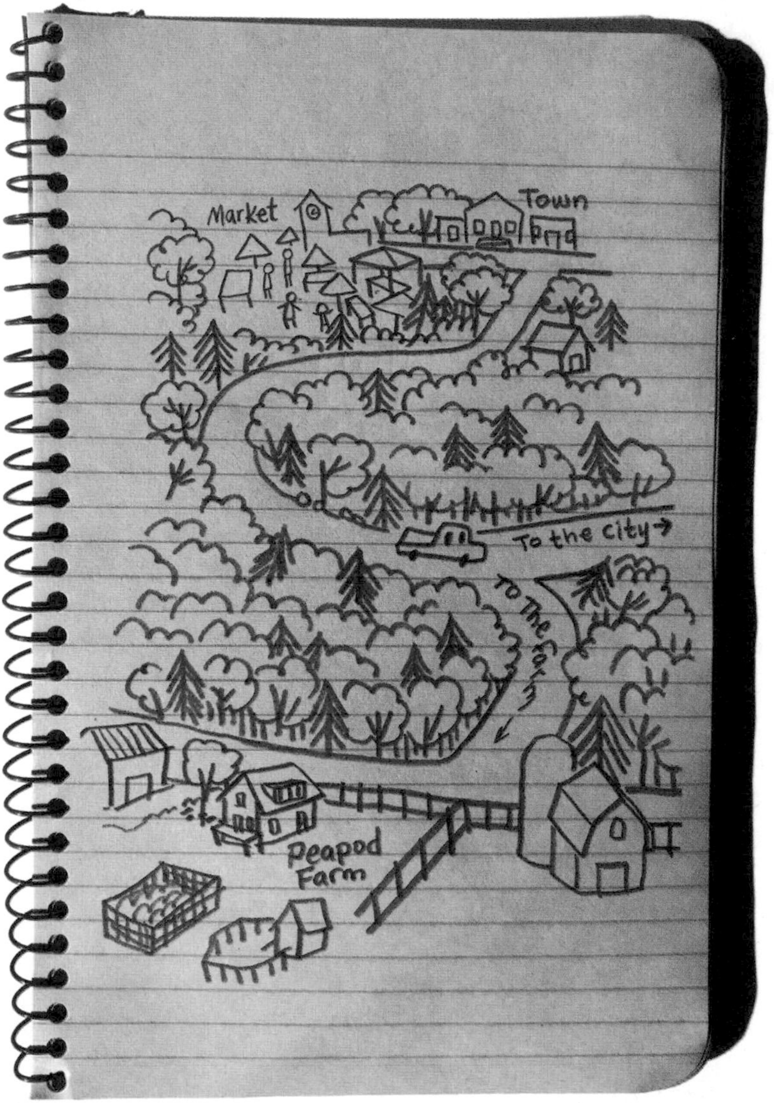
Market
Town
To the city →
To the farm
Peapod
Farm

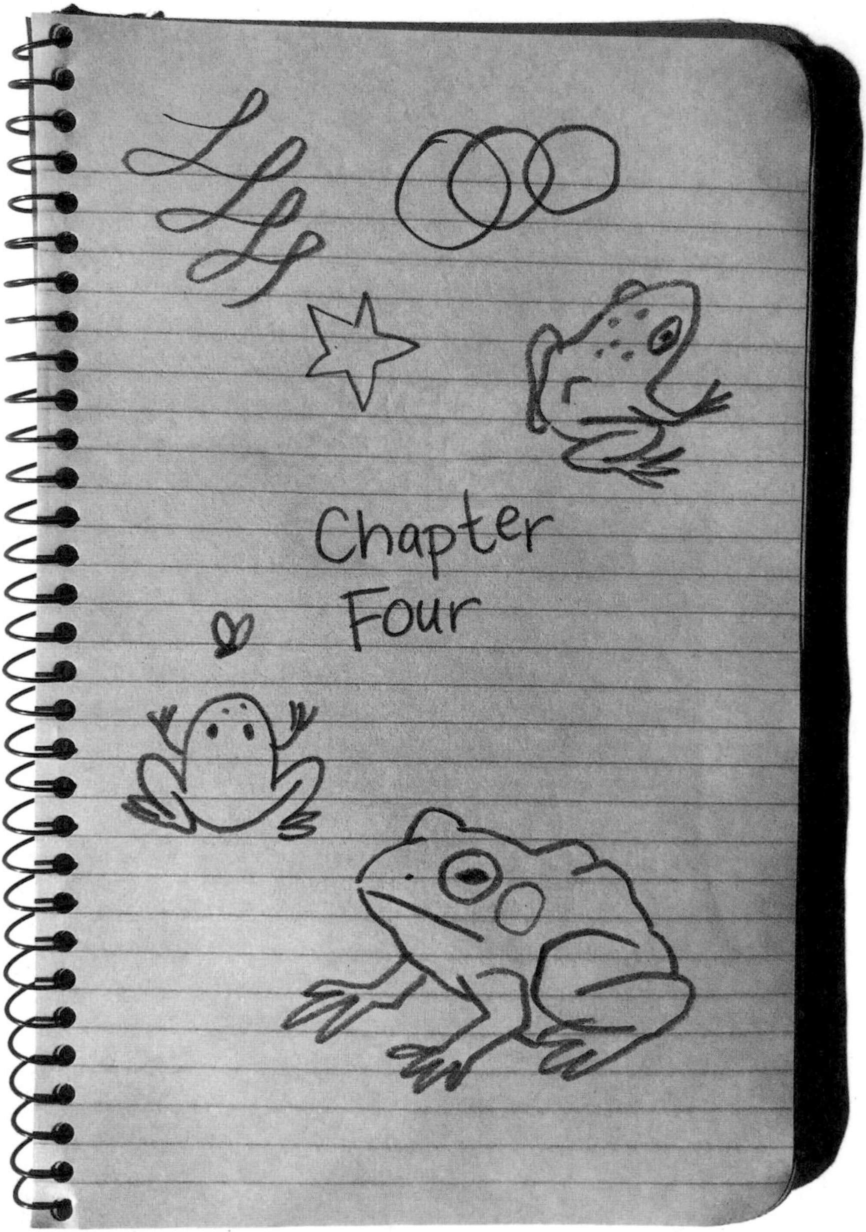
Chapter Four

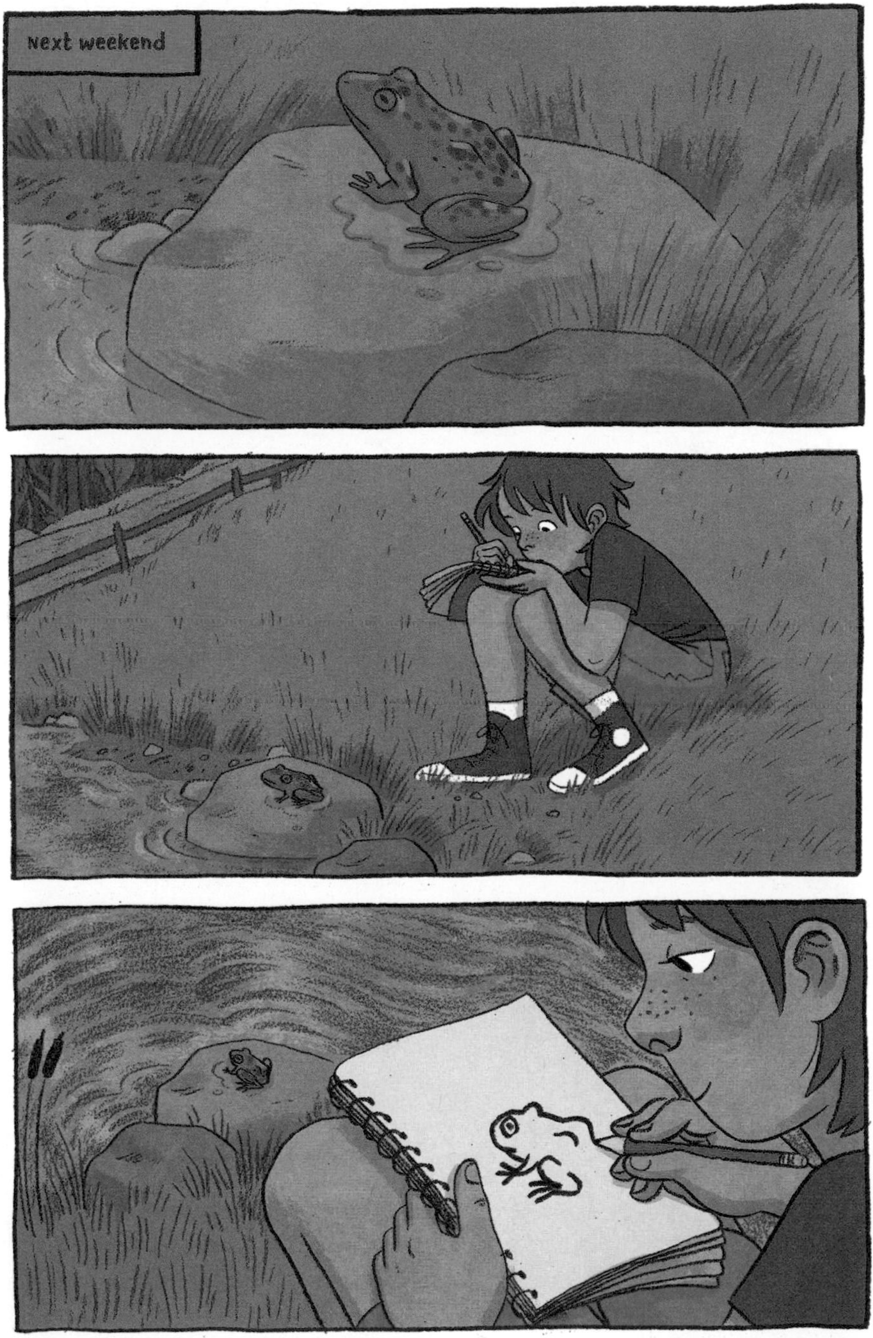
next weekend

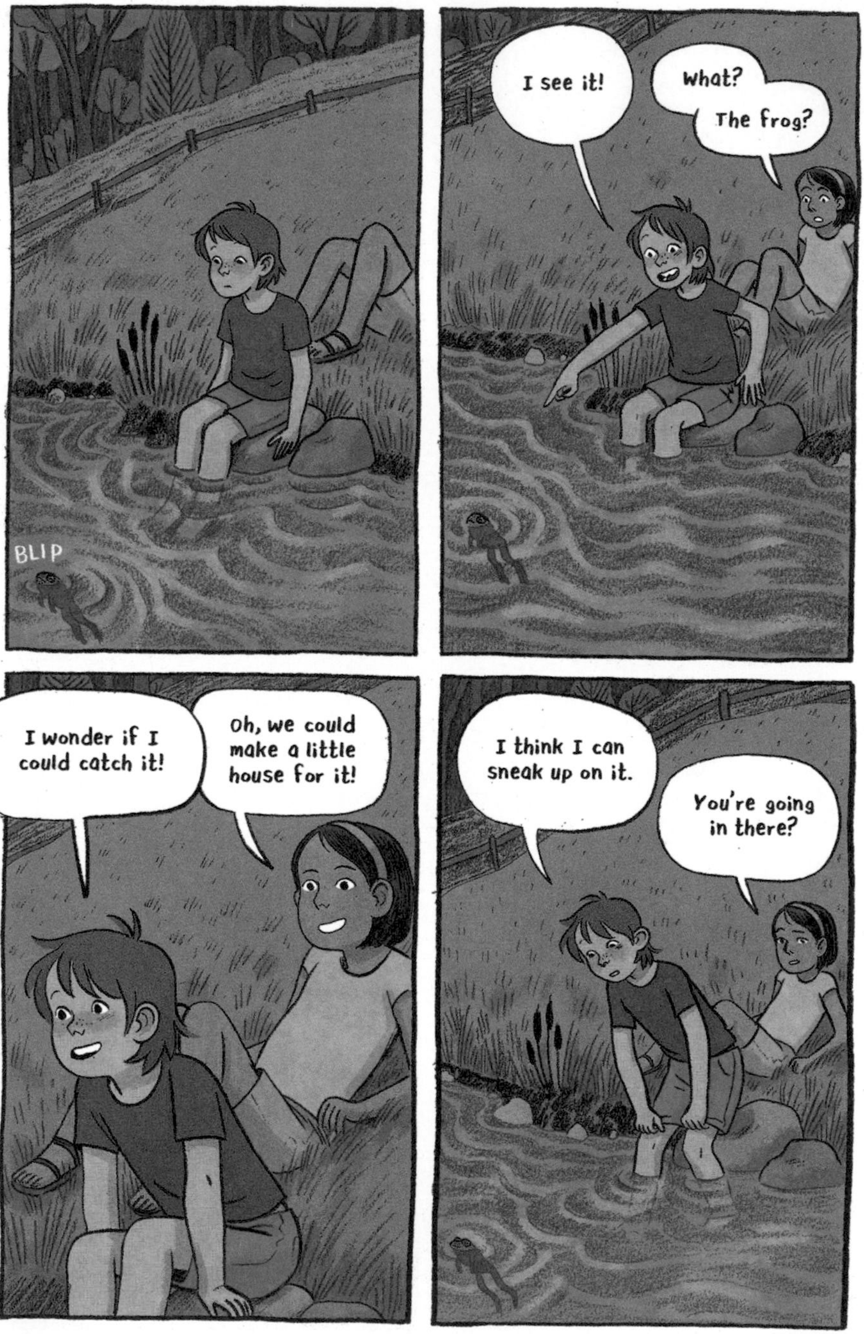

BLIP
I see it!
What?
The frog?
I wonder if I could catch it!
Oh, we could make a little house for it!
I think I can sneak up on it.
You're going in there?

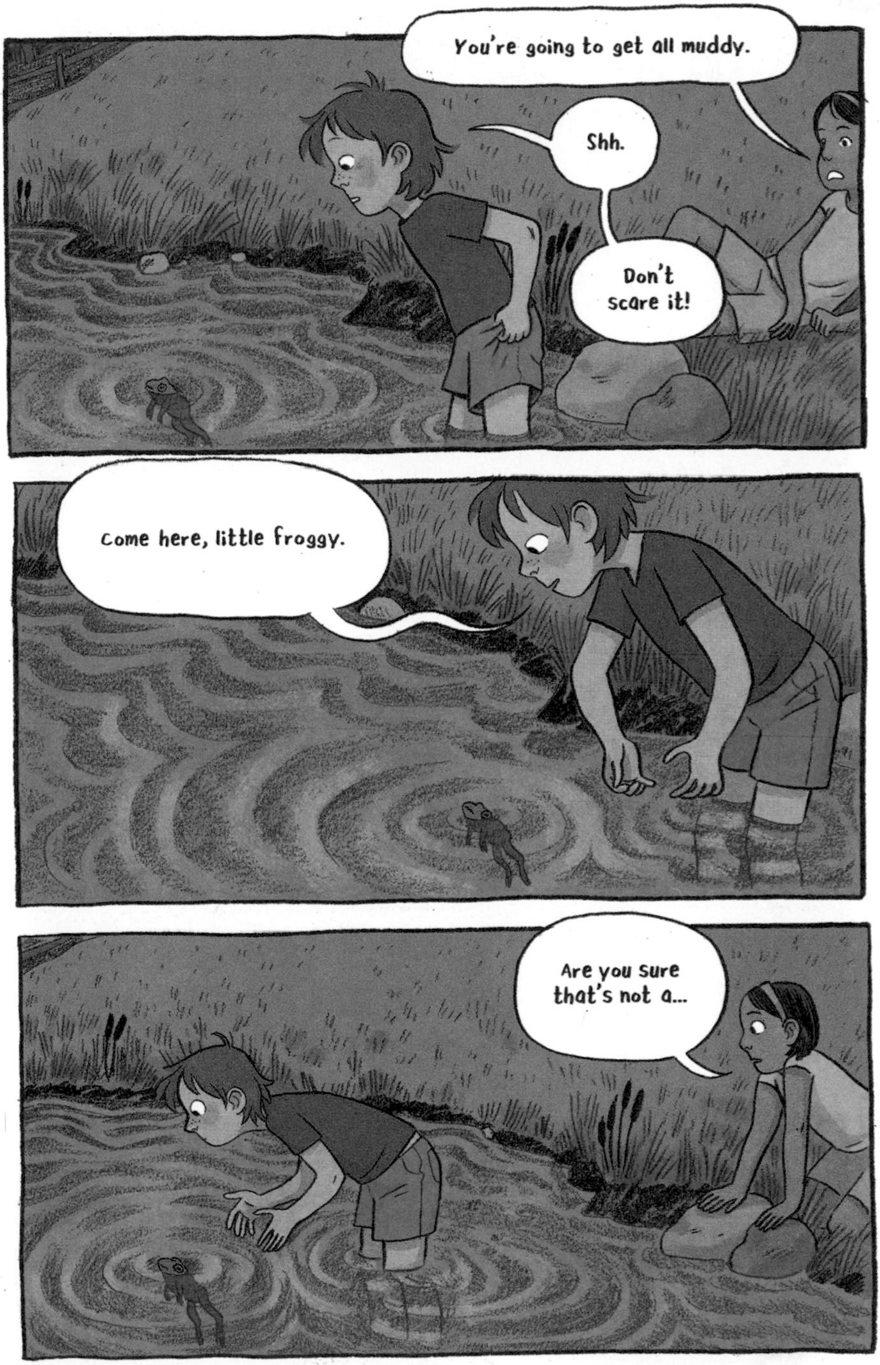
You're going to get all muddy.
Shh.
Don't scare it!
Come here, little froggy.
Are you sure that's not a...

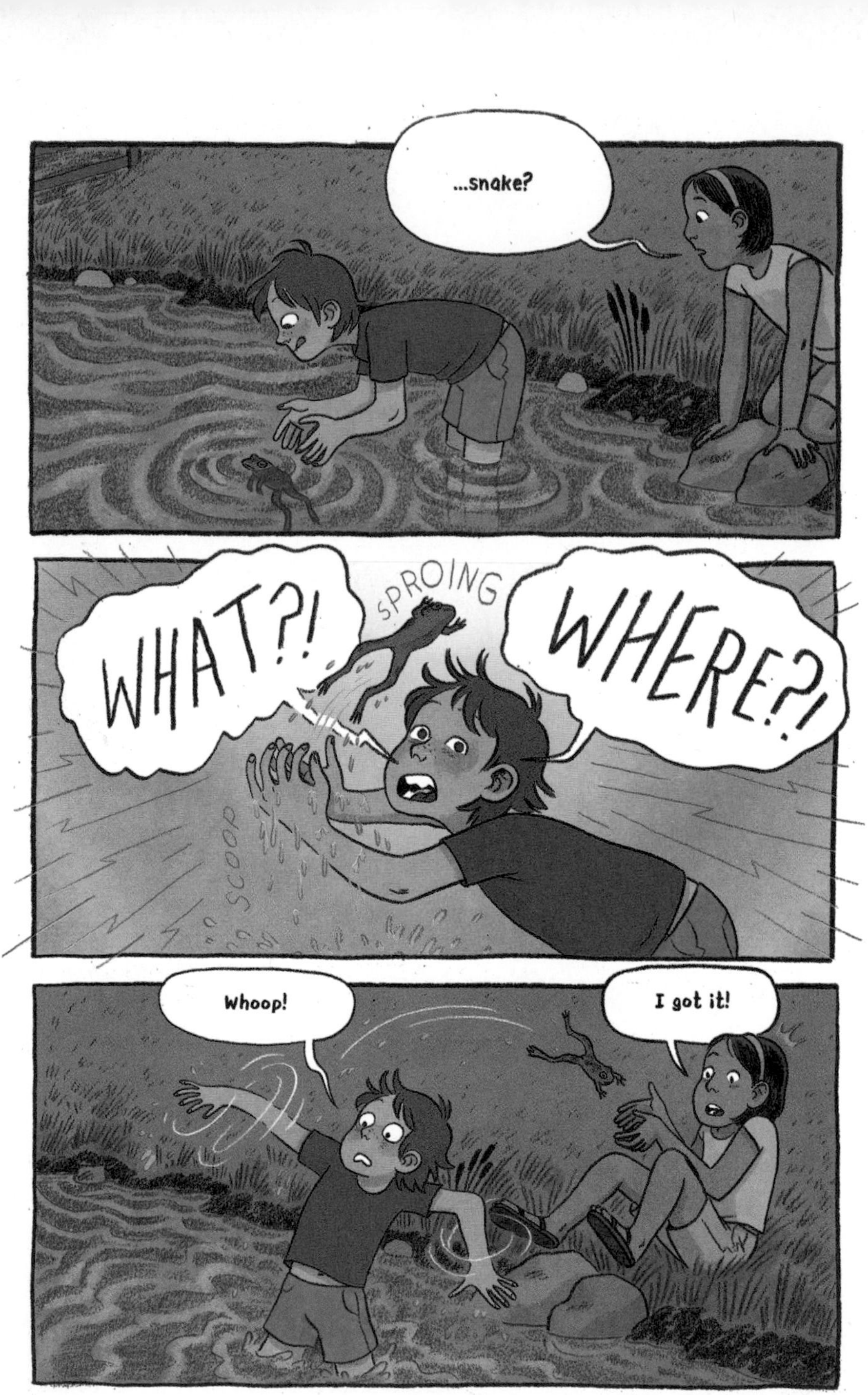
...snake?
WHAT?!
SPROING
WHERE?!
SCOOP
Whoop!
I got it!

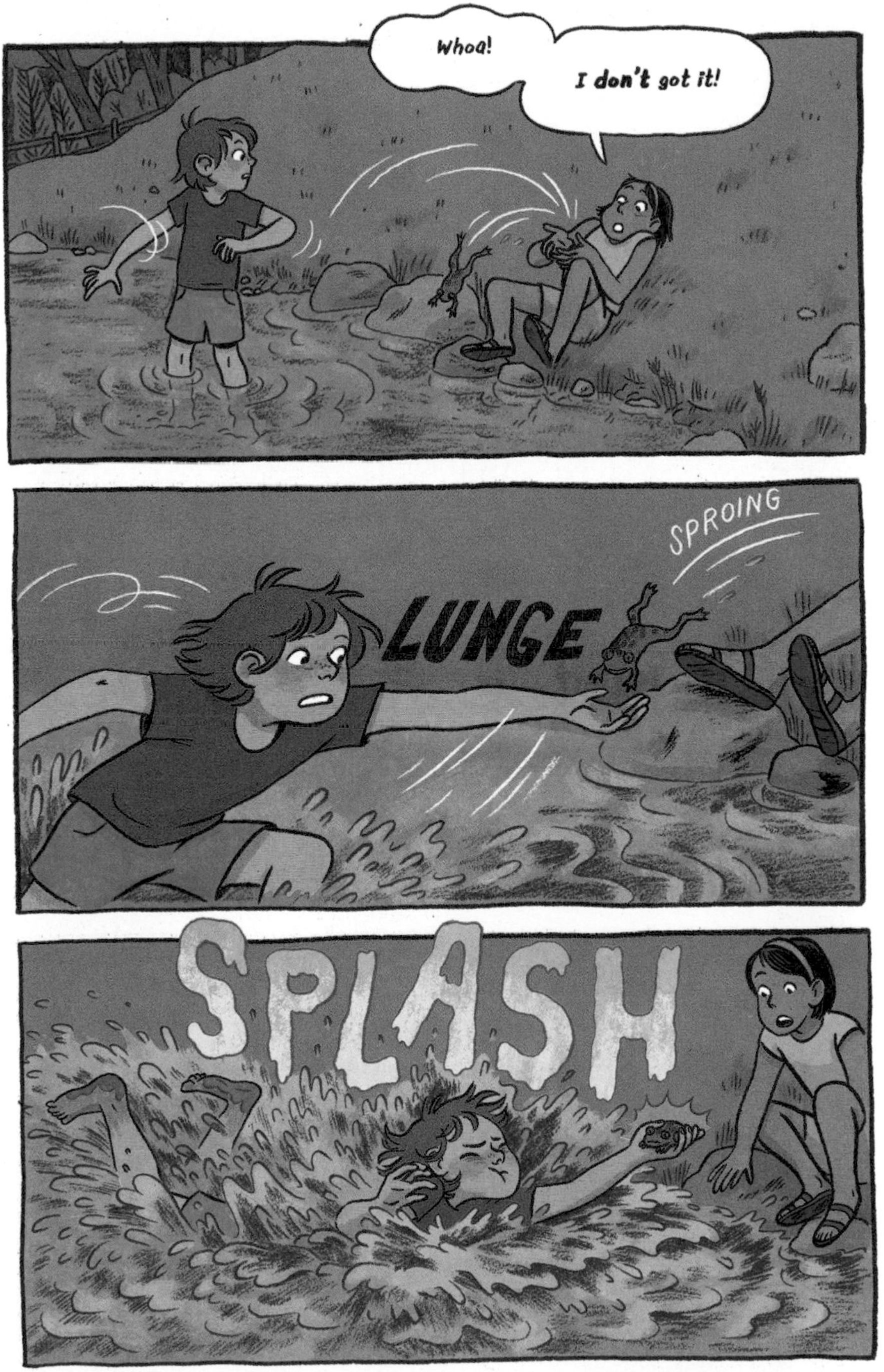
Whoa!
I don't got it!
SPROING
LUNGE
SPLASH

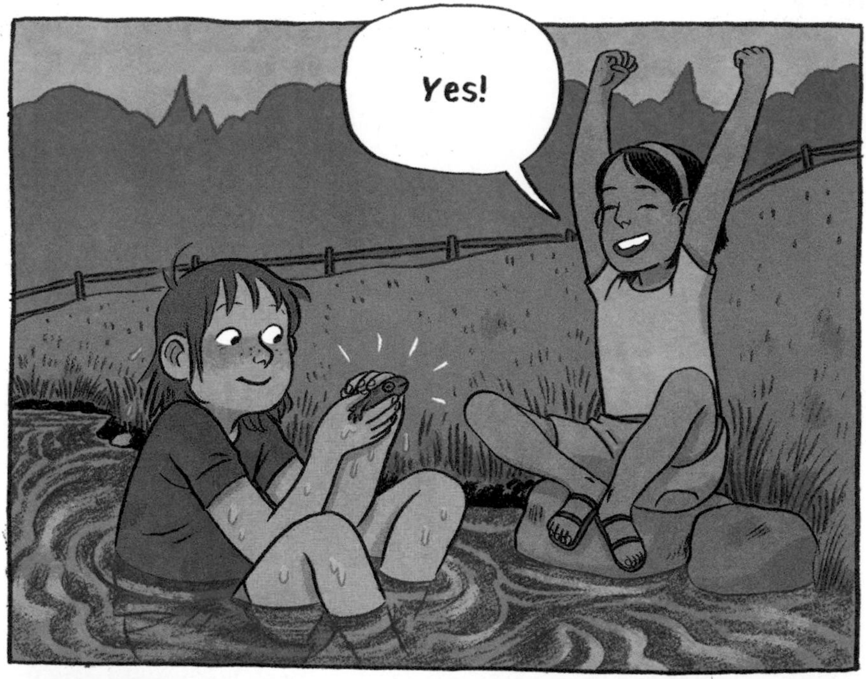
Yes!

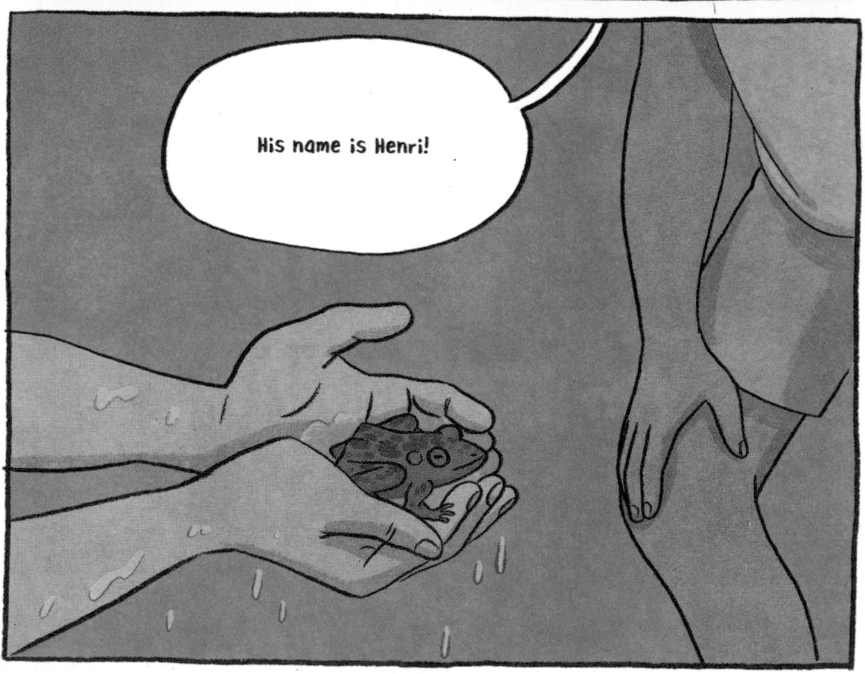
His name is Henri!

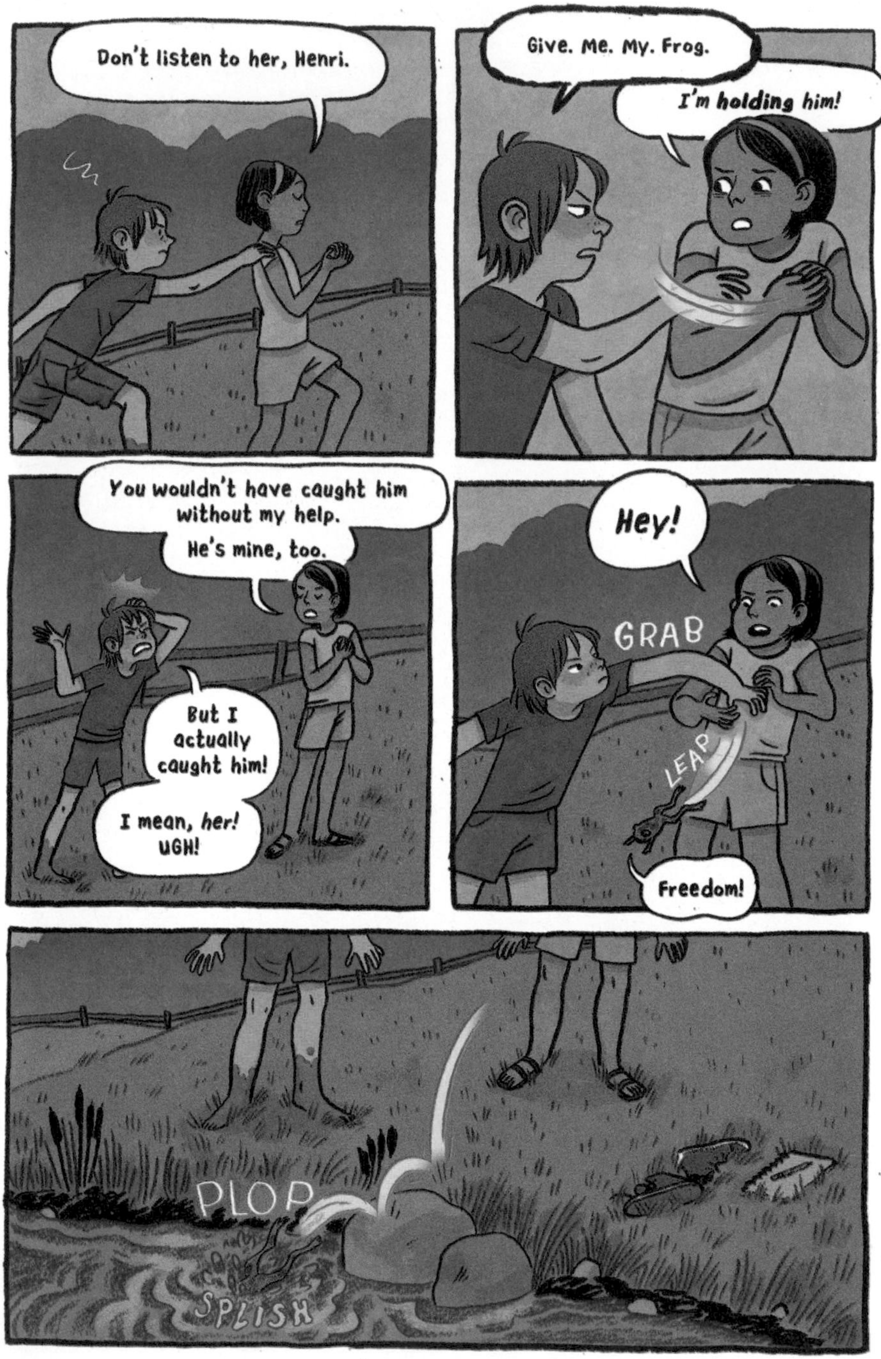
Don't listen to her, Henri.
Give. Me. My. Frog.
I'm holding him!
You wouldn't have caught him without my help.
He's mine, too.
But I actually caught him!
I mean, her! UGH!
Hey!
GRAB
LEAP
Freedom!
PLOP
SPLISH

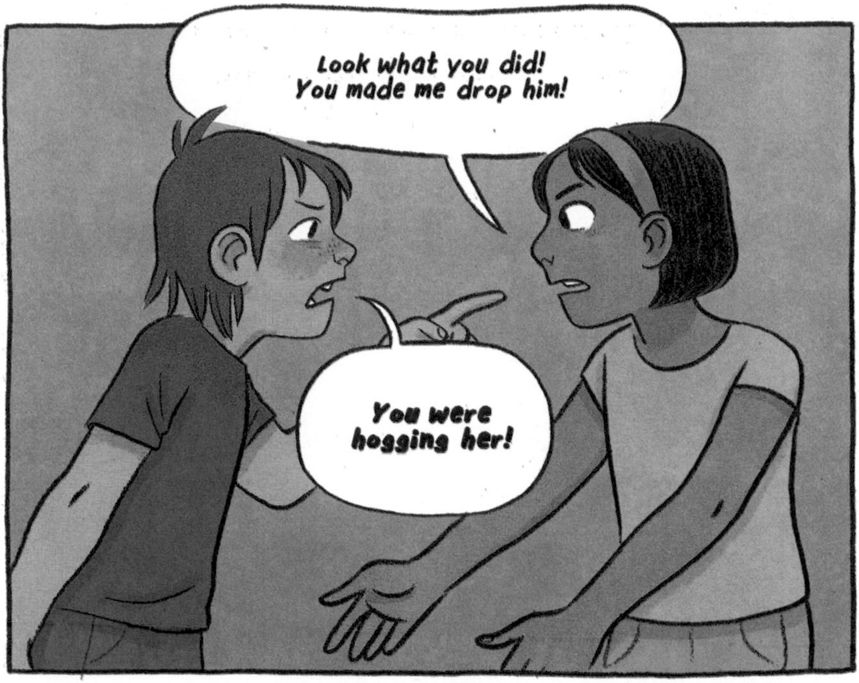
Look what you did!
You made me drop him!
You were hogging her!

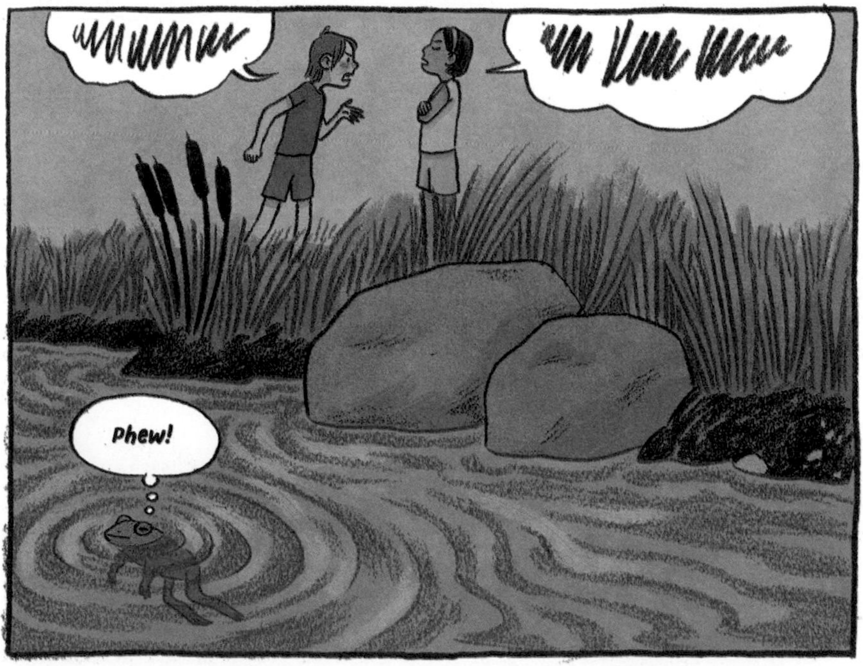
Phew!

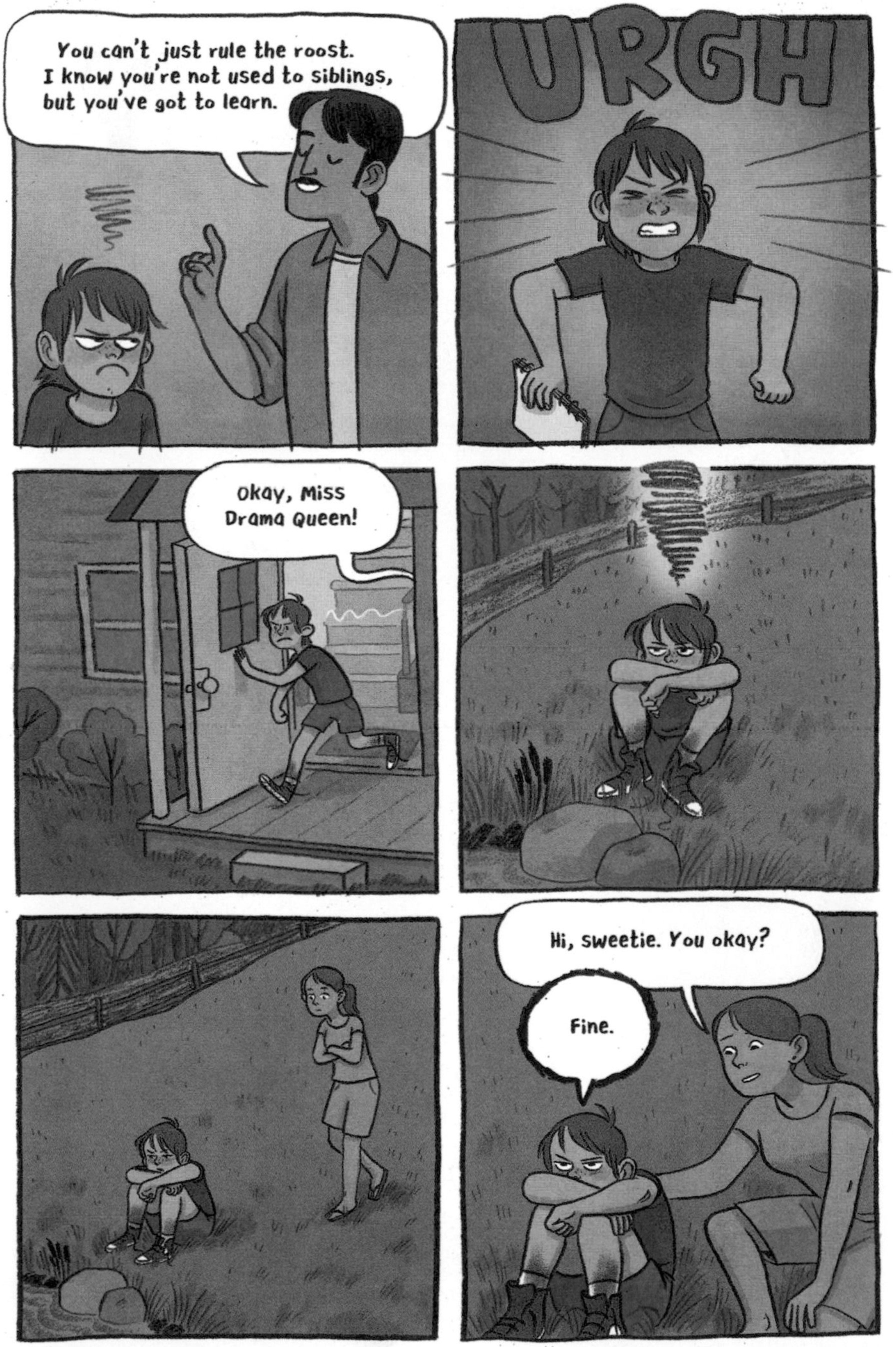
You can't just rule the roost. I know you're not used to siblings, but you've got to learn.
URGH
Okay, Miss Drama Queen!
Hi, sweetie. You okay?
Fine.

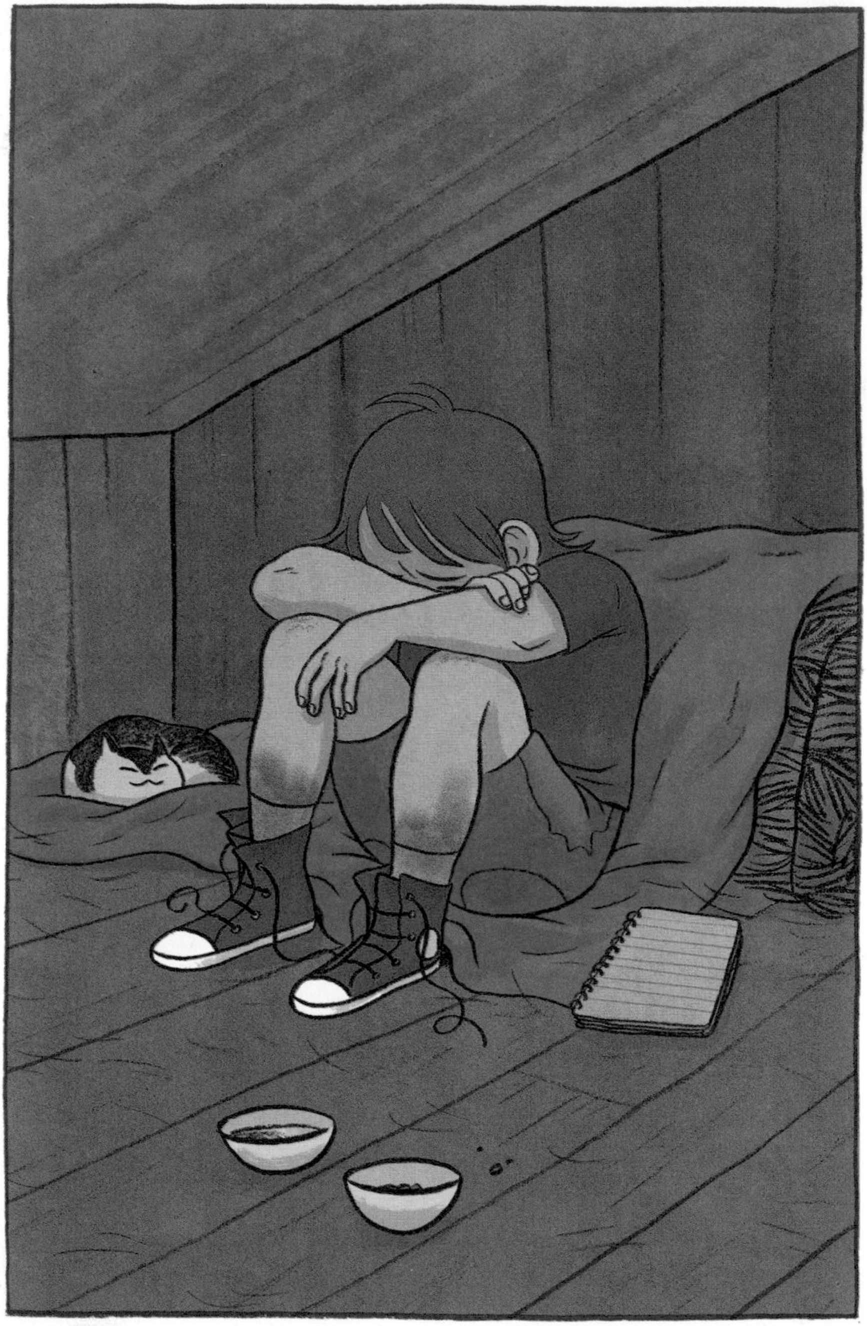

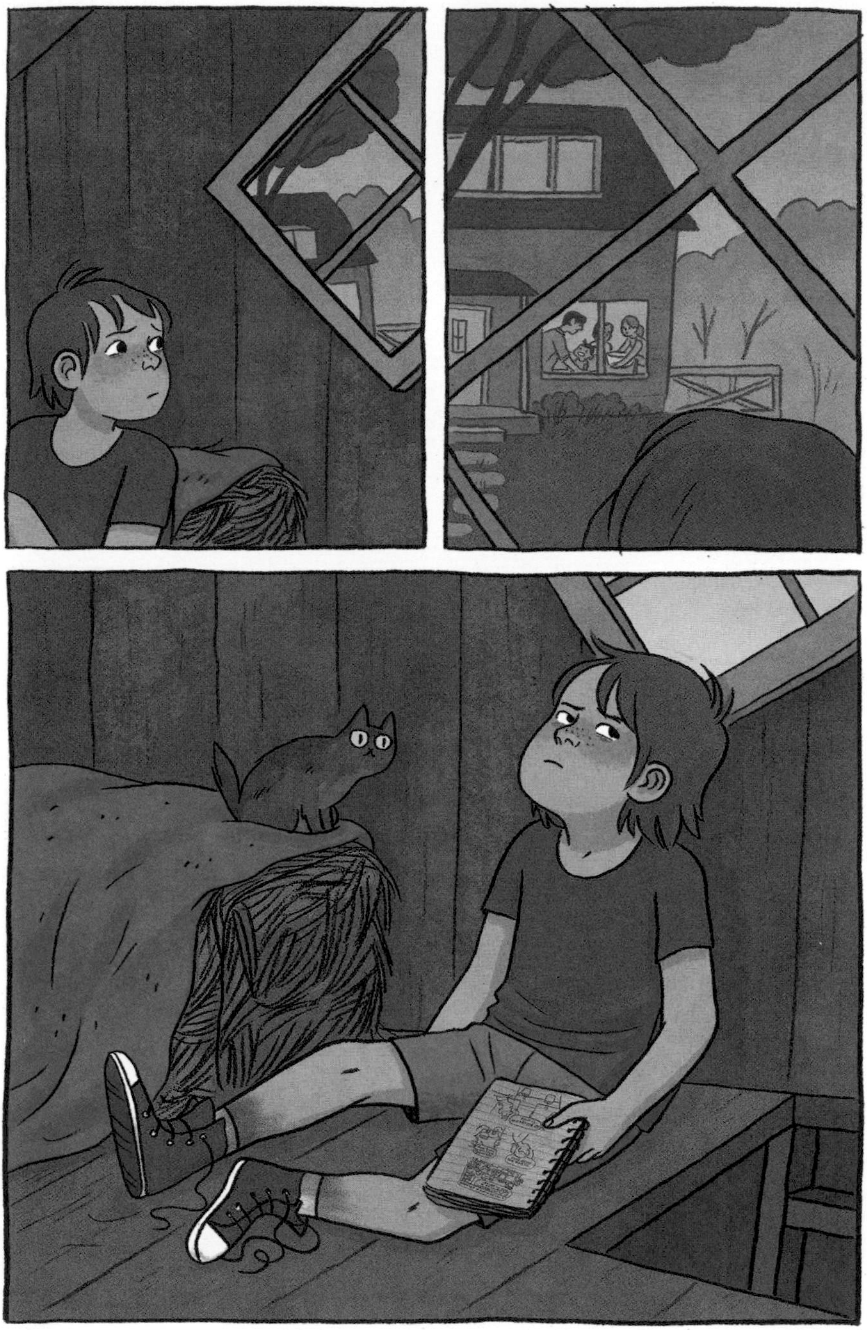

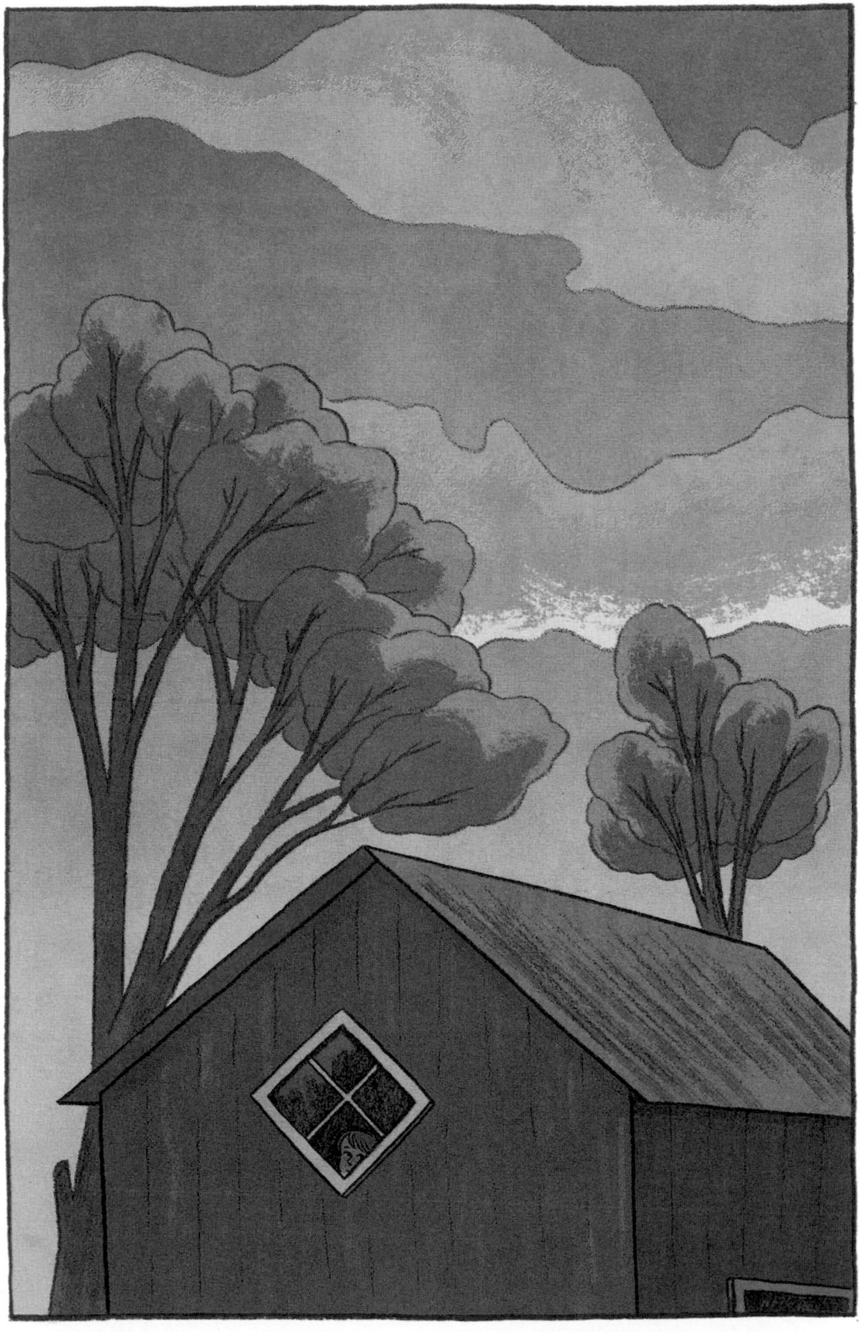

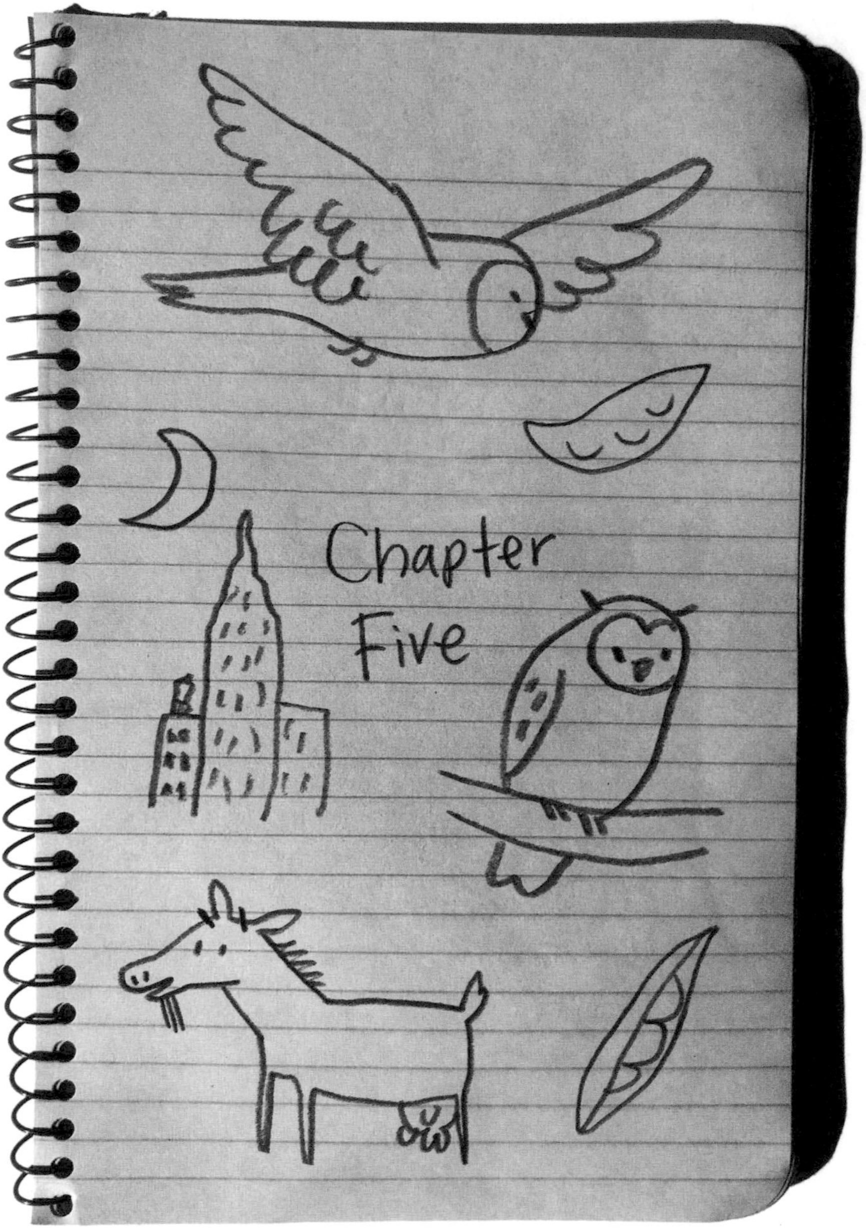
Chapter
Five

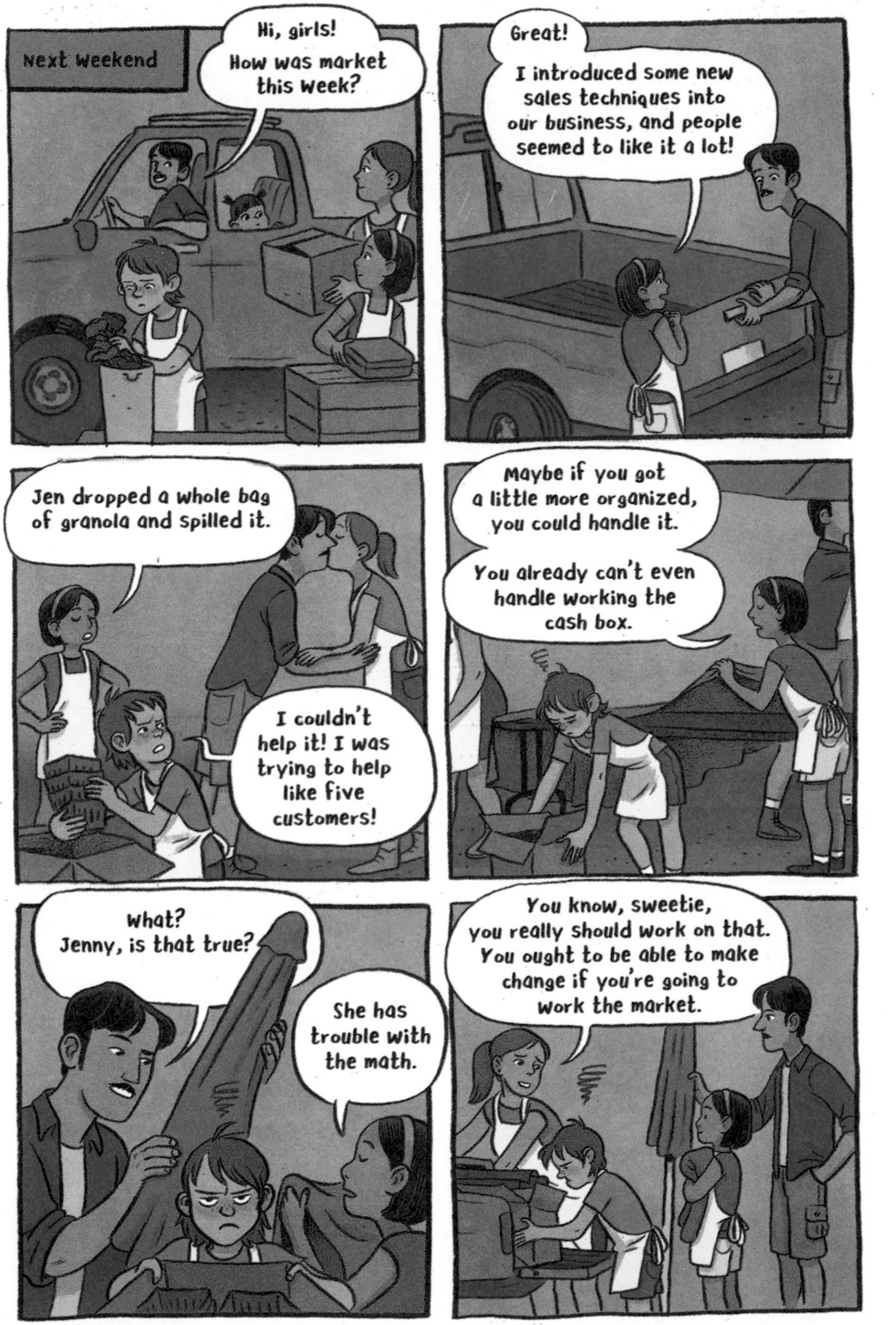
Next Weekend
Hi, girls! How was market this week?
Great! I introduced some new sales techniques into our business, and people seemed to like it a lot!
Jen dropped a whole bag of granola and spilled it.
I couldn't help it! I was trying to help like five customers!
Maybe if you got a little more organized, you could handle it.
You already can't even handle working the cash box.
What? Jenny, is that true?
She has trouble with the math.
You know, sweetie, you really should work on that. You ought to be able to make change if you're going to work the market.

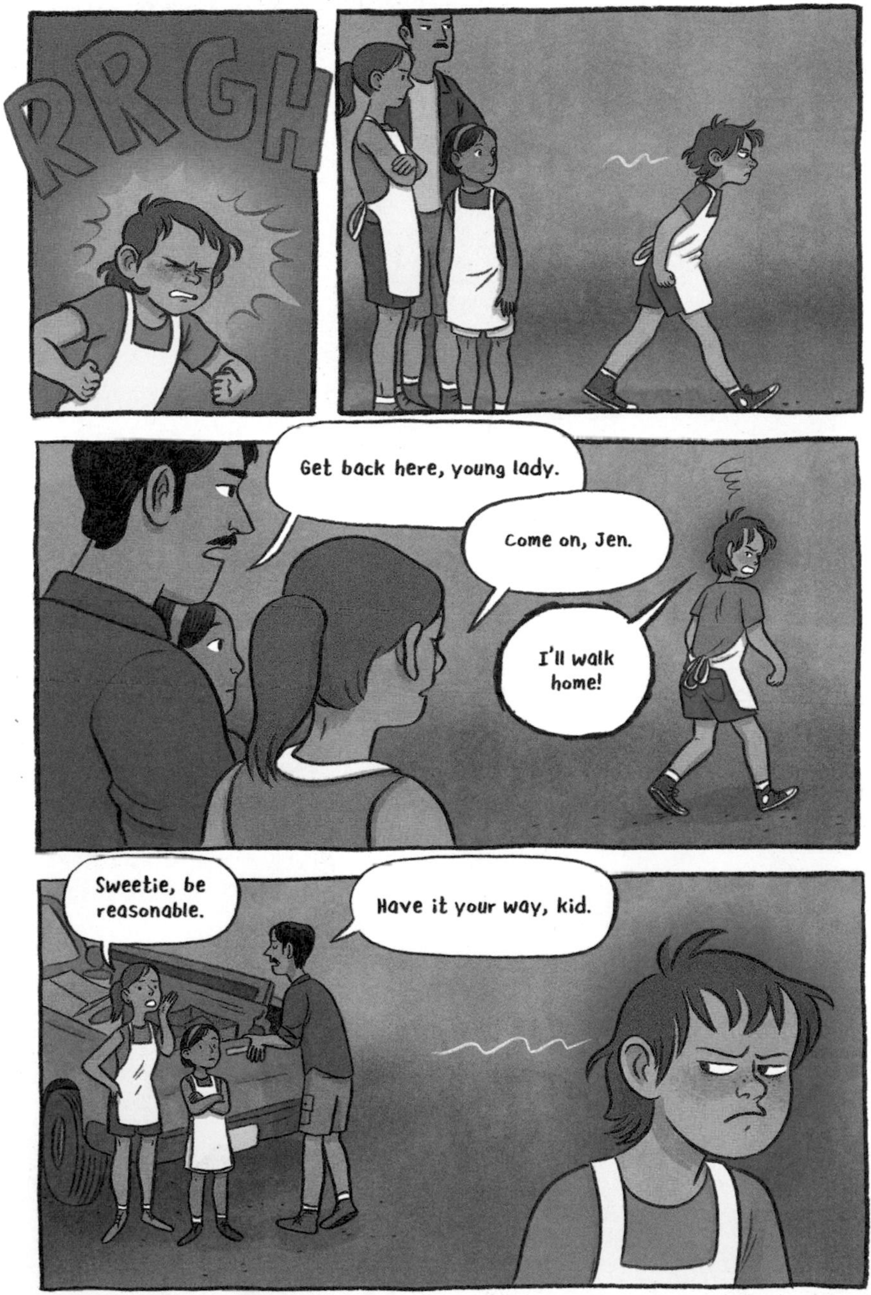
RRGH
Get back here, young lady.
Come on, Jen.
I'll walk home!
Sweetie, be reasonable.
Have it your way, kid.

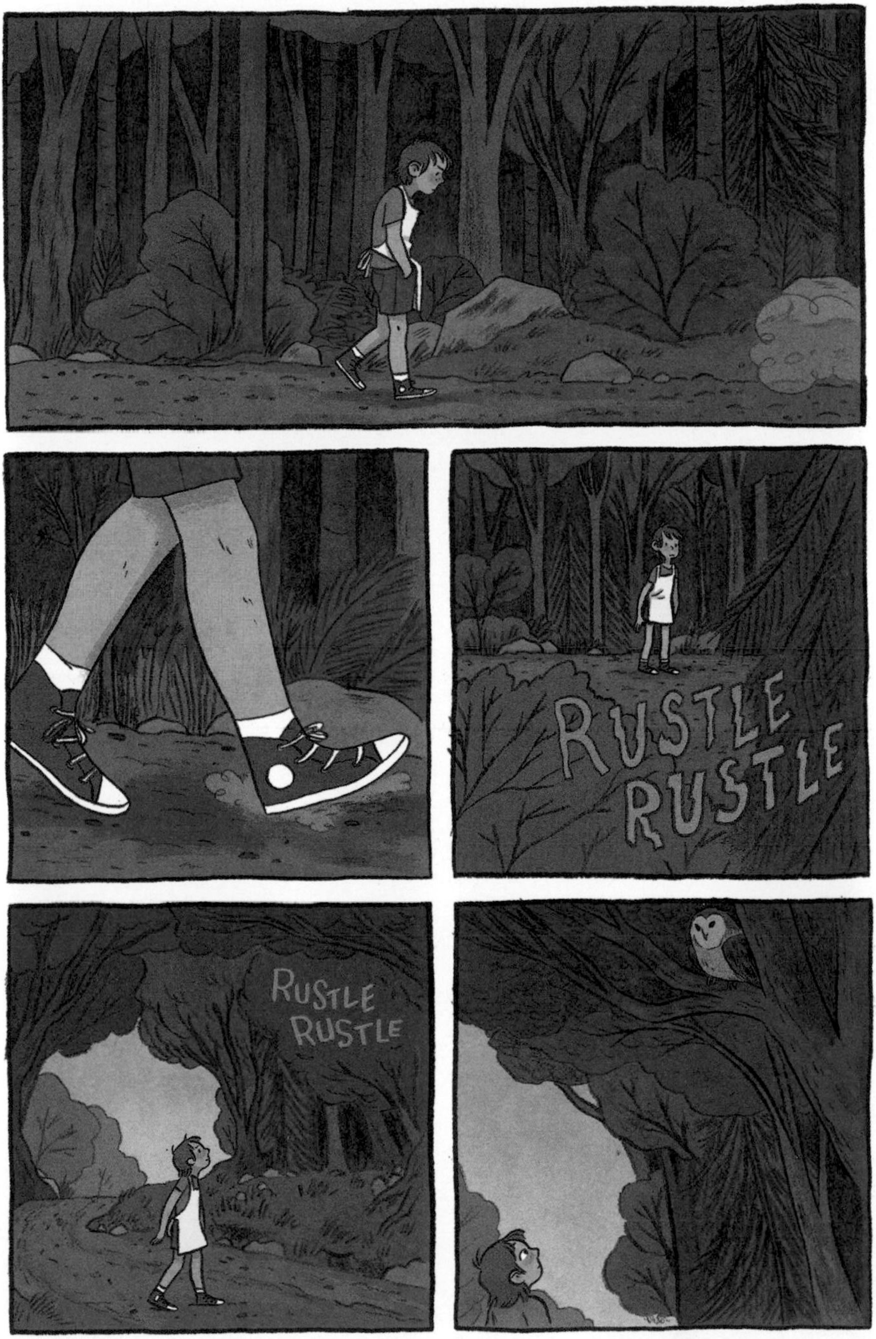
RUSTLE
RUSTLE
RUSTLE
RUSTLE

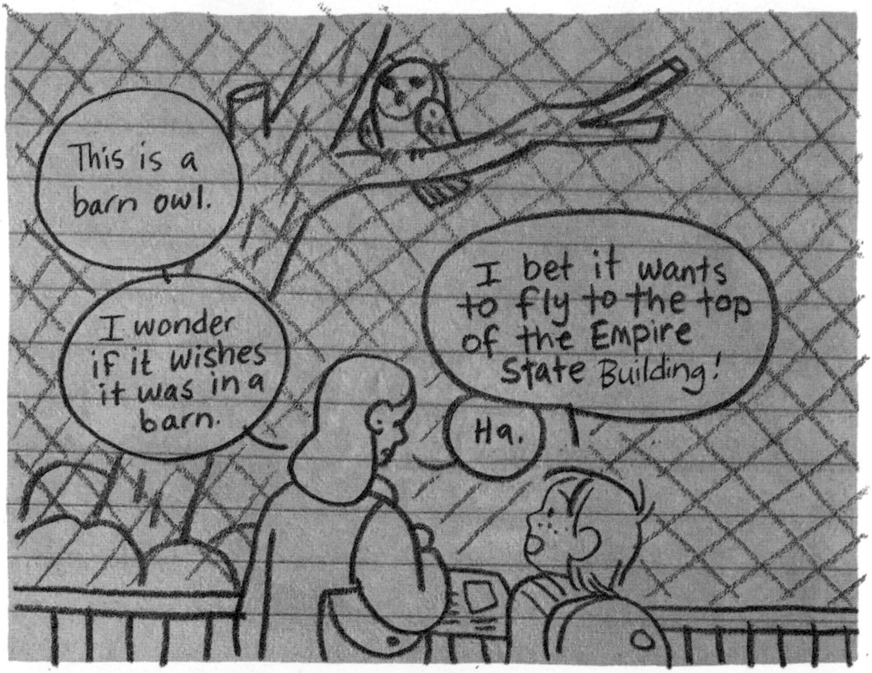
This is a barn owl.
I wonder if it wishes it was in a barn.
I bet it wants to fly to the top of the Empire State Building!
Ha.

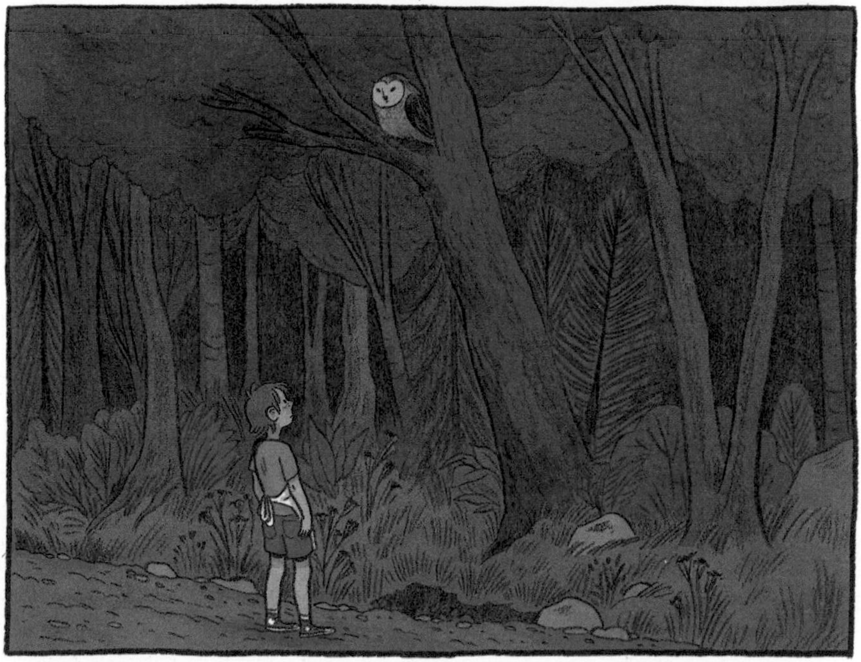

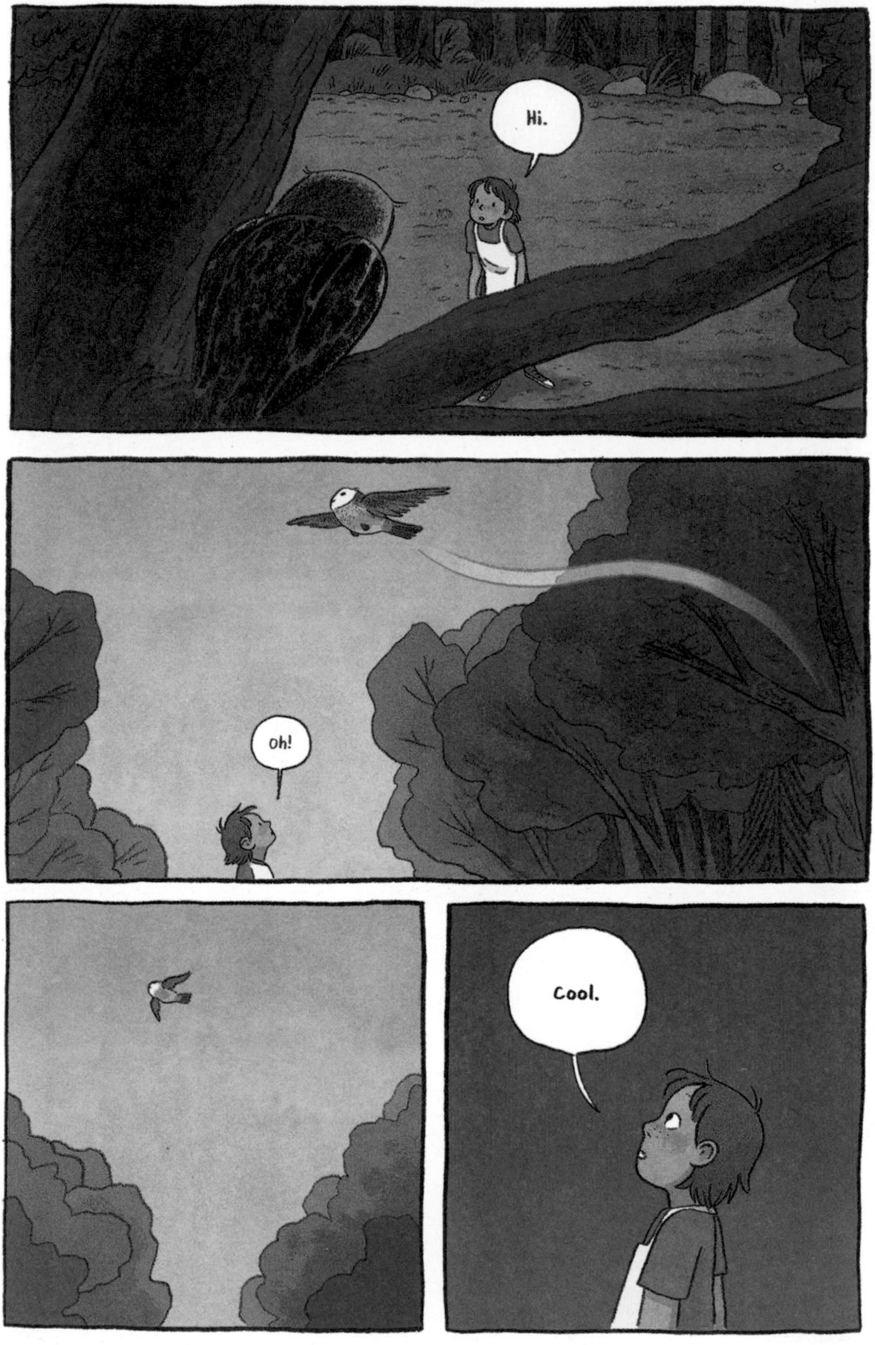
Hi.
Oh!
Cool.

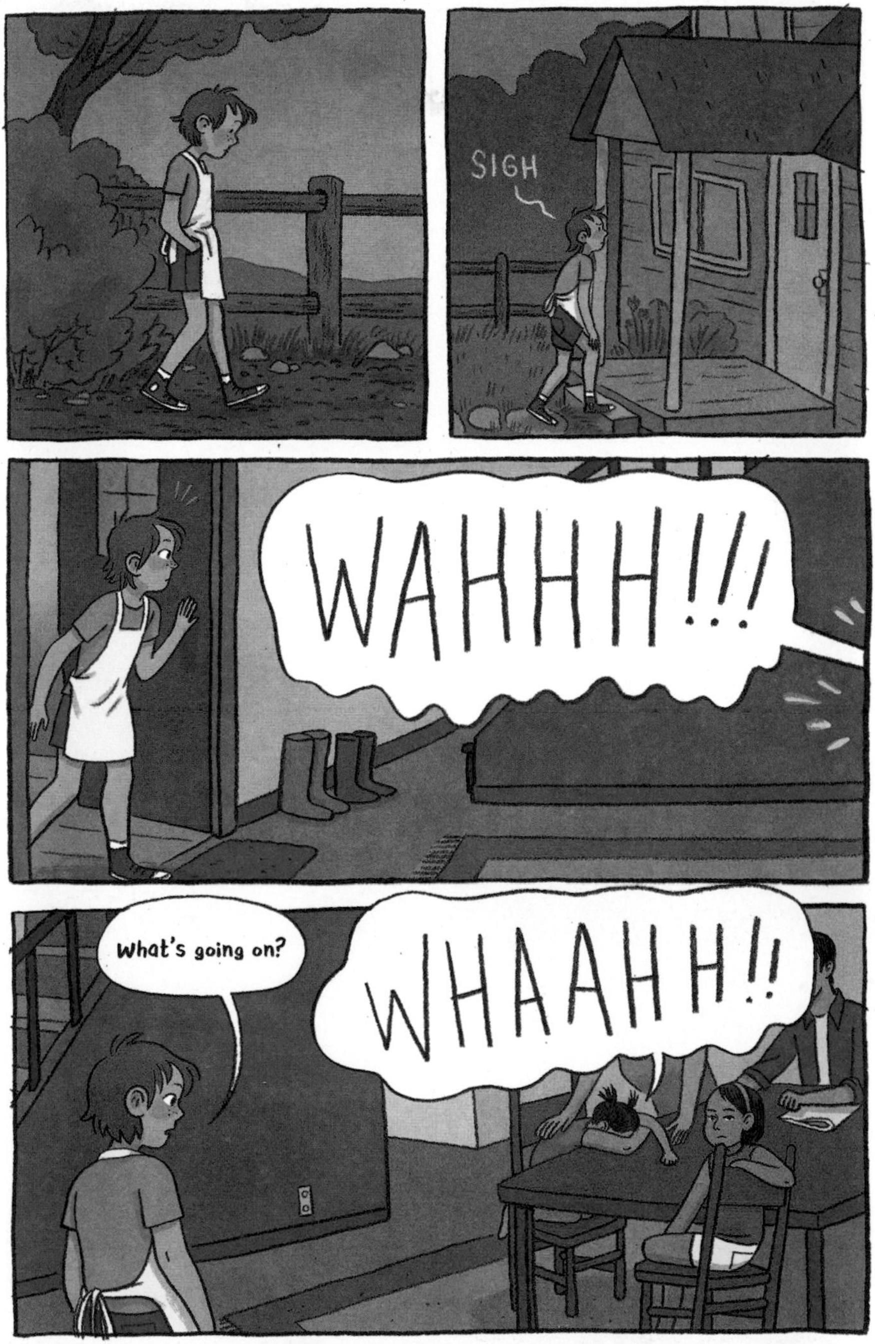
SIGH
WAHHH!!!
What's going on?
WHAAHH!!

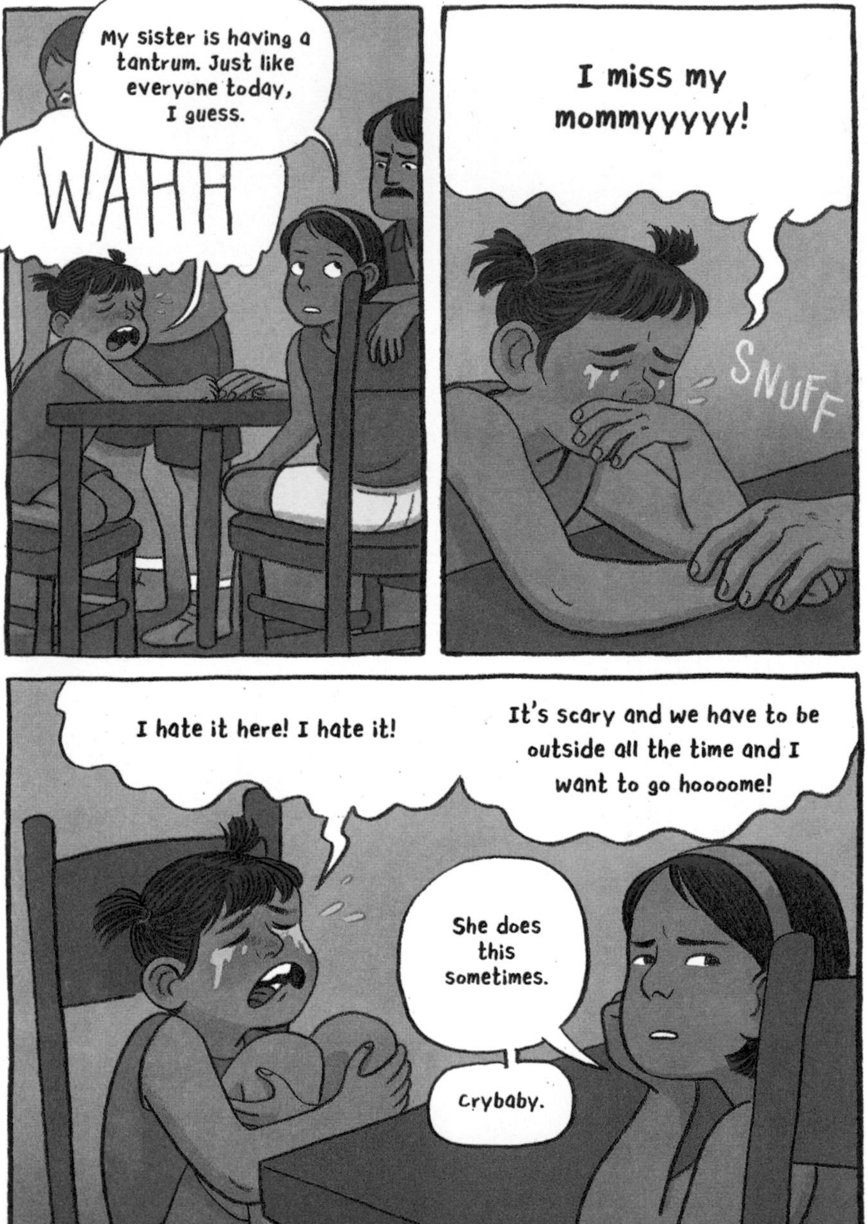
My sister is having a tantrum. Just like everyone today, I guess.
WAHH
I miss my mommyyyyy!
SNUFF
I hate it here! I hate it!
It's scary and we have to be outside all the time and I want to go hoooome!
She does this sometimes.
Crybaby.

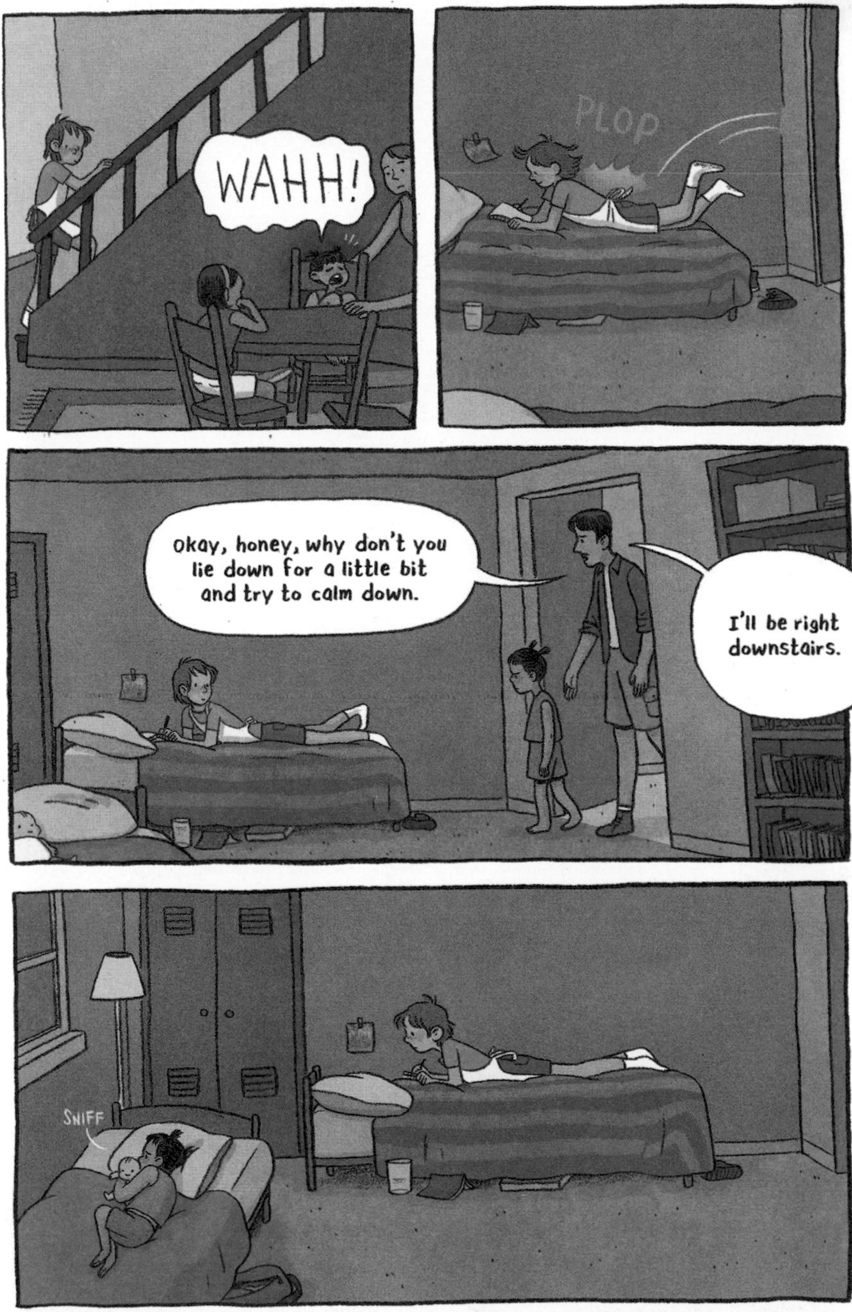
WAHH!
PLOP
Okay, honey, why don't you lie down for a little bit and try to calm down.
I'll be right downstairs.
SNIFF

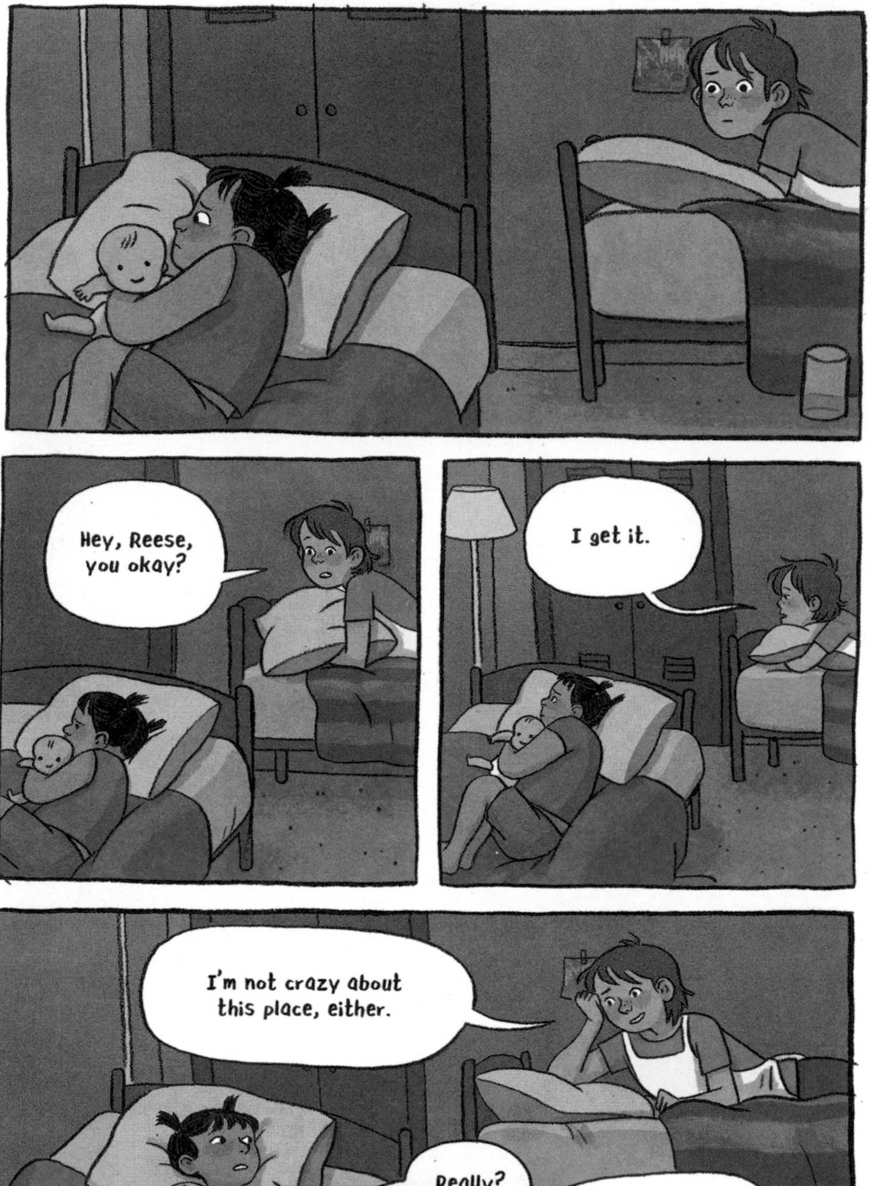
Hey, Reese, you okay?
I get it.
I'm not crazy about this place, either.
Really?
But you're like... a farmer.

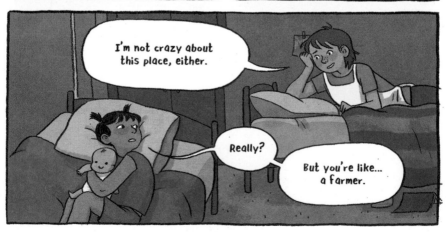

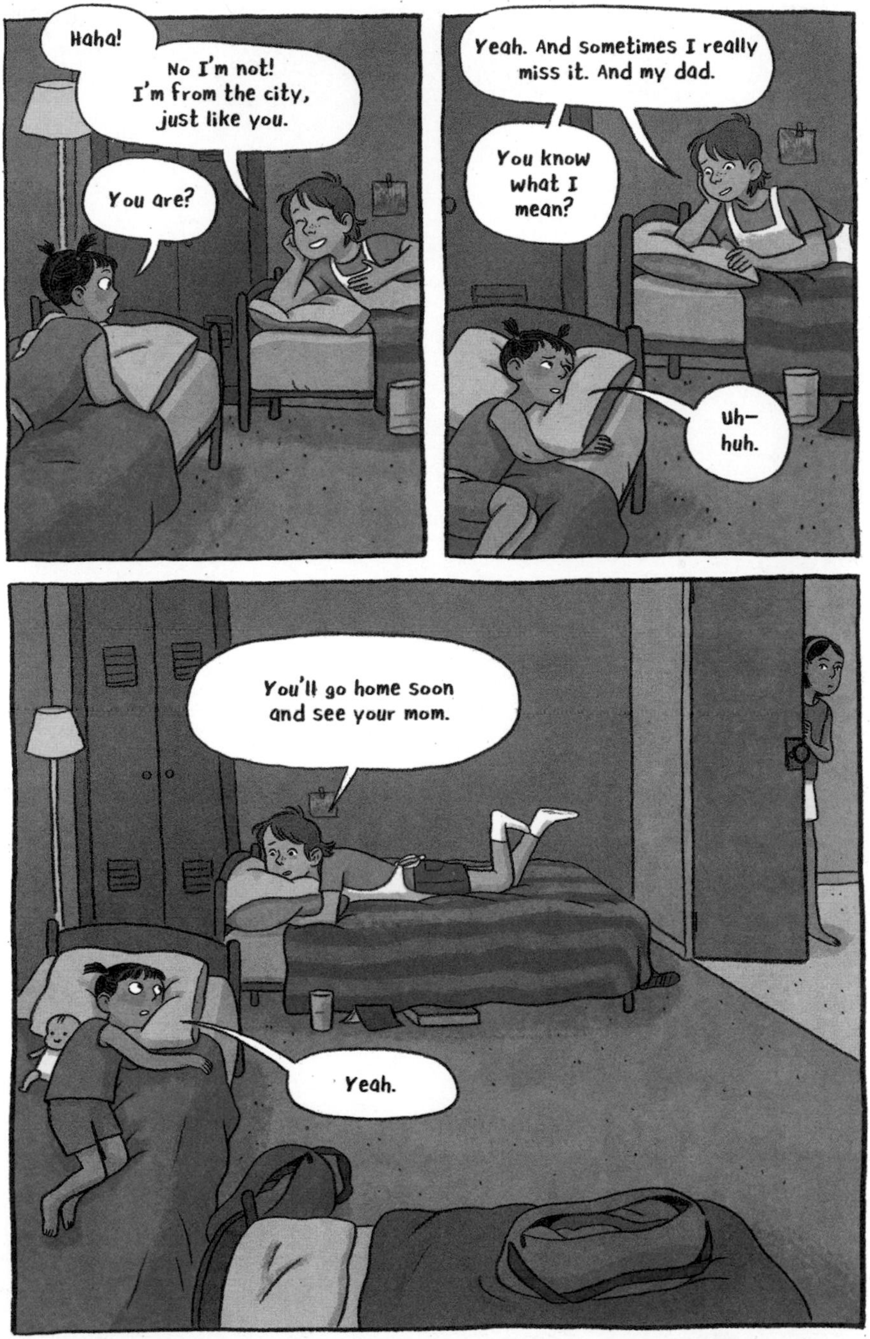
Haha!
No I'm not! I'm from the city, just like you.
You are?
Yeah. And sometimes I really miss it. And my dad.
You know what I mean?
Uh-huh.
You'll go home soon and see your mom.
Yeah.

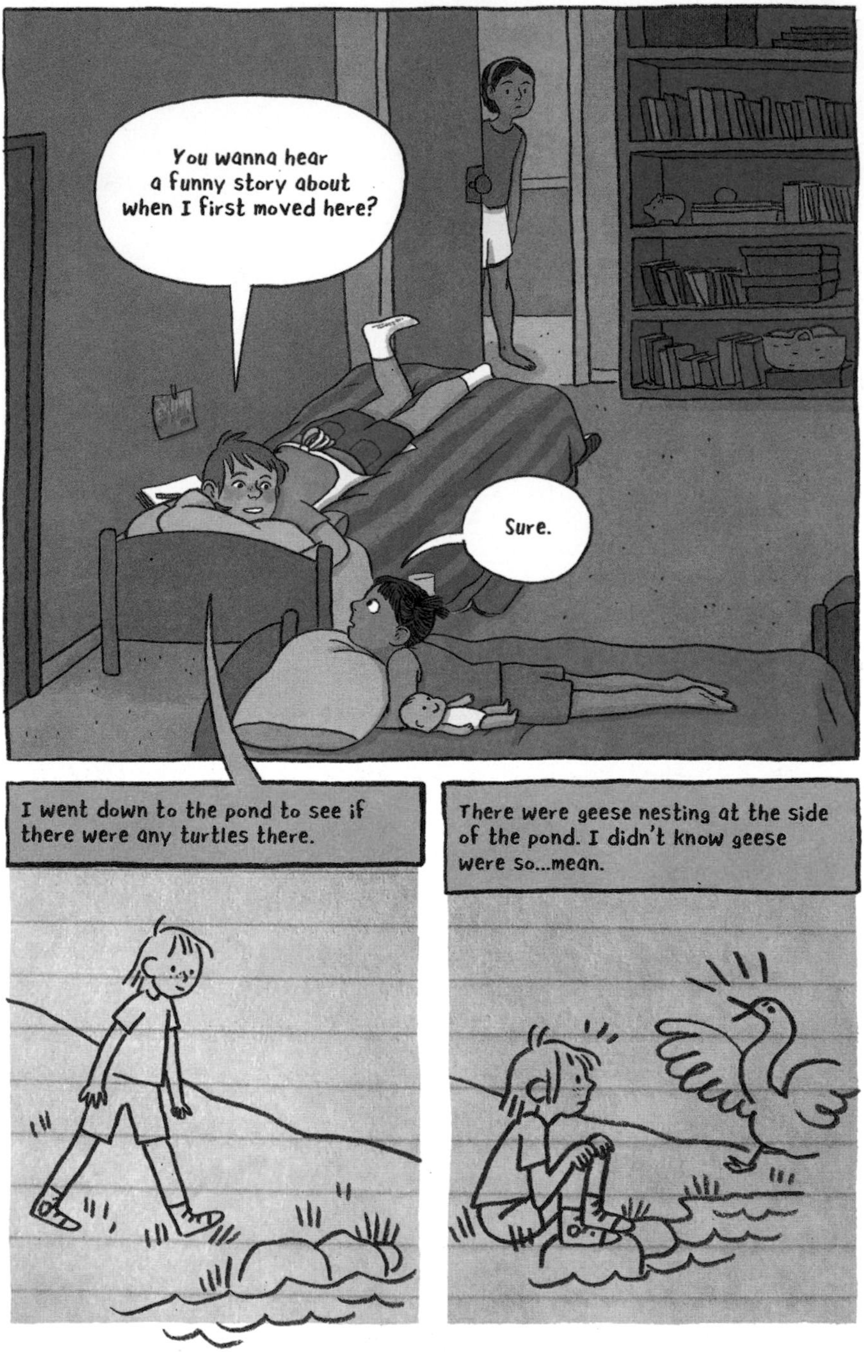
You wanna hear a funny story about when I first moved here?
Sure.
I went down to the pond to see if there were any turtles there.
There were geese nesting at the side of the pond. I didn't know geese were so...mean.

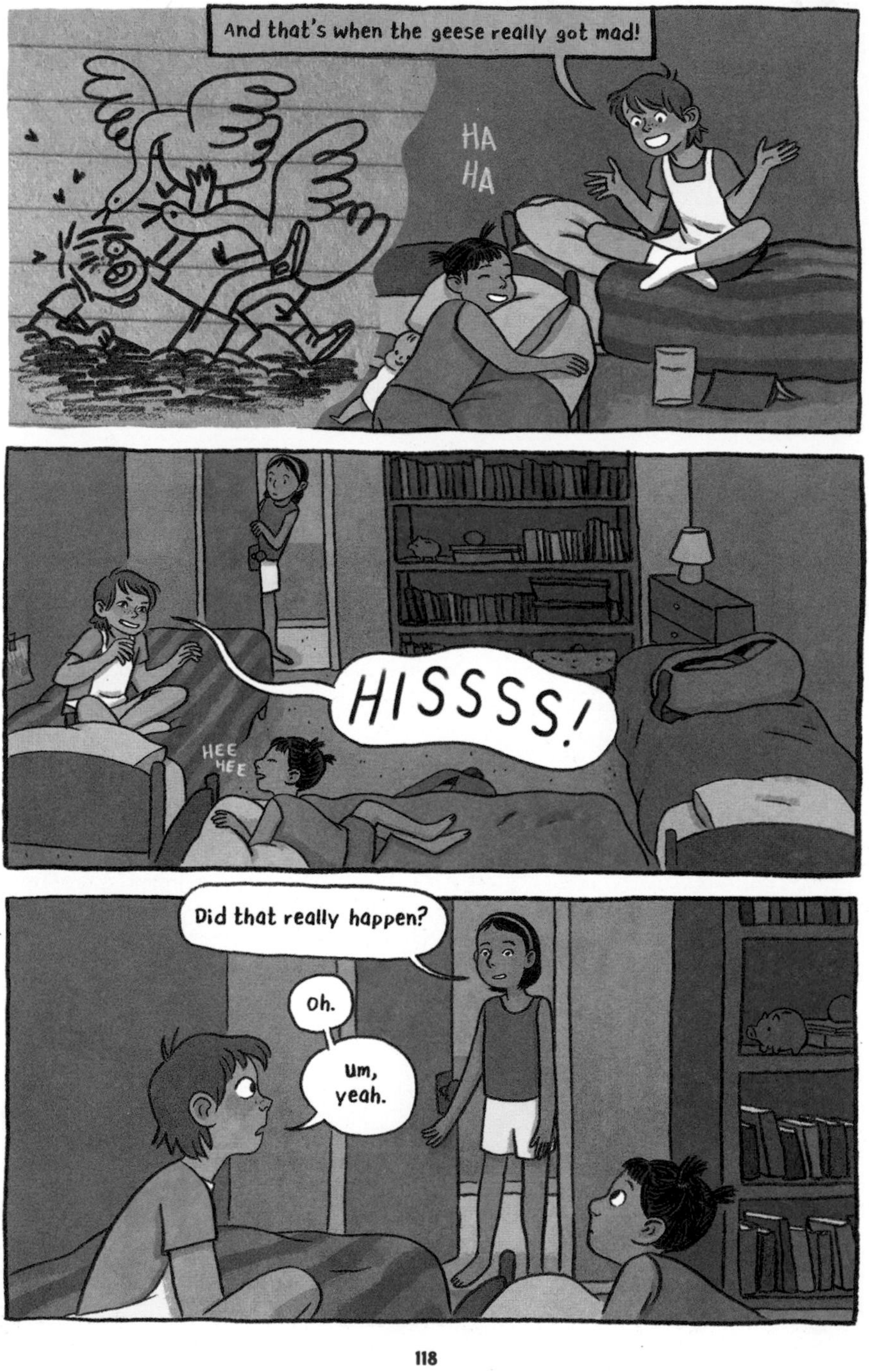
And that's when the geese really got mad!
HA
HA
HISSSS!
HEE
HEE
Did that really happen?
Oh.
Um, yeah.

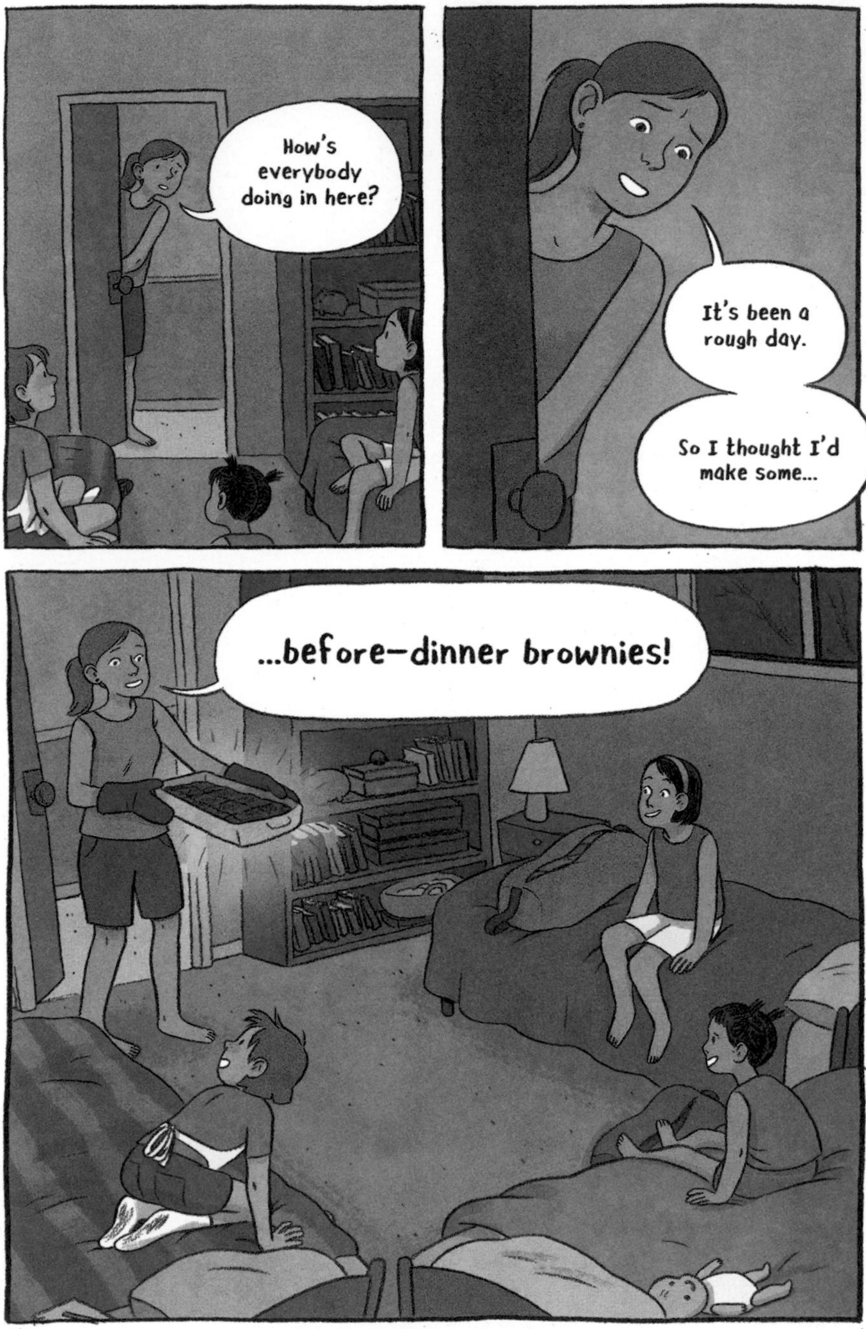
How's everybody doing in here?
It's been a rough day.
So I thought I'd make some...
...before-dinner brownies!

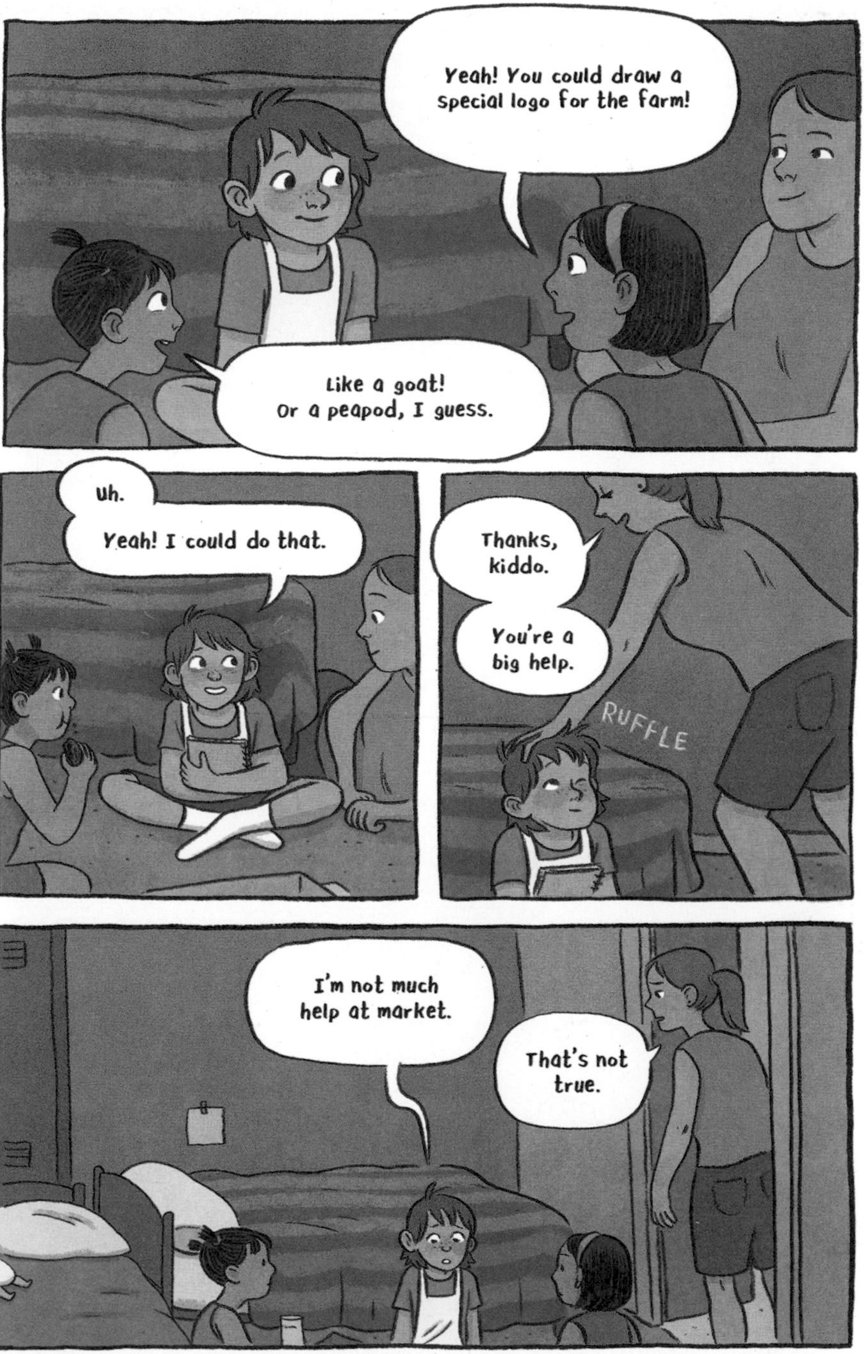
Yeah! You could draw a special logo for the farm!
Like a goat! Or a peapod, I guess.
Uh.
Yeah! I could do that.
Thanks, kiddo.
You're a big help.
RUFFLE
I'm not much help at market.
That's not true.

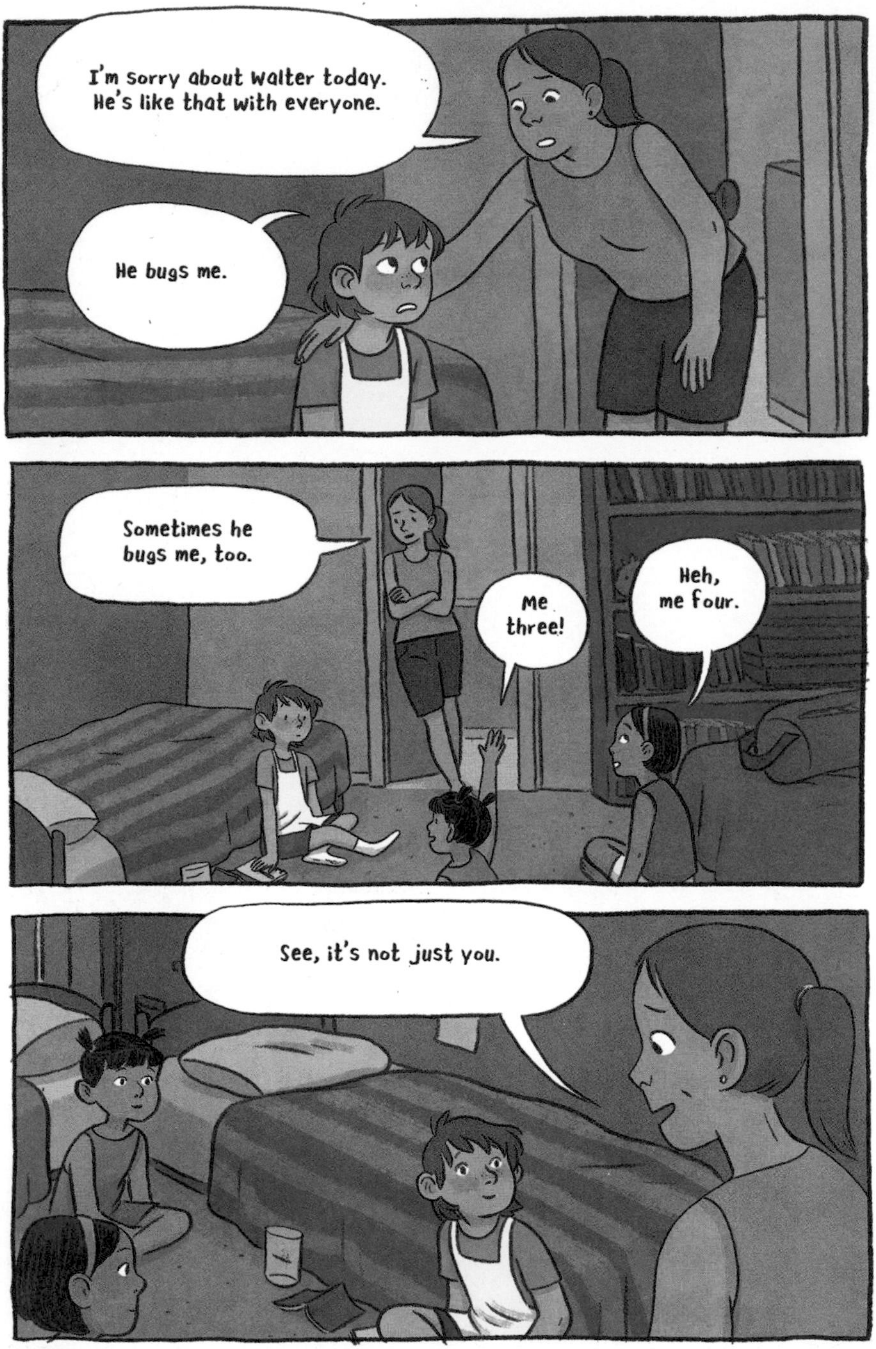
I'm sorry about Walter today. He's like that with everyone.
He bugs me.
Sometimes he bugs me, too.
Me three!
Heh, me four.
See, it's not just you.

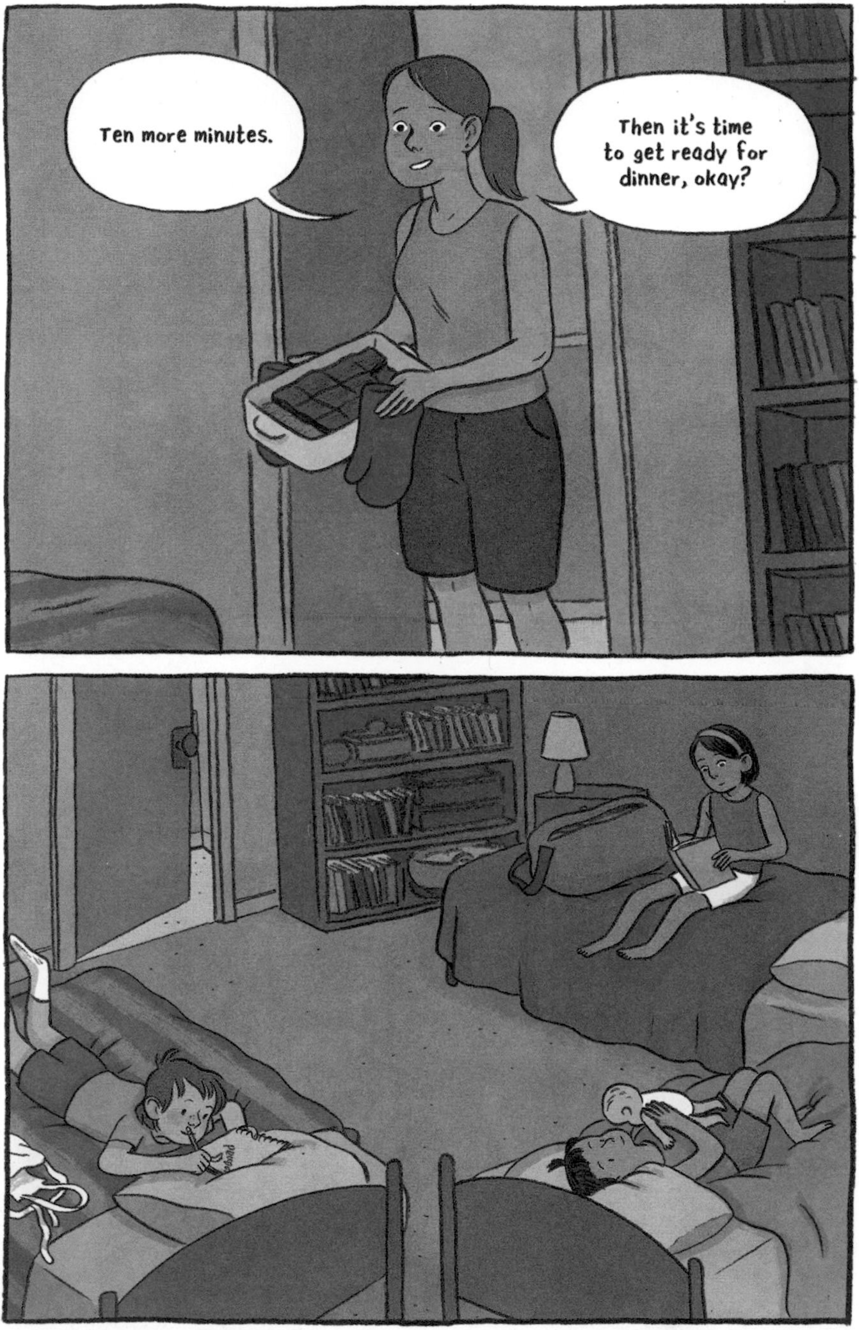
Ten more minutes.
Then it's time to get ready for dinner, okay?

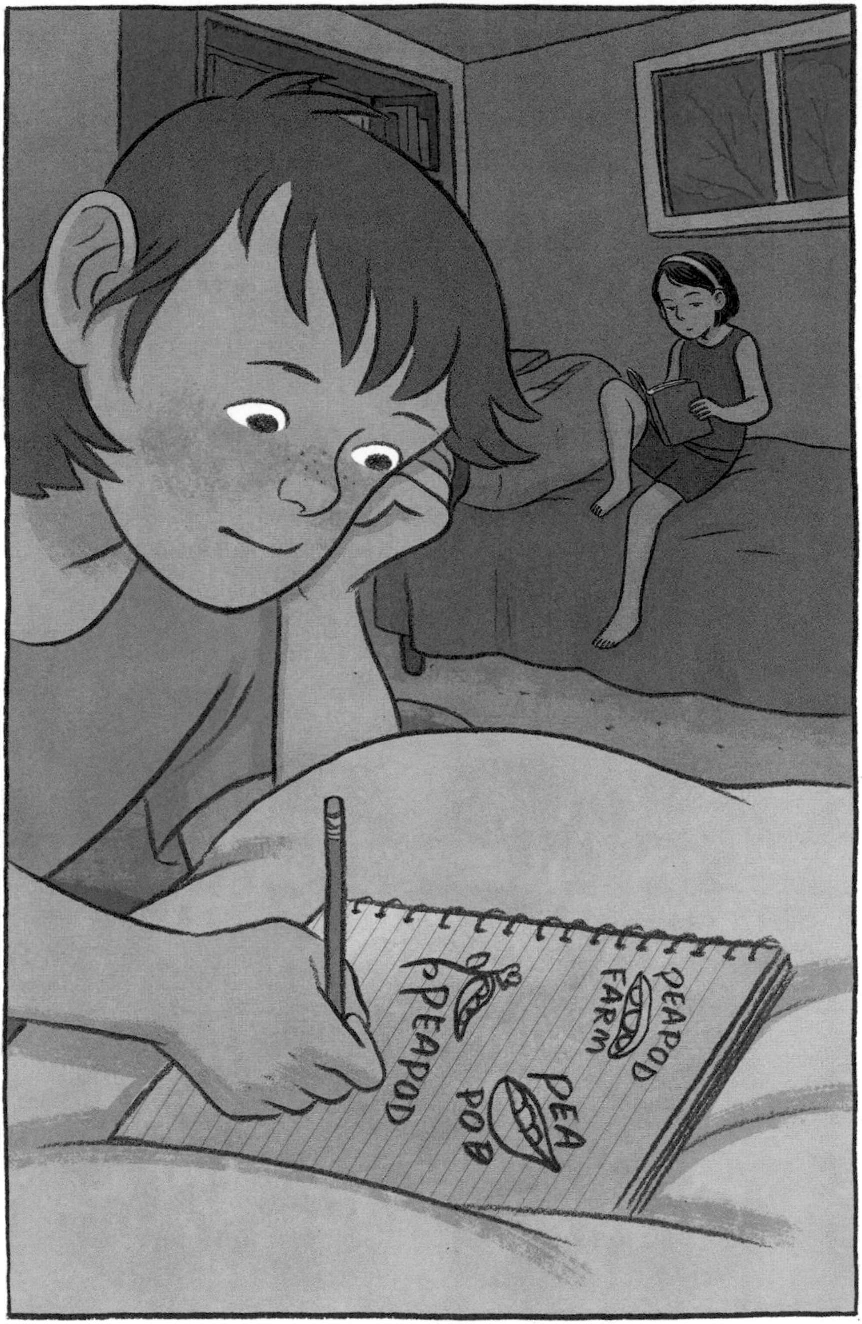
PEAPOD FARM
PEA POD
PEAPOD

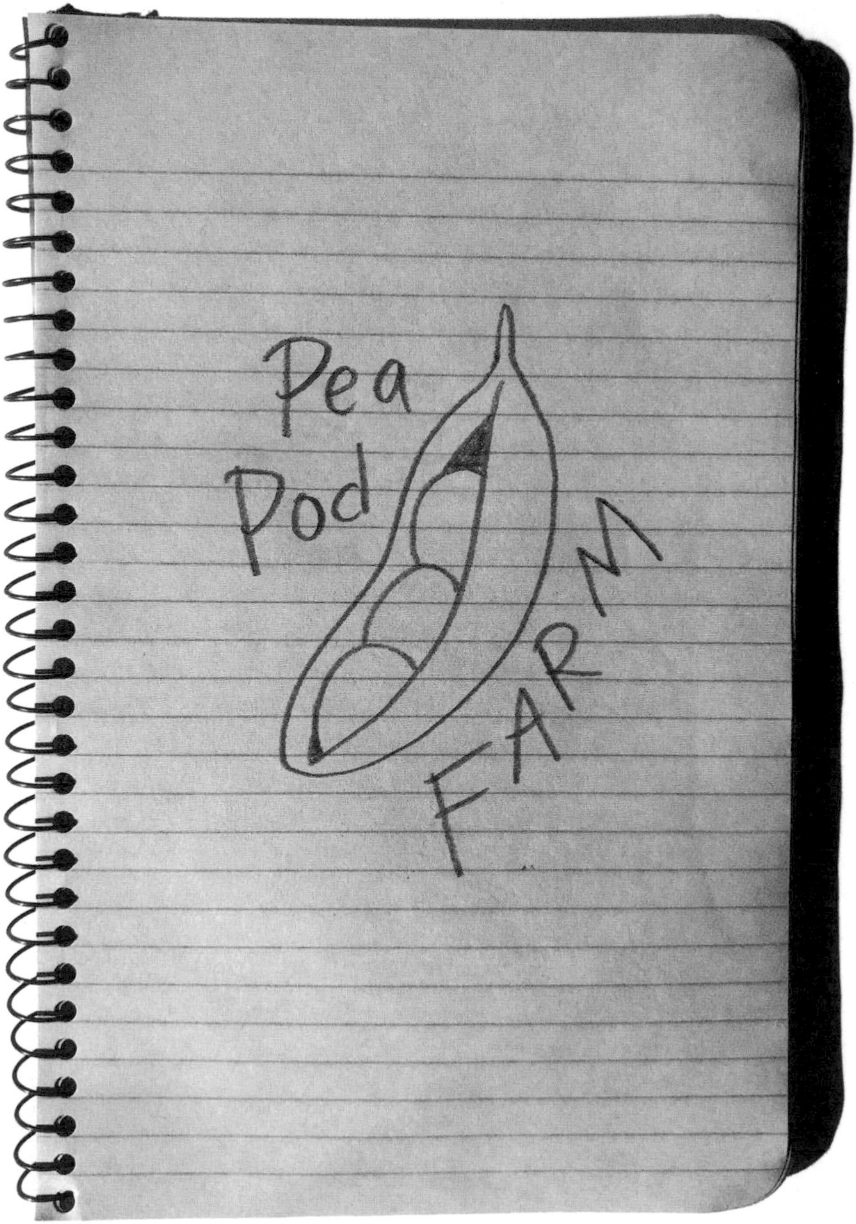
Pea
Pod
FARM

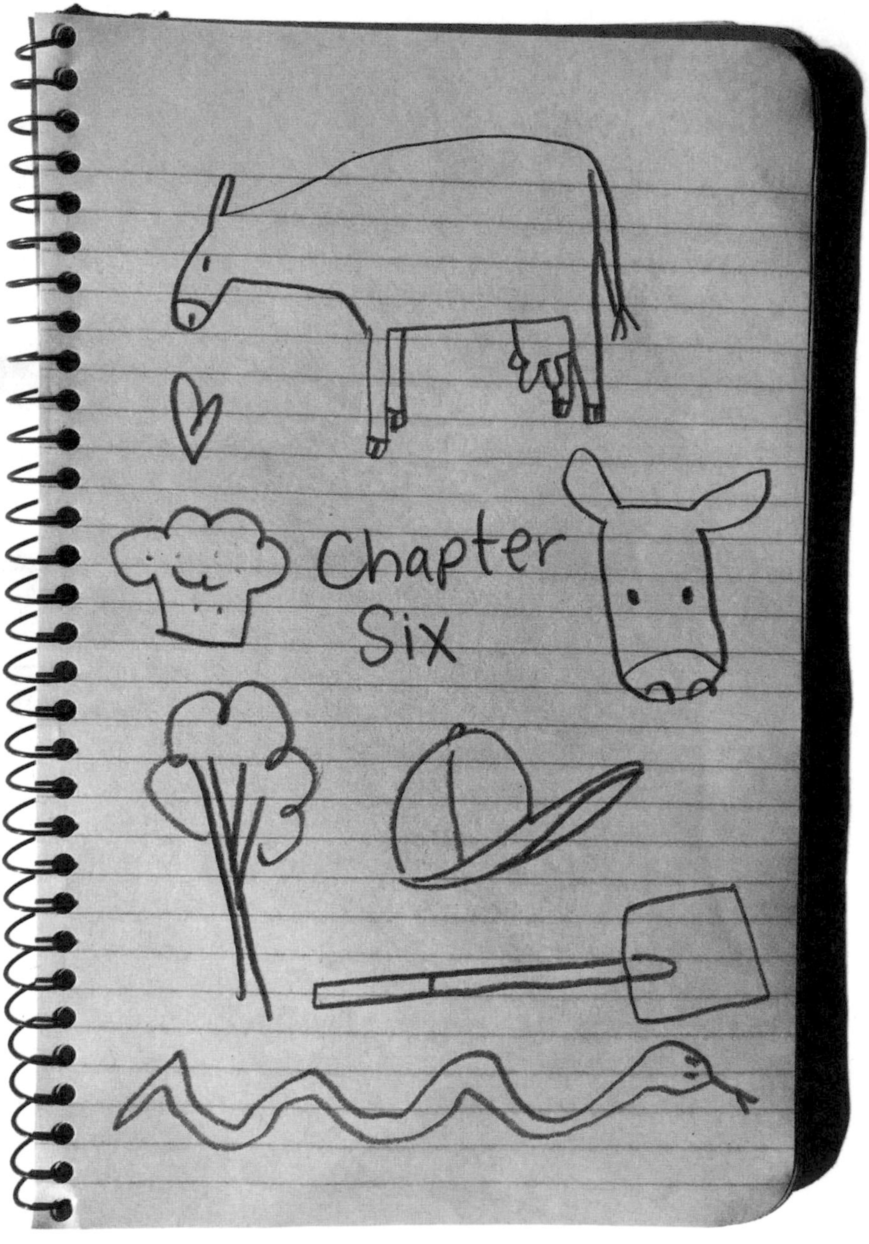
Chapter
Six

Next weekend

Ya don't just wanna yank on it.

You gotta be gentle.

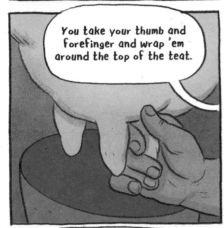

You take your thumb and forefinger and wrap 'em around the top of the teat.

Then you close your fist toward your palm, like so.

So! Who wants to go first?

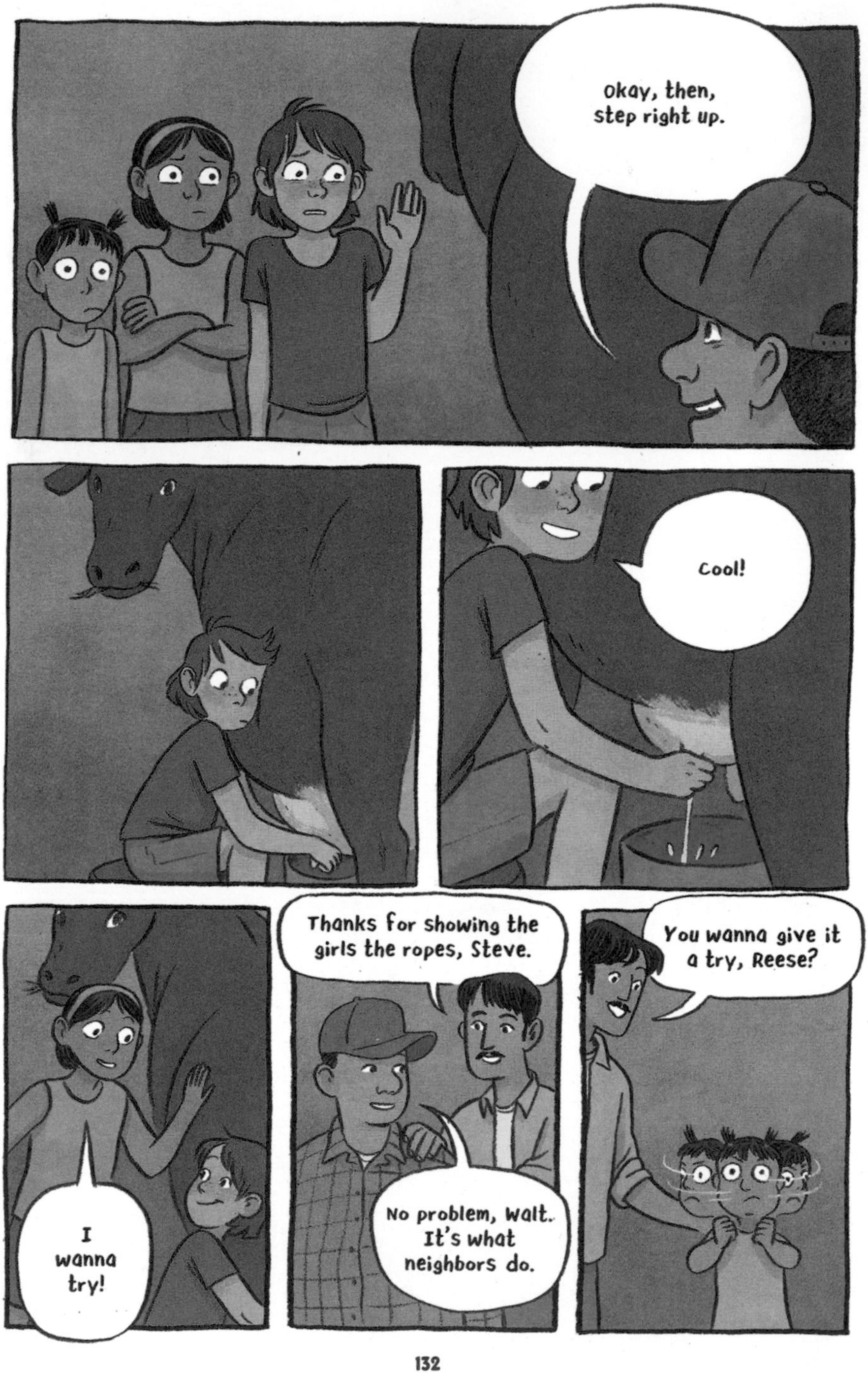
Okay, then, step right up.
Cool!
I wanna try!
Thanks for showing the girls the ropes, Steve.
No problem, Walt. It's what neighbors do.
You wanna give it a try, Reese?

Ten shaky minutes later...

Okay, let's see how it tastes on one of Mike's blueberry muffins.

You girls are in for a treat!

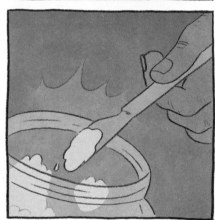

And there you have it! Fresh churned butter, straight from the cow.

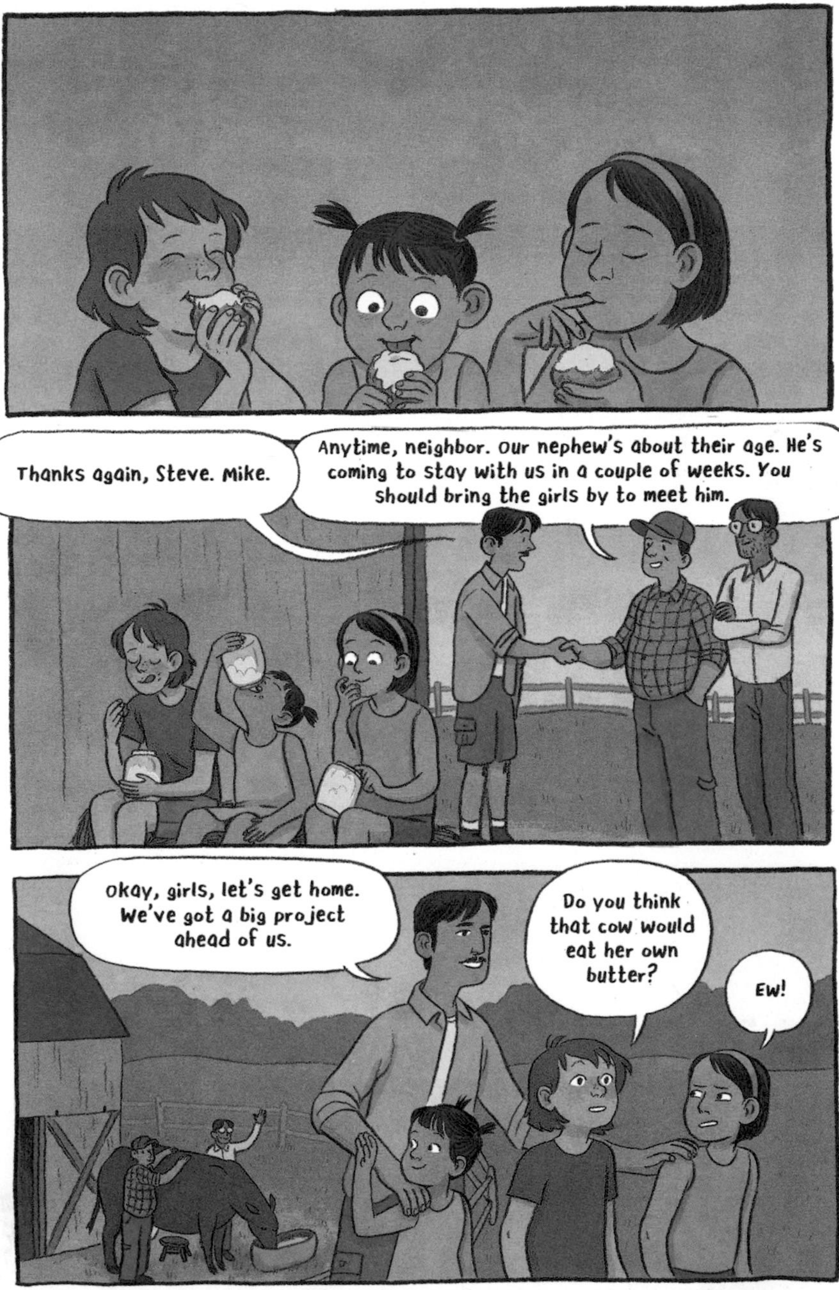
Thanks again, Steve. Mike.
Anytime, neighbor. Our nephew's about their age. He's coming to stay with us in a couple of weeks. You should bring the girls by to meet him.
Okay, girls, let's get home. We've got a big project ahead of us.
Do you think that cow would eat her own butter?
Ew!

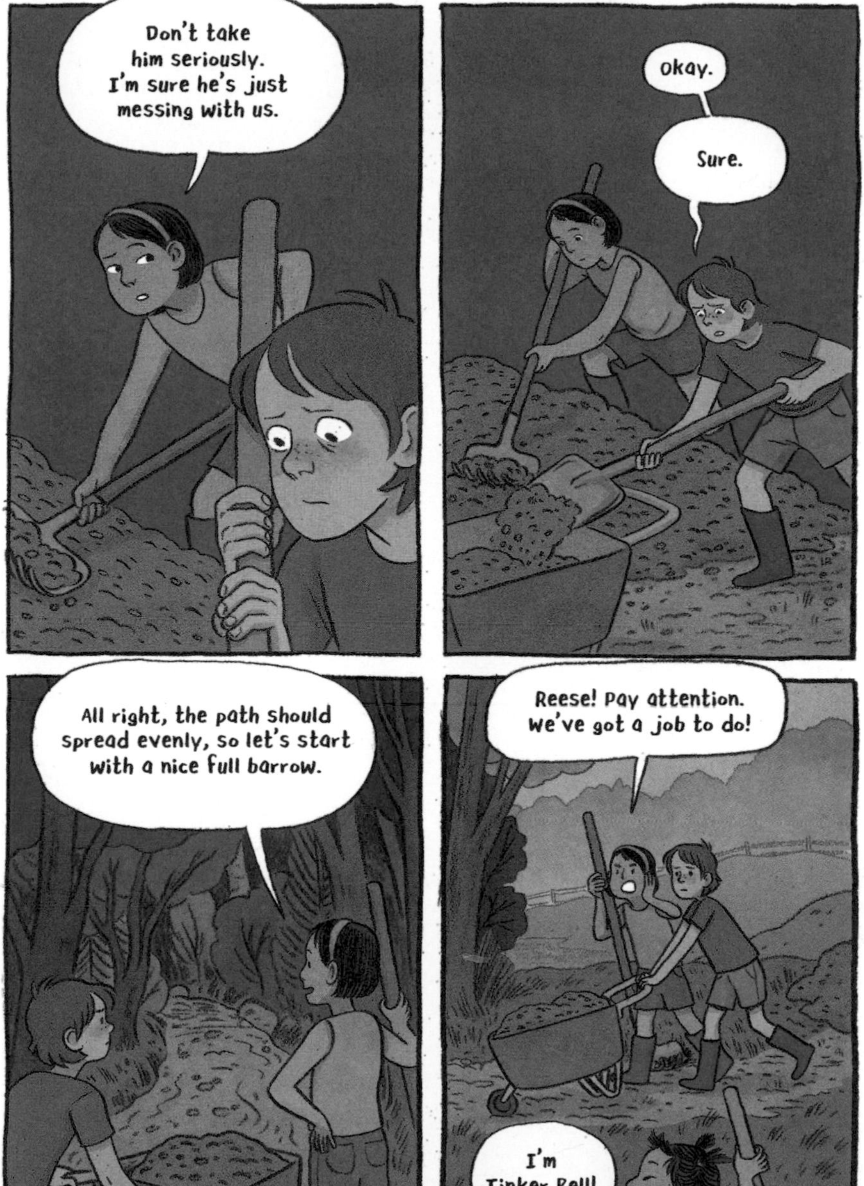

Don't take him seriously. I'm sure he's just messing with us.
Okay.
Sure.
All right, the path should spread evenly, so let's start with a nice full barrow.
Reese! Pay attention. We've got a job to do!
I'm Tinker Bell!

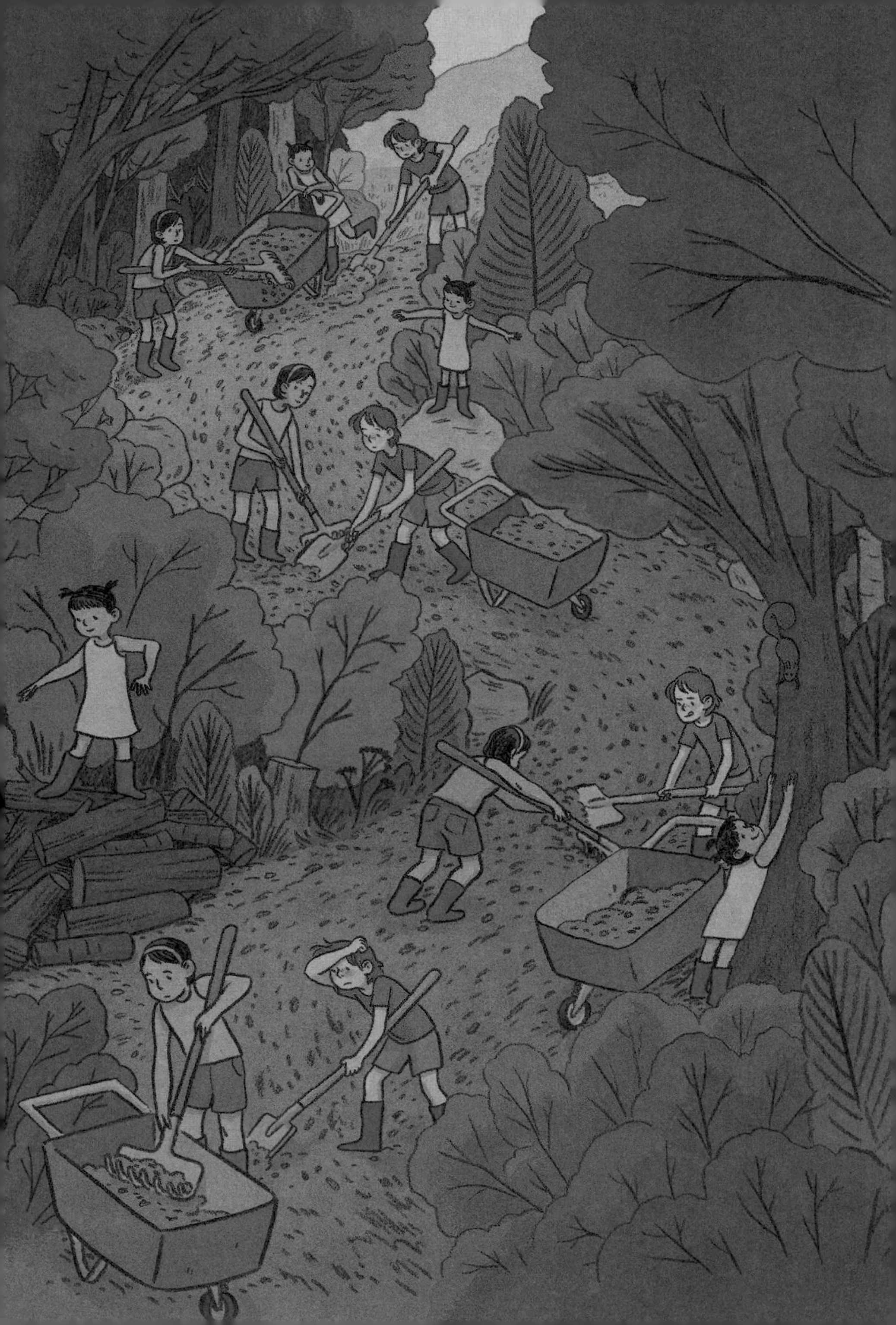

141

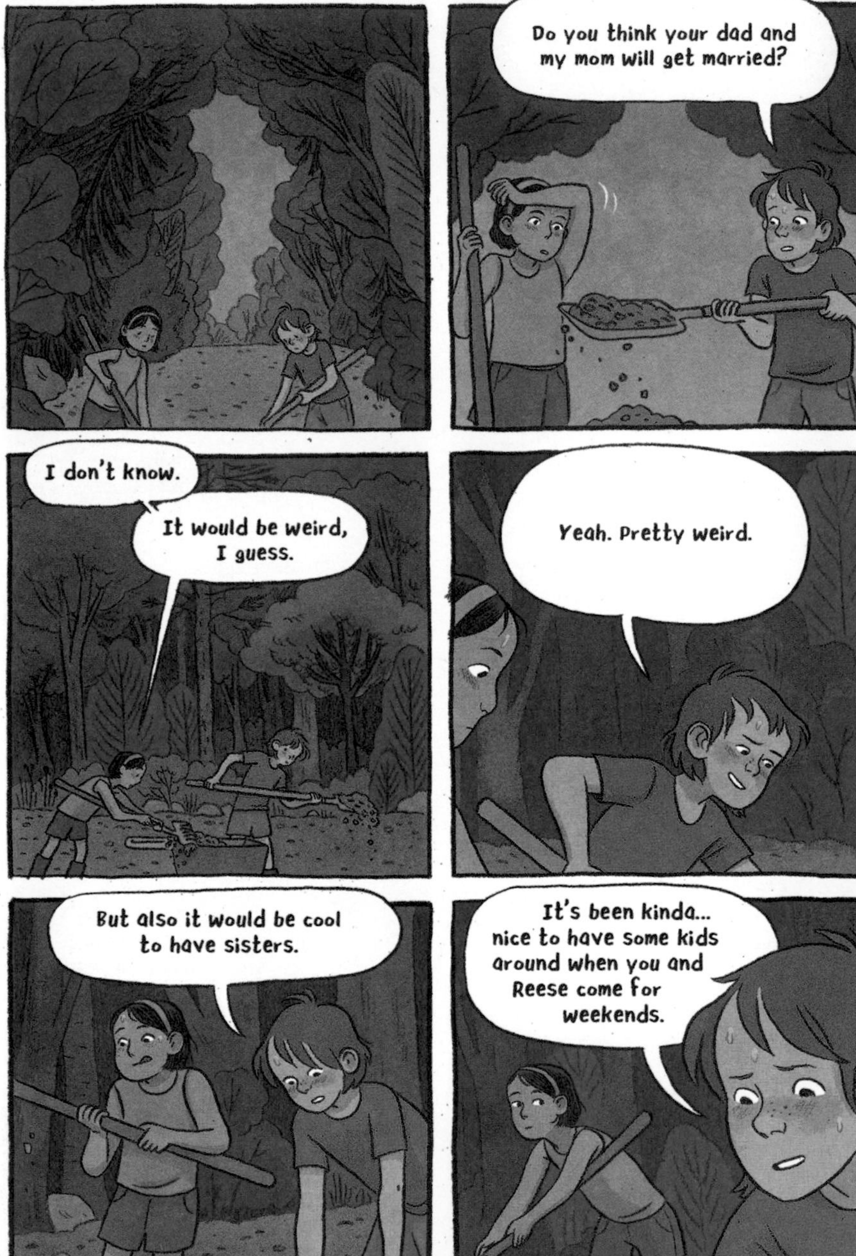
Do you think your dad and my mom will get married?
I don't know.
It would be weird, I guess.
Yeah. Pretty weird.
But also it would be cool to have sisters.
It's been kinda... nice to have some kids around when you and Reese come for weekends.

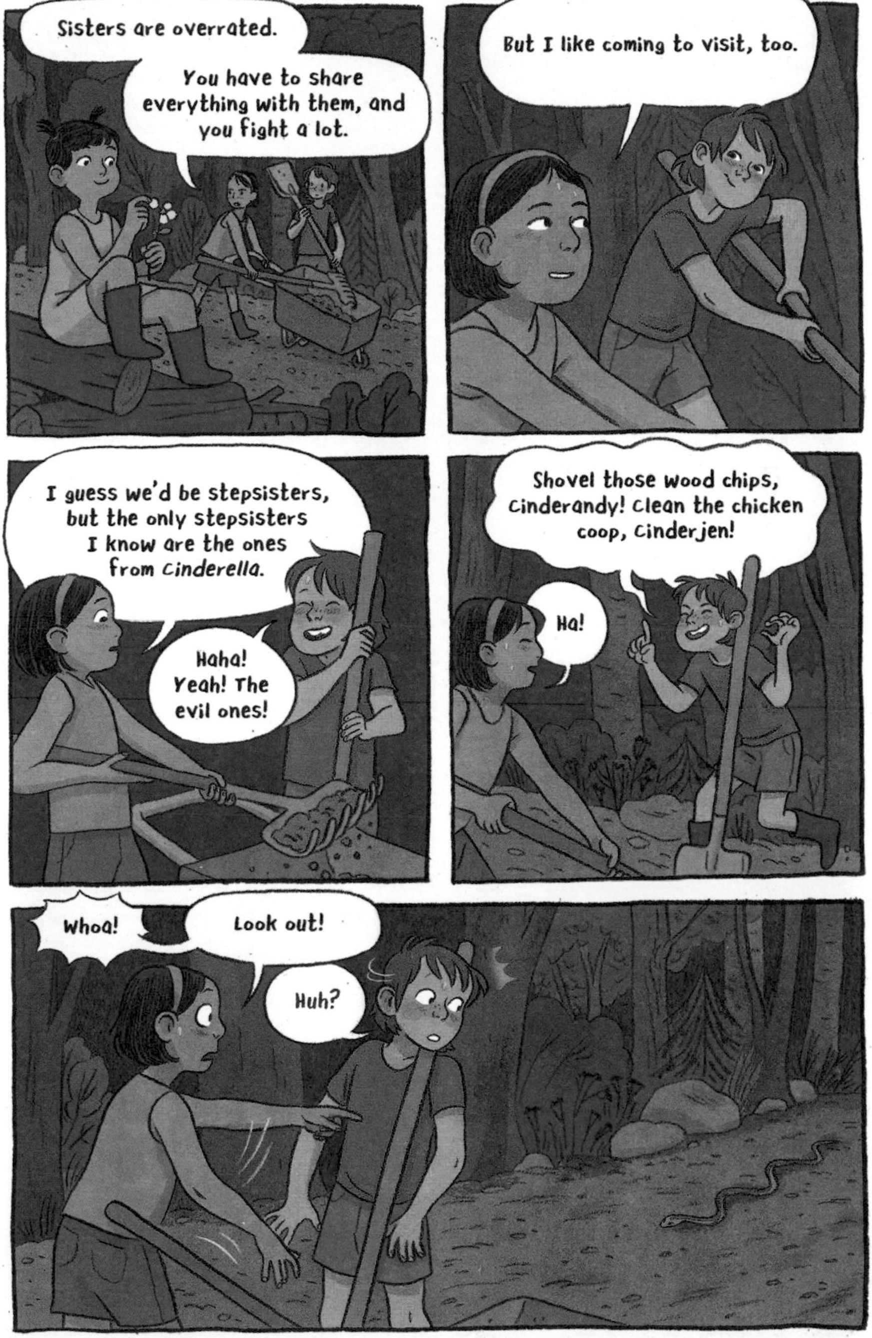
Sisters are overrated.
You have to share everything with them, and you fight a lot.
But I like coming to visit, too.
I guess we'd be stepsisters, but the only stepsisters I know are the ones from Cinderella.
Haha! Yeah! The evil ones!
Shovel those wood chips, Cinderandy! Clean the chicken coop, Cinderjen!
Ha!
Whoa!
Look out!
Huh?

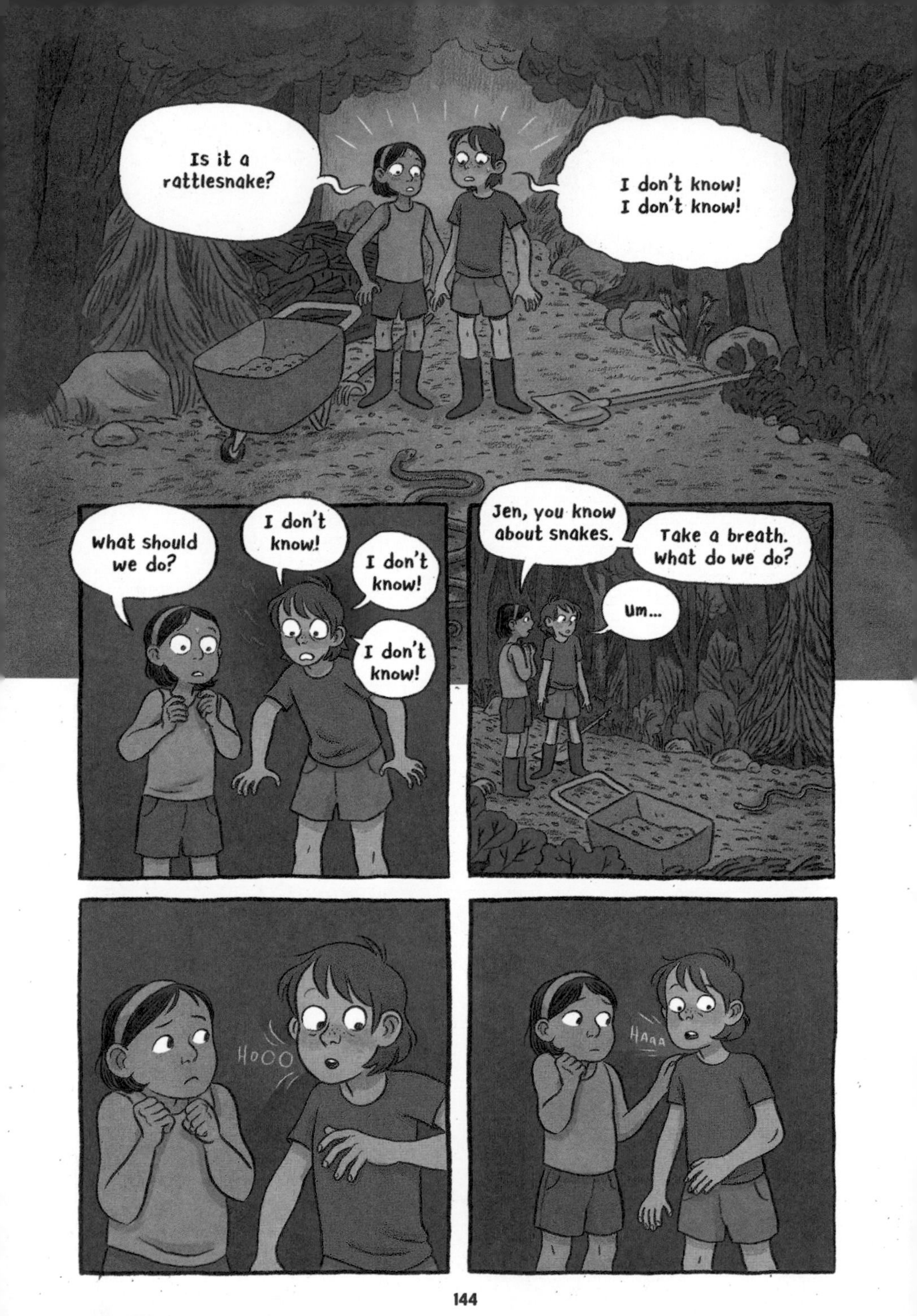
Is it a rattlesnake?
I don't know! I don't know!
What should we do?
I don't know!
I don't know!
I don't know!
Jen, you know about snakes.
Take a breath. What do we do?
Um...
HOOO
HAAA

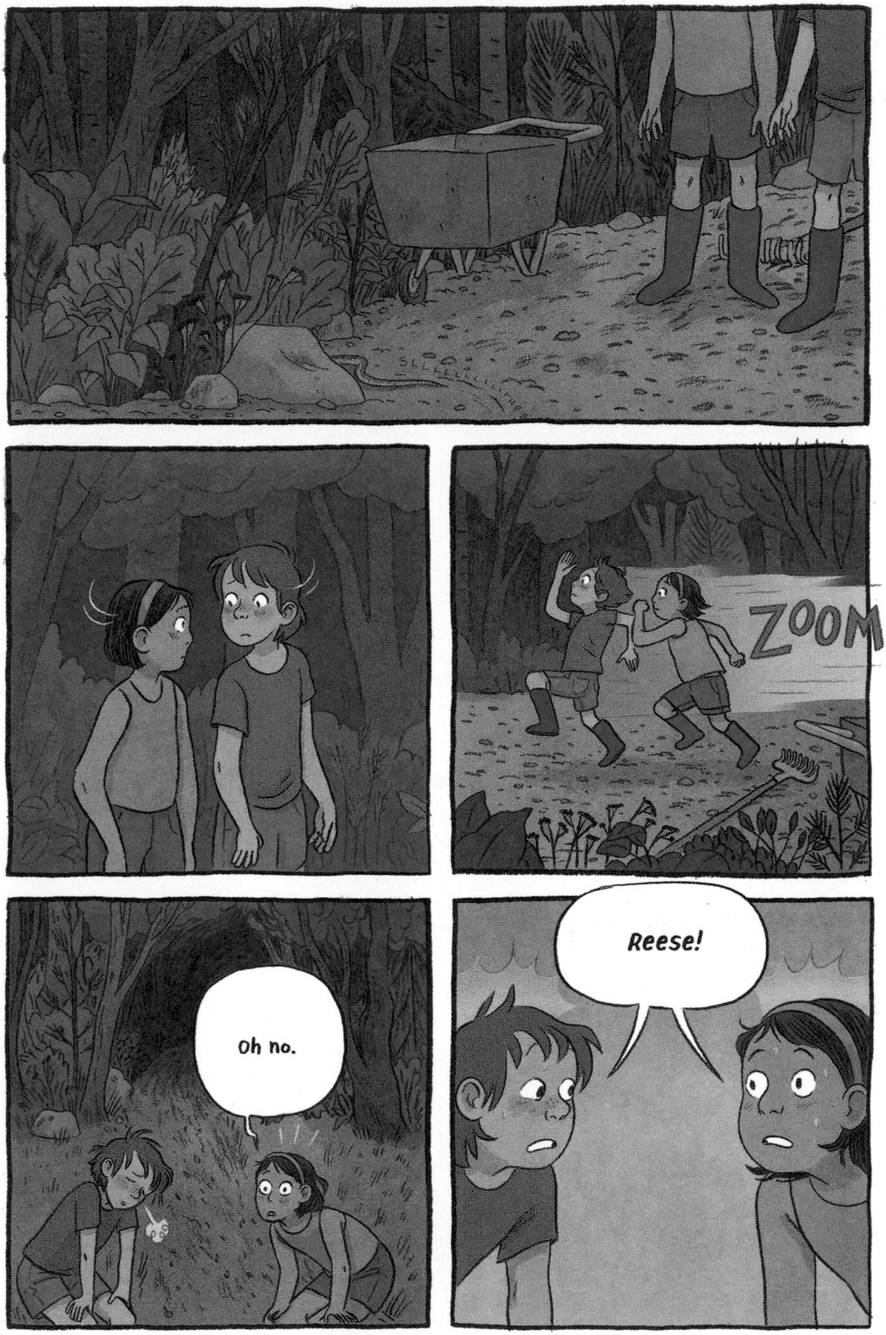
ZOOM
Oh no.
Reese!

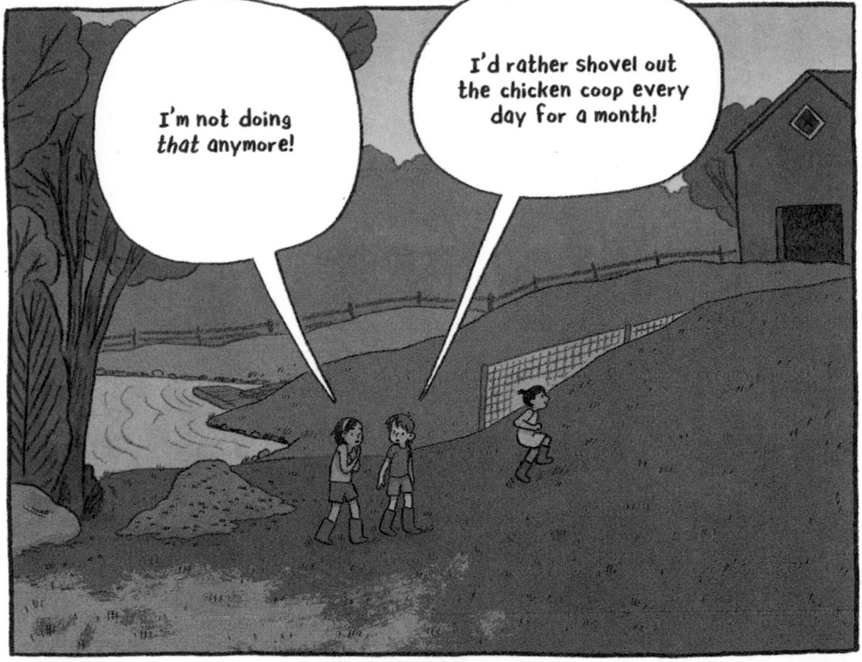
I'm not doing *that* anymore!
I'd rather shovel out the chicken coop every day for a month!

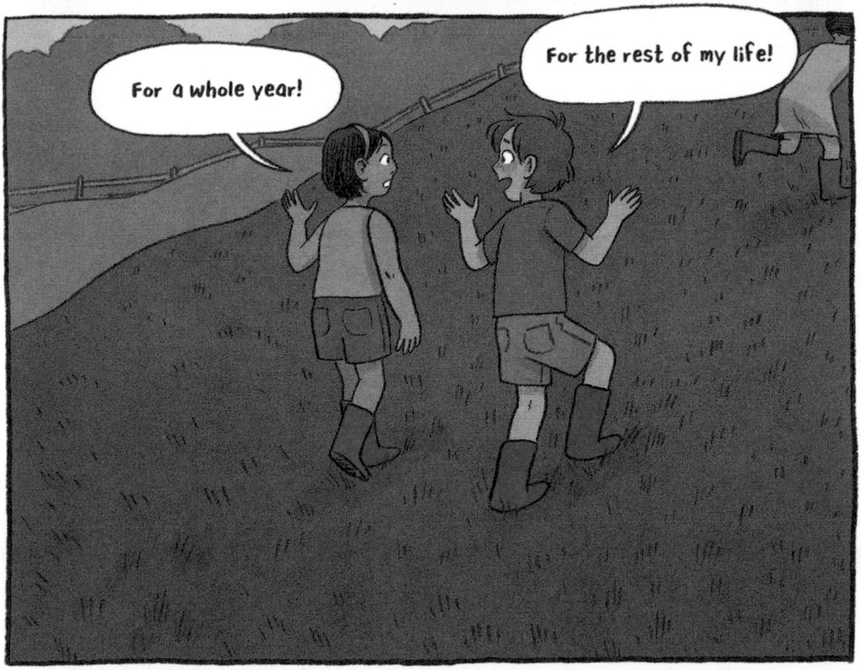
For a whole year!
For the rest of my life!

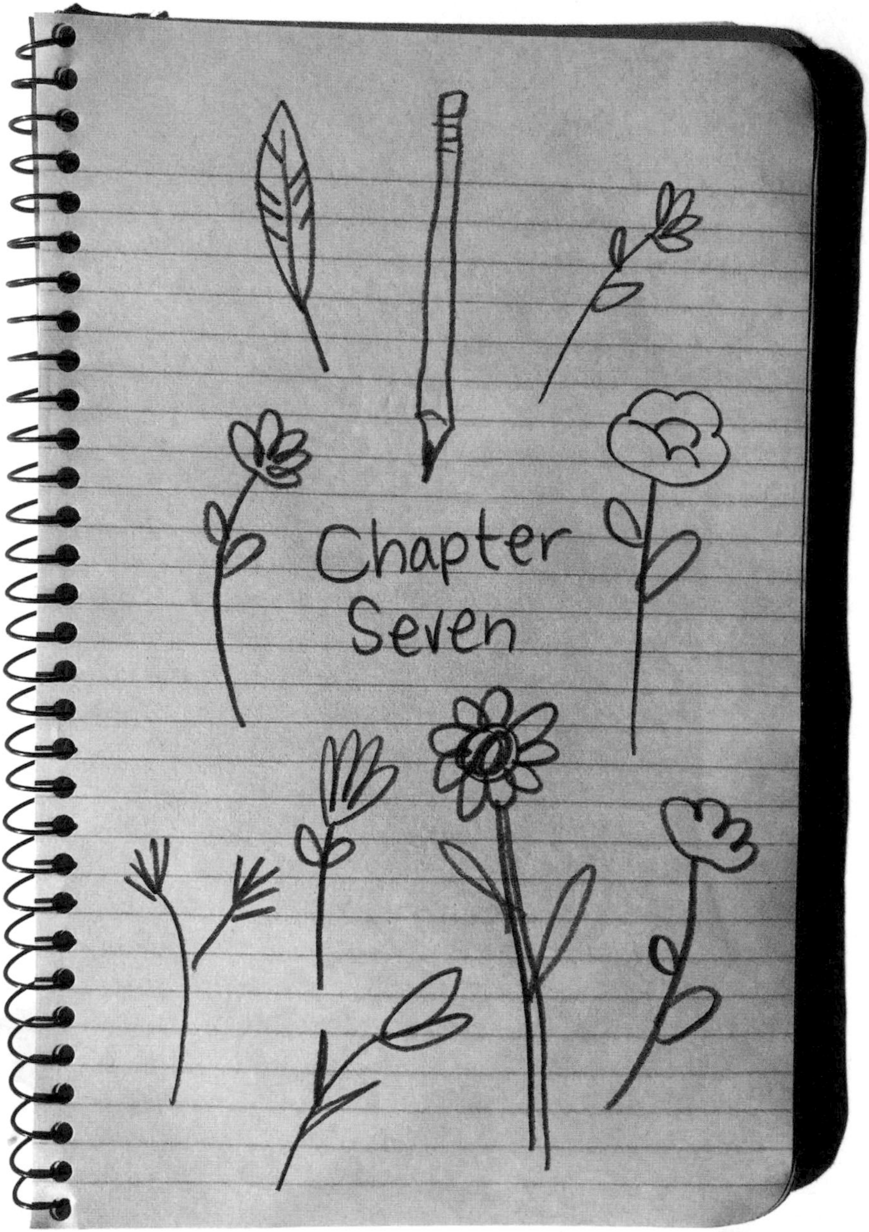
Chapter
Seven

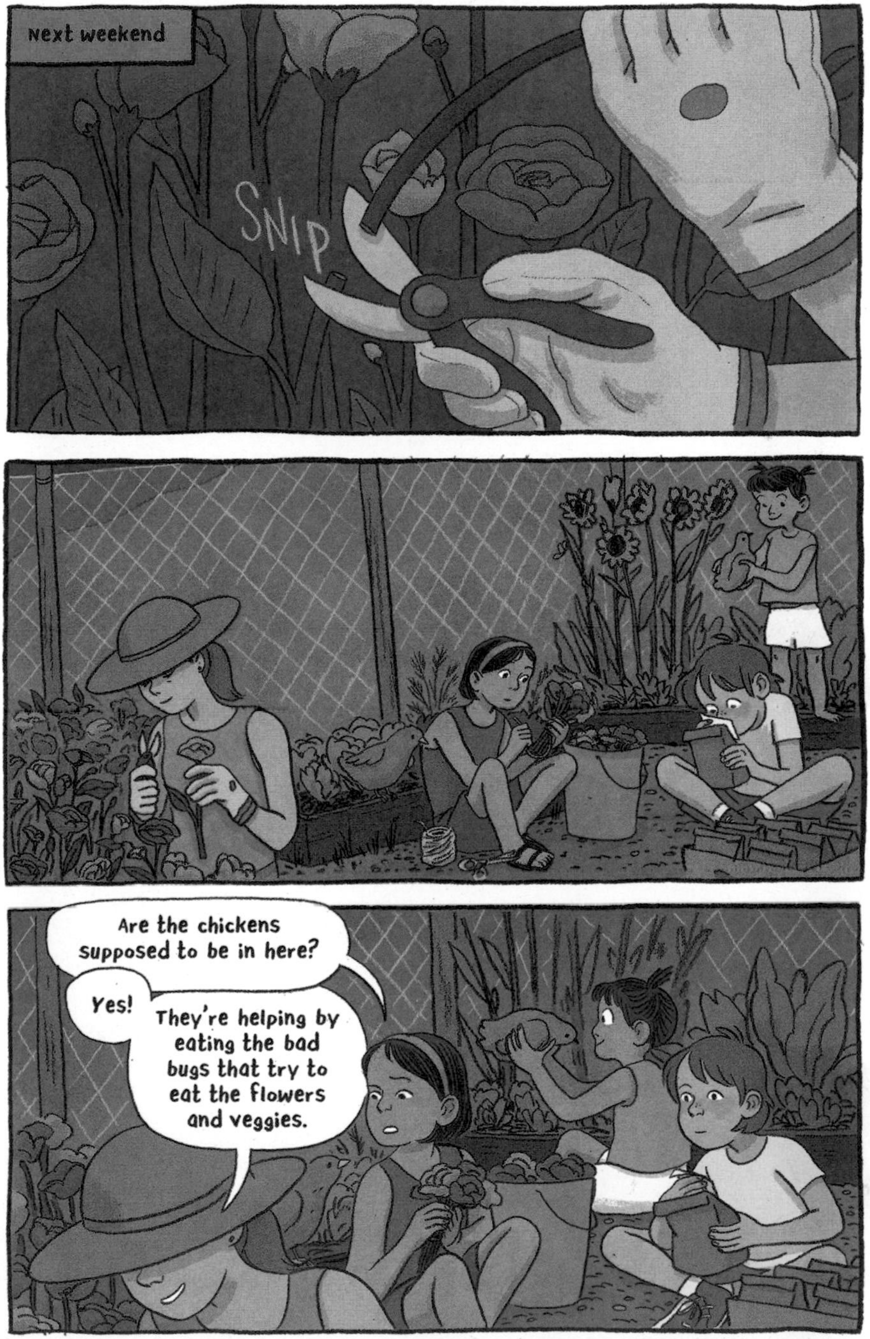
next weekend
SNIP
Are the chickens supposed to be in here?
Yes!
They're helping by eating the bad bugs that try to eat the flowers and veggies.

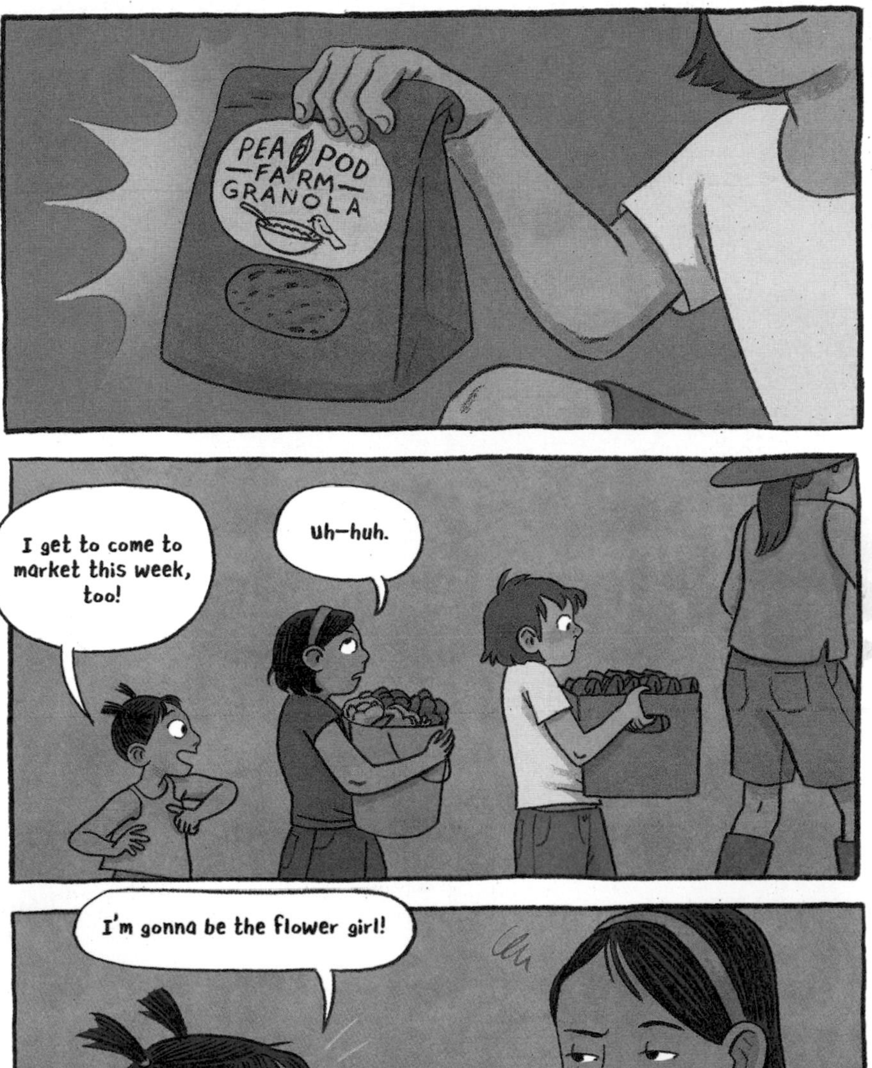
PEA POD FARM GRANOLA
I get to come to market this week, too!
uh-huh.
I'm gonna be the flower girl!
That's for a wedding, not market, silly.

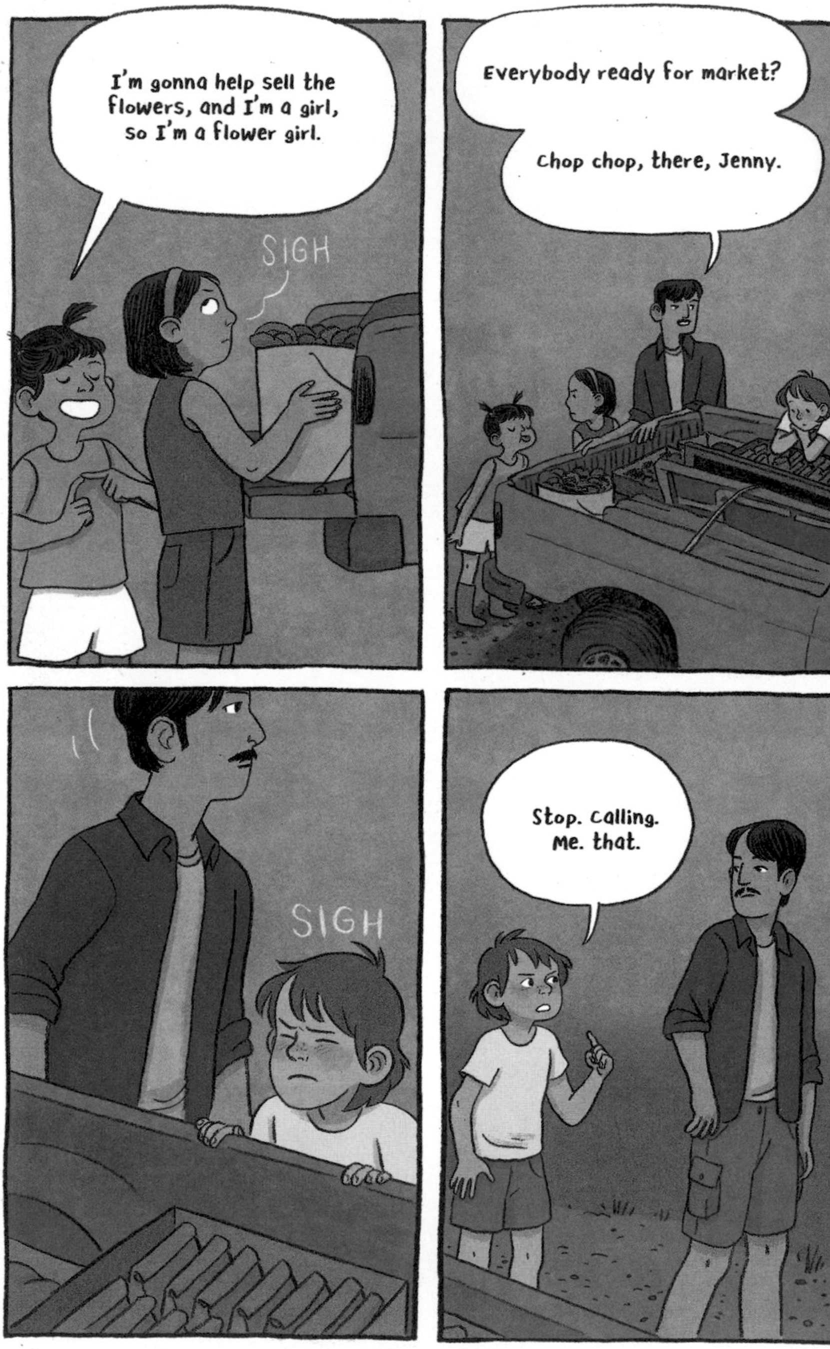
I'm gonna help sell the flowers, and I'm a girl, so I'm a flower girl.
SIGH
Everybody ready for market?
Chop chop, there, Jenny.
SIGH
Stop. Calling. Me. that.

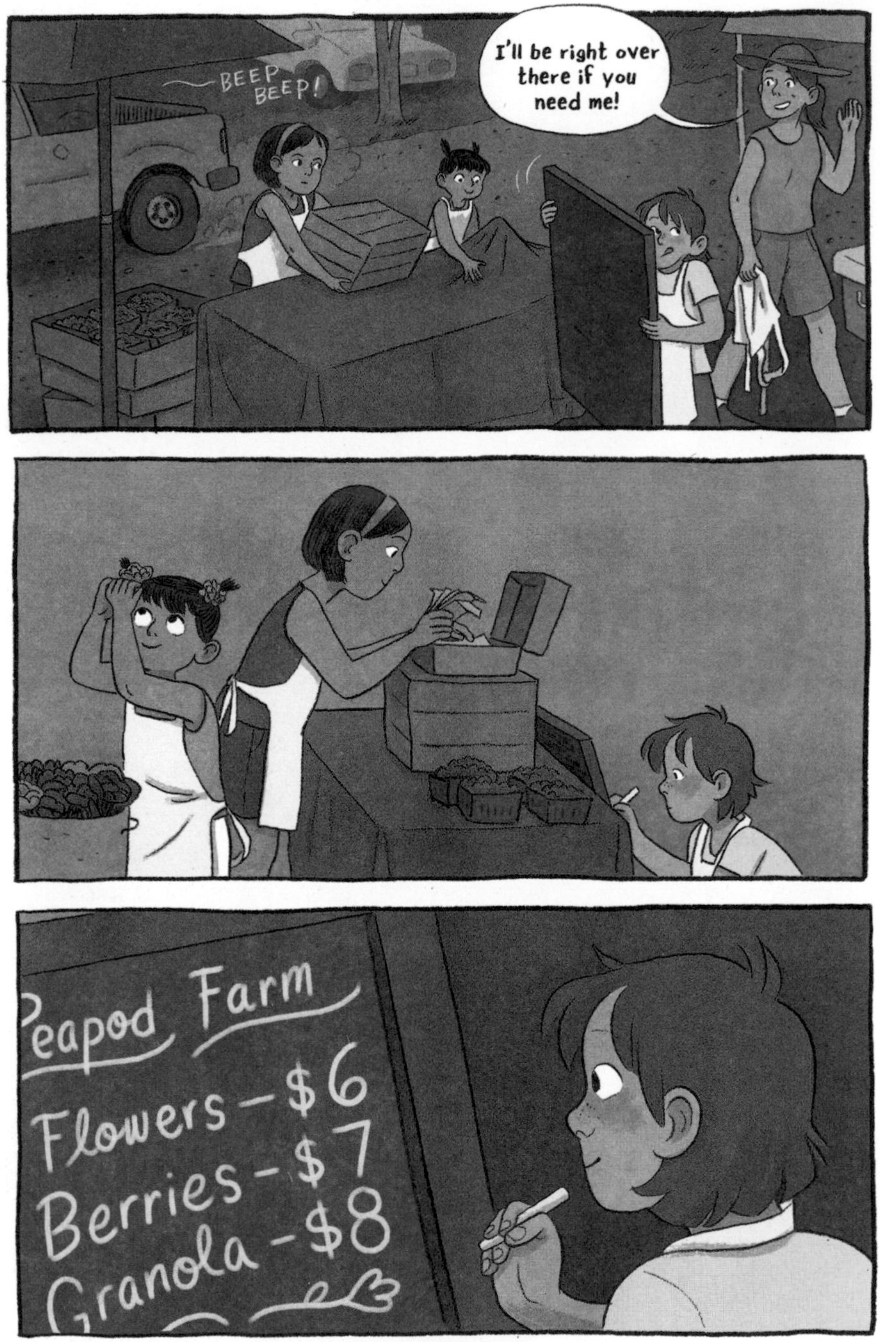
BEEP BEEP!
I'll be right over there if you need me!
Peapod Farm
Flowers - $6
Berries - $7
Granola - $8

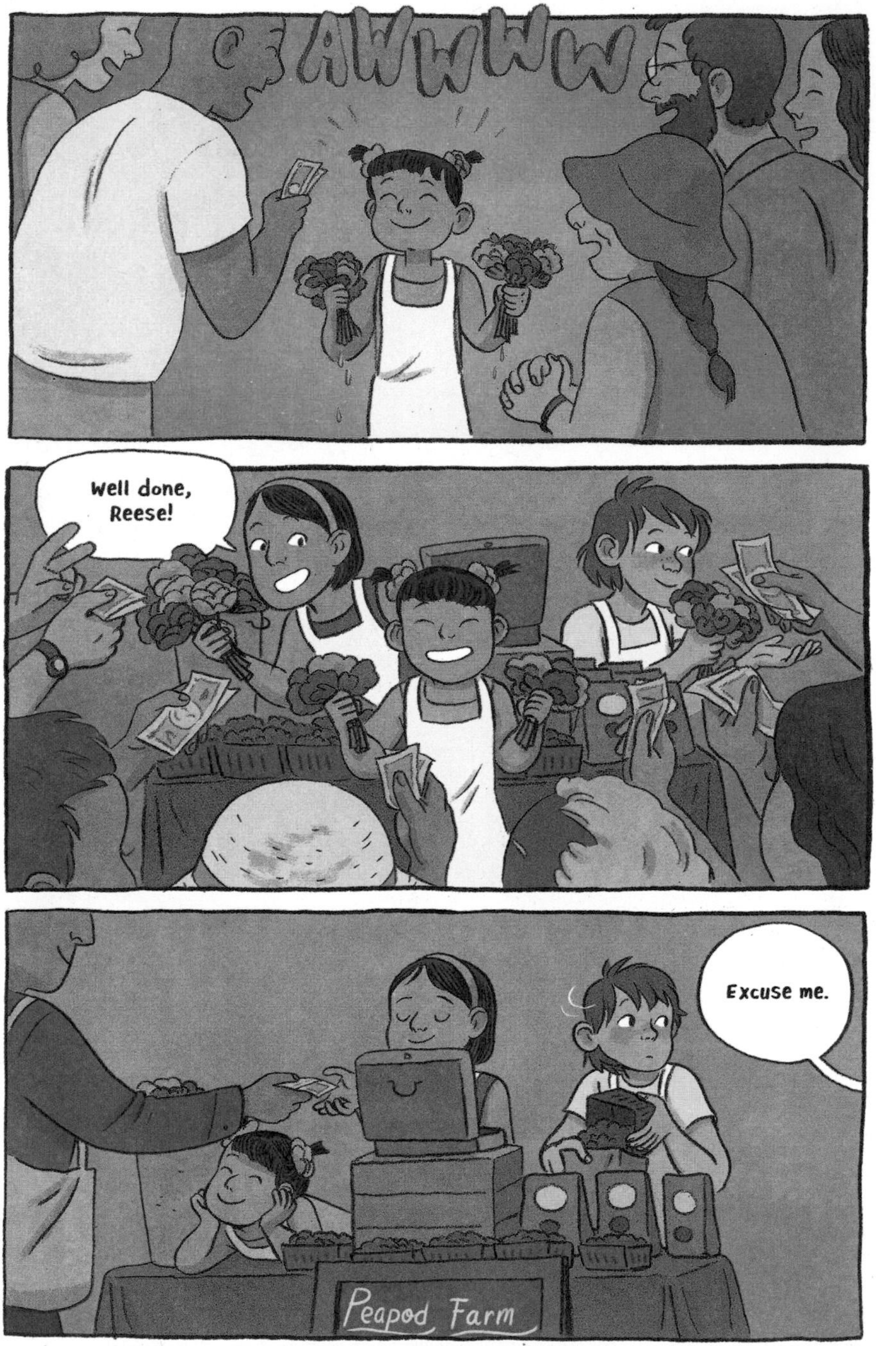
AWWWW
Well done, Reese!
Excuse me.
Peapod Farm

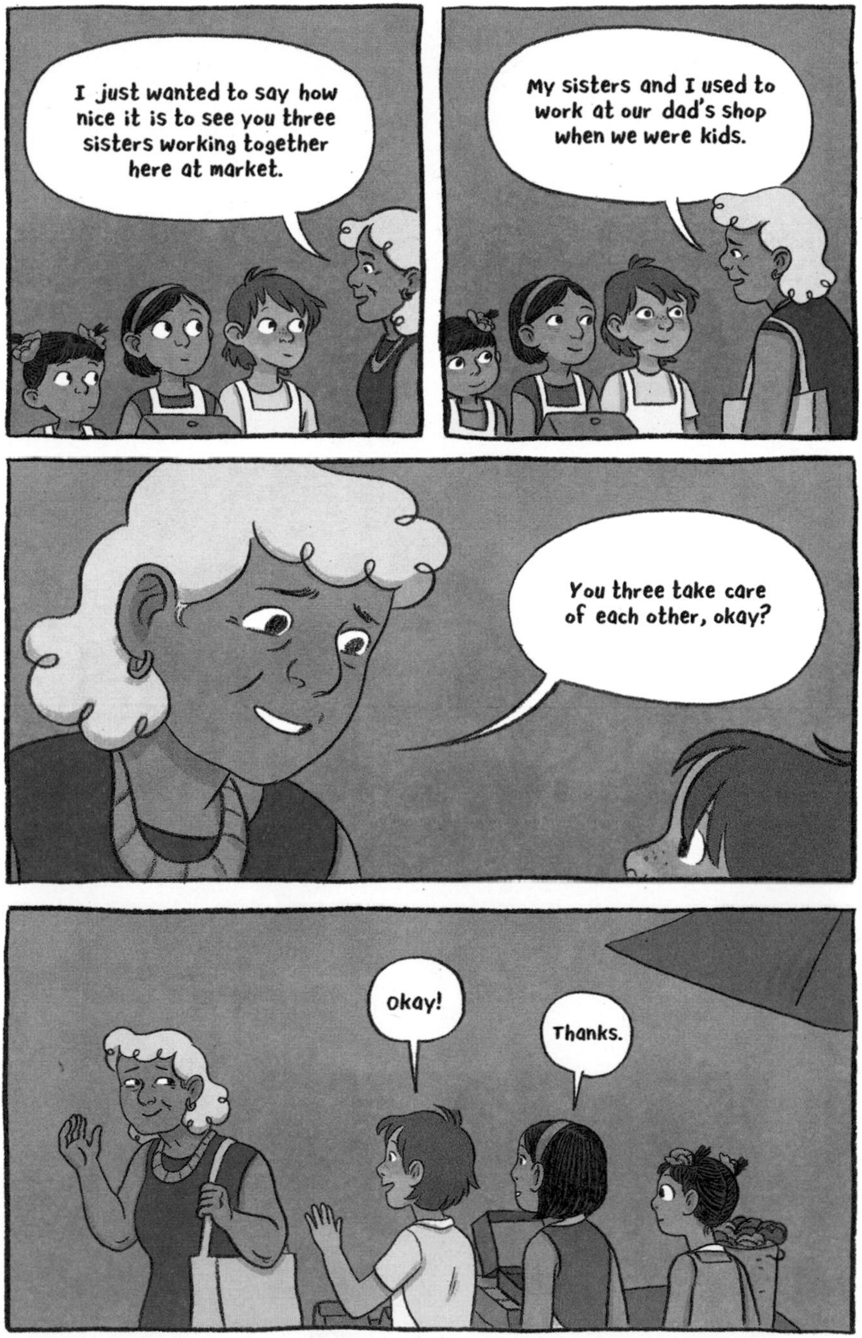
I just wanted to say how nice it is to see you three sisters working together here at market.
My sisters and I used to work at our dad's shop when we were kids.
You three take care of each other, okay?
Okay!
Thanks.

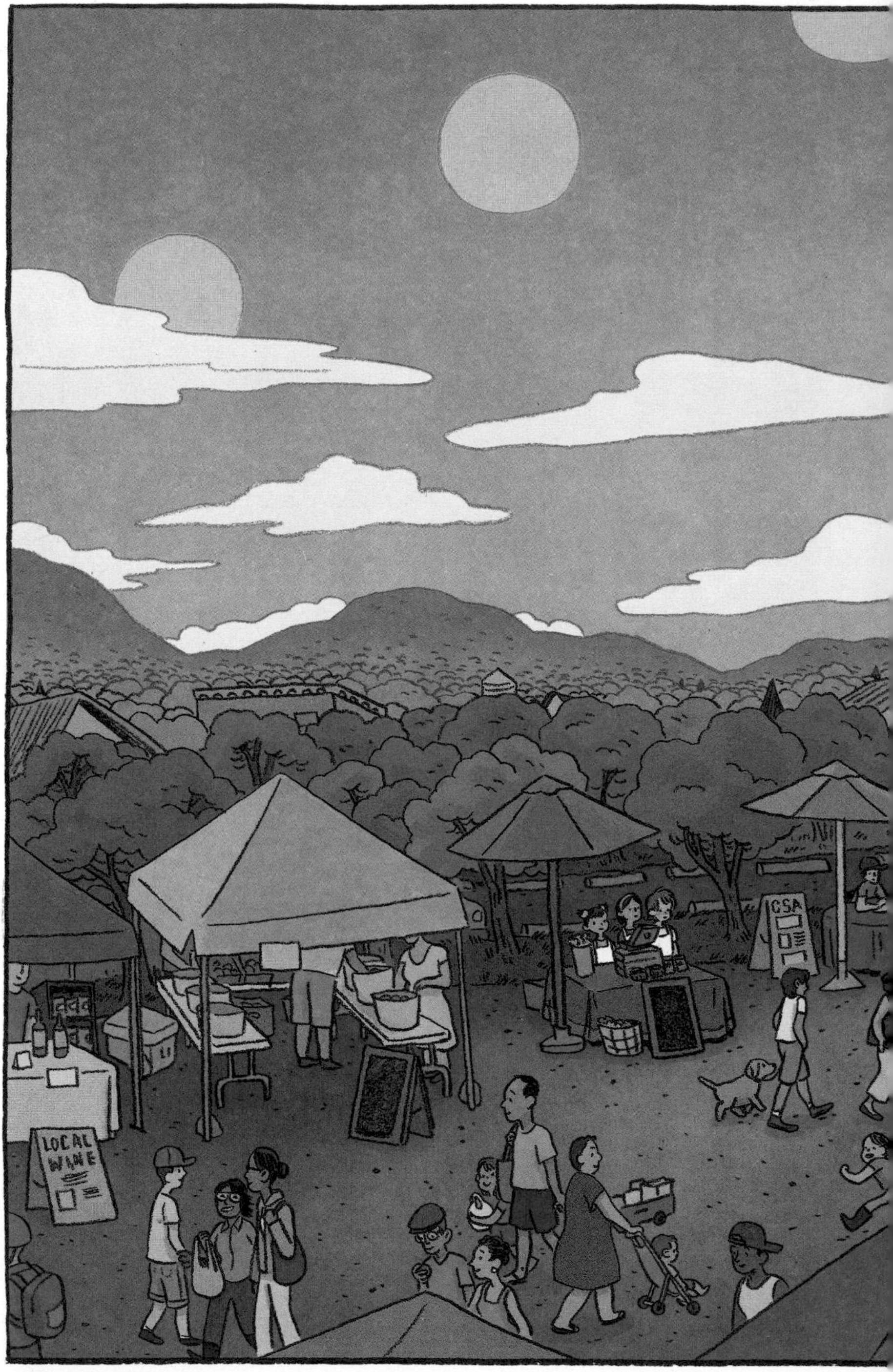
CSA
LOCAL WINE

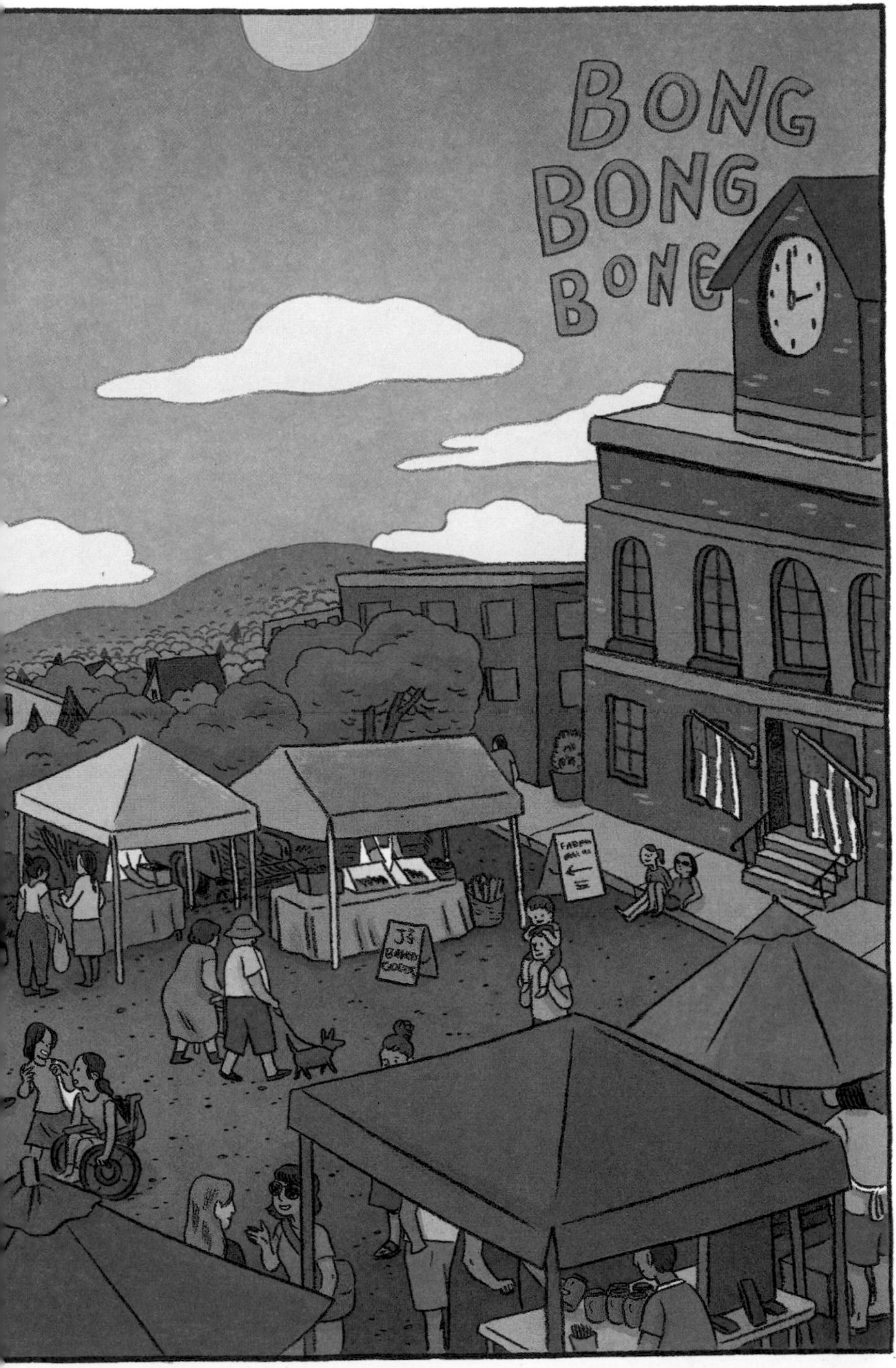
BONG
BONG
BONG

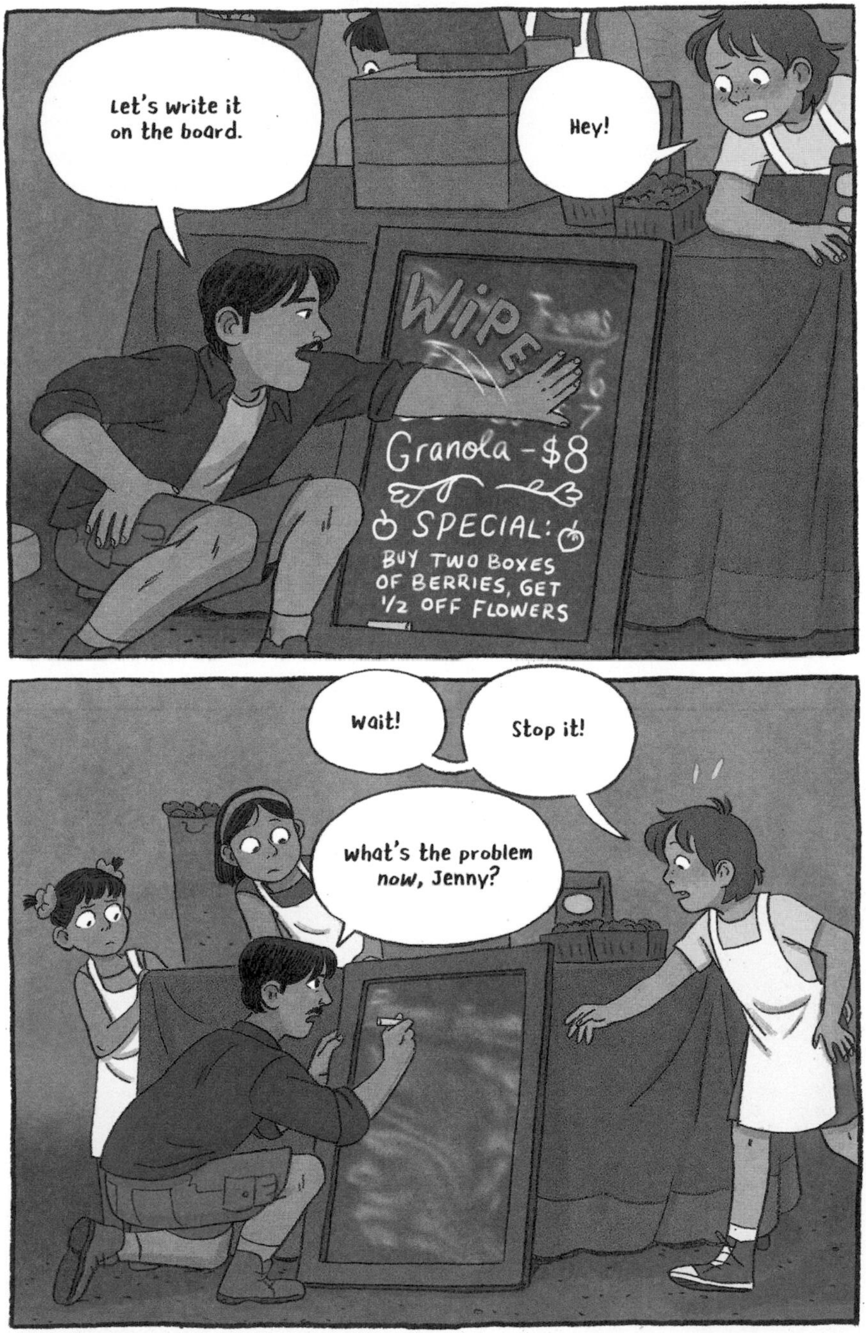
Let's write it on the board.
Hey!
WIPE
Granola - $8
SPECIAL:
BUY TWO BOXES OF BERRIES, GET 1/2 OFF FLOWERS
Wait!
Stop it!
What's the problem now, Jenny?

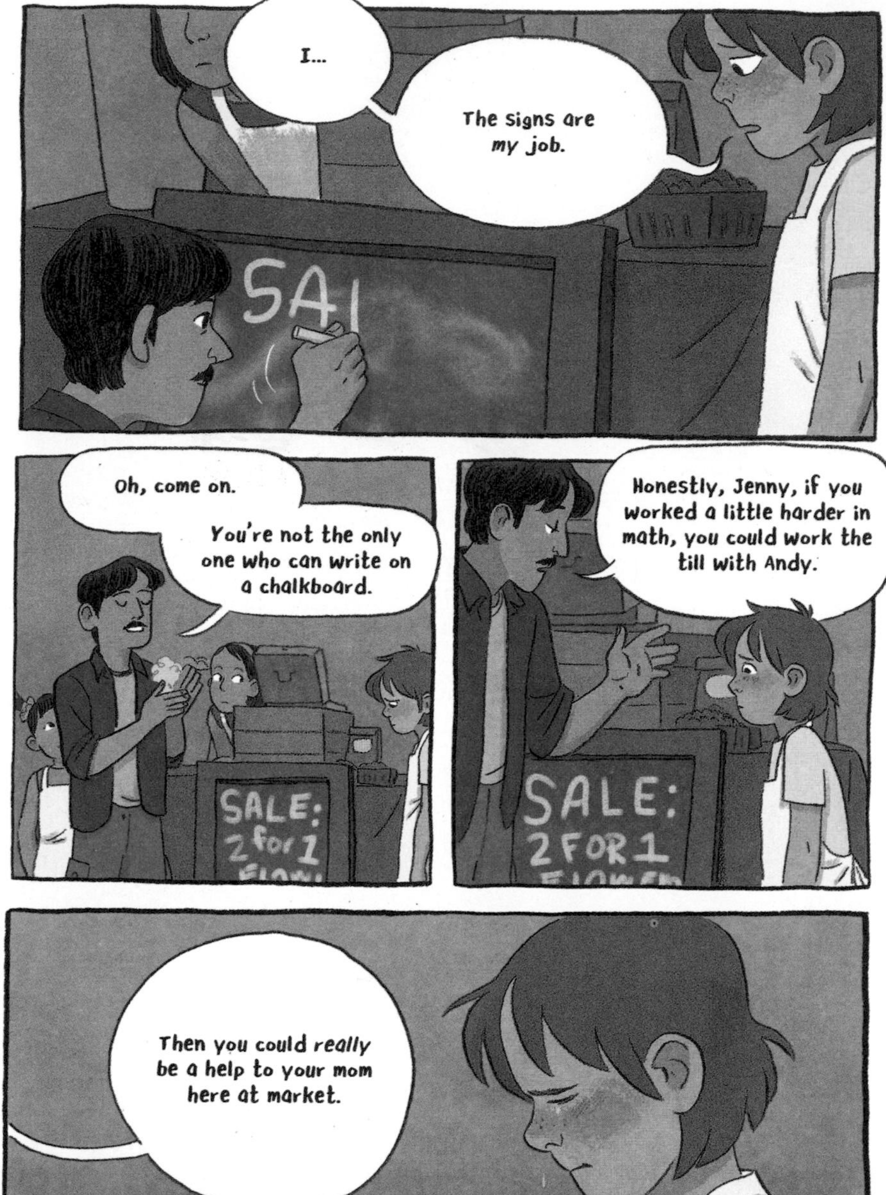
I...
The signs are my job.
SAl
Oh, come on.
You're not the only one who can write on a chalkboard.
SALE: 2 for 1
Honestly, Jenny, if you worked a little harder in math, you could work the till with Andy.
SALE: 2 FOR 1
Then you could *really* be a help to your mom here at market.

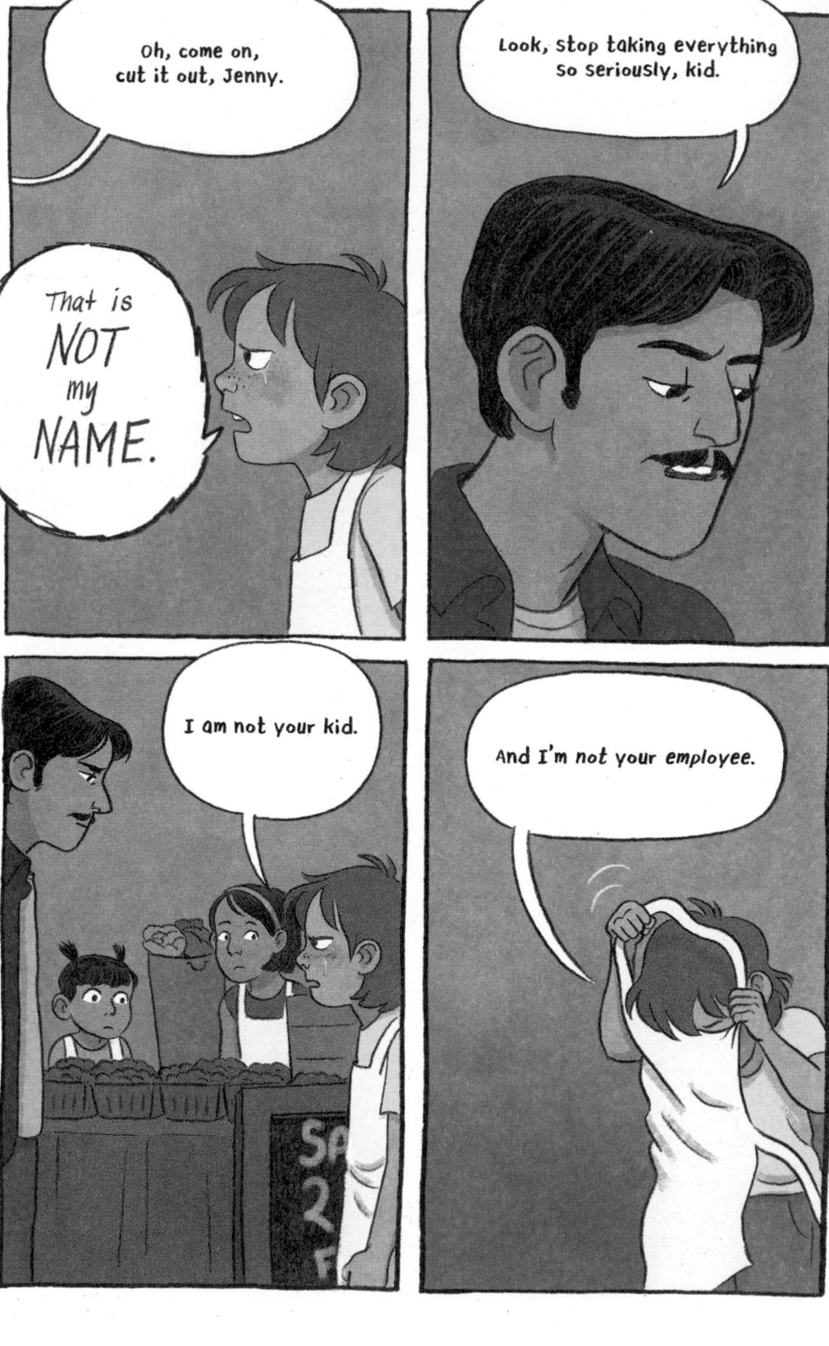
Oh, come on, cut it out, Jenny.
That is NOT my NAME.
Look, stop taking everything so seriously, kid.
I am not your kid.
And I'm *not* your *employee*.

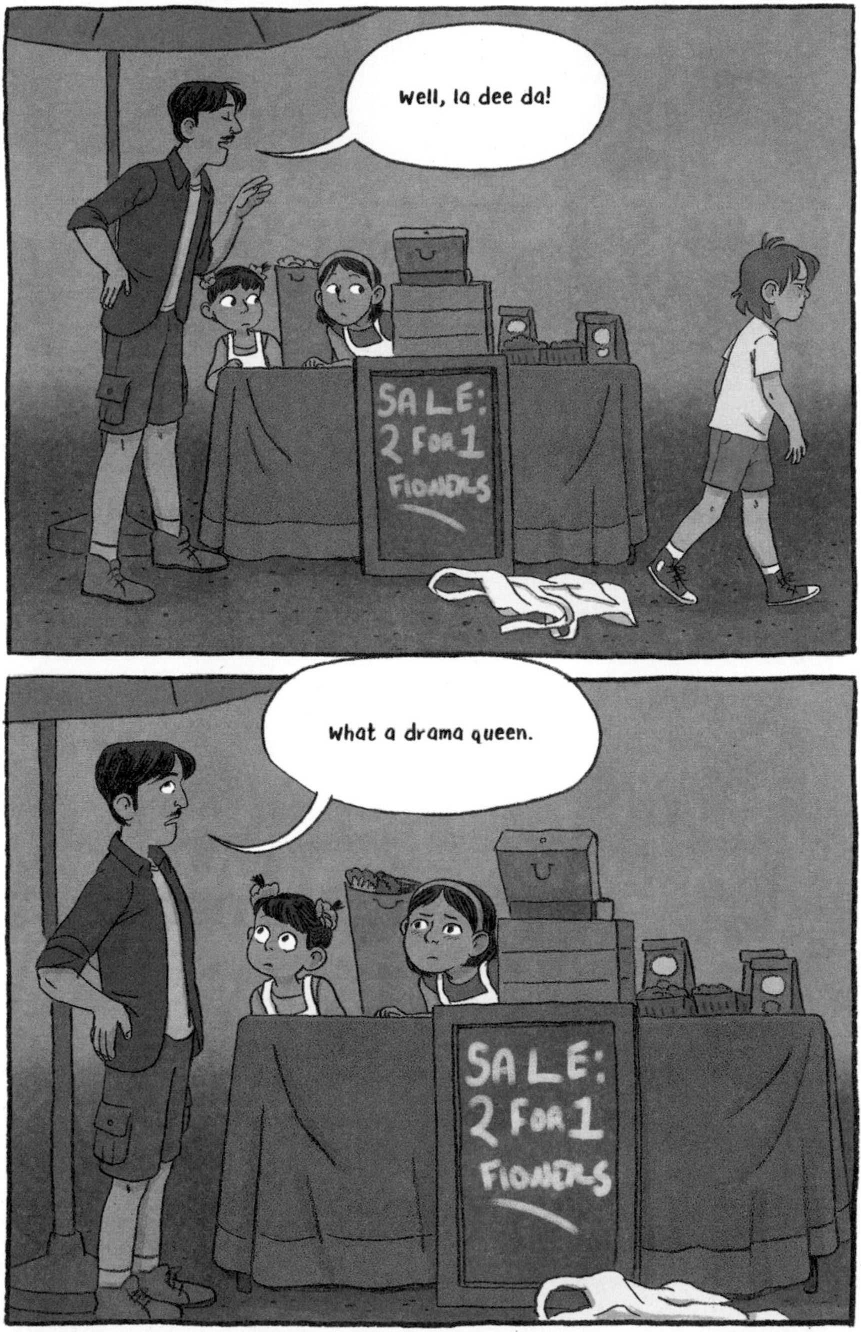
Well, la dee da!
SALE: 2 FOR 1 FLOWERS
What a drama queen.
SALE: 2 FOR 1 FLOWERS

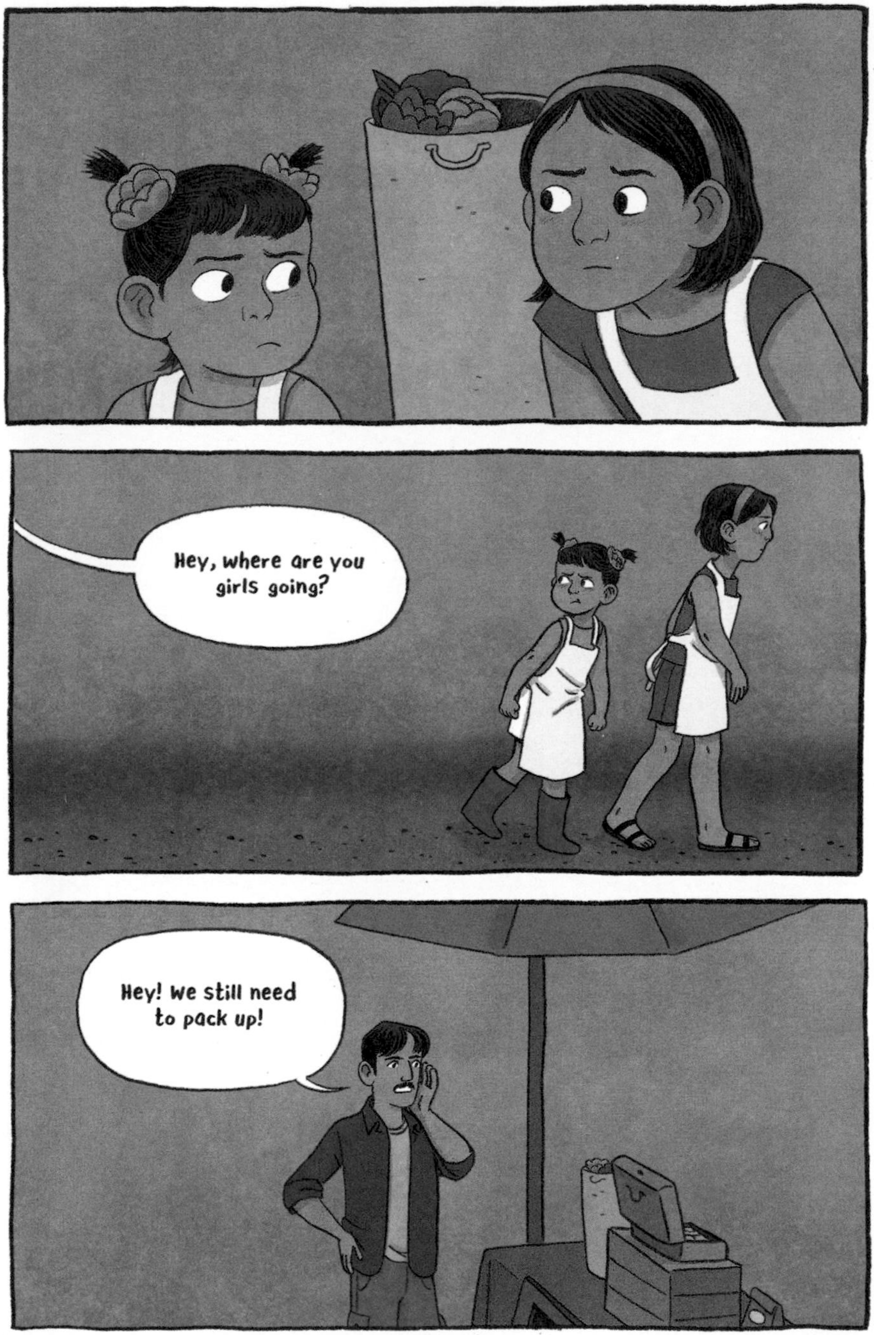
Hey, where are you girls going?
Hey! We still need to pack up!

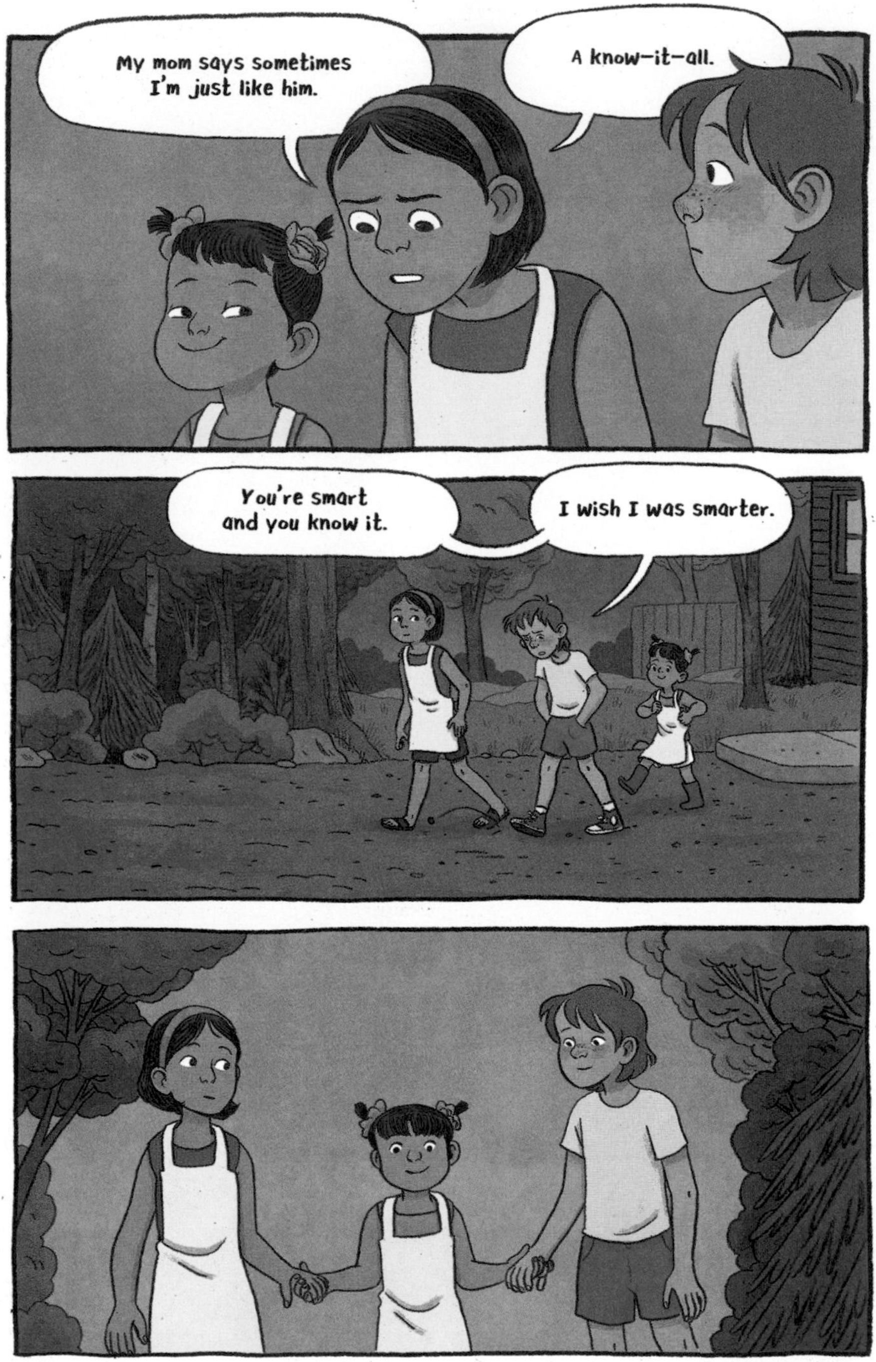
My mom says sometimes I'm just like him.
A know-it-all.
You're smart and you know it.
I wish I was smarter.

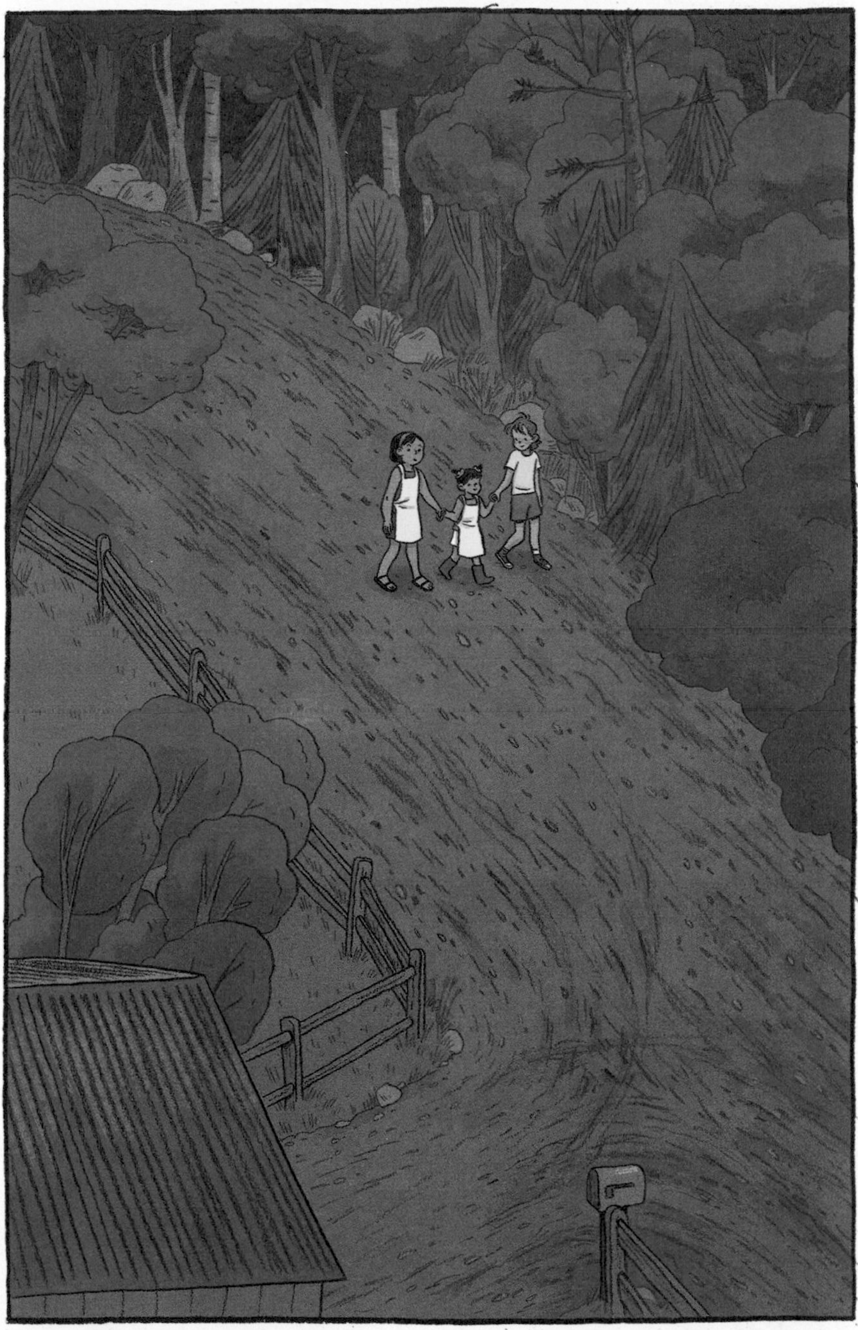

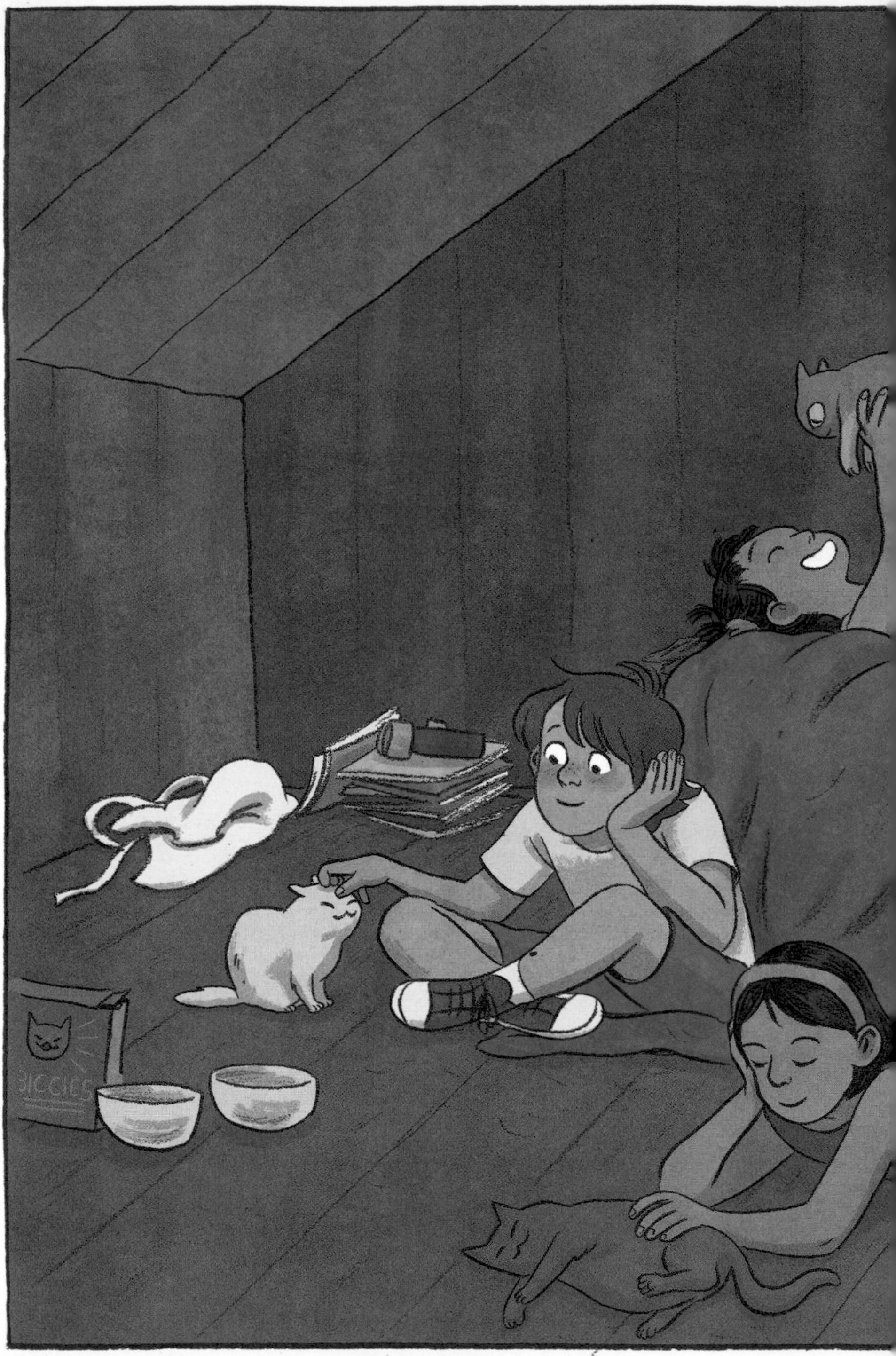

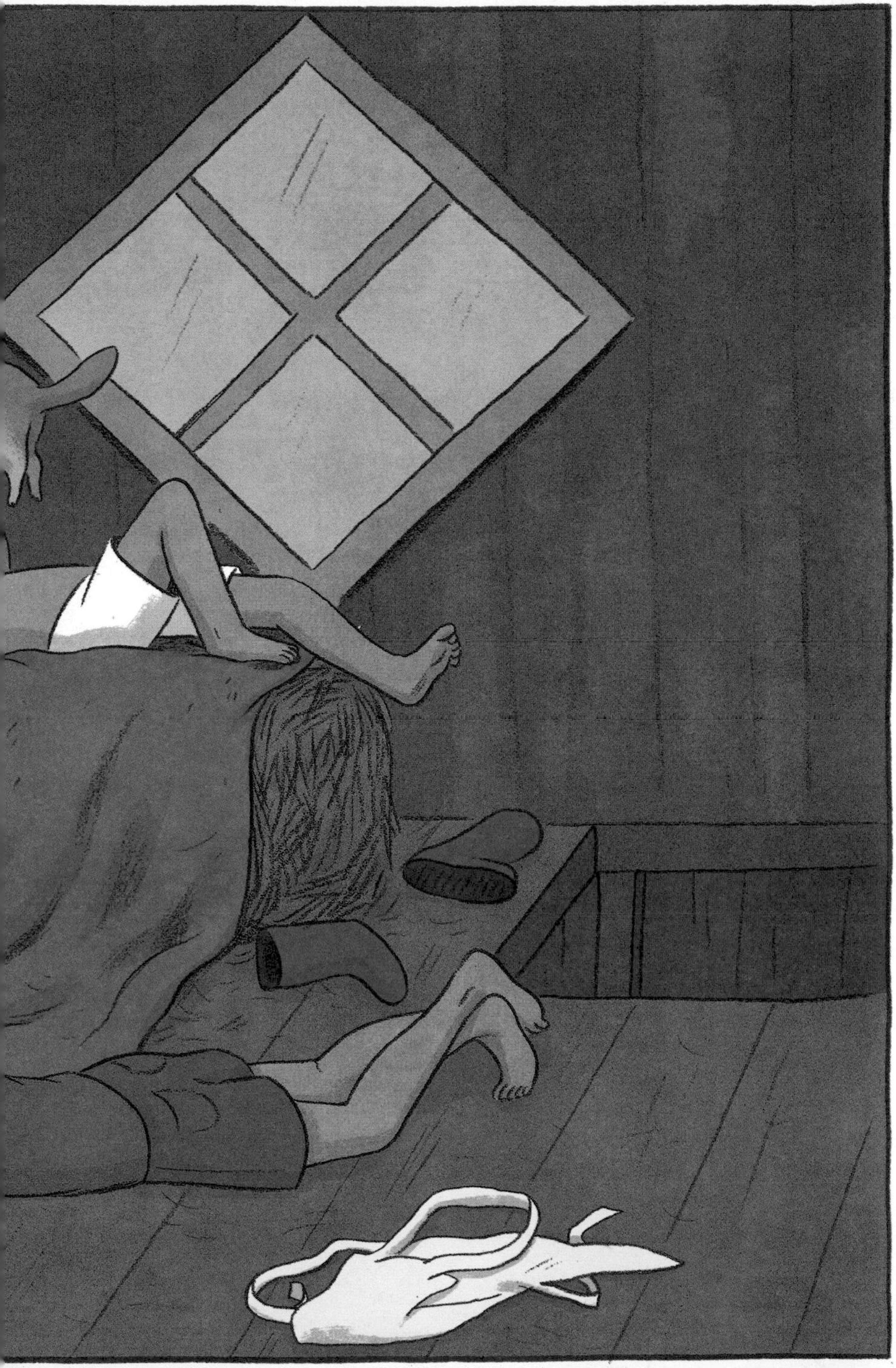

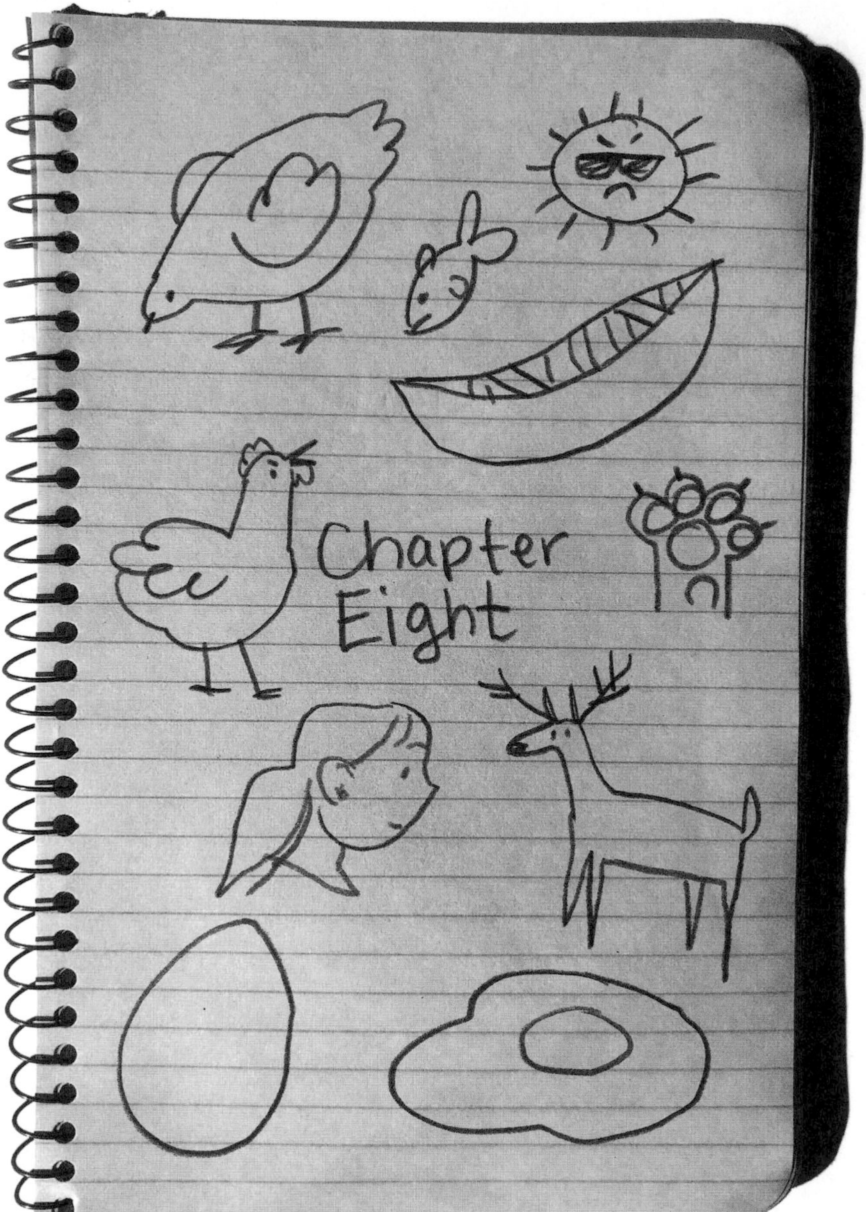
Chapter
Eight

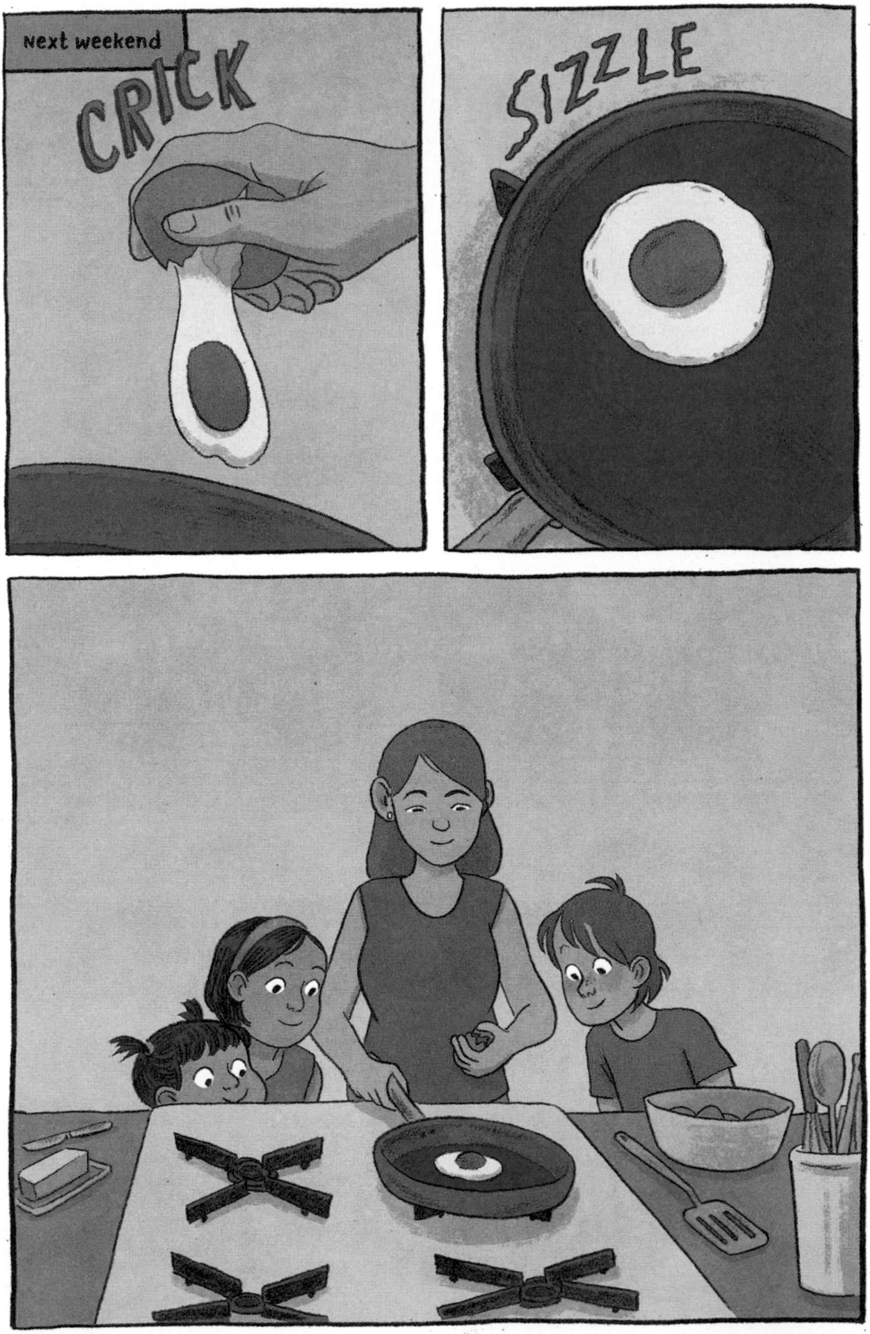
next weekend
CRICK
SIZZLE

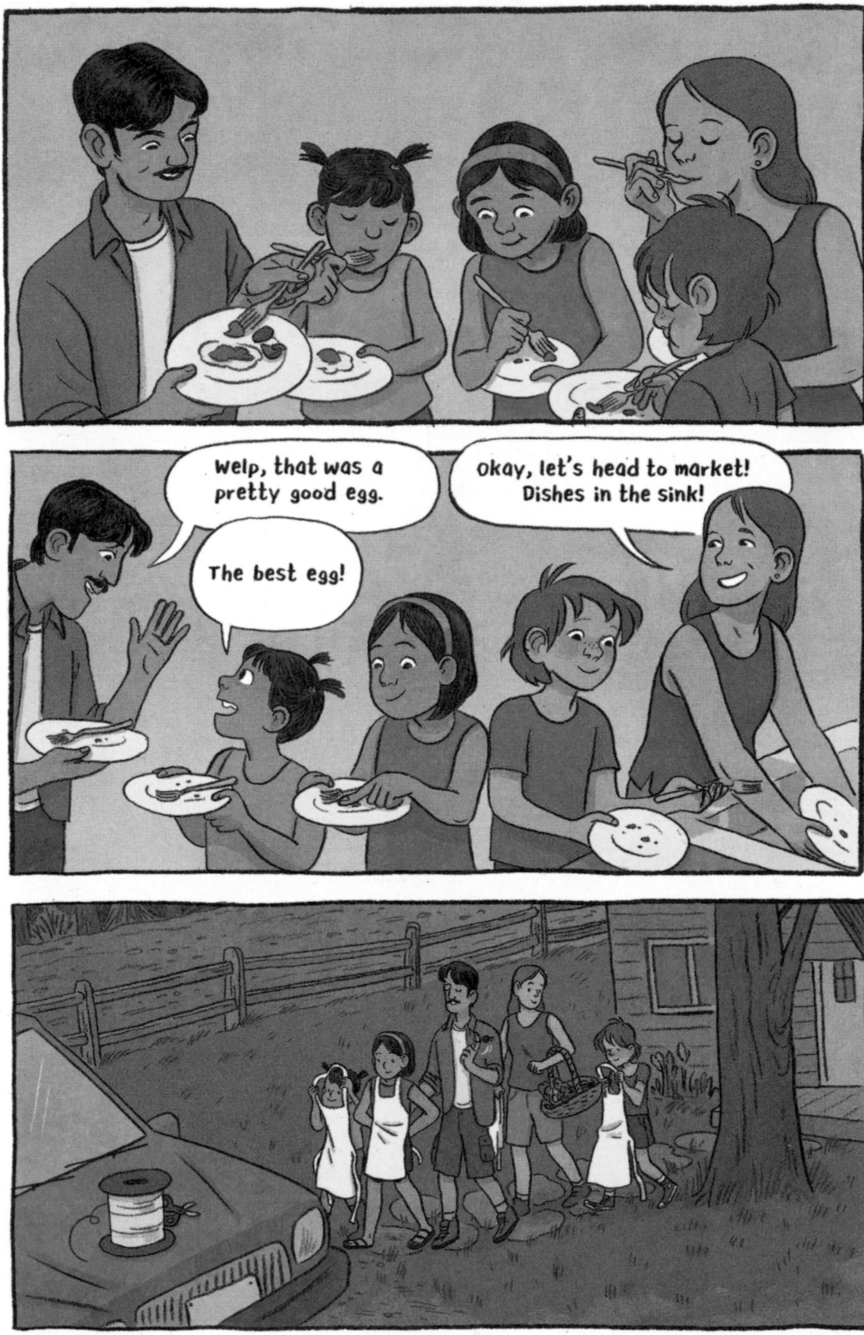
Welp, that was a pretty good egg.
The best egg!
Okay, let's head to market! Dishes in the sink!

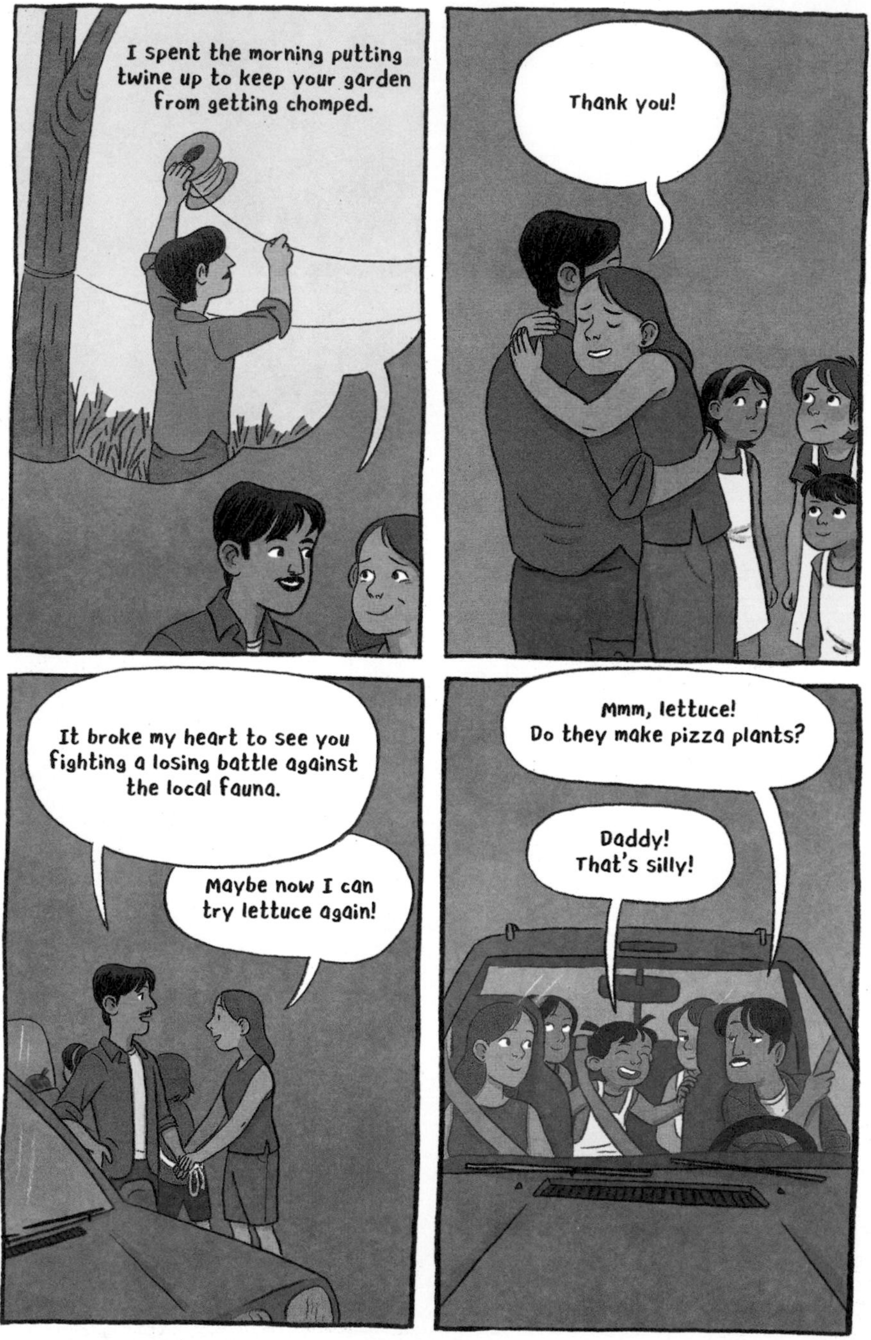
I spent the morning putting twine up to keep your garden from getting chomped.
Thank you!
It broke my heart to see you fighting a losing battle against the local fauna.
Maybe now I can try lettuce again!
Mmm, lettuce! Do they make pizza plants?
Daddy! That's silly!

Hello there!
Pea Pod Farm
BERRIES-$7
GRANOLA-$8
FLOWERS-$6
Oh, hello, Mr. Fisher. Can I interest you in our special today?
Haha, thanks, but your parents give me plenty already!
You lot are good neighbors to have around!
I just wanted to introduce you to our nephew, Eddie.
He comes to help us with the harvest.
TUG

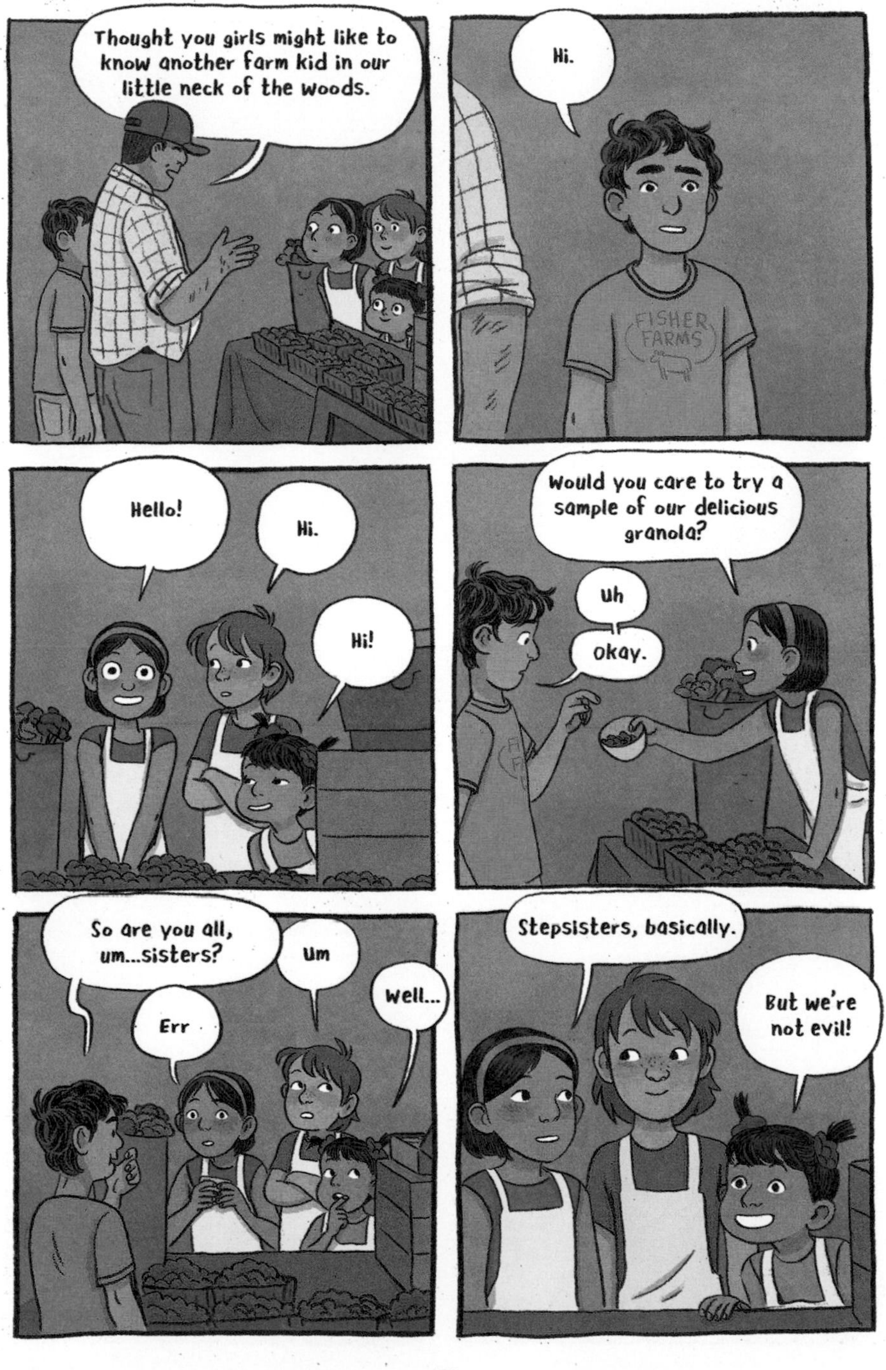
Thought you girls might like to know another farm kid in our little neck of the woods.
Hi.
FISHER FARMS
Hello!
Hi.
Hi!
Would you care to try a sample of our delicious granola?
Uh
Okay.
So are you all, um...sisters?
Err
Um
Well...
Stepsisters, basically.
But we're not evil!

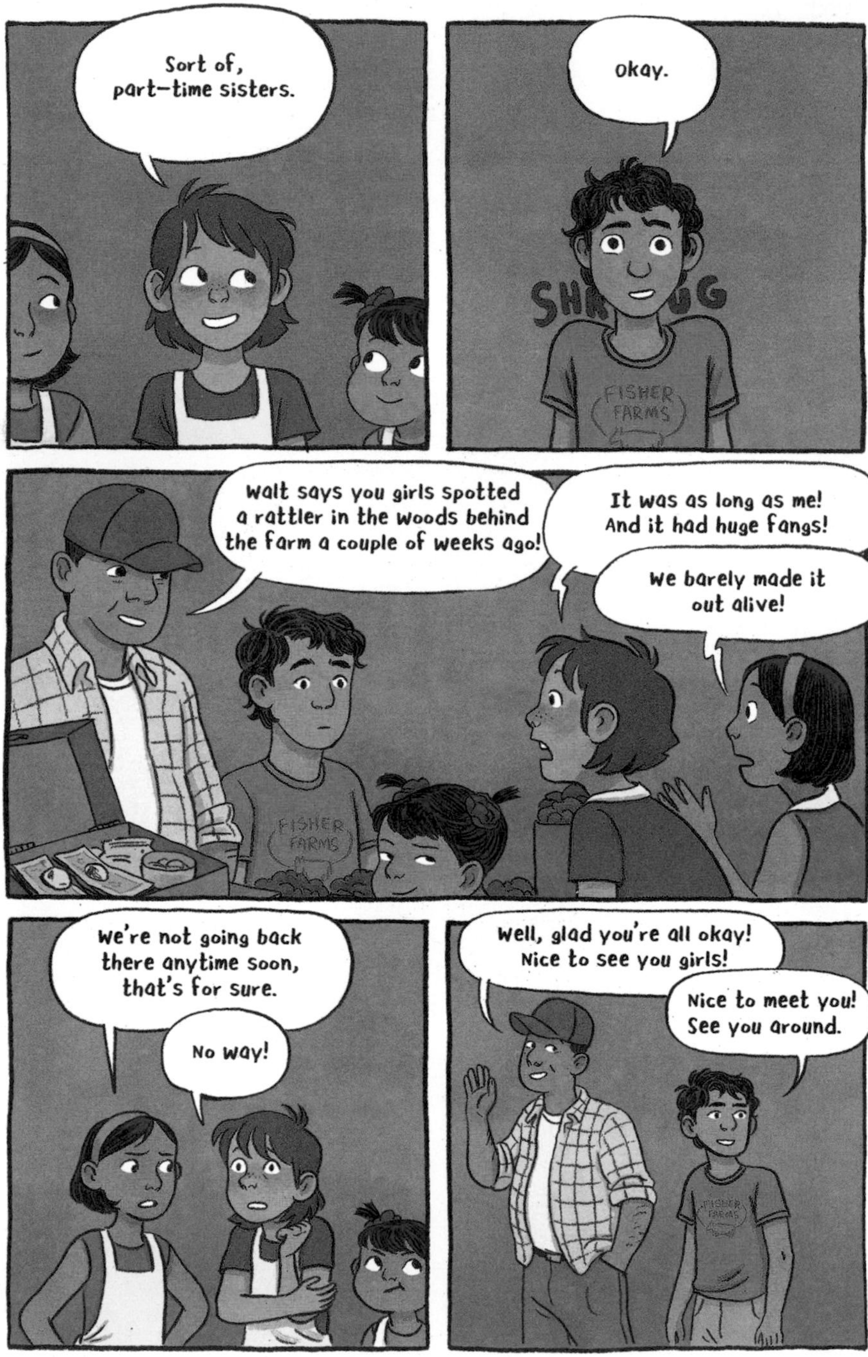
Sort of, part-time sisters.
Okay.
SHRUG
FISHER FARMS
Walt says you girls spotted a rattler in the woods behind the farm a couple of weeks ago!
It was as long as me! And it had huge fangs!
We barely made it out alive!
FISHER FARMS
We're not going back there anytime soon, that's for sure.
No way!
Well, glad you're all okay! Nice to see you girls!
Nice to meet you! See you around.

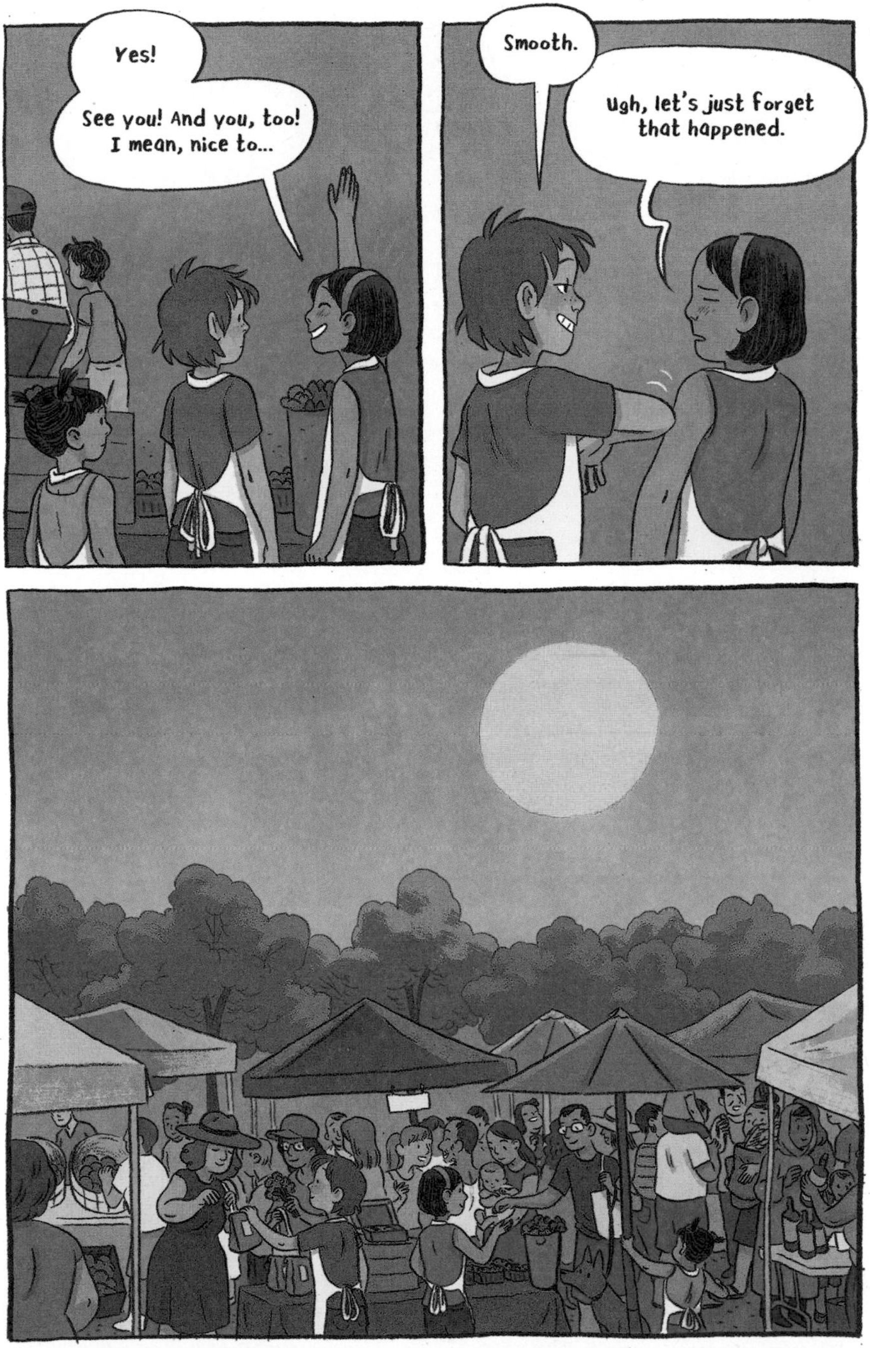

Yes!
See you! And you, too! I mean, nice to...
Smooth.
Ugh, let's just forget that happened.

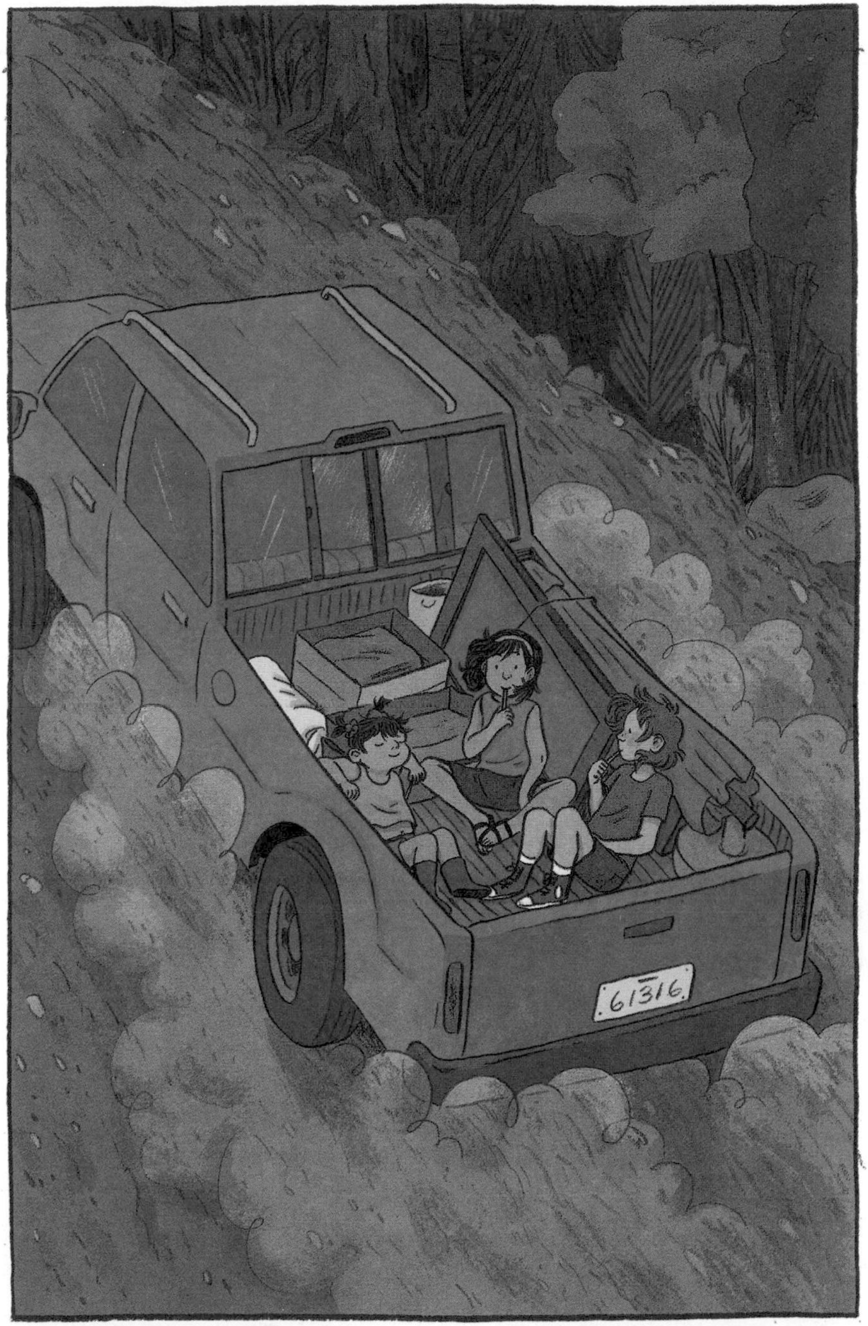
61316

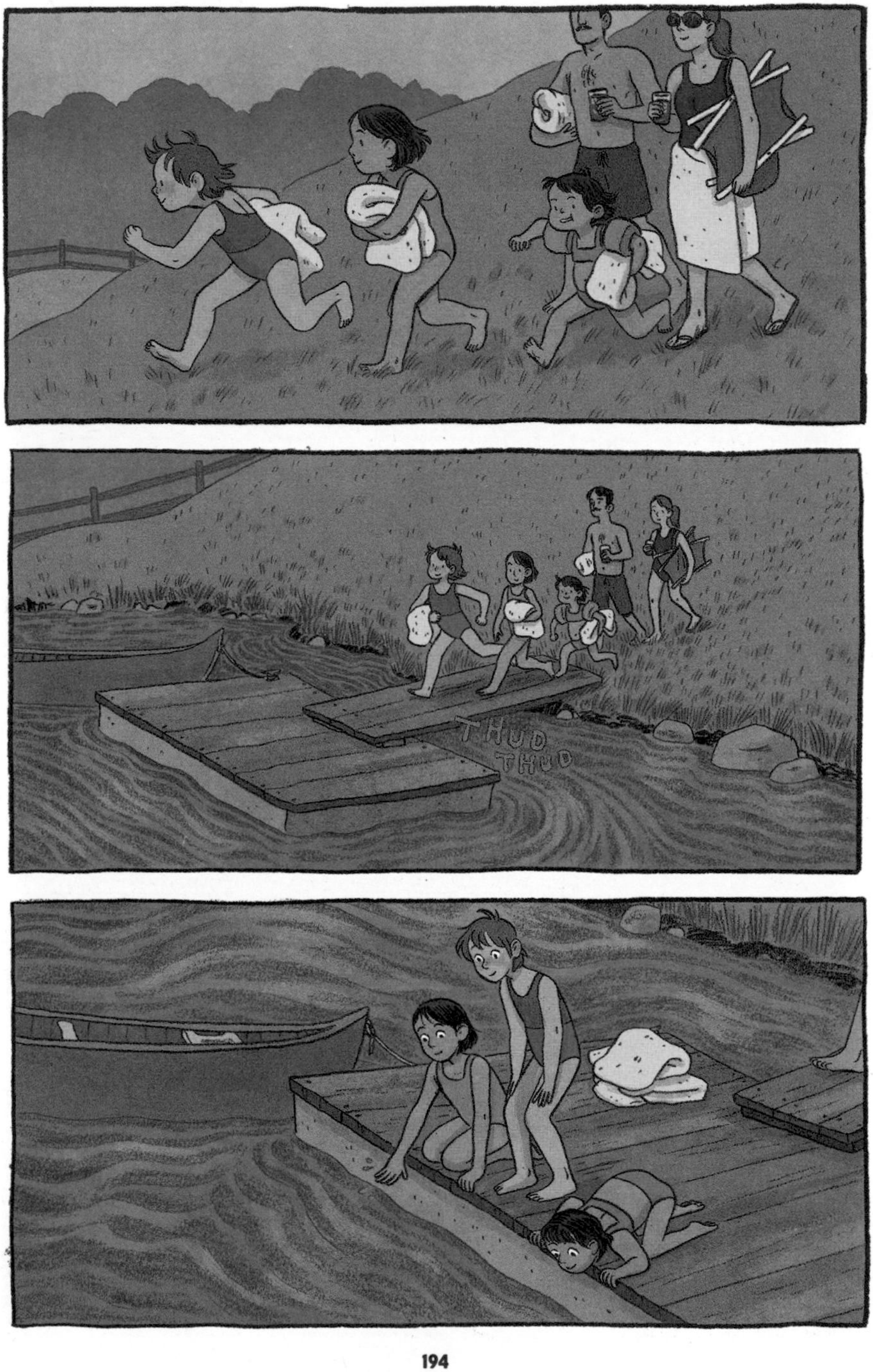
THUD
THUD

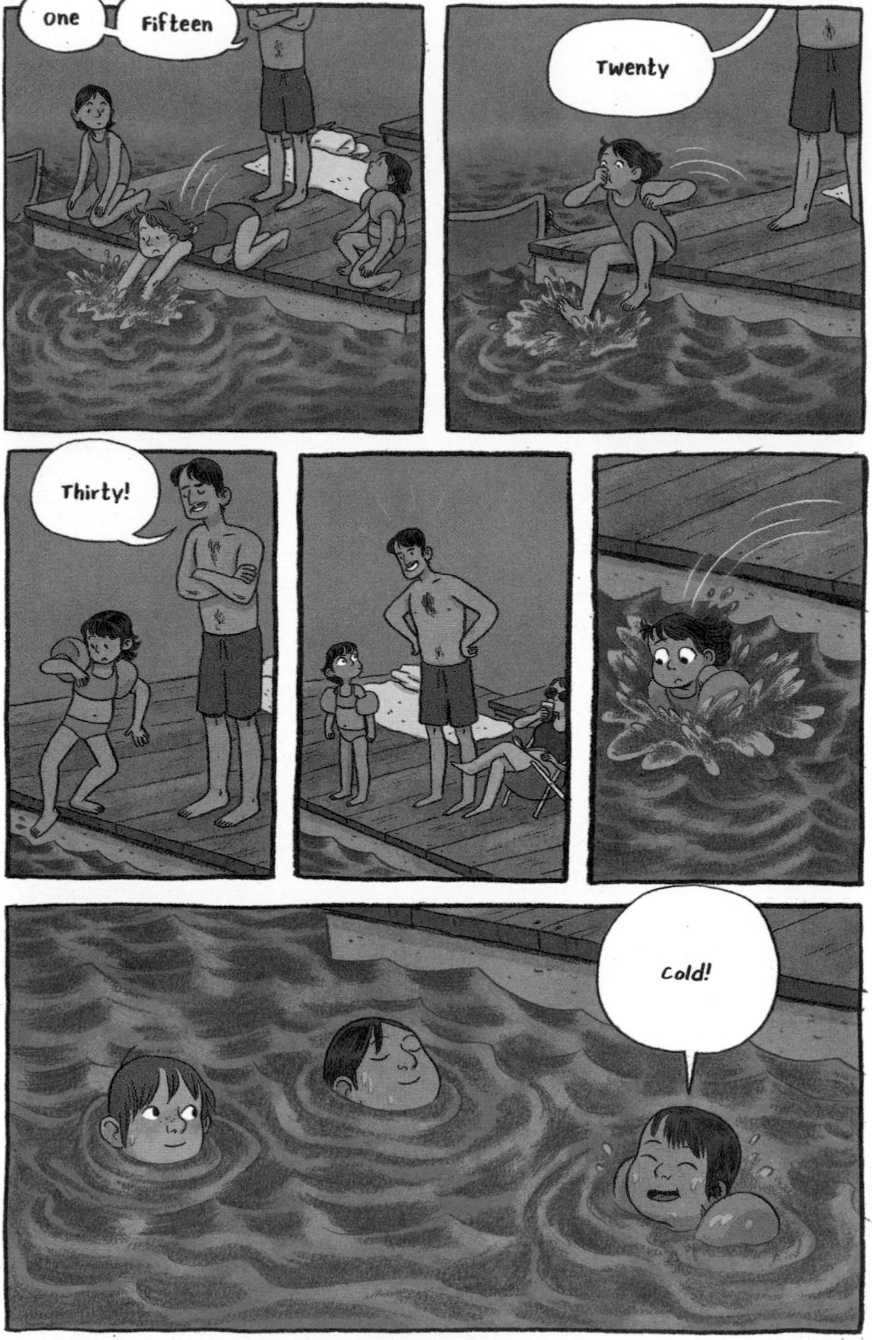
One
Fifteen
Twenty
Thirty!
Cold!

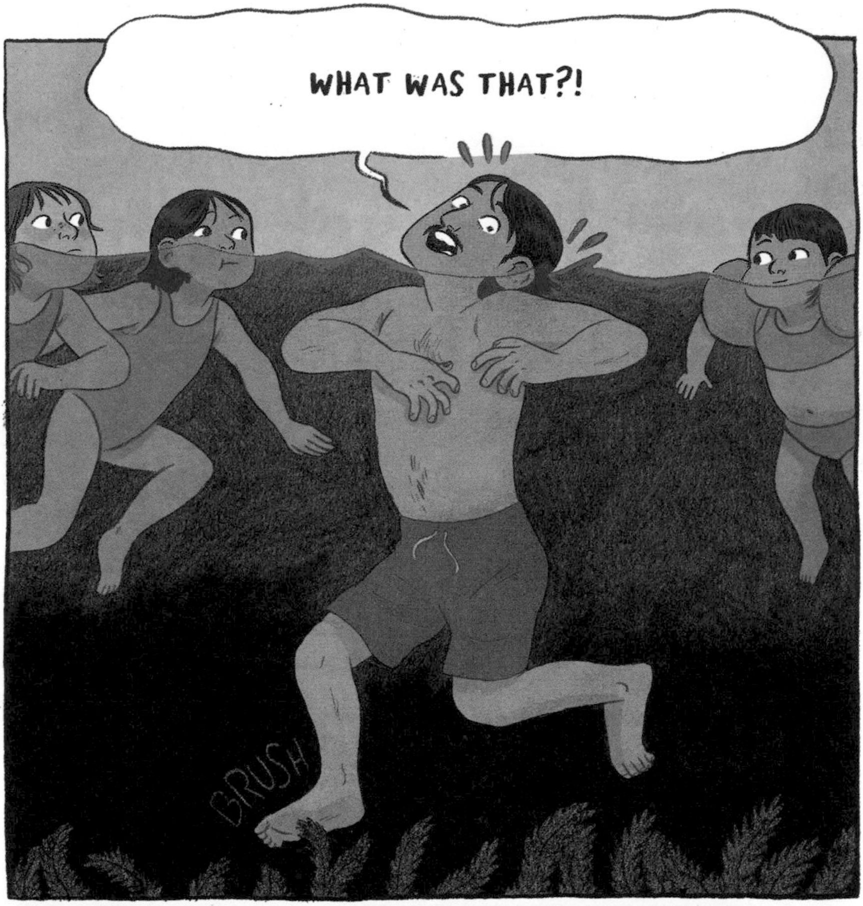
WHAT WAS THAT?!
BRUSH
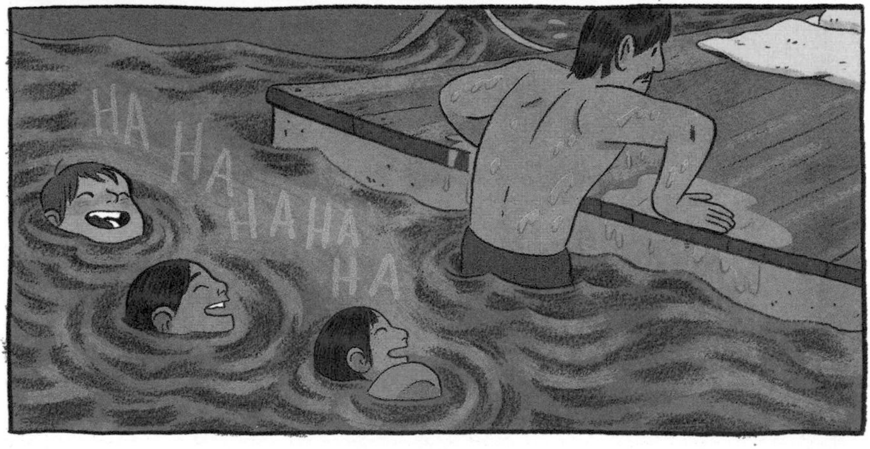
HA HA HAHA HA HA

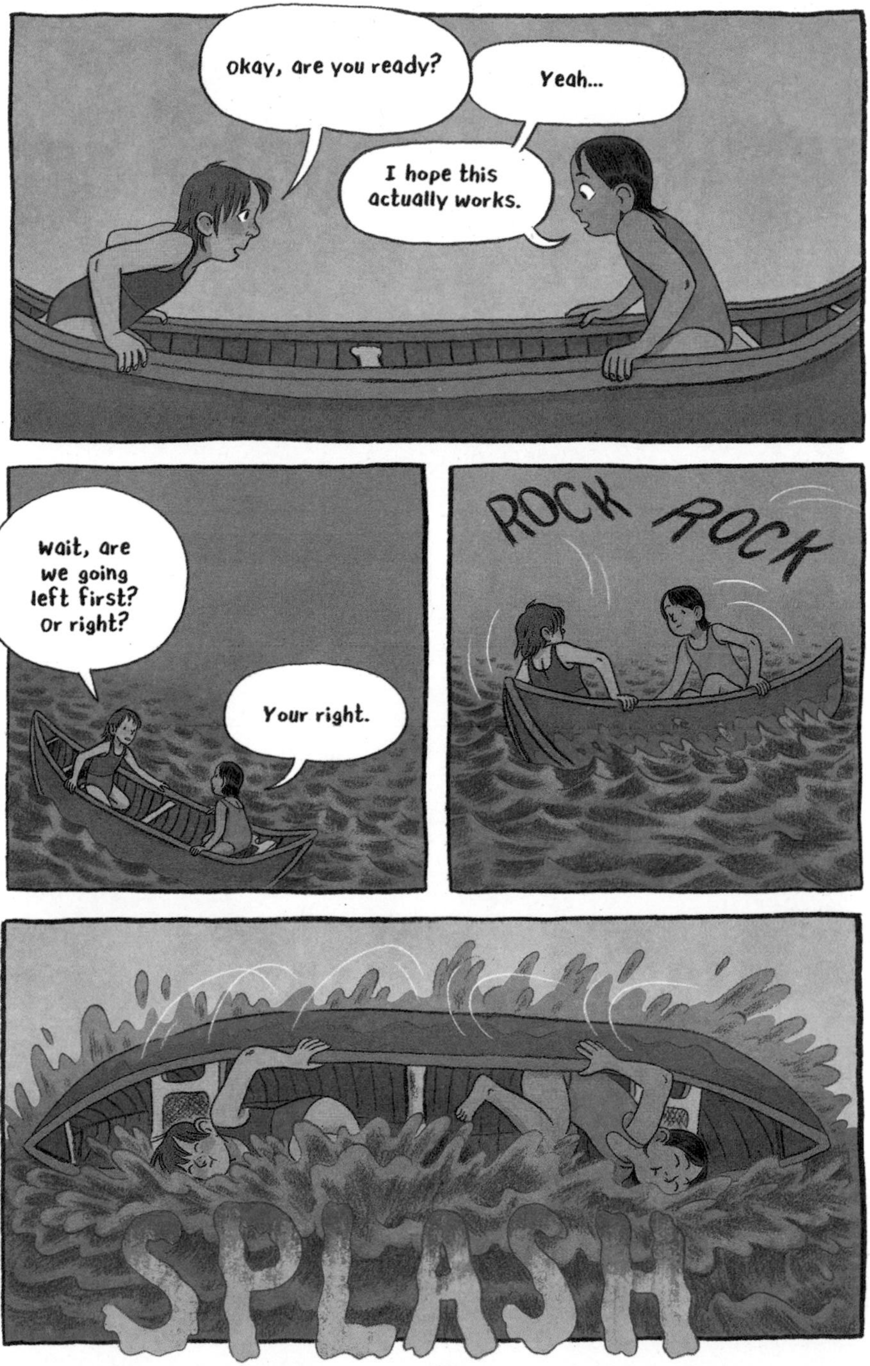

Okay, are you ready?
Yeah...
I hope this actually works.
Wait, are we going left first? Or right?
Your right.
ROCK ROCK
SPLASH

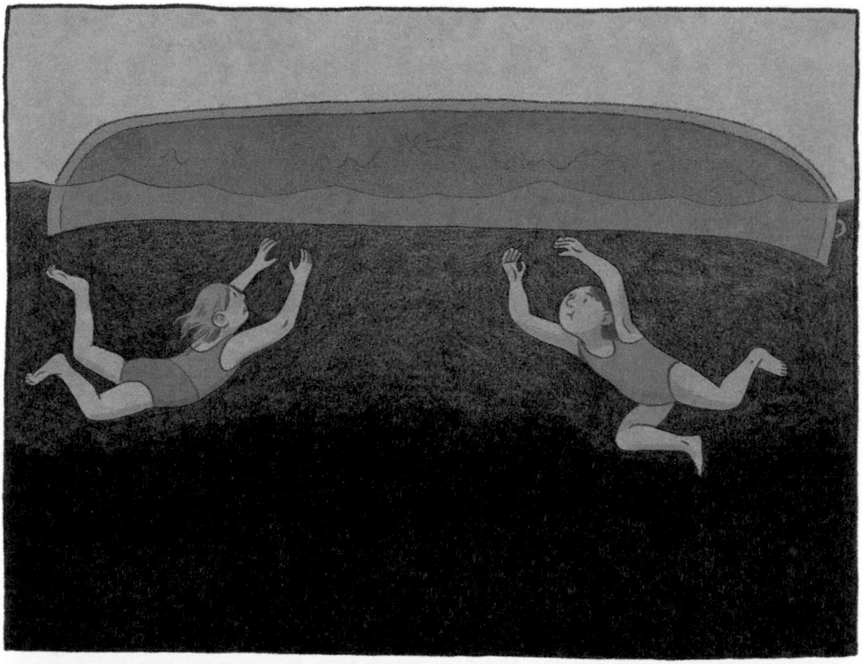

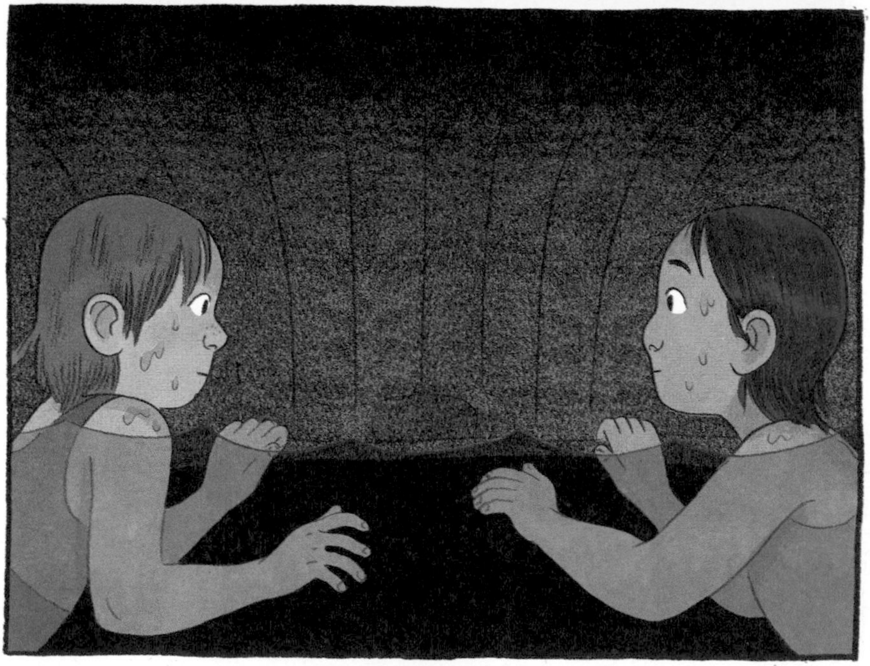

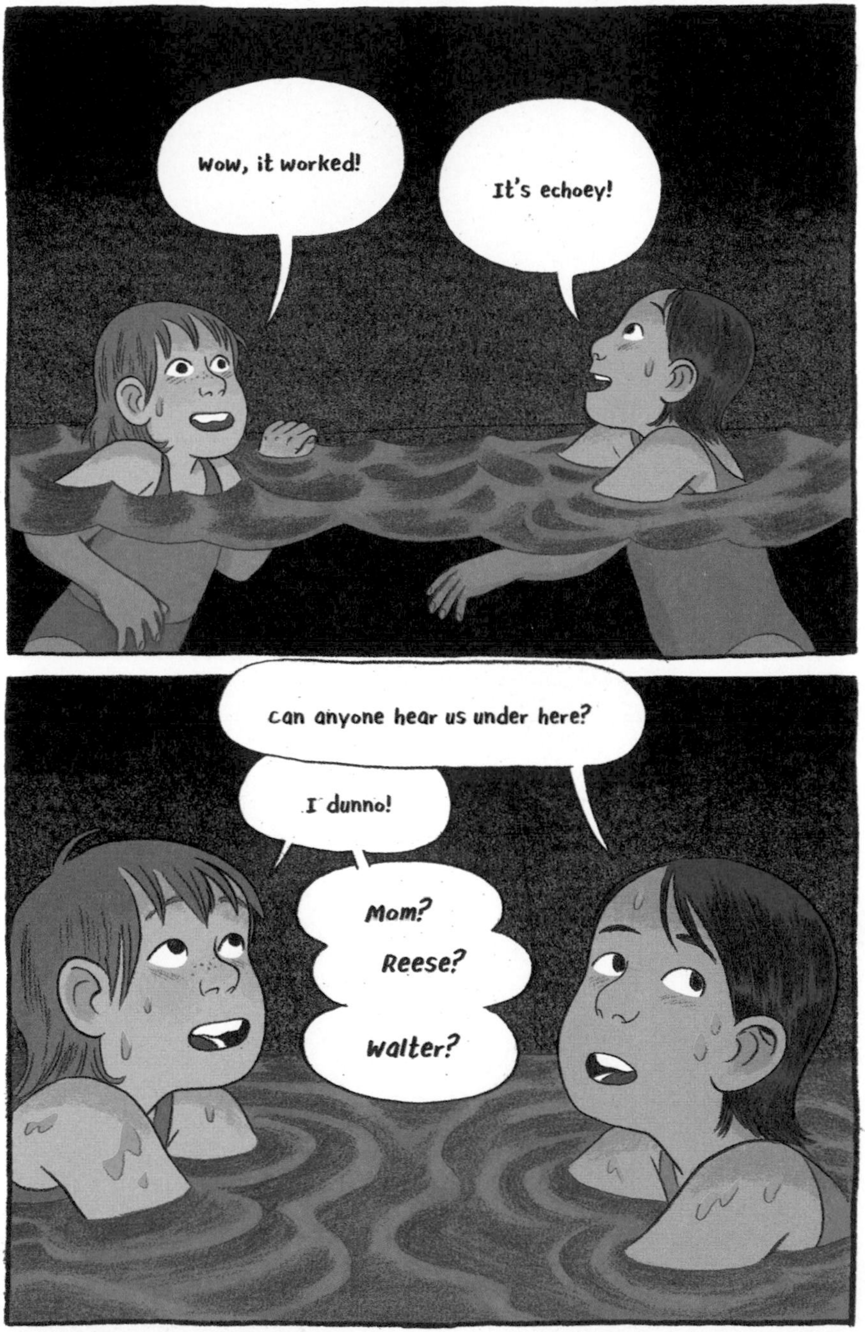
Wow, it worked!
It's echoey!
can anyone hear us under here?
I dunno!
Mom?
Reese?
Walter?

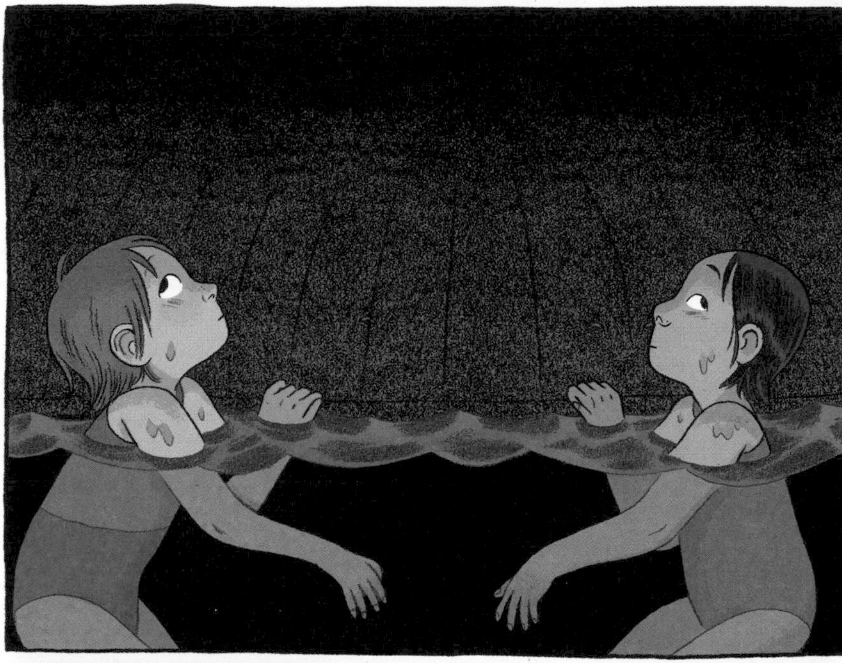

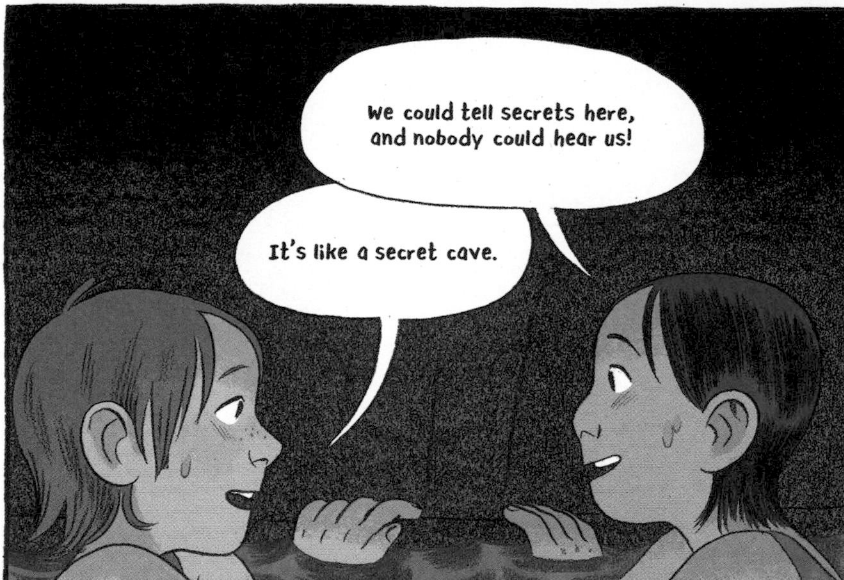
It's like a secret cave.
We could tell secrets here, and nobody could hear us!

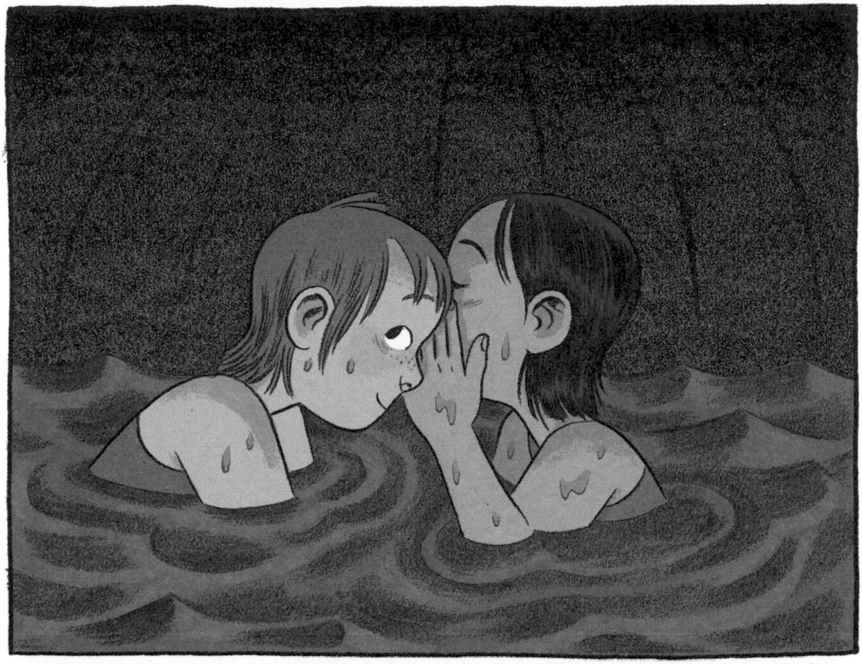

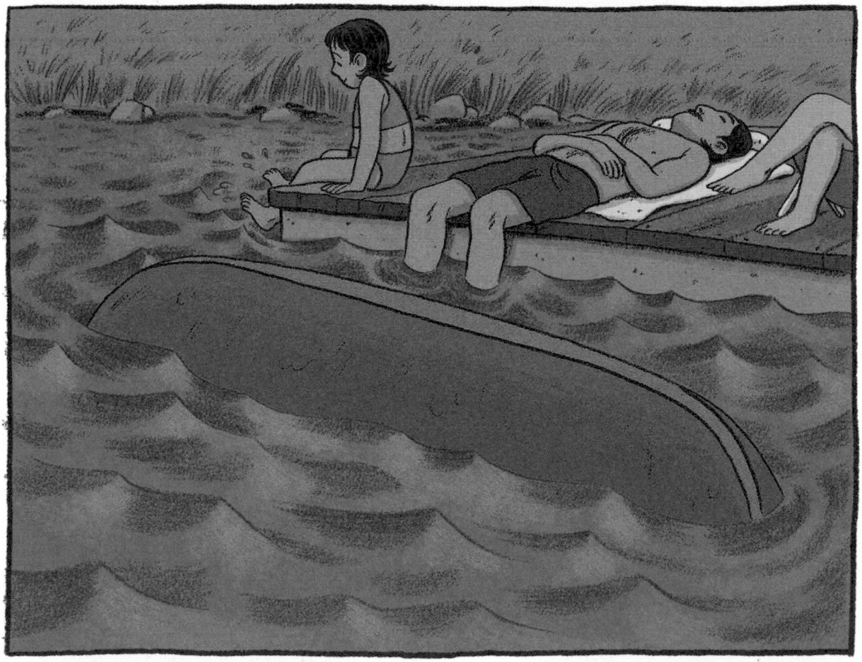

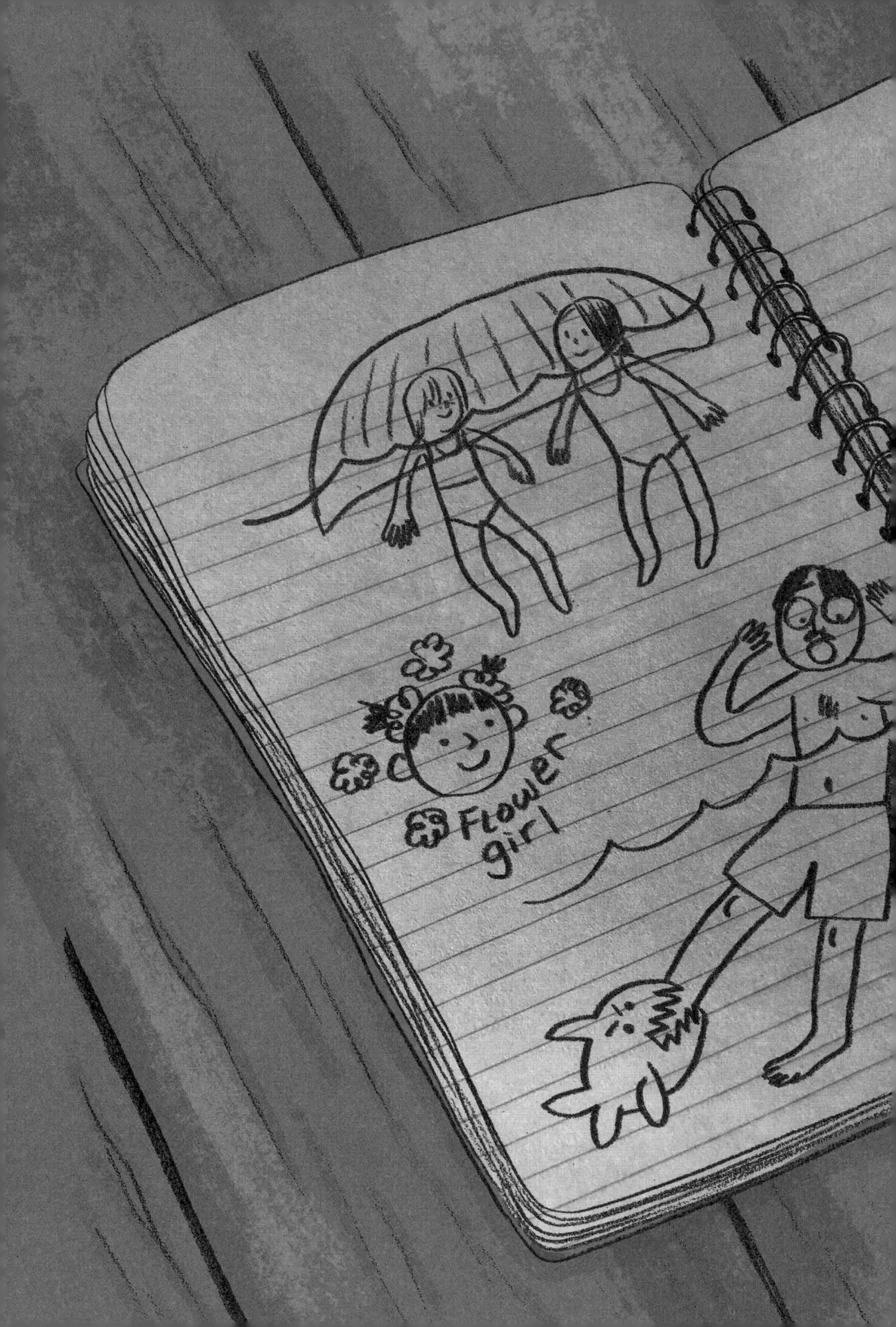
Flower girl

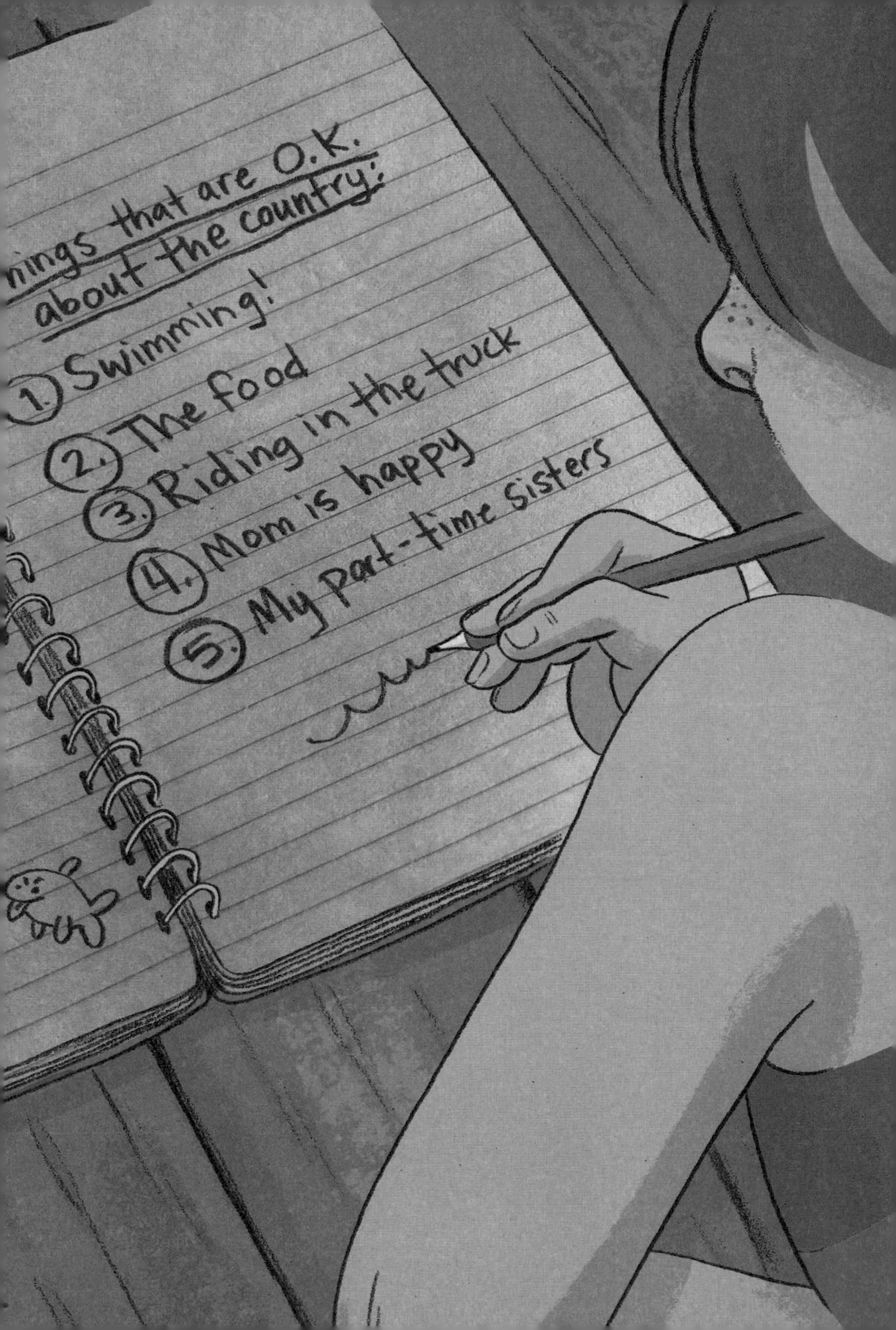
nings that are O.K.
about the country:
1. Swimming!
2. The food
3. Riding in the truck
4. Mom is happy
5. My part-time sisters

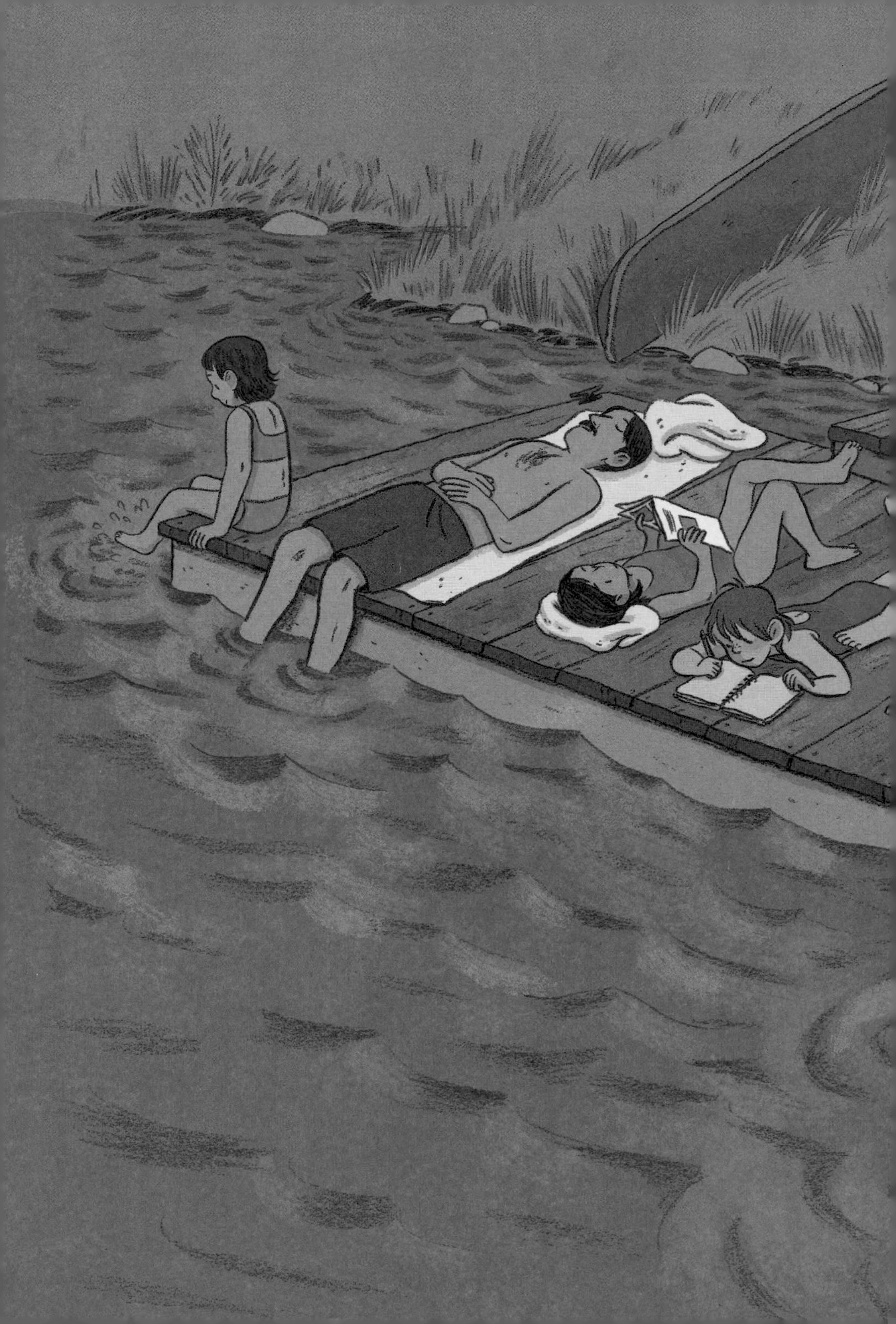

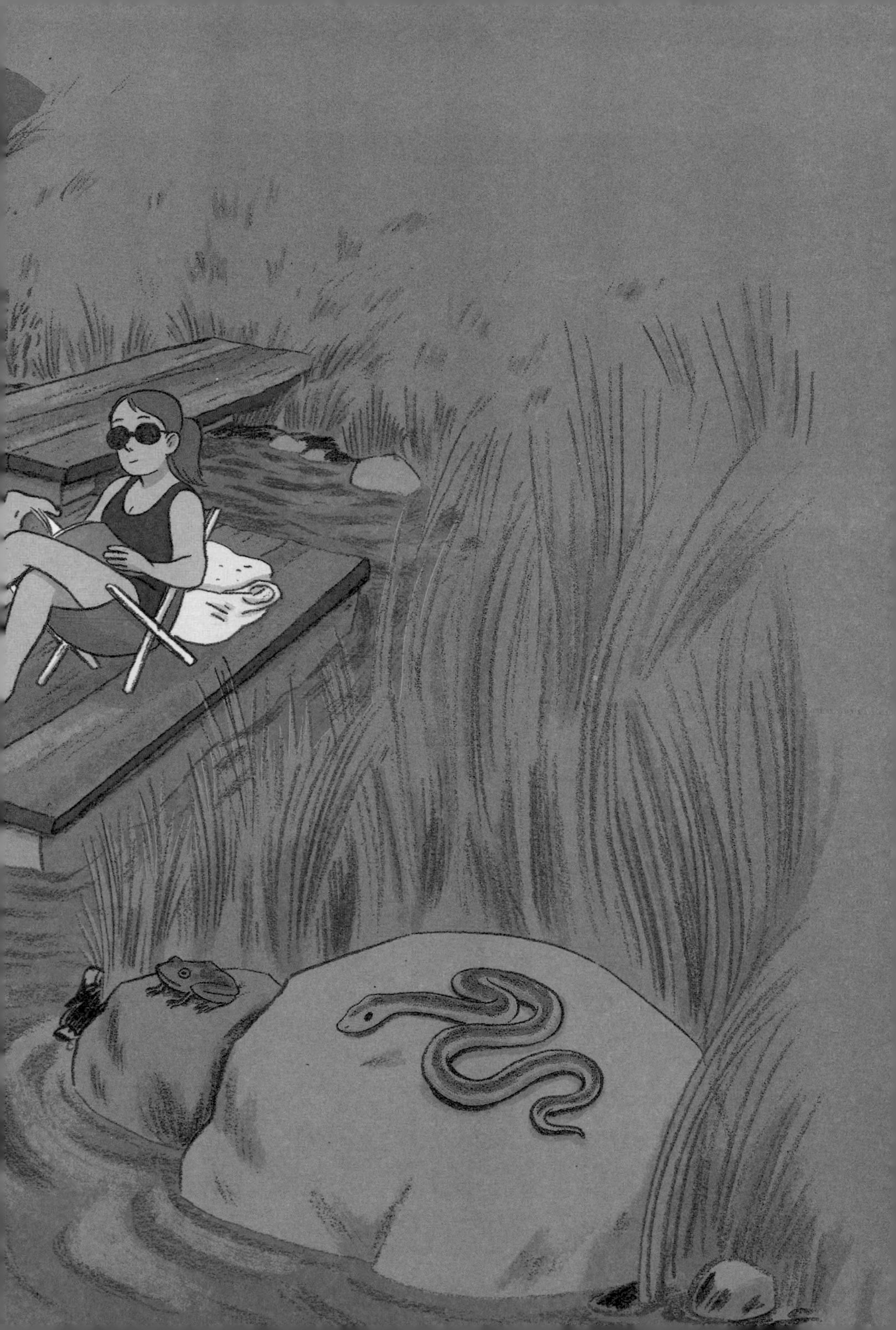

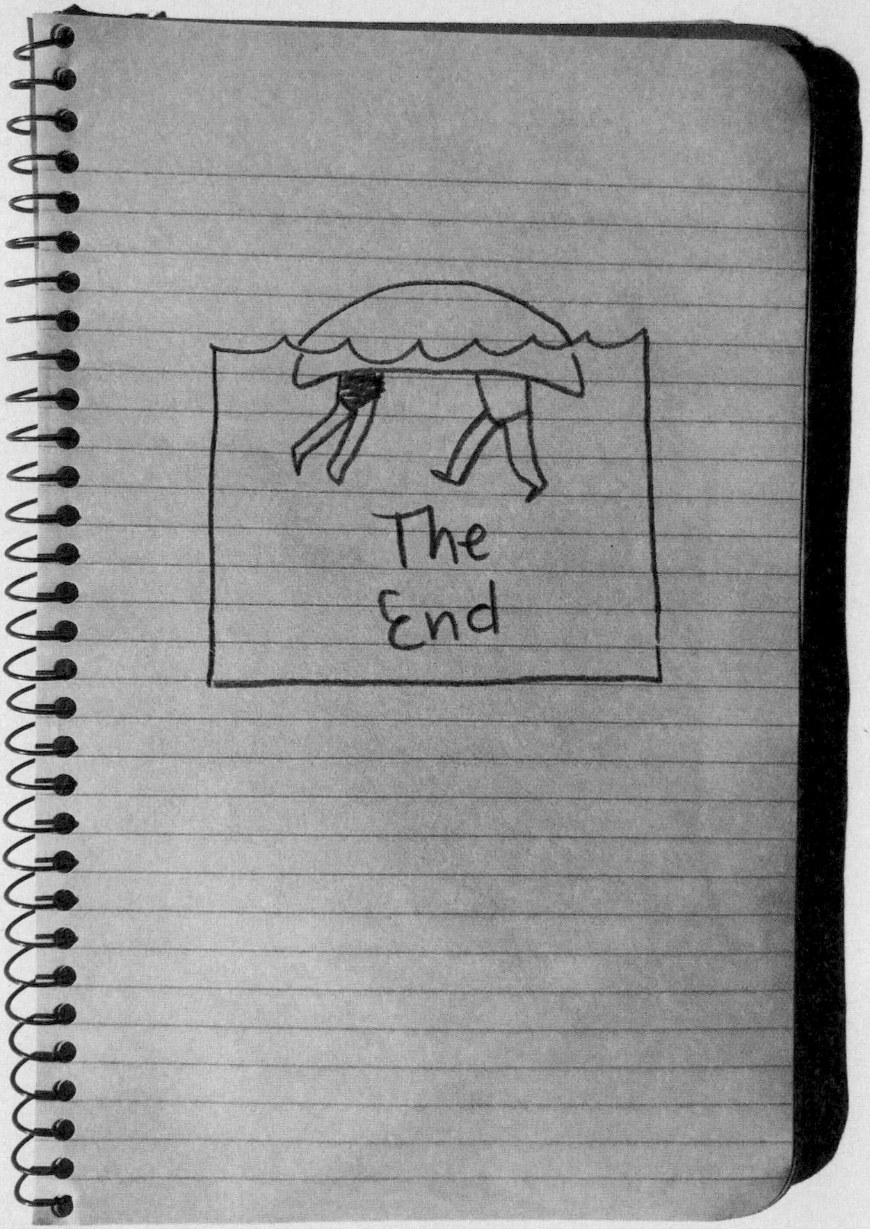
The End

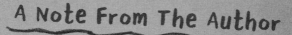

A Note From The Author

When I was a kid, my parents split up and my mom and I moved from New York City to a little farm in the country.

She wanted to grow flowers and berries and get her hands dirty. I wanted to read comic books INSIDE where it was CLEAN, but sometimes when you're a kid, you're just along for the ride.

Mom →

← Me

I wasn't always thrilled with my mom's decision to become a super farmer lady, but I didn't have much of a choice about becoming a not-so-super farm kid.

Then my mom got a boyfriend. He was loud, bossy, and annoying. I'd never met such an annoying grown-up! And his daughters! A loud, bossy kid and her whiny little sister! Suddenly, I was sharing my room every weekend with these total strangers.

One of the worst things about being a kid is finding yourself in these situations where you have no control over the decisions the adults are making that affect you. But sometimes it's also one of the best things— to find yourself in a situation you couldn't possibly have chosen for yourself, totally at sea. It can sometimes bring unexpected beauty, and introduce strangers that become family.

My "Andy" is still loud and bossy, but she's also brilliant and funny. My "Reese" is much less whiney now, and much cooler than all of us, as she has always been.

My "Walter" was both annoying and beloved until his dying day.

My mom is still getting her hands dirty and loving her life in the country, and I am so thankful to her for forcing me to endure such a beautiful childhood full of rattlesnakes and ponds and lots more stories to tell.

(Another little note)

Big shocker: I am bad at math.

$$4 \times 7 \over 28$$

I'm not just BAD at math, though;
I'm dyscalculiac! It's a little like
dyslexia, but rather than reading, this one
impairs your ability to process numbers
and magnitude.

When I graduated, I breathed a sigh of
relief that I'd never have to do math
again, but then I became a comic artist
and had to learn how to measure and
divide a page of panels! It was like
algebra RETURNING FROM THE GRAVE TO
HAUNT ME.

1234 *I'M BACK!*

Being "good" at something is less
important than trying or practicing. After
all, I became a comic artist after years
and YEARS of practicing my drawing and
writing. And I'm much better at math than
I used to be! My "Andy," of course, is an
engineer, and sometimes she has to draw
diagrams and she's rotten at it, but she's
getting better, too. Who'da thunk it?

Acknowledgments:

Thank you to Taylor, Chelsea, and Georgia.
Thank you to the Rhinebeck Farmers' Market.
Thank you to my fellow children of divorce.

Thank you to my publishing team at Random
House Graphic! Gina Gagliano and
Whitney Leopard and Patrick Crotty!
Thank you to Whitney Coger
for beautiful colors.
Thank you to Holly Bemiss
for being my champion.

Thank you to bees for your honey and
gardens for your flowers and bushes for
your berries and cows for your milk and
barns for your kittens.

Thank you to Warren, who I miss and who
would have been very sweet and very
annoying about this whole book.

Thank you to John and Pal,
who are my faves.

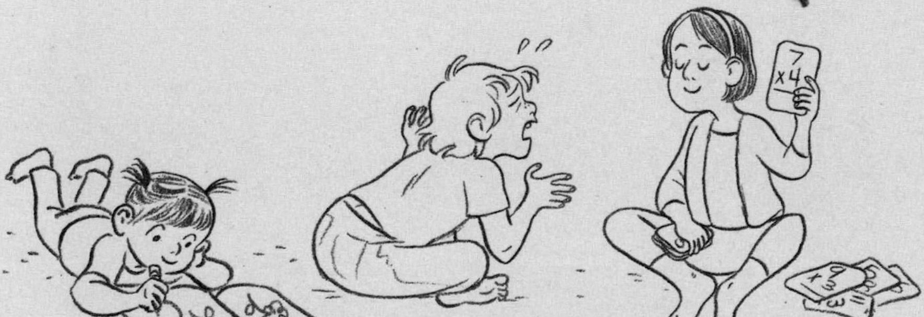
7
x4

Author shown with pencil stubs
used during the making of this book!

About The Author

Lucy Knisley grew up with one foot in New York City and the other on an upstate farm.

An only child with divorced parents, she was an avid comic book and fantasy reader, who began to navigate the unfamiliar world of step-familial melodrama when she was eleven.

She graduated from the School of the Art Institute of Chicago, followed by the Center for Cartoon Studies, and began publishing graphic novels (a travelogue) at the age of twenty-two.

She has always tried to use her work to make people feel less alone through her honest and confessional comics. Her topics range from travel, adulthood, ailing grandparents, foreign romance, wedding planning, food, and reproductive health.

She lives in Chicago, where she likes riding her bike with her son and partner, and reading fantasy novels and comic books.

LucyKnisley.com

RH GRAPHIC
· THE SUMMER 2020 LIST ·

CRABAPPLE TROUBLE
By Kaeti Vandorn
· · · · · · · · · ·
Life isn't easy when you're an apple.

Callaway and Thistle must figure out how to work together—with delicious and magical results.

Young Chapter Book

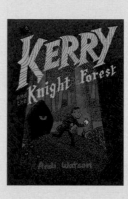

KERRY AND THE KNIGHT OF THE FOREST
By Andi Watson
· · · · · · · · · ·
Kerry needs to get home!

To get back to his parents, Kerry gets lost in a shortcut. He will have to make tough choices and figure out who to trust—or remain lost in the forest . . . forever.

Middle-Grade

STEPPING STONES
By Lucy Knisley
· · · · · · · · · ·
Jen did not want to leave the city.

She did not want to move to a farm.

And Jen definitely did not want to get two new "sisters."

Middle-Grade

SUNCATCHER
By Jose Pimienta
· · · · · · · · · ·
Beatriz loves music—more than her school, more than her friends—and she won't let anything stop her from achieving her dreams.

Even if it means losing everything else.

Young Adult

FIND US ONLINE AT
@RHKIDSGRAPHIC AND
RHKIDSGRAPHIC.COM